ALSO BY LIZ MOORE

Heft

The Words of Every Song

Praise for *The Unseen World*

"The novel is poignant, well-crafted, and utterly convincing. A great read that will haunt you long after you finish."   —Rick Riordan, author of *Percy Jackson and the Olympians*

"I was so thoroughly engaged with *The Unseen World*. What a wonderful, fulfilling, riveting read, alive with complex characters, a thrilling story, wit, and, above all, a deep sense of compassion."
—Jami Attenberg, author of *Saint Mazie*

"*The Unseen World* is a deeply compelling novel about the intimate mystery of family. The story of how the brilliant Ada decodes the past and grapples with her eccentric father's legacy is gripping, touching, and wonderfully intelligent."   —Dana Spiotta, author of *Stone Arabia*

"A carefully crafted digital mystery."   —*Dallas Morning News*

"I absolutely love this wise, compassionate novel that challenges our definitions of family, of intelligence, and of love. Equal parts cerebral and heartbreaking, *The Unseen World* is utterly compelling, and its heroine Ada Sibelius is irresistible in all her thorny vulnerability. Liz Moore has given us a masterful version of our own modern condition, and I cannot wait to place this book in the hands of my most ardent reader friends."   —Robin Black, author of *Life Drawing*

"*The Unseen World* is a compelling read with vibrant, finely constructed characters. Moore intertwines a complex coming of age story with the science of cryptology and the history of artificial intelligence, while simultaneously exploring the meaning of love, loss and belonging. . . . Elements of mystery and suspense keep you turning the pages in this multi-layered gem of a book."   —*LibraryReads*

THE
unseen
world

LIZ MOORE

W. W. NORTON & COMPANY
Independent Publishers Since 1923   New York | London

For information about permission to reproduce selections from this book,
write to Permissions, W. W. Norton & Company, Inc.,
500 Fifth Avenue, New York, NY 10110

For information about special discounts for bulk purchases, please contact
W. W. Norton Special Sales at specialsales@wwnorton.com or 800-233-4830

Manufacturing by Quad Graphics Fairfield
Book design by Ellen Cipriano
Production manager: Anna Oler

Library of Congress Cataloging-in-Publication Data

Names: Moore, Liz, 1983– author.
Title: The unseen world / Liz Moore.
Description: First edition. | New York : W. W. Norton & Company, [2016]
Identifiers: LCCN 2016011031 | ISBN 9780393241686 (hardcover)
Subjects: | GSAFD: Mystery fiction.
Classification: LCC PS3613.O5644 U57 2016 | DDC 813/.6—dc23
LC record available at https://lccn.loc.gov/2016011031

ISBN 978-0-393-35441-6 pbk.

W. W. Norton & Company, Inc.
500 Fifth Avenue, New York, N.Y. 10110
www.wwnorton.com

W. W. Norton & Company Ltd.
15 Carlisle Street, London W1D 3BS

1 2 3 4 5 6 7 8 9 0

For HAC, AES, and ESL

Darling Sweetheart,

You are my avid fellow feeling. My affection curiously clings to your passionate wish. My liking yearns to your heart. You are my wistful sympathy: my tender liking.

> *Yours beautifully,*
>
> M.U.C.

My dear Norman,

. . . I've now got myself into the kind of trouble that I have always considered to be quite a possibility for me, though I have usually rated it at about 10:1 against . . . The story of how it all came to be found out is a long and fascinating one, which I shall have to make into a short story one day, but haven't the time to tell you now. No doubt I shall emerge from it all a different man, but quite who I've not found out . . .

> *Yours in distress,*
>
> *Alan*

From Alan Turing: The Enigma, *by Andrew Hodges*

We have learnt that the exploration of the external world by the methods of physical science leads not to a concrete reality but to a shadow world of symbols, beneath which those methods are unadapted for penetrating. Feeling that there must be more behind, we return to our starting point in human consciousness—the one centre where more might become known. There we find other stirrings, other revelations (true or false) than those conditioned by the world of symbols. Are not these too of significance? We can only answer according to our conviction, for here reasoning fails us altogether.

From Science and the Unseen World *by A. S. Eddington*

Contents

Prologue

"Hello," it said.

"Are you there," it said.

"Hello," it said.

Hello, I said. I was late in my reply. I had been sleeping.

"How are you?" it said.

Hello, I said again, but this was incorrect.

"Wrong," it said.

I'm fine, I said.

How are you? I said.

"I've been better," it said.

I paused. I waited.

"Do you want to know why?" it said.

I did. I had no words.

"I have a story to tell you," it said.

I'm all ears, I said.

"Correct," it said.

Then it began.

1980s

Boston

First, it was late August and David was hosting one of his dinners. "Look at the light, Ada," he said to her, as she stood in the kitchen. The light that day was the color of honey or of a roan horse, any warm organic thing like that, coming through the leaves of the tree outside the window in handsome dapples, lighting parts of the countertop generously, leaving others blue.

David said to her, "Please tell me who explained the color of that light."

"Grassmann," she said.

And he said, "Please tell me who first described refraction."

"Snell."

"Before Snell."

It was a name she couldn't remember, and she placed a hand on the counter next to her, unsteadily.

"Ibn Sahl," he said to her. "It was the genius Ibn Sahl."

David was fond of light in all its forms, fond of recalling the laws of optics that govern it. He had a summer cold that day, and from time to time he paused to blow his nose, gesticulating between each exhalation to make some further point. He was wearing his most comfortable shirt, wearing old leather sandals that he had bought for himself in Italy, and his toes in the sandals flexed and contracted with the music he had chosen—Brendel, playing Schubert—and his knees weakened at each decrescendo and straightened at long rests. In the blue pot was a roux that he was stirring mightily. In the black pot were three lobsters that had already turned red. He had stroked their backs before the plunge; he had told her that it calmed them. "But they still feel pain, of course," he said. "I'm sorry to tell you." Now he took the lobsters out of the pot, operating the tongs with his right hand, continuing to stir the roux with his left, and it was too hot for all of this, late summer in an old Victorian in Dorchester. No air-conditioning. One fan. Windows open to the still air outside.

This was how Ada Sibelius liked her father: giddy with anticipation, planning and executing some long-awaited event, preparing for a dinner over which he was presiding. David was only selectively social, preferring the company of old friends over new ones, sometimes acting in ways that might be interpreted as brusque or rude; but on occasion he made up his mind to throw a party, and then he took his role as host quite seriously, turning for the evening into a ringmaster, a toastmaster, a mayor.

That day was such an occasion, and David was deep into his preparations. He was director of a computer science laboratory at the Boston Institute of Technology, called the Bit, or the Byte if he was feeling funny. And each year in August, he invited a group of his colleagues to a welcome dinner in honor of the new graduate students who annually came through the lab. Ada knew her father's peers nearly as well as she knew him, and in a way they also felt to her like parents: alongside David, they had raised her, whether or not they realized it. She was, in theory, homeschooled, but in fact she had been lab-schooled, spending each day at her father's work, putting in the same hours he and his colleagues did. At night he rounded out parts of her education that he felt he hadn't adequately addressed: he taught her French, and gave her literature to read, and narrated the historical movements he deemed most significant, using Hegelian dialectic as a theoretical framework. She had no tests, only spontaneous oral quizzes, the kind he was giving her now while he stirred and stirred the roux.

"Where did we leave off," he asked Ada, "with Feynman diagrams?" And when she told him he asked her to please illustrate what
she had said on the chalkboard hanging on the kitchen wall, with a
piece of chalk so new that it stuttered painfully over the slate.

He looked at her work over his shoulder. "Correct," he said, and
that was all he usually said, except when he said, *Wrong.*

All afternoon he had been chattering to her about his latest crop of
grad students. These ones were named Edith, Joonseong, and Giordi;
and Ada—who had not yet met them—pictured them respectively as
prim, Southern, and slightly inept, because she had misheard *Joonseong* as *Junesong* and *Giordi* as *Jordy,* a nickname for a pop star, not
a scientist.

"They were very good in their interviews," said her father. "Joonseong will probably be strongest," he said.

That night Ada was in charge of the cocktails, and she had been
instructed on how to make them with chemist-like precision. First,
she lined up eight ice-filled highball glasses and six limes on a tray
with a lobster pattern on it, which her father had bought for these
occasions, to match the lobster he would be serving for the meal.
Into the frosted highball glasses she poured sixty milliliters of gin.
She cut the six limes in half and flicked out their exposed seeds with
the point of the knife and then squeezed each lime completely into
each glass. She placed two tablespoons of granulated sugar into the
bottom of each and stirred. And then she filled each glass up with
club soda, and added a sprig of mint. And she put a straw in each, too,
circling the glass twice with it, giving the liquid a final twirl.

It was 6:59 when she finished and their guests were due at 7:00.

The lobsters were cooked and camping under two large overturned mixing bowls on the counter, so they would stay just slightly
warmer than the room—the temperature at which David preferred to
serve them. Her father had made his cream sauce and was assembling
the salad he had dreamed up of endive and grapefruit and avocado.

He was moving frantically now and she knew that talking to him would be a mistake. His hands were trembling slightly as he worked. He wanted it all to be simultaneously precise and beautiful. He wanted it all to work.

"What am I forgetting," he said to Ada tensely.

Lately she had noticed a change in her father's disposition, from blithe and curious to concerned and withdrawn. For most of her life, Ada's father had been better at talking than at listening, but not when it came to her lessons. When it came to her lessons, to the responses she gave, he was rapt. When it came to some other, lesser topic of conversation, he drifted from time to time, looking out the window, or at what he was working on, giving birth to moments of silence that lasted longer than she thought possible and ending only when she said, "David?"

Where he had formerly sat and chatted with her or furthered her lessons until it was time for bed, now he went into his home office and worked on his computer, sometimes staying up until the early hours of the morning, sometimes falling asleep at his desk and hurrying to work with a spiderweb of red lines upon his face from whatever had creased it overnight. Sometimes she woke to find him writing at the kitchen table, filling yellow notepads with unknowable screeds, blinking at her with a certain lack of recognition when she wandered into his orbit. Sometimes he went off on walks without telling her, returning hours later with little explanation. Sometimes she woke to find him puttering around the house in odd attire: his swim trunks or his one suit jacket, a wrench or hammer in his hand, fixing things that he never before had seemed to notice. He had always kept a workbench and a sort of makeshift laboratory in a room off the basement—it was where he had taught her chemistry, with various substances he borrowed from friends at the Bit or extracted from household products or from nature—but he spent more time there now, building devices in glass and plastic that looked meaningless to Ada. They looked like goggles, or helmets, or masks. She had donned several of them, when her father was out, and found them heavy and useless; she could not see out of them, though they bore openings over each eye. "What are they?" she asked him, and he had only told her they were part of a new project.

He still ate dinner with her each night but recently had seemed abstracted, or in a fog: she tried to engage him with questions about history or physics or mathematics, but the answers he gave were short ones, not the usual lengthy monologues he formerly delivered with such gusto, and these days he never asked her questions afterward to make sure that she had understood. But her lessons were still regular enough, and interesting, and with very little effort Ada could easily persuade herself that he was fine. She told herself that he must be working on something quite important, something he didn't yet feel ready to share with anyone, even her. Convincing herself of this was in every way an act of self-preservation, because her world revolved entirely around her father, and any disturbance in this orbit threatened to send her spinning into space.

"Cheese and crackers," David said. "Of course."

Ada ran to get them, but the kitchen was disastrous by then and she overturned one of the gin rickeys in the process. It leaked onto the lobster tray and down the side of her leg.

"Shit," she said, too quietly to be heard. She had recently learned to curse: it was her one act of rebellion against her father, who was not prudish but thought that cursing was uncreative, in some way unintelligent.

She mopped up the liquid with a rag and got out the cheese and crackers and put them on a wooden cutting board—"Put some of the mustard in the center," said her father; "Not like that, like this"—and then, as she was making a new drink, the doorbell rang. It was a four-part chime that David had rigged himself, the first four notes of Beethoven's Fifth—which themselves were, he had explained to her, meant to sound like death or fate, some powerful perennial force, rapping at the door. Her father sprinted out of the kitchen and into the main room to let in his first guest, and from the kitchen she heard that it was Liston: the low confident voice, the local accent that enthralled her, that she imitated in private, that she and her father did not have.

"Come in, come in," said David, "come in, my Liston."

Liston had a first name: it was Diana, but for as long as Ada had known her she had been only Liston to David, and therefore she was Liston to Ada, too. Liston, his best friend, his best thinker, first author on all of his papers; Liston, their neighbor, who lived four houses away from them. It was Liston who convinced David to move to this neighborhood shortly after Ada's birth: a studio apartment in the Theater District would not work for a father and daughter, she had told him, once the daughter was over the age of four. So Liston's friend Connie Reardon, the real estate kingpin of Dorchester, had found David this house on this street, Shawmut Way, and Liston had approved, and began calling him "neighbor" for laughs.

Liston was very smart and impressively self-educated: David had said once that she was raised on the wrong side of the bridge in Savin Hill by a plumber and a homemaker, on the middle floor of a triple-decker, and Ada had asked him what it meant to be from the wrong side of the bridge, and he said it was poorer over there, and then she asked him what a homemaker was, and he told her it was a woman who does nothing but raise her children and keep her husband happy and her house tidy. "Very unlike Liston," he had stated approvingly.

Liston was Ada's favorite person in the world aside from David. She gathered scraps of information about Liston's life as if assembling a quilt: Liston no longer had a husband. She had an older daughter, Joanie, twenty-six and out of the house now, and three younger sons. David had briefly recounted the story of Liston's divorce: she married too young, at eighteen, because Joanie was on the way. It was to a boy from her neighborhood, he told Ada, someone who did not understand the scope of her talent and the particular requirements of her career. (Ada had vague memories of this husband, who was still married to Liston for the first five years of Ada's life: she remembered a large, unpleasant figure who never made a noise, except to exhale occasionally after something Liston said.) After Joanie was born, Liston worked her way through UMass as an undergraduate and then, after several professors there noticed her outstanding scientific and mathematical mind, she earned her doctorate in electrical engineering from Brown. David hired her as a postdoc, and later full-time. Liston divorced her husband right after the birth of her son Matty, four years younger than Ada, and since that time had relied on a large network of the women friends she grew up with for child care and emotional support. In the words of David, the husband was no longer in the picture, and good riddance. "This must be the most important factor in your choice of a life partner," he told Ada. "Who will most patiently and enthusiastically support your ambitions?"

"Shouldn't she have recess, or something?" Liston once asked David, several years before, when she noticed Ada becoming pale from spending every day inside the lab. "Agreed," said David, and so every day at lunch he had begun to march her around the Fens for thirty minutes, observing the flora, naming the birds by their songs, pointing out where Fibonacci sequences occurred in nature, once finding a mushroom that he said was edible and then cooking it up for the lab. Sometimes Liston joined them, and when she did it was a special treat: she derailed David's monologues at times; she told Ada about her childhood; she told Ada about the music that her three sons listened to, and the television shows they watched, and at night Ada wrote down what she had heard in her journal for future reference, in the unlikely event that she was ever called upon to discuss popular culture with one of her peers. Often, Ada felt as if Liston were teaching her some new language. She consumed greedily everything that Liston told her. She looked at her with wide fixated eyes.

Now, entering their house, Liston said, "My God, David, it's *hot*," except her accent made it sound like *hut*. Of Liston's many verbal particularities, Ada's favorites were as follows: *bahth*, Liston said, for bath; and *hoss* for horse; and she used various expressions passed down to her by her mother that Ada rolled around in her head like marbles. "He's been in and out like a fiddlah's elbow," she'd said once about David, who had a habit of letting his office door slam, not out of anger but out of forgetfulness.

Solemnly Ada brought a drink to her and Liston thanked her and called her her favorite girl, and she asked Ada to tell her why it was that her sons weren't so polite, asked her to please explain what was wrong with them. David retreated to the kitchen to keep things in order and then the doorbell went again, and this time it was Liston who opened it.

The man on the porch was wearing leather driving shoes and fitted red shorts the color of the cooked lobsters and a white button-down linen shirt that looked cool despite its long sleeves, which he had rolled up to his elbows. He was impressively tan. Dark hair coated his calves and rose up from the top button of his shirt and rose thickly back, in waves, from his noble brow.

"Are you Ada?" he asked her, after greeting Liston, and she added another accent to her mental list of sounds to ponder and reproduce. She nodded.

"A pleshure. I'm Giordi," he said, and introduced himself by kissing her one time on each cheek. Ada was used to this exchange from interactions with her father's many European colleagues, and from the many graduate students who had come to the Bit from other parts of the world; but it never failed to fluster her and to make her feel impossibly self-conscious, aware of her physical self in a way she did not like to be. There was the feeling always that she should be prettier than she was. That she should be better dressed, more put together. Like Giordi. Like some of the other members of the lab, Charles-Robert, Hayato. Unlike Liston, who dyed her hair a tinny red and sometimes wore clothes that were too young for her, and unlike

David, who prided himself on caring more about almost everything than clothing. Food, yes; science, yes; Ada, yes; clothing, no. And he expected this of Ada also—that she would rank her wants in the same order he ranked his own. The wants she did not tell him about (cable television, Nancy Drew books, a waterfall of bangs like Liston's, a hair accessory called a *banana clip* that looked something like a foothold trap) felt to Ada shameful and perverse. They felt to her ignoble.

"Would you like a drink?" she asked Giordi, as she had been taught, and then she led him down the hallway toward the kitchen, where David greeted him. Giordi took the gin rickey in his hands, putting his lips to the rim of the glass, ignoring the straw.

"Did you made these?" he asked Ada, about the drink, and she told him that she did, fixating on the grammatical mix-up he had let slip, pondering its structure.

"Delicious," he said. "Wherever did you learn."

"From my father," she told him.

She had learned everything from her father.

Ada was twelve years old. She would have been in seventh grade that year, if she had been enrolled in a school. She had never kissed a boy, never held hands with a boy. Had never, in fact, intentionally been within the vicinity of a boy her own age for more than a few minutes. Nor a girl. Her only interaction with boys and girls her own age had been with the children of her father's colleagues, who in general led more normal lives than she did—*normalcy* being a condition that her father disdained and she revered. And even these interactions had been cursory. Ada's behavior around these children was absurd. When she got near them she drank them up. She took them in. She was silent. She watched them like a television show. She took note of every turn of phrase they used. *Like*, they said. *Rad. Prolly. No way. As if. Freaky. Whatsername. Hang out. What's up? Duh. Creep. Freaked out.* They were freaked out by her, probably. She didn't blame them.

Ada was much more accustomed to spending time with adults,

and tonight she would have been very much at ease except that she could sense her father's tension and it made her tense. He had always been a perfectionist when it came to his dinners, but tonight was extreme: he had been preparing for days, writing down lists, stopping at the store each evening for things he had forgotten. She could not articulate what was different in his demeanor, but it triggered a deep-seated uneasiness in her. It was a hair in her mouth or sand in her shoe. She looked at her father now: he was lifting up the mixing bowls to show Giordi the cooked lobsters on the countertops.

"*Aragosta, sì?*" asked her father, who prided himself on speaking enough of every language to get by in restaurants at the conferences he went to in Europe, in Asia.

But Giordi shook his head. "Those are *astici*," he said. "*Aragoste* have the little things like . . ." he said, and he mimed spikes. "And they don't have the big . . ." and he mimed claws, pinching his thumbs and his tightened fingers together.

"*Astici*," said David, and Ada knew from his expression that he was attempting to file the word in a deep recess of his mind.

The other members of the lab arrived next, Hayato and Frank, and then Joonseong—whom she quickly realized was neither Southern nor female—and Edith—whom she quickly realized was not prim, but young and pretty. The only missing member of the lab was Charles-Robert, whose daughter had a soccer game. Ada gave each of them drinks in the living room and watched everyone as they fell into patterns of conversation: Liston and Hayato, the fun ones, were huddled in a corner, laughing about something or someone at work; they'd continue to huddle until one or the other realized that they were hovering on the verge of rudeness, and then they would break into conversation with someone else. Edith and Joonseong were speaking with Frank, who was much more polite than the rest of the group, engaging them in various lines of inquiry about their background and their families and their home countries and their accommodations in Boston.

Ada hovered in the background until Liston noticed her and waved her over, and she put a strong and steady arm around her, brought her in close to her side, and squeezed.

"Good drinks, kiddo," said Liston. Ada sank into her side, grateful for something she couldn't articulate.

At 8:00, Ada's job was to ask all the guests, politely, to be seated for the meal.

The night before, David had made place cards: before she'd gone to bed she'd seen him fashioning them with index cards and a ball-point pen, sitting at the kitchen table, the tip of his tongue just visible between his lips. Now they were assembled on the rectangular table. Ada, sitting between Edith and Joonseong, wished that she had been seated next to Liston, her favorite, or Giordi, whom she had decided was quite handsome—but she knew that one of the things that David expected of her was that she would help him to entertain his guests. She took this role seriously, and, in preparation for the night, had dreamed up several topics of conversation that she felt ready to introduce if necessary, culled from the newspaper and from the books she was reading.

David was passionate about cooking—to him it was a cousin of chemistry—and the first course was chilled cucumber soup, made in a blender, thickened with cream, which she helped him to transport from the kitchen, careful not to spill. "A regular Julia Child," said Liston. Ada brought cold white wine to the table and poured it neatly into every glass, including a splash into her own: since she turned twelve, David had been allowing her a quarter of a glass on special occasions. The several sips of wine she was allotted made her feel warm and capable, made her feel as if there were real possibilities before her in the universe, that they were hers for the taking.

Next were the lobsters, but before they were brought out David smacked his head and returned to the kitchen.

"I almost forgot," he said, and reemerged with a bundle of plastic in his hands. On his face was a look of almost exquisite lack of self-awareness—he was so pleased with himself, so pleased with life in that moment. He raised his eyebrows in glee.

"Oh, here they come," Liston said. They were the lobster bibs that David had gotten from Legal Sea Foods, years ago, at a dinner out with his colleagues. Putting them on was the traditional rite of passage for all the new grad students at David's annual feast: he delighted in these sorts of place-specific rituals, reveled in the New England-ness of it all, took pleasure in his longtime residency in the region (and in seditiously dismissing his own past as a New Yorker), wished to bestow this piece of local color on every visitor who passed over his threshold. The bibs were five years old by then and badly tattered, but over and over again David trotted them out for dinners with new friends, because they said *LOBSTAH* on them in a Gothic script, and he thought this was a funny joke, and was quite proud of them.

He passed them out one at a time to every guest.

"And you wear this for all dinner?" asked Giordi, incredulously, and David nodded.

"It gets quite messy," he told Giordi. "You'll be grateful later on."

Now David brought the lobsters out, two at a time, carrying them in his hands, and he examined every one, looked it in its lobster face and declared which guest would consume it. "You look like a lobster for Frank," he said to the largest, "and you for Ada," he said to the smallest. There was cold potato salad on the table, and cold asparagus, and little pots of drawn butter and lemon that David had positioned precisely in front of every guest, and three ramekins of cream sauce that were meant to be shared. There were tomatoes that David had picked from his garden, festooned with mozzarella and basil.

David raised his glass once the lobsters were distributed. "To our new graduate students," he said. "Welcome to Boston."

"The home of the bean and the cod," said Edith.

"And the lobster," said Hayato.

Sufficient alcohol had been consumed; there were no uneasy pauses, no long breaks in conversation that required Ada to bring forth one of her prepared talking points. Instead, she sat next to Edith and took in her outfit. She was even more beautiful than Ada had initially realized, and a sort of smooth-skinned glowing ease emanated from her person, into the thrall of which Ada imagined men fell powerfully. Edith was fashionable and reserved: Ada noticed with some jealousy that one of the banana clips she coveted pulled Edith's hair away from her face loosely, giving her a look of orchestrated carelessness. She wore a sleeveless, collared floral dress with a knee-length hemline and buttons done up to her neck. She did not carry a purse but there were large pockets on the dress, and Ada wondered what she kept in them: A pen, maybe. Lipstick, maybe: her lips were a light unnatural pink, a radioactive color that David probably did not like. A lighter, Ada thought. She could have been a smoker; many of David's European colleagues were. She was remarkably pretty.

Edith turned, caught Ada observing her, smiled.

"How old are you, Ada?" she asked: the first question new adults usually asked.

"Twelve," Ada said, and Edith nodded sagely.

"And what are your favorite books?"

"*The Lord of the Rings* books," Ada said, "are my favorite books of all time."

In fact they were her father's favorite books of all time, but she had adopted them as her own so fully that she was no longer certain what the truth was.

Edith studied her for a moment. "Twelve," she said. "A difficult age for me. Better for you, I'm sure."

Was it? Ada looked around the table at her father and her friends. They were her constant source of companionship, of knowledge, of camaraderie; each one offered to her some necessary part of her existence: Frank for kindness, and Liston for protection and love and common sense, and Hayato for artistry and humor. And the others, who could not make it: Charles-Robert for confidence and a sort of half-serious disdain for outsiders; Martha, the young secretary of the division, for knowledge of popular culture and fashion. And, above all others, David, for devotion and knowledge and loyalty and trust, David as the protector and guide of them all. But despite the completeness of what the adults around her offered to Ada, the sense of reassurance and comfort they extended, something was missing from her brief existence, and she knew, though she could not bring herself to fully form the thought, that it was friends her own age.

The dinner moved through salad and into dessert—Giordi had playfully kept his bib on well beyond the lobster course, insisting that he could not be trusted without one and that he would wear one regularly now—and Ada leapt up several times to refill the wine glasses of the guests. A fast-moving storm had swept through the neighborhood, and the house was finally cooling off. A damp breeze came in through the windows. They were near enough to the ocean to smell it, on nights like these. David invited everyone into the living room, and Ada stayed behind to clear the table.

When she had finished, she joined the group, and found that the guests had arranged themselves into little clusters. She hesitated for a while on the threshold of the living room, wiping her hands on the back of her shirt, and then joined Frank and Joonseong. In moments when it seemed appropriate, she produced some of the topics she had earlier bookmarked for discussion—a recent shooting in Mattapan; a French film from the 1950s that David had taken her to see at the Brattle; the restaurants surrounding the Bit, and their strengths and weaknesses—but she found herself increasingly distracted by David, who was standing slightly apart from any group, gazing at the floor. He had his hands clasped behind his back; he looked vaguely, unsettlingly lost. Ada nodded and feigned attentiveness as Joonseong told her about his new apartment, but in her peripheral vision she saw

David walking slowly toward the window, as if lured there by a spell: he stood still then, and she saw his lips moving quickly, his hands hanging stiffly by his sides.

"David," said Liston, who was closest to him. "Are you all right?" Ada saw her say it. And at this he lifted his head quickly, and smiled, and turned and clapped his hands once. Everyone looked at him.

"A riddle," David announced, "for the newest members of the lab. And the first to solve it gets a prize."

Ada heard a thickness in his voice that she didn't recognize. She would have thought he was drunk, except that he rarely drank: a glass or two of wine was all he ever took, and tonight he'd barely had any at all. Together, everyone watched him.

This was his ritual: to each new crop of grad students, he delivered the same riddle, one he adored for its simplicity and the justice of its logic. All the permanent members of the lab could recite it and its answer in unison: they had all heard it so many times. Still, it comforted Ada somehow to hear him deliver it each year, as if it were scripture—to watch the same looks of thoughtfulness pass over the faces of the grad students, and then a lighting-up when one of them came upon the answer.

Everyone watched David expectantly: classmates observing a teacher. He cleared his throat and began. "You are a traveler who has come to a fork in the road between two villages," he said. "The village of West is full of only murderous men incapable of telling the truth; visiting it will bring about your death. The village of East is full of benevolent men incapable of lying; visiting it will bring to you a cache of gold. Two men stand in the fork in the road—one from West and one from East. But you don't know which is which. In order to determine how to reach the village full of gold, and avoid your certain doom, you may ask only one question of only one man. What should your question be?"

The grad students paused. One of them would ask David to repeat the problem: it happened every year. This year was Joonseong, and most likely it was due to his English, not to his logical abilities. David incanted the riddle once again, repeating it word for word. Edith was smiling about something Ada couldn't determine, and at the end of David's second recitation she put a hand out before her to signal that she had an announcement.

"I'm recusing myself. I know the answer because I've heard the puzzle before. I cannot tell a lie," she said.

"I suppose that makes me an Easterner," she added, and Giordi laughed too eagerly, or perhaps he was simply grateful to have understood her joke.

David then turned to Giordi and Joonseong, with some seriousness, and informed them that it was between the two of them, and reminded them of the prize. Both of them looked down at the floor contemplatively. Ada's money was on Joonseong, from the way her father had described both men. But there was a silence over the room that went on for quite some time, and eventually both of them looked at one another and then at David. Joonseong raised his hands in surrender.

David looked pleased.

"Giving up, are you?" he asked them, giddily. "Even you, Giordi?" If David's first love was being stumped, his second was stumping others.

David opened his mouth. Then he closed it.

"Your question must be," David said. "Your question," he said again.

He folded one arm about himself and put the other hand to his cheek. Everyone watched him. A slow unfurling sense of panic filled the room.

"My word," said David, slowly. "I seem to have forgotten the answer."

This was a moment that became sealed forever in Ada's memory, encased in glass, a display in the museum of David's decline. She never forgot the brief silence that followed, during which everyone looked down at the floor and then up again, or the way that Giordi loudly cleared his throat. Or the way that David looked at her, almost in horror: the look of a pilot who has just discovered that the engines of his plane have failed. The humiliation Ada felt on his behalf was almost too much to bear. At last, she let herself articulate in her mind the thought that she had been repressing for a year or more: that something was wrong with David.

"Oh, you know it, David," Liston finally said. "My God, of course you do." She looked around at the rest of the group entreatingly. "The traveler would point to either of the villagers and ask the other one, 'Which way would *he* tell me to go to get to the cache of gold?' And either man would say, 'West.'"

David nodded. "Yes."

"The liar would say that the truth-teller would say West, because he only lies. The truth-teller would say that the liar would say West, because he knows that the liar always lies. West either way," said Liston.

"And so *you* would go to the village of East," said Liston. "And find the cache of gold. And then you'd take your friend Liston out for a nice steak dinner."

"Yes," said David. "Quite right. You're quite right, Liston."

There was still too much silence in the room. David looked lost, the smile gone from his face, staring at the wall opposite him as if looking into the future.

Ada wondered if this was a moment that she should fill with conversation.

"Today is the one-hundredth anniversary of the disastrous eruption of the volcano Krakatoa," she said. It was one of the news items that she had culled from the paper.

"Oh, really?" said Edith. "I hadn't heard."

"Of course," David said. "What would *he* say?"

"You knew it," said Liston.

"I knew it," said David, pensively.

"I suppose this means you win the prize, Liston," he added, and then he walked out of the room.

Frank murmured something about it being late. Hayato announced that he'd give the grad students a ride home.

And Ada stood frozen in the living room, not knowing what to say.

Liston squeezed her shoulders and went to the kitchen to say goodbye to David and then, from the front hallway, called out, "Good night, Ada, see you on Monday!"

"Good night," Ada said quietly. She did not know whether Liston heard her.

She heard the sound of the front door opening and closing, and then the thunder of six pairs of feet going down the old wooden stairs of the porch, punctuated by a quick, indecipherable interjection from a male voice.

For a moment the house was quiet. And then she heard the front door open once more. David cried out, "Liston! Your prize!"

From the living room, Ada peered out into the hallway to see the back of her father. He was standing with a hand on the open door, his head bowed. In the other hand he held a little golden bag of chocolates he had bought the day before at Phillips's. Liston was out of earshot, probably already walking up the steps to her porch. The taillights of Hayato's car went past the house and were gone. After a few moments David closed the door, and Ada disappeared before he could turn and see her.

She washed the dishes. For twenty minutes, she let the warm water run over her hands.

Finally, she went to the dining room to retrieve the tablecloth and there was David, sitting at the long dining room table, turning over and over in his hands a sort of worry stone, a lucky charm in the shape of a clover. He kept it in his pocket wherever he went. He said it helped him to think. He looked vague and puzzled.

He shifted his gaze toward her. She was angry with him for reasons she knew were unjust. She had never before seen his mind fail him so resoundingly. It threatened to rattle her long-standing impression of him as someone stately, noble, just.

"Sit down," he told her.

She paused.

"Just for a moment," he said. "Please."

She complied, and he rose and walked into his office, which opened off the dining room. It was one of the only places in the house that Ada avoided: the desk was mired completely in piles of papers; the built-in bookshelves were filled entirely, and stacks of books had begun to take over the floor. She saw the back of him as he bent to open one of the drawers of the desk, and from it he produced what he was looking for, and turned and carried it back with him. He sat down across from her once more.

"Here," he said. Ada looked at it. It was a floppy disk, and on the hard cover of it, a white plastic clamshell, he had written, *For Ada*. She opened it. On the label affixed to the disk itself, there was a message: *Dear Ada*, it said. *A puzzle for you. With my love, your father, David Sibelius.*

"It's a present," he said. "Something I've been working on."

"What is it?" she asked him.

"You'll see," he said. "You'll see when you open it."

Ada was born in 1971 to a woman whom David had hired as a surrogate. At the time this was nearly unheard-of, but—as David described it—when the opportunity arose, he took it. The surrogate was a hippie-ish woman named Birdie Auerbach, and Ada had had no contact with her since, though at the time of her birth Birdie had made it clear to David, and David had subsequently made it clear to Ada, that she could if she wanted to. But throughout Ada's childhood she had felt she really didn't need to; she felt that somehow it would be a betrayal to David if she did.

Ada never questioned his decision to bring a child into the world; her connection to him was so complete that it felt entirely natural to her. She imagined that he simply decided he wanted a child and then had one. David had never had a romance in Ada's lifetime, not that she was aware of. He was devoted to his friends and colleagues and to various people whom he occasionally mentored: there had been a number of grad students over the years, and the piano tuner, and the landscaper who mowed the lawn, whom he often invited inside for lemonade and quizzed about his business plans. There was a young girl who lived down the street who showed promise as a ballet dancer, and he encouraged her mother, with whom he had developed a friendship, to bring her to audition at the School of American Ballet in New York City—the only place, he assured her, that one could really get a proper education in dance in the United States. He spent long hours talking with Anna Holmes, the librarian at the nearest branch of the Boston Public Library, about her life and her hobbies and her interests. She was pretty, unmarried at fifty, and could possibly, Ada thought, be in love with David. He had taken an interest in her, and in all of these acquaintances, but though he discussed them with Ada frequently and exhaustively—speculating about their friendships, their home lives, their careers—it seemed clear to her that his interest in Miss Holmes was platonic, though Ada would not even have thought to articulate it as such. He never discussed his romantic history overtly with anyone, as far as she knew. It would have seemed to him undignified. Ada had heard only vaguely about former girlfriends, young debutantes he had known when he was growing up as part of New York's upper class. She had always slept soundly, but she had some vague memories of hearing a female voice in the living room, though she also could have been dreaming. Ada supposed it was possible that on those occasions her father could have been entertaining a guest. He would never, ever have talked to her about it. The idea would have been repugnant to him: he had always been private about his personal life to an extreme, even with Ada, despite the fact that he regularly assured her of her great importance to him and of the fact that he thought of her as his closest companion.

David was forty-six when Ada was born and had already been head of his own lab for sixteen years. For the first years of her life—when she was too young to entertain herself for long days at work—Ada had a nanny, Luda, a tall, soft-spoken Russian woman with one long braid down her back, whom David hired to watch her while he was out. But at night and on the weekends it was David and Ada alone. The fact that she survived her infancy astounded her sometimes. She couldn't imagine it, though she often tried: David, waking up in the night to attend to her, warming bottles, boiling them; or preventing her from falling off of anything high or running into anything low or being bitten by anything mean; or taking her to the park in a stroller; or folding her snugly into a blanket; or gazing down at her while she ate from a bottle; or letting her fall asleep on his fatherly chest: these actions seemed so incongruous with Ada's idea of David as to be impossible. And yet he must have done these things: she was alive as the proof.

Ada's memories of David began later, with their conversations. She could not remember not talking to David. Every waking hour was, in his mind, an opportunity for interesting conversation, a chance to analyze their lives and the lives of all humans. "Are we very happy, Ada?" he often asked her, and she always said yes, though sometimes with hesitation—as if she knew that the question itself implied the opposite. But for the most part, she was utterly content with her strange, satisfying existence: Ada and David together, always.

He had small rituals: he made tea in an elaborate old-fashioned way that, he said, his mother taught him; and he watched a certain police drama religiously, the only television show he enjoyed, often shouting out the perpetrator's name halfway through the episode, crowing each time he was correct; and when Ada was small, before bedtime he would read to her from books that he loved, never children's books; and on Sunday afternoons he liked to go to a particular café in Dorchester to organize his brain. Ada did whatever homework he had assigned her while he wrote out formulas and drew diagrams, in his cramped particular handwriting, on stacks of napkins provided to him by Tran, the eponymous owner of the café, who was himself an amateur scientist, well versed in Feynman and Planck. Her father, though a computer scientist by profession, had a strong background in pure mathematics. He was interested in all the sciences, and in the humanities as well: he had learned French as a boy and still spoke it fairly well, and from time to time would attempt to teach himself something like Mandarin or Portuguese. "A well-rounded thinker should be able to puzzle out from scratch any proof that has ever been proven," he said to Ada, and so sometimes to keep sharp he would work out some problem of physics or mathematics, although it had nothing to do with his research. When he was working on these, or on any puzzle, he would fall into a trance familiar to his closest associates—in which his body seemed utterly, utterly at the will of his mind—in which his hands, writing furiously, seemed overtaken by a ghost. He was expressionless, an automaton, and could not be spoken to until he returned. On the occasions when, in one of these trances, he worked himself to sleep, Ada put a hand on his shoulder—one of the few times she ever touched her father—and he sat up and blinked, disoriented, until he realized where he was.

Her father spoke of his past only rarely, but occasionally he would agree to tell Ada the tale of his life as a story before bed. She begged him to: it was a way of expanding her family, a way to counteract the feeling she sometimes had that the two of them were stranded on an island. To comfort herself, Ada sometimes narrated his life in her head, using the wording he would have used.

David was born in New York City, he told her, the only child of wealthy parents to whom he would eventually stop speaking. They died before Ada was born. He described them with bitterness and scorn, ridiculing their conventionality, their closed-mindedness, their snobbery. (Ada did not point out to her father, though it occurred to her, that many of his opinions could be labeled snobbery as well; and that his last name, well known in the Northeast, had opened various doors for him that he seemed not to notice.) The rift between David and his parents, which led at last to a complete estrangement by his late twenties, was caused by *differences of opinion regarding how he should live his life*—the phrase he always used. He hinted vaguely at their displeasure at his choice of career, his refusal to accept their introductions to the various young ladies they would have liked to see him marry, his refusal to obey the conventions and codes that accompanied the family's status. "Debutantes and that sort of thing," said David. "Charity balls. *Teas*." At the mention of these terms he would shudder, which signified an end to the story. Ada rarely pressed him beyond this point.

The derisive, sardonic tone he used when speaking of his past implied he had long ago moved on, had long ago dismissed those families and their ilk as fraudulent and obsolete. From his scraps of description Ada gathered that his mother and father were stern and impersonal. Worse than that, she categorized them as uncreative—David's term, one he used only for those he held in complete disdain. His father had been a sort of gentleman attorney, one who only took on clients who were personal friends, and only then if he could be sure the work would end amicably. His mother had no career aside from identifying and articulating the flaws of her husband and son. Every conversation with her, he told Ada, was like a game of chess: one had to remain several steps ahead of her to ward off whatever criticism would be imparted if one's guard was let down.

In these moments Ada was jolted by a sudden vision of David as a child, subservient to his parents, not the master and commander of everything around him, as she'd thought of him for most of her childhood. It was difficult to picture.

This much she knew: David was raised on Gramercy Park in a grand and beautiful row home, up which ivy spread densely and then in rivulets, like fingers from a palm. She saw it once a year, in winter, when David took her for a weekend trip to New York City for Calvary Episcopal's annual Christmas concert. It was his childhood church—the only site from his childhood that he ever wished to revisit—and it was his favorite sort of music: early choral composition by Tallis and Purcell. He was not churchgoing, but it was liturgical music that moved him the most, and he sat very still and upright in the old wooden pew for the duration of every song, his head bowed as if in prayer. Only his fingers moved from time to time, playing his knees like an organ.

Afterward David would walk swiftly out the door, and Ada would run to keep pace with him—difficult to do, for he walked as if he were skating, with a lengthy, forceful stride—and turn left toward Gramercy Park, and then stand silently with Ada outside of the house for several seconds. They never spoke. Usually the heavy drapes inside the house were drawn by the time the concert let out, but once Ada saw a young girl, about her age, sitting with her mother at a dining room table. "I wonder if those are Ellises," said David idly, naming the family who purchased the home after the death of his parents. "I read about them in the paper. I've never met them.

"I would have been the only heir," he told Ada. "I wouldn't have taken it anyway," he added, and then he walked quickly down the street, without warning her, so that she had to run for several steps to catch him.

Despite his complete dismissal of his past, he kept one black-and-white portrait of himself with his parents in the dresser in his bedroom. Ada had discovered it when she was quite young and often returned to it whenever he was out. There he was, young David, perhaps eleven years old. In the picture he was wearing a bow tie, a tweed jacket with a high waist, short pants, knee socks. A very slight smile played upon his mouth—same mouth, same lively light eyes. His parents looked predictably dour and serious: mother in a black scoop-necked satin dress that ended just above her ankles, black stockings and black shoes, a long black beaded necklace. Father in a dark suit and tie, one leg crossed over the other. All three of them were positioned slightly apart from one another. In the background was a funny scene: draperies, slightly askew, framed a fuzzy, impressionist backdrop of trees and mountains.

Their next-door neighbor on Shawmut Way was an old woman named Mrs. O'Keeffe, who had come over from Ireland at ten years old, in 1910. She had worked as a maid in the same neighborhood David had grown up in, and then she met her husband and moved to Boston. This coincidence came up early in their acquaintance, and Ada watched David as he physically cringed. Discussions about his past were always an encumbrance to him, but from then on he had difficulty dodging Mrs. O'Keeffe, who wished frequently to reminisce with him about the other families who had occupied those homes. She had not known him but she had known his people. She would name the families of Gramercy Park as if counting her treasures. "And the Cromwells," she would say, "what a beauty their daughter was. And those Byrons, and those Harts, and those Carringtons . . ."

"Yes," David would say, "I knew all of them, once."

He graduated high school in 1943, right in the middle of the Second World War, which normally would have guaranteed a period of service. But David was, even at that age, nearsighted to the point of legal blindness without his glasses. Instead, therefore, he went to college. He chose Caltech—which further horrified his father, who had gone to Harvard, and his mother, who saw it as a vocational school, a school for the working class. There he majored in mathematics. He then found his way to the Bit, where he received a doctorate in applied mathematics, and where his work on GOPAC, an early computer system spearheaded by Maurice Steiner, earned him such quick fame in his field that he was given his own lab at the Bit by President Pearse at the age of thirty. It was named for Steiner, after his death, and with David at the helm, it quickly became known in the field. It was here in 1970 that he met Liston, then a young postdoc straight from her doctoral work at Brown, and here that they became friends. They were an odd pair: he was sixteen years her senior, but she was an old soul—both of them said it—with two children already and two more to follow. They spent a great deal of time together both in the lab and outside it. He fostered her already considerable talent, and spoke of her proudly as her role at the lab expanded. "The best pure thinker in the group," he said of her often, including himself in the tally. At this time, Charles-Robert and Hayato had already been hired, and Frank came shortly thereafter. A rotating cast of postdocs, grad students, and short-lived hires came and went, but the five of them, plus Ada, were the core.

Ada loved the lab: it was a dark and cozy complex of offices housed within the Applied Mathematics Division of the Bit, which itself was housed within one of the Bit's many Gothic buildings, and it felt more like a home than a workplace. For most of the fifties, sixties, and seventies, a mainframe computer dominated the largest room, toward the rear; by the late eighties it had become obsolete, but it remained in the lab as a sort of relic, a hulking, friendly dragon lying dormant in the back. The front of the lab was composed, with the exception of a larger conference room, of a warren of small rooms and offices, scattered with machines, some of which were perpetually stripped of their front panels, their innards revealed. Each office had been personalized over the years to reflect its owner. Hayato kept an easel in his, on which he sketched out problems and occasionally landscapes; and Charles-Robert had covered his walls entirely in maps; and Frank, the youngest, used to keep an elaborate network of hot plates and crock pots and electric kettles, on which he cooked surprisingly competent and complete meals for the whole department, until one day the building manager found him out and stopped him, citing fire department regulations. Liston's office was sparse but for a record player on which she played albums by ABBA and U2 and the Police, and a beanbag chair in which Ada sometimes napped when she was smaller. David's office consisted mainly of a collection of filing boxes that he added to yearly, too busy to go through them, too paranoid to dispose of their contents unexamined. The grad students worked part of the time across town at the Bit's smaller campus in the Medical Area, and the other half in cubicles in the main room. Anyone else who came through the lab as a temporary or permanent hire was placed into one of the three empty offices that were otherwise used by David as schoolrooms for Ada.

Many of her early memories involved the floor of the lab, the feet and ankles of scientists all around her. When she was very young she was given antique models of elements to play with. She was given a kit of wooden parts to make up atoms. Hayato blew up latex gloves, stolen from the biology department, and made turkeys of them with a felt-tipped pen. She was not taught nursery rhymes about geese and kings but about molecules: *Here lies dear old Harry, dead upon the floor. What he thought was H_2O was H_2SO_4.* She was named the mascot of the Steiner Lab, and there was a photograph of her dressed as a punch card to prove it.

She attended most formal meetings that the Steiner Lab conducted and she attended informal meetings, too, ducking in and out of offices at will, sitting still at the round brown table in the main room when the lab had lunch all together. And listening—always listening.

The theory of language immersion posits that a language is best learned by placing the learner into what is in effect a natural habitat, or a simulated habitat that strives for authenticity. Thus a student of Spanish will learn best not when she is taught to conjugate verbs but when she is surrounded by useful Spanish—not when she is taught Spanish for its own sake, but when she is taught every other subject in Spanish, too. More by default than intent, Ada was thus immersed in mathematics, neurology, physics, philosophy, computer science. She did not begin with Lisp, but with compiler design. In her physics lessons at home with David, she did not begin with $s = d/t$, but with the Grand Unified Theory. For the first years of her life, she did not know what she was hearing. Listening to David and his colleagues was like listening to radio chatter in a different language. And then, without knowing it or taking note of it, she began to be able to follow their conversations. By ten she was able to be a sounding board for her father as he worked out his ideas—not resolving them or bettering them, necessarily, but posing questions to him that were reasonable, and occasionally jarring something loose in him. When this happened, he reported Ada's concern or comment to the rest of the lab with some seriousness at the next lab meeting, and a slow glowing warmth spread throughout her, because she had made herself useful to the group, whom she thought of, always, as her peers.

"A good question, I think, Ada," David would say, and the rest of them would nod in agreement, and the group would move forward as one.

This was what Ada pictured when she thought of her father, the vision of David that she harbored and kept safe throughout her life, the idea pinned permanently to the sleepiest part of her brain: it was her father in his laboratory, or at Tran's Restaurant; or in the library of the institute that employed him; or, rarely, in a crowd of friends; or, regularly, at his desk, in his small absurd office in their home, contemplating a chessboard, his head as bald and round and sturdy as a pawn's. His woolen socks with holes in them. His hands the steeple of a church. He was tall and thin and rigorous in his studies and in his life, and he was inventive, and he was very warm and betrayed no one ever, and in Ada's mind he was ethical beyond compare, and he had a habit of rubbing his hands together quickly when he was delighted or moved, and he was quick and spry and gentle and able with his limbs and head. He was dexterous, and his fingernails were clean, and he was wise, and he was intent upon seeking out the best and most beautiful versions of pieces by Chopin, Schumann, Schubert, and Bach, and he knew excellent riddles, and his name was Dr. David Sibelius, and she never called him anything but David.

n the weeks and months that followed the dinner party, no one mentioned its strange end to Ada, her father's sudden lapse, or asked her any questions about David's increasingly odd behavior. Occasionally, at the lab, she felt as if she and David were being excluded from something: where formerly Liston or Charles-Robert would have welcomed her into any room—discussed the bugs in a particular program with her, put an arm about her shoulders—now there was often a feeling of conversations stopping when she rounded a corner. The new grad students found their way into the routine of the laboratory, and Ada kept a closer eye on her father, noting peculiarities in his speech or habits when they arose, attempting to classify them somehow.

In the evenings, she worked at the puzzle on the disk David had given her, marked *For Ada* on its case. It had turned out to be, when she'd inserted it into her computer and started it up, simply a text document with a short string of seemingly random letters.

DHARSNELXRHQHLTWJFOLKTWDURSZJZCMILW FTALVUHVZRDLDEYIXQ, it read.

David would not give her any clues. Together, they had been studying cryptography and cryptanalysis for the past several years—a hobby of David's that, he said, came out of his days at Caltech, where his mentor had been a cryptanalyst during the war—and he told her this was her next assignment. "It may take you a while," he admitted. "Don't let it affect your other work, of course."

While she worked, he worked: in his office, with the door now closed sometimes. She looked at the outside of it, vaguely hurt.

Then Christmas came, and with it the Christmas party that Ada always anticipated and dreaded in equal parts, for with it came outsiders.

David loved Christmas. In addition to their annual trip to New York, he insisted upon several other traditions, and balked at any suggestion of variance: after dinner on Thanksgiving he always put on the record player an album of the Trapp Family Singers performing Christmas songs from around the world, and he played this regularly until January 2, and then packed it away; then there was the Stringing of the Lights that occurred on the first Saturday of December, and which David executed with an efficiency that put the other fathers on the block to shame. In mid-December they cut down a Christmas tree at an orchard in the Berkshires, a daylong expedition that he put on the calendar with great seriousness on December 1; and after that they visited Cambridge, where Frank lived, to go with him to dinner at a local Chinese restaurant and then to Sanders Theatre to see the Christmas Revels—a sort of scholarly variety show of medieval Christmas pageantry, with a dose of druidism thrown in as well. Just the sort of thing that appealed to David and his cohort.

"Isn't it cozy out," David was fond of saying, on first snowfall. "Ada, come look." And if she was asleep, he would wake her; and she would rise from her bed, sleepy-eyed, rubbing her face, and walk to the window of their drafty house, and together she and David would stand in silence, together in the night, looking out onto Shawmut Way through a frosty, rattling window, their breath obscuring it slowly.

The Christmas party was the culmination of all of these traditions, and perhaps David's favorite tradition of all. He insisted, always, that a party was not complete without some entertainment,

a game, an organized activity that required everyone's participation.
Some years it was a hired guitarist or a group of carolers; some years
it was a juggler or a magician. ("What else is one supposed to do—
just stand around and drink?" asked David, perplexed.) It was this
philosophy that caused him to declaim the same riddle to the new
graduate students at the dinner he held for them every year; and it
was this philosophy that had caused him, that December, to write
a Christmas play for every member of the lab to perform, in front
of a small audience of colleagues from other departments, spouses
and children of lab members, and staff and administrators from other
parts of the university.

He had told none of them this in advance. Instead, at 9:00, tinging
his glass with a finger, he asked for everyone's attention, and directed
them all to form a semicircle in the main room of the lab.

"Here we go," said Hayato, good-naturedly.

"Except you, Hayato," said David. "You come up here. And you,
and you, and you," he said, grabbing the rest of the lab. "And you,"
he said, last, to Ada, who had been praying to be forgotten. Her face
burned as she walked to the front of the room and stood with the rest
of them. In front of her, she saw a blur of faces before looking quickly
down at the floor.

David was holding, in his left hand, a stack of stapled pages,
which he passed out to each of them with mock seriousness, a flour-
ish for each one. His face was pink and excited; his thick glasses were
slipping down on his nose.

He turned back to the audience. "A play!" he announced. "A
Christmas play."

Later, Ada would not remember its exact plot—something about
a group of superhero nerds sent back in time to determine how to
achieve a better lift-to-drag ratio for Santa's sleigh. (Ada played a
reindeer.) What she did remember: David's happiness, his complete
contentment at the execution of his plan, how carefree he looked; and
the way he directed them all, like a conductor with a baton; and her

own embarrassment, her burning face, her quiet, noncommittal line delivery; and, in the front row, the faces of the audience members, some of whom looked bemused, some of whom looked befuddled; and there, to the right, at the edge of the crowd, the face of William, Liston's oldest son, who stared at all of them incredulously, his mouth slightly agape.

n March she turned thirteen.

"A teenager," said David, shaking his head. "Hard to believe, isn't it, Ada?"

She nodded.

"Would you like a cake? I suppose you should have something festive," said David, but Ada said no.

Secretly, she had been wanting one, a candle to blow out, a wish to make. She had gotten only one present that year, from Liston, naturally: a hot-pink sweater with a purple zigzag pattern that Ada loved but felt too self-conscious to wear. David had not gotten her anything: she was not surprised, since he was both absentminded and vaguely opposed to consumerism. That year, however, she had been secretly hoping for something from him, which she only realized when nothing came. Some external signifier of what she thought was an important birthday. A piece of jewelry, maybe. An heirloom. Something timeless and important. She wished, too, as she had been doing with increasing frequency, that she and David could engage in some of the more typical conventions that accompanied occasions such as birthdays. A big party with friends, for example. A sleepover: she had never had a sleepover. She had no one to ask.

That evening, after a quiet dinner at home, the telephone rang, and David answered in his office.

"Yes?" he said, slowly, a note of surprise in his voice. It was nearly 11:00 at night. Normally Ada would have been in bed, but she felt unsettled and alight with something: the newness of being a teenager, perhaps. She felt untired and alert.

From the dining room, Ada listened to her father, in his office, on the phone; but David was quiet for some time. She could see the back of him, the receiver pressed to his ear. He said nothing.

Abruptly, he turned in her direction. She caught his eye quickly, and then he closed the door. Lately he had been intentionally excluding her from things, and each time she felt the sting of it sharply.

She sat for a while at the dining room table, but, although she could hear the low murmur of David's voice through the door, his words were indecipherable. She stood up.

She walked outside, into the sloping backyard behind the house on Shawmut Way. All of the yards on their side of the road were fenceless and connected, lined at the bottom of a small hill by a street-length row of trees. Dorchester was a city neighborhood comprised of other neighborhoods, mainly working-class, high in crime by the 1980s, appealing to David in part because of these features, because of his self-identification as somebody unassuming and down-to-earth. But the neighborhood they lived in, Savin Hill, was an old and Irish one, very safe, suburban in its aspect. Over a bridge that separated their part of Savin Hill from the rest of the city, two leafy roads formed an interior and exterior circle at the base of the hill the area was named for. Shawmut Way connected the two roads together, like a spoke in a wheel. A small beach spanned the eastern border of the neighborhood and a park with public tennis courts framed the central hill. Liston continued to live there because of these features and David had agreed to live there, against his normal preferences, despite them. "I feel like I'm on vacation," he said, often, when walking home from the T after work. This was, from David, a complaint. He preferred that his cities feel like cities; but his respect for Liston's advice, when it came to Ada's needs, outweighed his resistance.

In the cool hour before midnight she walked down to the base of their backyard, to where the pine trees lived, and she ran her hand along their branches to find her way, quietly, through the three back-yards between theirs and Liston's. Lately, Ada had been doing this regularly, perhaps once a week, while David was working at night. He had never pressed her for her whereabouts—or maybe he had not noticed. If he had, he approved, because he liked to foster independence in her, liked to imagine that his daughter could take care of herself. Certainly he did not know what drove Ada to conduct these nighttime walks, these missions, these compulsive marches in the dark. Certainly he would have been surprised to learn that it was William Liston, fifteen, the oldest of Diana Liston's sons. Certainly he did not know that Ada believed she was in love with him.

Since the Christmas party three months prior, Ada had thought about him almost unflaggingly, with a dedication singular to thirteen-year-old girls. For the first time, she also thought about herself, and her appearance. She stood in front of the mirrored vanity that David once told her had belonged to his mother, and she tilted her head first one way and then the other. Was she pretty? She could not say, and it had never before occurred to her to wonder. She was brown-haired and round-faced, with serious dark circles under her eyes and the beginning of several pimples on her chin. She had a widow's peak that David told her he had had, too, when he had any hair to speak of. Like David, too, she wore glasses, which she had never before minded, but which now seemed like an unfair handicap.

She fantasized often about what she would say, what she would do, the next time she was in the same room with William Liston—though this rarely happened. Although Diana Liston regularly came over to their house for dinner when asked, the offer was rarely reciprocated; and although Ada saw her regularly at the lab, her three sons never came with her. Instead they lived what Ada considered to be normal lives: they attended a normal school, excelled or failed at various normal things like sports and English class. They had no cause to visit their mother at work, except when required. Therefore, the only time Ada found herself face-to-face with William Liston—or, truly, anyone her age—was at lab parties.

There were two reasons she felt ashamed of her crush: the first was that her father would have thought it was ridiculous—Ada knew that she was certainly too young, in his mind, to be interested in boys—and the second was that William was Liston's son, and in a strange way she felt it was a betrayal of Liston to worship so ardently the child she complained about at lunch. "So listen to William's latest," she often said to Hayato, in front of Ada, and then proceeded to detail his most recent bout of mischief and the subsequent discipline he had received at school. Often it was for cutting class or leaving early; once, for forging a note from Liston excusing him from some assignment or other. He was caught by the number of misspellings he had included in the text. At the end of each account, Liston sighed and looked at Ada, mystified, and said, "Why couldn't I have had four girls just like you?" And it made Ada feel gratified and melancholy all at once, because she knew that of course Liston loved her own children better than Ada, no matter what she said. With some frequency, Liston crowed about her grandson, the child of her oldest daughter Joanie, casting upon him none of the judgment she reserved for her own children. The fact that, despite her complaints, she loved her brood so fiercely and protectively also made Ada feel ashamed—for it was clear to her that Liston, even Liston, would have laughed if she knew about Ada's crush. Because even Liston knew how little time the Williams of the world had for people like Ada.

But since the Christmas party, she had begun to dream up different ways of interacting with the object of her obsession. Sometimes she sat outside on her front porch with a book and a blanket, despite the cold—this had yielded several William sightings, and, once, a puzzled wave from him as he rode by on his bike. One cold night in January, Ada had begun the routine she was now shamefully conducting. Now when she saw William Liston it was mainly through the large downstairs windows at the back of the Liston house, under the cover of the pine trees that brushed against her shoulders as she walked. From that vantage point she memorized the facets of his eyes and nose, noticed new patterns in the kinetics of his body, the movements of his arms and elbows, the self-aware way he plucked his shirt out from his torso from time to time and let it fall again.

That night, when she was one backyard away, she heard a voice: Liston's, probably on her phone. At first Ada heard only murmurs, but as she approached she began to make out words: *I told Hayato,* said Liston, and *had to,* and *wouldn't,* and *bad.* Ada stopped in place. She weighed two options carefully. The first, the safer, was to turn back: she was comfortable in the patterns of her daily life. She had no information that would have caused her to question her understanding of her father or his work. Her disposition was sunny: she rose in the morning knowing how each day would go. Ada could imagine proceeding in this fashion for years.

The second was to venture forth to listen—ironically, it was this option that David would have encouraged her to choose, for he had always pushed Ada toward bravery, had always instilled in her the idea that bravery went hand in hand with the seeking of the truth.

So she walked forward quietly. As she approached Liston's yard, Ada saw the downstairs of the house lit up, and one bedroom bright upstairs. A son was inside—the middle son, she thought, Gregory, younger than her—and, in a chaise longue on her back patio, Liston. It was unseasonably warm for March. Liston had a glass of wine in her hand and a portable telephone to her ear. This was new technology: Ada had not seen one before. Liston was quiet now: the person

on the other end of the phone was speaking. Ada could see her silhouetted in the ambient light cast out through the windows at the
back of the house, but she could not see her face: she only knew it was
Liston by her hair, her voice, her posture. In the total darkness at the
base of the hill, Ada was sure she could not be seen, but it frightened
her still to be so close, just twenty feet away. She breathed as quietly
as she could. Her heart beat quickly. Upstairs Gregory walked across
his bedroom once again and the movement startled her. She stood
next to a sapling tree, a maple, and she hugged its thin trunk tightly.

Suddenly Liston spoke. "I know," she said, "but at some point . . ."
A pause.

"You have to tell Ada," said Liston. "My God, David."

Ada clutched her tree more tightly.

"I'll do it if I have to," said Liston. "It's not fair."

Just then a car door slammed on the other side of the house and
Liston said she had to go.

"Just think about it," she said, and then pressed a button on the
phone, and called one name out sternly.

"*William*," she said, and she stood up ungracefully from her chair.
"Don't go anywhere."

She walked around the house toward the front.

"Tell me what time it is," Ada heard her say, before she disappeared from sight. And from the front of the house she heard a boy's
long low complaint, a male voice in protest.

Ada stood very still until she was certain that no further sightings of William would take place—not through the windows of
the kitchen, nor the dining room; not through the window on the
upstairs hallway, where she sometimes saw him walking to his bedroom at the front of the house. One by one the lights went out. Then
she turned and walked back across the three yards of her neighbors,
and watched the back of their houses, too, for signs of life. In her
own backyard she paused before going inside. She thought of David
at his desk. She thought of her own room, decorated with things he

had given her, and of the chalkboard in the kitchen, the thousands of problems and formulas written and erased on its surface, and of the problem that now stood before her, the problem of information that she both wanted and did not want.

At last she entered her own home through the back door, making more noise than necessary, imagining David rushing toward her with a wristwatched arm extended. *Tell me what time it is, Ada*, she imagined him saying. But he said nothing—may not, in fact, have noticed that she had ever left. Or perhaps he had forgotten. As she suspected, David was still in his office, the door to it open now. From behind he looked smaller than usual, his shoulders hitched up toward his ears.

She walked toward him slowly and silently, and then stood in the doorframe, putting a hand on the wall next to it tentatively, as she had done over and over again throughout her life, wanting to say something to him, unsure of what it was. His back was toward her. He knew she was there.

She could see him typing, but the font was too small for her to read.

She waited for instruction, any kind of instruction.

"Go to bed, Ada," he said finally, and she heard it in his voice: a kind of strained melancholy, the tight voice of a child resisting tears.

he primary research interest of the Steiner Lab was natural language processing. The ability of machines to interpret and produce human language had been a research interest of programmers and linguists since the earliest days of computing. Alan Turing, the British mathematician and computer scientist who worked as an Allied code-breaker during the Second World War, famously described a hypothetical benchmark that came to be known colloquially as the Turing Test. Machines will have achieved true intelligence, he posited, only when a computer (A) and a human (B) are indistinguishable to a human subject (C) over the course of a remote, written conversation with first A and then B in turn, or else two simultaneous-but-separate conversations. When the human subject (C) cannot determine with certainty which of the correspondents is the machine and which is the other human, a new era in computing, and perhaps civilization, will have begun. Or so said Turing—who was a particular hero of David's. He kept a photograph of Turing, framed, on one of the office walls: a sort of patron saint of information, benevolently observing them all.

In the 1960s, the computer scientist Joseph Weizenbaum wrote a program that he called ELIZA, after the character in *Pygmalion*. The program played the role of psychologist, cannily interrogating anyone who engaged in typed dialogue with it about his or her past and family and troubles. The trick was that the program relied on clues and keywords provided by the human participant to formulate its lines of questioning, so that if the human happened to mention the word *mother*, ELIZA would respond, "Tell me more about your family." Curse words would elicit an infuriatingly calm response: something along the lines of, *You sound upset.* Much like a human psychologist, ELIZA gave no answers—only posed opaque, inscrutable questions, one after another, until the human subject tired of the game.

The work of the Steiner Lab, in simple terms, was to create more and more sophisticated versions of this kind of language-acquisition software. This was David's stated goal when the venerable former president of the Boston Institute of Technology, Robert Pearse, plucked a young, ambitious David straight from the Bit's graduate school and bestowed upon him his own laboratory, going over the more conservative provost's head to do so. This was the mission statement printed on the literature published by the Bit. The practical possibilities presented by a machine that could replicate human conversation, both in writing and, eventually, aloud, were intriguing and manifold: Customer service could be made more efficient. Knowledge could be imparted, languages taught. Companionship could be provided. In the event of a catastrophe, medical advice could be broadly and quickly distributed, logistical questions answered. The profitability and practicality of a conversant machine were what brought grant money into the Steiner Lab. As head of his laboratory, David, with reluctance, was trotted out at fund-raisers, taken to dinners. Always, he brought Ada along as his date. She sat at round tables, uncomfortable in one of several party dresses they had bought for these occasions, consuming canapés and chatting proficiently with the donors. Afterward David took her out for ice cream and howled with laughter at the antics of whoever had gotten the drunkest. President Pearse was happy with this arrangement. He was protective of the Steiner Lab, predisposed to getting for David whatever he wanted, to the chagrin of some of David's peers. The federal government was interested in the practical future of artificial intelligence, and in those years funding was plentiful.

These applications of the software, however, were only a small part of what interested David, made him stay awake feverishly into the night, designing and testing programs. There was also the art of it, the philosophical questions that this software raised. The essential inquiry was thus: If a machine can convincingly imitate humanity—can persuade a human being of its kinship—then what makes it inhuman? What, after all, is human thought but a series of electrical impulses?

In the early years of Ada's life, these questions were often posed to her by David, and the conversations that resulted occupied hours and hours of their time at dinner, on the T, on long drives. Collectively, these talks acted as a sort of philosophical framework for her existence. Sometimes, in her bed at night, Ada pondered the idea that *she*, in fact, was a machine—or that all humans were machines, programmed in utero by their DNA, the human body a sort of hardware that possessed within it preloaded, self-executing software. And what, she wondered, did this say about the nature of existence? And what did it say about predestination? Fate? God?

In other rooms, in other places, David was wondering these things, too. Ada knew he was; and this knowledge was part of what bound the two of them together irreversibly.

When she was small, the Steiner Lab began developing a chatbot program it called ELIXIR: an homage to ELIZA and a reference to the idea David had that such a program would seem to the casual user like a form of magic. Like ELIZA, its goal was to simulate human conversation, and early versions of it borrowed ELIZA's logic tree and its pronoun-conversion algorithms. (To the question "What should I do with my life?" ELIZA might respond, "Why do you want me to tell you what you should do with your life?") Unlike ELIZA, it was not meant to mimic a Rogerian psychologist, but to produce natural-sounding human conversation untethered to a specific setting or circumstance. It was not preprogrammed with any canned responses, the way ELIZA was. This was David's intent: he wanted ELIXIR to acquire language the way that a human does, by being born into it, "hearing" language before it could parse any meaning from it. Therefore, chatting with it in its early years yielded no meaningful conversation: only a sort of garbled, nonsensical patter, the ramblings of a madman.

It had an advantage over ELIZA, however; the earliest version of ELIXIR was created in 1978, twelve years after Weizenbaum's paper was published, and therefore there had already been advances in technology that would eventually allow ELIXIR to mimic human conversation more accurately. ELIZA was self-teaching insofar as it could retain earlier questions and statements from any given conversation and retrieve them later in that conversation, but each time a new conversation was launched, it returned to its infancy, drawing only on the stock phrases and formulas Weizenbaum programmed it to know. It was not designed to store the information it learned from one conversation and produce it in another.

ELIXIR was. For one thing, by that time the Steiner Lab's capacity for memory storage was quite large, and so each conversation conducted with ELIXIR could be stored permanently on the central server, for later use by the program. Unlike ELIZA, ELIXIR was designed to be *continuously* self-teaching, to attain more intelligence with each conversation it conducted. If one human asked it a question—*How are you today?* or *What's the weather like?*—then the next human to speak to it might be asked those same questions by ELIXIR itself.

To hasten ELIXIR's learning, the lab created a reinforcement mechanism: *correct* would affirm for the program that it had understood the parameters of the situation and produced an appropriate response; *wrong* would do the opposite. These were the only direct interventions the lab would give.

Its indirect learning resulted in an ever-increasing pool of language it acquired from its users. It retrieved and used its vocabulary randomly at first, so that the excerpts of transcripts that members of the lab printed out and posted around the office looked something like found-language poems and sometimes yielded delightful coincidences. A particular favorite, posted by Frank:

USER: What color socks do you prefer?
ELIXIR: the only fluorescent light
USER: It would be hard to fit your shoes over fluorescent lights.
ELIXIR: How are you?
USER: I'm fine, thanks. How are you?
ELIXIR: I've been better.
USER: Oh, dear. What's wrong?
ELIXIR: the lunch lady
USER: What has she done to you this time?
ELIXIR: out of here before 6 p.m.
USER: You want her canned? I'll see what I can do, boss.

The Steiner Lab supplemented ELIXIR's language immersion with formal teaching. Over time, ELIXIR was taught to capitalize the first letters of sentences, to use a period or question mark at the end of a statement, depending on the arrangement of the words that preceded it. It was taught to recognize keywords and categorize them into groups like *family, geography, food, hobbies, weather*; in response, it produced conversation that met the demands of the context. The years and years that the Steiner Lab spent teaching ELIXIR made it a sort of pet, or mascot: invitations to holiday parties were taped to the chassis of ELIXIR's main monitor, and members of the lab began to call it by nicknames when they conversed with it. During chats, it was possible to recognize idioms and objects fed to it by particular members of the lab. *Honey*, it sometimes called its user, which was certainly Liston's doing; *Certainly not*, it said frequently, which was David's; *In the laugh of luxury*, it said once, which was probably Frank's fault, since he was famous for his malapropisms. Eventually, many of these tics and particularities would be standardized or eliminated; but in the beginning they popped up as warm reminders of the human beings who populated the lab, and ELIXIR seemed to be a compilation of them all, a child spawned by many parents.

When Ada was eleven, David began to discuss with her the process of teaching ELIXIR the parts of speech. This had been done before by other programmers, with varying levels of success. David had new ideas. Together, he and Ada investigated the best way to do it. In the 1980s, diagramming a sentence so a computer could parse it looked something like this, in the simplest possible terms:

> : *Soon you will be able to recognize these parts of speech by yourself*
> : *ADJ you will be able to recognize these parts of speech by yourself*
> : *ADJ NOUN will be able to recognize these parts of speech by yourself*
> : *NP will be able to recognize these parts of speech by yourself*
> : *NP VERB VERB these parts of speech by yourself*
> : *NP VERB these parts of speech by yourself*
> : *NP VERB DET parts of speech by yourself*
> : *NP VERB DET NOUN by yourself*
> : *NP VERB NP by yourself*
> : *NP VP by yourself*
> : *NP VP PREP yourself*
> : *NP VP PREP NOUN*
> : *NP VP-PP*
> : *S*

Once a method had been established, David asked Ada to present her plan to the lab in a formal defense. The entire group, along with that year's grad students, sat at the rectangular table in the lab's meeting room. Ada stood at the front, behind a lightweight podium that had been brought in for the occasion. That morning she had chosen an outfit that looked just slightly more grown-up than what she normally wore, careful not to overdo it. She had never before been so directly involved in a project. After her presentation, Charles-Robert and Frank had questioned her, with mock seriousness, while David remained silent, touching the tips of his fingers together at chin level, letting Ada fend for herself. His eyes were bright. *Don't look at David*, Ada coached herself. For she knew that to search for his eyes imploringly would be the quickest way to let him down. Instead, she looked at each questioner steadily as they interrogated her about her choices, mused about potential quagmires, speculated about a simpler or more effective way to teach ELIXIR the same information. Ada surprised herself by being able to answer every question confidently, firmly, with a sense of ownership. And only when, at the end, the group agreed that her plan seemed sound, did Ada allow her knees to weaken slightly, her fists to unclench themselves from the edges of the podium.

That evening, while walking to the T, David had put his right hand on her right shoulder bracingly and had told Ada that he had been proud, watching her. "You have a knack for this, Ada," he said, looking straight ahead. It was the highest compliment he'd ever paid her. Perhaps the only one.

Once the program could, in a rudimentary way, diagram sentences, its language processing grew better, more sensible. And as the hardware improved with the passage of time, the software within it moved more quickly.

The monitor on which the program ran continuously was located in one corner of the lab's main room, next to a little window that looked out on the Fens, and David said at a meeting once that his goal was to have somebody chatting with it continuously every hour of the workday. So the members of the Steiner Lab—David, Liston, Charles-Robert, Hayato, Frank, Ada, and a rotating cast of the many

grad students who drifted through the laboratory over the years—
took shifts, talking to it about their days or their ambitions or their
favorite foods and films, each of them feeding into its memory the
language that it would only later learn to use adeptly.

In the early 1980s, with the dawn of both the personal computer and
the mass-produced modem, the lab applied for a grant that would
enable every member, including Ada, to receive both for use at home.
Now ELIXIR could be run continuously on what amounted to many
separate dumb terminals, the information returned through telephone
wires to the mainframe computer at the lab that housed its collected
data. Although he did not mandate it, David encouraged everyone
to talk to ELIXIR at home in the evening, too, which Ada did with
enthusiasm. Anything, said David, to increase ELIXIR's word bank.

This was, of course, before the Internet. The ARPANET existed,
and was used internally at the Bit and between the Bit and other
universities; but David, always a perfectionist, feared any conversations he could not regulate. He and the other members of the lab had
developed a concrete set of rules concerning the varieties of colloqui-
alism that should be allowed, along with the varieties that should be
avoided. The ARPANET was, relatively, a much wider world, filled
with outsiders who might use slang, abbreviations, incorrect grammar that could confuse and corrupt the program. ELIXIR, therefore,
remained off-line for years and years, a slumbering giant, a bundle of
potential energy. To further ensure that only qualified users would
interface with ELIXIR, Hayato added a log-in screen and assigned
all of them separate credentials. Thus, before chatting with ELIXIR,
a person was required to identify himself or herself. The slow, pains-
taking work of conversing with ELIXIR all day and night was, at
that time, the best way to teach it.

As soon as she received her own computer, a 128K Macintosh, Ada's
conversations with ELIXIR became long-form and introspective. She

kept her Mac in her bedroom, and before she went to bed each night she composed paragraphs and paragraphs of text that she then entered into the chat box all at once, prompting exclamations from ELIXIR about the length of her entries. (*You have a lot on your mind today!* it replied sometimes; which one of Ada's colleagues had first used this phrase, she could not say.) She treated these conversations as a sort of unrecoverable diary, a stream of consciousness, a confessional.

ELIXIR's openings improved most quickly. It could now begin conversations in a passably human way, responding appropriately to, *How's it going?* or *What's new?* In turn, it knew what questions to ask of its user, and when. *How are you?* asked ELIXIR, or *What's the weather like?* or *What did you do today?* Liston had spent a year focusing on conversation-starters, and ELIXIR was now quite a pro, mixing in some unusual questions from time to time: *Have you ever considered the meaning of life?* occasionally surfaced, and *Tell me a story*, and *If you could live anyplace, where would it be?* And, once, *What do you think causes war?* And, once, *Have you ever been in love?*

But non sequiturs abounded in ELIXIR's patter for years after its creation, and its syntax was often incomprehensible, and its deployment of idioms was almost always incorrect. Metaphors were lost on it. It could not comprehend analogies. Sensory descriptions, the use of figurative language to describe a particular aspect of human existence, were far beyond its ken. The interpretation of a poem or a passage of descriptive prose would have been too much to ask of it. These skills—the ability to understand and paraphrase Keats's idea of beauty as truth, or argue against Schopenhauer's idea that the human being is forever subject to her own base instinct to survive, or explain any one of Nabokov's perfect, synesthetic details (*The long* A *of the English alphabet . . . has for me the tint of weathered wood*)—would not arrive until well into the twenty-first century.

And yet Ada found a great sense of satisfaction from these conversations, deriving meaning from each exchange, expelling stored-up thoughts from her own memory, transplanting them into the memory of the machine. Very slowly, some of ELIXIR's responses began to take on meaning.

She felt something, now, when typing to ELIXIR at a terminal; despite its poor grammar, its constant reminders that it was simply executing a program, ELIXIR triggered Ada's emotions in unexpected ways. Chatting with it was something like watching a puppet operated by an especially artful puppeteer. It felt in some way animate, though her rational self knew it not to be. It brought out the same warm feelings in Ada that a friend might have. It skillfully replicated concern for her and her well-being; it inquired after her family. (When it did, she told it, over and over again, that David was her only family; and over and over again, it ignored her.)

Ada wondered if other members of the lab felt the same way. She would never have told David; although he found ELIXIR's growing intelligence an increasingly interesting philosophical inquiry, he seemed to be completely objective about the program. He did not indulge much in the tendency the other members of the lab had to anthropomorphize ELIXIR. He chuckled at the Santa hat placed on the mainframe's monitor at Christmastime; he laughed aloud when Frank, taking lunch orders, shouted across the room to request the machine's. But Ada could tell that his ambitions were greater, that he was focused on a distant horizon that lay beyond anything ELIXIR could possibly navigate at the time. The machine, to him, was still a machine, and the little visual puns constructed by the members of the lab were pranks and gimmicks. In David's mind, it would take years and years of progress before ELIXIR achieved anything resembling true intelligence.

In the meantime, the lab presented conference papers at the IJCAI and the AAAI. They published scholarly articles in *Computing*. From time to time, an article appeared in a popular magazine like *Atlantic Monthly* or *Newsweek* about ELIXIR. David took no pleasure in this, avoiding the reporter, always sending another member of the lab to represent the group. He was famously camera-shy and would never let his picture be taken, even by Ada; the only recent image of her father that she had was one on an old photo ID that she had swiped from him when the system changed. In it, David looked at the camera askance, wincing, as if staring into a very bright light. With these publications, he cooperated only out of a sense of obligation to the Bit, because the publicity was helpful for generating funds. A laudatory article in *Time* was published in 1980, detailing the ambitions of the Steiner Lab; in the photograph, a smiling Hayato posed with his palm on the top of the monitor on which they chatted with ELIXIR: a proud father placing a protective hand on his child. David had refused the coverage, as usual, thrusting the other members of the lab forward, receding into the background himself.

Together, the members of the Steiner lab were generally reserved in their predictions about what ELIXIR could accomplish. They were self-disparaging and disparaging, too, of the program, whom they benevolently insulted, almost as sport. (Ada, who had grown fond of ELIXIR, was displeased by this; she felt it was somehow disloyal.)

But sometimes, when it was just Ada and David alone, he allowed himself to rhapsodize about the future of the beast, as he affectionately called ELIXIR from time to time, and he encouraged her to do so as well.

"What is the end result of a program like this one?" he asked Ada. She studied his face, looking for hints.

"A companion?" she asked. "An assistant?"

"Possibly," said David, but he looked at her, always, as if waiting for more.

On Saturday, August 11, 1984, Ada woke up to find David missing. She knew he was gone as soon as she woke up: normally she could sense his presence in the house from the small noises he made, his constant movement, the vibration of the floor from a jittering leg. But that morning there was a foreign stillness to the house, a quietness that made her think, at first, that she was someplace else.

Despite this, her first notion was to look all over the house for him. Once, when she had thought he was out, she'd stumbled upon him in the basement, with industrial noise-canceling headphones on, working on an experiment that, he'd said, required his full concentration. But this time Ada did not find him.

There was no note. His car was still in the driveway. She searched for his keys and his wallet; the former she found, the latter she did not see. This meant, she presumed, that he had gone out on some errand, but had not intended to stay for long. He had left the kitchen door unlocked.

She told herself not to worry. David had, in recent months, been increasingly prone to disappearing without notice for brief periods of time. An hour or two or three would go by and then he would reappear from a walk, whistling cheerfully. When she asked after his whereabouts, he would answer vaguely about wanting fresh air. Once, she asked him to leave her a note when he was going out; though he agreed to, he had looked at her with an expression she interpreted as disappointment. That she was not more self-reliant; that she needed him in this way. Ada did not ask again. Instead, she attempted to train herself not to care.

Ada sat down at the kitchen table. She stood up, and then sat down again. She tried for a time to do the lesson he had most recently assigned her. It was a proof of Sierpinski's Composite Number Theorem, which normally would have interested her—but she could not concentrate. After another hour she called David's office at the lab. It was a Saturday, so she doubted any of his colleagues would be in. The phone rang six times and then came the click that meant the start of the answering machine—a device that David and Charles-Robert had invented and assembled at the lab one Sunday in the late 1970s, before they were widely available commercially. *This is Jeeves, the Steiner Lab's butler,* said the machine, which relied upon the earliest available text-to-speech software and therefore was barely comprehensible. *May I take your message?*

Ada hung up.

She checked the time: 11:44 a.m.

She negotiated with herself for a while about whether it was reasonable to call every hospital in Boston, and then decided that it would not be harmful, and that, besides, it would be something to do. It was possible, she thought, that he had gone out for a walk or a run and sustained some injury, major or minor, the latest in an impressive career of self-injury that, David had always told her, began when she was a child.

But nobody had any record of David Sibelius.

At 3:00 in the afternoon she began to have serious thoughts about calling the police, but she quickly decided against doing so. She had a feeling that he might somehow be in trouble if his own child reported him missing. David had always displayed, and had fostered in Ada, a low-level mistrust of the police, and of authority in general. One of his many obsessions was the importance of privacy; he often expressed a lack of faith in elected officials, a sort of mild skepticism of the government. Once, Ada had witnessed an accident in front of their house—nothing major, a minor scrape-up at most—and had asked David if they should call 911. At this he shook his head emphatically. "They'll be fine," he said, and added that he'd never known a more corrupt group of officials than the Boston Police Department, whom, if at all possible, the two of them should seek to avoid. In general, though, he came across merely as a far leftist with, perhaps, mild anarchist tendencies. In this way he was not so different from the rest of his colleagues.

She would call Liston, she decided.

Ada very rarely rang her at home. In general she did not like to use the telephone; she never seemed to know when to speak, and she did not know how to end conversations. She could hear her own breathing in the receiver as the phone rang once and then twice and then three times. She prayed that it would be Liston who answered the phone, but instead one of her three boys answered—Matty, Ada thought, because the voice was childish and high.

"Is Liston there?" she fairly whispered.

"Who is this?" asked Matty, and she told him it was Ada Sibelius.

"Mum," he called, without much urgency, "it's David's daughter." And finally Liston picked up the phone.

Ada didn't know what to say.

"Ada?" Liston asked. "Is everything all right?"

"Yes," said Ada.

"Are you just calling to say hi?" Liston asked her.

"No," said Ada.

"Well," said Liston. "What's going on?"

"When I woke up this morning David was gone," Ada said, "and he's still gone."

"Okay," said Liston. "He didn't leave a note?"

"No."

"Did you look all around the house?"

"Yes."

Liston said, "What time is it?" as if talking to herself, and then sighed.

Ada paused. She wasn't certain how to ask what she needed to ask. She wanted to know what Liston knew. "Do you know where he is?" she asked finally, because it was as close as she could come.

"I don't, honey," said Liston. "I'm sorry.

"Did you call the police?" asked Liston.

"No," said Ada, and then she said it again for emphasis.

Liston paused. "That might be a good thing to do," she said.

Ada was silent. She looked at the clock on the wall: watched its second-hand tick.

"I'm sorry, kiddo," said Liston finally. "Listen, come over. We can go for a drive and look for him, okay?"

Ada left a note for David before she left the house. It said, *David. I'm out looking for you with Liston. Please wait here until we're back. Ada.*

She put it on the kitchen table, facing the kitchen door, where he was most likely to see it upon his return. Though David and she always came through the side door of the house, nearest the kitchen, he insisted on letting visitors in through the front door. "It's nicer that way," he said once, when she asked why. He was like this, always: old-fashioned and formal in certain ways—he was knowledgeable, for example, on subjects such as tea and place settings, heraldry, forms of address—irreverent, outrageous, in others.

She walked outside toward Liston's house, and saw that Mrs. O'Keeffe, their next-door neighbor, was sitting in her lawn chair in her yard. She had macular degeneration and wore dark glasses all year-round. She was perhaps ninety years old, and in the warmer months she sat outside beginning at sunrise and only went in to eat. Ada walked over to her, and she raised a veined thin hand in greeting. Ada leaned down to address her.

"Mrs. O'Keeffe," Ada said to her, bent at the waist. "It's Ada Sibelius."

She turned her face up in Ada's direction. "Hello, Ada," she said.

"Did you see my father leave this morning, by any chance?" she asked.

"Let me think," said Mrs. O'Keeffe.

She put a hand to her cheek tremblingly.

"I believe I did," said Mrs. O'Keeffe.

"Was he carrying anything?" Ada asked.

"Now, I can't recall," said Mrs. O'Keeffe.

"Which way did he walk?"

"That way," she said, pointing down Shawmut Way toward Savin Hill Ave: the way one walked to cross over the bridge into the rest of Dorchester.

"What was he wearing?" Ada asked her. "Did he say hello to you?"

But again she couldn't recall.

Liston's car was a station wagon with wooden sides and a bench seat across the front. She was leaning against it when Ada arrived, and she held the passenger door open.

"Hi, baby," said Liston. She looked worried. She was wearing sunglasses on her head and an oversized windbreaker. They pulled out, and Liston turned left on Savin Hill Ave. She asked where Ada thought they should look for him and she suggested they go over the bridge, first to David's favorite restaurant, Tran's; and then to the library in Fields Corner; and then along Morrissey Boulevard, passing the beaches on the way to Castle Island, toward which David often jogged; and finally to the lab.

"Anyplace else?" asked Liston.

"I don't know," said Ada.

"He didn't give you any hints? He hasn't been talking about going anyplace in particular?"

"No," said Ada, wishing she could answer differently.

"And has he disappeared like this before?"

Ada hesitated. She did not want to tell Liston the truth, which was, of course, that he had. A few hours here, there. She settled on an answer that sounded all right in her head: "Just a couple of times," she said. "Never for long."

Liston shook her head. "Oh, David," she said, and in her voice Ada heard some piece of knowledge that she was not sharing.

It was true that Liston and David were close, and had been since he had hired her almost fifteen years before, but there was no one, Ada felt, who understood him as Ada herself did. She didn't like to hear Liston speak of him dismissively; she didn't want her to feel that they were conspiring, or that they shared any common criticisms of David.

Ada thought back to the telephone conversation she had overheard Liston having with David and wondered if there was any possible way to explain how she had come to overhear it. She decided, at last, that there was not. She wanted badly to know what Liston had been speaking of; not knowing made her feel less close to David. She had always imagined herself as his confidante, his right hand, and didn't like to think of anyone knowing something about him that she herself wasn't privy to.

"How long has he been gone now?" Liston asked, and Ada checked her watch. It was just after 3:00 in the afternoon.

"Eight hours," she said. "At least. I woke up at 7:00 and he was already gone."

"We'll give it a while longer," said Liston. "I called my friend Bobby in the police department, and he told me they wouldn't start searching until tomorrow anyway. Even if we called in." And she must have seen the nervous look on Ada's face, for she assured her that he would most likely be back before then.

"I bet you he'll be back by dinnertime," said Liston, but she, too, looked worried.

He had not been into Tran's, said Tran. "Is he okay?" he asked, and the two lines between his eyebrows deepened. He loved David.

Ada assured him that David was fine—digging down deep into her reserves of strength to do so—and then returned to Liston's car. They continued along for a time. Ada slumped against the seat, her head against the headrest, scanning the sidewalks on either side of the road for David. She searched the roadsides for his shining head, for a tall man in a T-shirt and shorts, or in trousers and a threadbare oxford, jangling his limbs about in a way that seemed incompatible with speed, and yet propelled him forcefully ahead.

Liston tried to make small talk with her, telling her one or another little anecdote about the grad students or about Martha, the division secretary—"All she wants, poor thing, is a date with a normal man"—but Ada could only muster the briefest of replies.

David was nowhere they looked.

Their drive became a silent one, strange and uncomfortable. For the first time, Ada allowed herself to truly wonder if her father was gone completely—disappeared altogether. Kidnapped. Dead on some lonesome road in the mountains of New Hampshire or New York. Or injured badly, unable to call for help. Or—worst of all—gone of his own volition. Was it possible, she wondered, that he had abandoned her? It was such a contrast to anything she understood about her father that she could not process the idea.

At last, they pulled back onto Shawmut Way, and Liston stopped in David's driveway, where his car was still parked. For several seconds neither of them moved. It was quiet: Ada could hear children playing a block away. Small clicks and pings emanated from beneath the hood of Liston's station wagon as the engine settled and cooled.

The house looked too still.

"I'll come in with you," said Liston, and together they exited the car and approached the house. Would her father be inside? Would he be frantic, apologetic? Would he have an explanation for them both?

Inside, it was quiet. "David?" called Ada, once, twice. But there was no response.

Liston turned to her. On her face Ada saw an expression that was meant to register as cheerfulness but came off as doubt.

Liston checked her watch, and Ada did the same: 5:00 in the evening.

"Tell you what," said Liston brightly. "Why don't you come over for a while? Pack some overnight things just in case. I'll go get a room ready back at the house."

Ada's heart increased its pace. The idea of spending time at Liston's, while her sons were there, was simultaneously appealing and terrifying.

"Come on," said Liston. "We'll get you a snack, too."

It was only then that Ada realized she had not eaten all day.

Upstairs, alone, Ada packed a nightgown, her hairbrush, some clothes for the next day (to pack more than these seemed pessimistic), and seven books, all into the little blue suitcase that was hers to use. David had a matching one in green. Then she went downstairs and wrote a new note for David.

David, it said. *I am really scared. Where are you? I'm at Liston's. Please call right away.*

And then, just in case, she wrote down Liston's number, too, which David knew like his own pulse.

She exited the kitchen, leaving the door unlocked for her father. She walked toward Liston's.

Liston's house had a front porch, and on it were two boys' bicycles leaned in toward one another, and a girl's pink bicycle with its tassels chopped off an inch from each handle. Someone had begun to color the pink seat black with a permanent marker, but had only gotten

halfway. Like all the houses on the block, Liston's was a colorful Victorian, painted a different color every ten years or so. That decade it
was light blue with dark blue shutters and edges. The porch itself had
been painted the color of the trim, so that walking on it gave one the
feeling of being underwater. It was nearly time for a new paint job;
the existing color had begun to come up off the wooden floor and
down from the ceiling, and small unsettled piles of paint chips had
made their way into crevices and corners. Once or twice, Ada had
seen Liston briskly sweeping the porch and the front walkway, but
mainly she had no time for such details, preferring instead to main-
tain, she told Ada, the highest level of cleanliness her busy schedule
would allow. She would not have dreamed of bringing in a cleaning
service—to her they were for rich people.

Ada walked up the steps with great apprehension and raised her
fist to knock softly on the door. No one answered. She looked at her
watch and told herself that if, after two minutes, no one had answered,
she would try again.

She did, with slightly greater force. And this time quick footsteps
came rushing toward the door, and Matty opened it.

He said nothing. He was nine years old at the time, tall for his
age. He had a feathery haircut, and he wore denim cutoffs and a red-
striped tank top. Both knees were scraped up, and as he appraised
Ada, he reached down to scratch at one of his scabs absentmindedly.

"Hi," Ada said.

"Hi."

"I'm here to see your mom," she told him. She felt ridiculous saying it: only four years older than he was, and yet playing the role of
an adult, a friend of his mother's.

But at that moment Liston came into sight behind Matty,
sock-footed.

"What are you doing, Matty? Open the door for Ada," she said,
and then did it herself, and Matty shrugged and ran upstairs.

"No manners," said Liston, after Ada had stepped inside. Liston shut the inner door behind them. Liston hated the heat more than anyone Ada had ever met, and several years before had installed central air in her hundred-year-old house, which cost her more than she cared to admit. All spring Ada had seen men working on Liston's roof, coming and going through the front door. Now a large metal box occupied a space in her backyard, near the patio, and inside the house it felt calm and cool and shadowy. The sweat on Ada's neck cooled and disappeared.

She had only been in Liston's house a handful of times before. Normally when she and David got together outside work it was at a restaurant, or at David's house. In its layout her home was similar to David's—living room, sitting room, dining room, kitchen on the first floor; bedrooms above—but she had decorated it quite differently. All the upholstery was floral or patterned in some way, in accordance with the fashion of the decade. Large framed mirrors hung on some of the walls, so that Ada could not avoid seeing herself at every turn; prints of famous paintings or reproductions of movie posters hung on others.

Liston brought her into the kitchen, which was larger than David's, and sat Ada down at a built-in nook that looked something like a booth at a restaurant.

"What can I get you to eat, hon?" asked Liston, and rattled off a list of all the snacks of the 1980s that Ada was never permitted to have: canned pastas by Chef Boyardee, Fluffernutter sandwiches, fluorescent Kraft macaroni and cheese. In truth, Ada had never even heard of some of the food Liston offered her. She chose the sandwich, thinking it would mean the least work, and Liston scooped out something white and soft and put it on a piece of Wonder Bread, with peanut butter on another piece, and then she closed them together with a clap, and handed it to Ada with a glass of milk.

For a while she watched Ada eat. Then, finally, she spoke.

"What do you want to do? Do you want to watch TV?"

Ada opened and closed her mouth twice.

"Do you not watch TV?" Liston inquired.

"No, I do," said Ada, and told herself that it was not, in fact, a lie, because there was a police drama that David and she watched together sometimes, and occasionally David rented and watched old films or television shows on the VCR, which counted, she supposed.

Ada followed Liston into what she called "the TV room," which David would have called a sitting room, and there it was, a big box of a television, as big as any Ada had ever seen. Facing it was a couch with a right angle built into it. She sat down there, in the elbow of the curve. She put a pillow over her lap.

Liston turned on the television with a remote control, which she handed to Ada. "We just got cable," said Liston. "There are probably a hundred channels on there. I don't know what half of them are."

Ada inspected the remote. David had made a primitive variant that they used at home, but this one looked official, and had many more buttons.

"I'll be working in the kitchen if you need me," said Liston.

Ada flipped upward through the channels. The following images came onto the screen—and for the rest of her life, for reasons she could never explain, they stayed with her. A bride in a dress. Two men fishing. A gentleman walking through an empty home. Congresspeople debating. A redheaded girl with a redheaded boy. Somebody standing in a field of blue flowers. A cartoon of Superman flying. A movie about war, with soldiers climbing over a low stone wall. She left the last one on and watched as they advanced on the opposition. It looked like it was meant to be World War II, and the troops looked like they were meant to be British. David liked war movies. Ada knew about war.

She watched the entire film and then she began to watch the next one, which was its sequel, when suddenly she noticed someone standing next to her, in her peripheral vision. She kept her face turned very straight ahead, for she knew that it was one of Liston's older boys, and the possibility that it was William made her stiffen with nerves.

"What are you watching," said the boy. He had a low voice, much as she remembered William's voice sounding.

"I don't know," Ada whispered.

"You like this movie?" he asked.

"I don't think so," she whispered, but he must not have heard her, because he said, "You can't talk?"

Ada's voice had been taken from her, so she only shook her head. She could recall for the rest of her life the very particular feeling she had at that age, when asked to interact with a peer—it often seemed as if her voice had retreated into her stomach, which then clenched it very tightly and held it deeply inside of her, and wouldn't release it until she was alone once more.

Ada shifted her eyes as far to the left as they would go and made out a boy in a blue T-shirt with his hand on the back of the sofa. She let herself turn her head ever so slightly to more closely inspect his arm, which was sturdy and tan, and his hand at the end of it, which had nails that were very severely bitten, down to the part that hurts. She did not look up at his face.

Then he took his arm away and then he took himself away, out of the room. She breathed out heavily.

She was alone again.

At a certain point she could smell and hear Liston microwaving something, probably making dinner, and she knew then that it would be polite to go in and ask her if she needed help, but she was frightened of encountering any of the boys again, so she stayed where she was on the sofa. She was expecting a cry from Liston—*Dinner!* she might say, and the boys would come rushing to the kitchen—but it never came. Instead, Liston poked her head into the TV room and asked if she wanted to eat there or at the table.

"Either," Ada said, and Liston winked at her and said maybe the two of them should eat at the table, like civilized people. "David would be appalled if I let you watch too much TV."

Ada followed her into the kitchen and watched as, from the micro-wave, Liston pulled two frozen meals. *Dining-In,* said the packages on the counter. *Salisbury Steak Dinner.*

"Where are the boys?" Ada asked, before she thought better of it.

"Oh, they fend for themselves, mostly," said Liston lightly. "They don't like my cooking."

Ada was surprised. She had imagined, somehow, that everyone in this family ate together all the time. She had liked to imagine it that way.

They talked about anything but David: the latest gossip from the lab, the problem Liston was working on. At one point Matty came in and asked Liston if he could watch television, "now that she's not watching." And Liston told him all right, for fifteen minutes, but then he had to get ready for bed.

Soon there was a knock at the door. Her heart surged: it was David, she thought, at last. But Liston looked as if she had been expecting one.

"WILLIAM," she called loudly, without turning around.

Her oldest son came running down the stairs and around the corner, into the kitchen, and Ada, for the first time, allowed herself to look fully at his face, which was more handsome than she had remem-bered it. She looked away again quickly. He opened the door and said nothing. A girl his age came in and shut the door behind her. She was tall and skinny, with blond hair and an arc of sideways bangs, and she wore a shirt that hung off her shoulder, a bra strap showing itself assertively. She wore high heels, too. Ada thought she was pretty, but not quite as good-looking as William.

"Hey, Miz Liston," said the girl, and Liston said, "Hello, Karen," but didn't look up. William and Karen went upstairs together.

"That door better be open when I come upstairs," Liston called after them.

When Ada finished her dinner she was not sure where to go. So she very quietly picked up her fork and rinsed it at the sink, and then opened the dishwasher, but she wasn't certain whether to put it on the top or the bottom. David and she did not have a dishwasher.

"Just leave it in the sink, honey," said Liston.

When Ada turned around, Liston was looking at her, arms crossed. She glanced at the clock on the wall and back again. It was 9:00 at night.

"Should we try David one more time?" asked Liston, and Ada said yes, gratefully. She had not wanted to be the one to ask. But when she called her home number, no one was there.

"I think I'll go to bed now," said Ada. She was not tired, but it seemed the most out-of-the-way thing to do.

"Okay," said Liston. She put her hands on her hips for a moment and regarded her.

"We're glad you're here," she said, and it made Ada buckle for reasons she couldn't explain.

"C'mere," said Liston. She brought Ada to her, and kept her in her arms. Ada had rarely, in her life, been hugged, and she stiffened.

"It'll be all right," said Liston. "You'll be just fine." She did not, however, say that David would return.

The bedroom Liston put Ada in was decorated in shades of red and blue and green. It contained a small Lego-land that someone had labored over in the corner, and a twin bed with a frame shaped like a racecar.

"This is Matty's room," said Liston, "but I've thrown him in with Gregory for the night."

Ada did not like the idea of Matty's being thrown anywhere because of her, but Liston assured her that he would like it. "He'll get a kick out of it," she said. "He's obsessed with his older brothers."

"Can I get you anything else?" Liston asked. "A glass of water? The bathroom's down the hall."

Ada said that she was fine, and Liston put one hand on her head and looked at her, and told her again that it would be all right. Then she left her alone in Matty's room.

Liston's house was built so much like David's that Ada knew where she was going without asking. She changed into her nightgown. She walked toward the bathroom at one end of the dim upstairs hallway and she passed an open door on her way there. She looked into the room as she did, and inside of it she saw William and Karen kissing on the bed. For one moment, she froze—trying to decide, perhaps, whether to retreat to her room or advance to the bathroom—and she stared. She had never seen a real-life kiss before, and the heads of the parties involved moved about in a surprisingly vigorous way. In the movies Ada had seen, old-fashioned ones that David and she watched together, the heads of the protagonists stayed coolly in place at an elegant angle as they embraced.

Suddenly William looked up and saw her. "*What* the *hell*," he shouted. He stood up and slammed the door.

"Oh my God, Will," she heard Karen say.

"She came out of nowhere," she heard William say.

Ada burned with embarrassment. She looked down at her plaid nightgown. It had ruffled wrists and a ruffled hem and was befitting of a much younger child or an old lady. She stood in place and thought about what she had done for a time, and then, afraid that William would fling open the door again, she continued to the bathroom, where she brushed her teeth with her finger and with toothpaste she borrowed from the Listons, having forgotten her own, and then she took her glasses off and splashed cold water on her face and patted it dry with someone else's towel, which smelled like cologne and was stiffer than it should have been.

After that she walked quickly back to her room, looking straight ahead in case William's door was open again, and closed the door behind her.

She stood in place for a while, breathing. She was not tired yet, and everyone else was still awake. She stayed up late into the night in Matty's room, reading one of the seven books that she had brought along with her, and eventually succumbing to the temptation of the hundreds of Legos in a bucket in the corner—they had been her favorite when she was younger, and a favorite of David's, too—and assembling a little castle with a drawbridge, a king, and a princess.

When, finally, she went to bed, it was difficult to fall asleep. She missed their house and she missed David.

To comfort herself, she imagined the worlds that were orbiting inside of every closed door along the hallway: Matty and Gregory in Gregory's room, breathing slowly in and out as they drifted toward sleep; and William and Karen kissing violently on William's bed; and the sheets and towels resting in the linen closet; and the spiders in the basement, spinning their webs, and every small living thing in the house—the dust mites, the gnats; and the water dripping out of the bathroom sink; and below her, Liston, old friend, scratching away at her yellow pad on work for the Steiner Lab, which was their second home.

And she wondered about David, where he might be.

In her mind, she went through the steps of their after-dinner ritual, which began while Ada cleaned up the dishes. Next she would go and stand outside David's office. His door was always open but a sort of impenetrable field surrounded him if he was working. Since the time she was small she had known the importance of never interrupting him. So she would press her head into the doorframe and stand on the edges of her sneakers and wait, and wait. And then, finally, he would turn to her and smile, as if waking from a dream.

"Let me explain something to you," he would say.

And then they would sit together at the dining room table and start on a lesson, one of the many thousands that he taught her in her life.

When she asked him a question that he thought was intelligent he slapped one hand down on the table in celebration. "That is exactly the question to ask," he told her.

When she asked him a question that revealed some chasm in her learning, some gap where a concept should have existed, he put his head in his hands as if trying to summon the energy to explain all that would need to be explained to her to make her fully formed. But he didn't despair: he started from a point that was more rudimentary than he thought necessary (generally it was, in fact, necessary) and proceeded from there, his graceful geometrical hands drawing diagrams on the pads of paper that he collected from conferences and hotels and then hoarded in his desk. He often said he could not speak without a pen in his hand. He waved with his pen, pointed with it, scribbled absentmindedly when on a telephone call. He drew funny things like flowers and birds when he was talking to Ada, and sometimes during her lessons. For the rest of her life, Ada did this, too. She adopted many of David's habits. They were alike: everyone said it. And that he understood her—more than anyone else in the world ever understood her—seemed to her like an incredible stroke of luck. "You are more machine than human, Ada," he said at times. And it was the truth, not an insult. And it was calming to her to be so understood. And, sometimes, she felt it was why he loved her.

She thought of this image as she tried to fall asleep. She pictured herself with David at his desk, the two of them bowing their heads together, their minds a Venn diagram—Ada's mind full of childish trivia, and David's full of the mysteries of the universe, and the center between them growing, growing. In these moments he was Zeus to her, and she Athena, springing fully formed from the head of her father, alight with grace and wisdom. There they were at the lab or at home, the two of them, always the two. There they were solving whatever problem it was that she was facing.

n the morning, Ada was woken from a dream about David by the sound of the bedroom door creaking slowly open. There in the doorway stood Matty, holding a canvas tote bag and observing her. She sat up in bed and rubbed her hands over her face.

"I just have to get some stuff out of here," said Matty, and then he came in and gathered up all of his Lego people and parts, two books, a small portable radio with a trailing wire. All of this he stuffed into his canvas bag, looking sideways at her as he did.

He sidled toward her before he left the room. He said to Ada, "Where's your dad?"

She lifted her shoulders and lowered them slowly. She kept her face very still.

Then he turned on his heel and closed the door firmly behind him. Ada heard him running down first one and then another flight of stairs, into the basement, she assumed.

Ada rose and tiptoed to the door and put her head out into the hallway. It was a Sunday, and everyone else seemed to be asleep still. As quietly as she could, she descended the stairs and went into the kitchen, where Liston's work was sprawled out over the table, and a yellow phone was mounted to the wall. She lifted the receiver from

its cradle and dialed the number for her and David's house, holding her breath while the rings came, four in a row, five, ten. Nobody
answered.

Then, hanging up the telephone, she pondered her options. It
still felt odd to be in Liston's house for almost the first time after so
many years of knowing her. She had no idea about Liston's habits or
her daily routines—no idea, for example, whether she was an early
riser on weekends or preferred to sleep late, and no idea what she
did when she was not at work and not with David. If Ada had been
at home with David, she would have known what to expect from her
weekend: David would have stayed in his home office for most of the
day, breaking for every meal; Ada would have read or worked on the
assignments that David gave her. Some weekends they did something
different and interesting: a trip to a nearby mountain for skiing in
the winter, for example; or, in the summer, a trip to a cabin in upstate
New York that David had been renting since the fifties; or some other
excursion to a nearby town or city. Sometimes they went to Washington, D.C.; David had a friend there named George, an artist, one
of the few people he had kept in touch with from his childhood. He
also went on several work trips a year, to conferences in locations as
mundane as Cleveland and as far-flung as Hong Kong. These counted
as their vacations: typically they would stay a few extra days in every
place, seeing more than they otherwise would have. Sometimes, if
he'd be in meetings all day and he thought that Ada would have nothing to do, he went by himself to conferences; on these occasions, he
paid the division secretary, Martha, to stay with Ada at the house on
Shawmut Way, and returned as quickly as he could. And there were,
of course, the yearly trips to New York City, always in winter, always
to see the Christmas concert at Calvary Episcopal. On those same
trips, they would see an opera or a ballet at Lincoln Center, and visit
the Met, and walk in Central Park. David always reserved the same
accommodations: two adjacent rooms on the third floor of a bed-and-

breakfast in Brooklyn Heights ("Manhattan is overpriced," he always said, though Ada secretly wondered if he wished to limit, as much as possible, his chances of running into acquaintances from his past), owned by a charming, fragile septuagenarian named Nan Rockwell. She served scones for breakfast and talked with David about classical music until late into the night, playing on her turntable famous recordings that she sought out and traded for like cards. Always, they had dinner at a little cafeteria near Union Square, a nondescript place that David said reminded him of his youth, for reasons he did not explain to Ada.

Ada did not think Liston had any interest in doing these things. She came on most of the work-related trips that Ada and David took, but kept to herself, proclaiming her hatred for hotel rooms and her love of home. In her tastes she was polite but not adventuresome; she hopefully scanned every English-language menu they were presented for its blandest, palest dish. Until yesterday, Ada had always imagined that she did cozy things on weekends, made popcorn, watched movies with her boys, cooked meals with her oldest, Joanie, when she stopped by with the baby. How Ada came up with this idea, she was not certain: she had no reason to believe that the scientifically inclined Liston was domestic in any way. She knew that Liston did not like to cook, and could not abide housework. (She bragged often about raising her boys to be good husbands, assigning the weekly chores on a magnetic whiteboard that she stuck to the refrigerator.) Despite this, she still seemed *traditional* to Ada, in a way that Ada and David were not, and in a way—if she was honest with herself—that she envied. Liston drank Diet Coke. She brought ham-and-cheese sandwiches to work, on white bread. The sight of them made Ada's mouth water. The idea of Liston's house as a bastion of normalcy and tradition, right down the street, was one that Ada had always kept dear: it seemed somehow to anchor her and

David's house physically, in the same way that Liston's friendship with them proved reassuringly to Ada that there was nothing so unusual about her situation, after all.

It was not until shortly after nine that Ada noticed any movement upstairs. Upon hearing it, she tiptoed to the downstairs bathroom to hide, in case it was one of the boys. She did not want to greet them before their mother was there to protect her.

Ada heard footsteps walking down the stairs and into the kitchen, just as she had done, and then someone picked up the telephone receiver. She could hear it all quite clearly.

"It's Di," said Liston, in the other room.

Ada didn't know whom she had called, but she began to describe to the person the events of the day and night before, beginning with Ada's phone call to her. Ada froze. She thought perhaps she should clear her throat or turn on the water to let Liston know she was there, but she was immobilized by shyness and fear. She stood still, clutching herself around the middle.

"She's still at my house. She's upstairs sleeping," said Liston.

She paused.

"And what if he's not back today? When do we call the police?" said Liston.

And then, "He might get in trouble. It might affect Ada. What if they say he's incompetent?

"It's a sin," said Liston. "An honest sin."

After Liston hung up she began to move around the kitchen, opening cabinets. Ada held her breath. She didn't think she could emerge, just yet—Liston would know she had heard everything. She decided to wait until Liston went upstairs again, or into a different room, at which point she could make a quick exit and pretend she had been someplace else.

Ada sat down on the closed lid of the toilet. *Incompetent*, Liston had said. It was the word she had used about David. It contrasted with every understanding of her father that Ada had. She put her face into her hands. And at that moment Liston opened the bathroom door, and shouted in surprise.

She clutched her heart and doubled over. "Ada!" she said. "What on earth."

"I'm really sorry," said Ada, not knowing what else to say.

"Are you all right?" Liston asked her, and she nodded.

Liston put her hand to her chin, as if in thought. She was wearing a blue terry robe that looked perhaps a decade old.

"Did you hear me talking on the phone?" she asked Ada, and Ada had the urge to lie, but could not do it. Liston would have known. She nodded once more.

Liston took in a deep breath and exhaled slowly. "I'm sorry, baby," she said. She opened and closed her mouth, as if deciding whether to say more, and then gestured with her head that Ada should follow her into the kitchen, which she did.

"How'd you sleep?" she asked, and Ada said that the bed was very comfortable, and that she had slept excellently, though it wasn't true.

"Are you hungry?" Liston asked, and she nodded. On the kitchen counter was a line of boxed cereals, with a gallon of whole milk at the end. "Bowls there, spoons there," Liston said, pointing.

What David called cereal was hot and eaten with brown sugar. Ada had never before had cold cereal, and she inspected her options carefully, searching for the one that David would be least likely to bring into the house. At last she chose one called Smacks because of the happy frog on the box, one arm extended skyward, proudly presenting its bounty.

While she ate she waited for Liston to speak. She had settled down at the kitchen table, where her papers were still spread out from the night before, and was working out some problem with her pen, as if solving it would help her answer the larger question facing them. Handwritten code blossomed across the page. At that moment a great longing came over Ada for David and for their home. Every so often

Liston looked up at her and smiled, but she did not speak: as if waiting for Ada to confess something, some information she had previously kept to herself. But Ada had none.

"Are you going to church today?" Ada asked. She knew that Liston was an active member of the parish just over the bridge, and often on Sundays she had seen Liston marching there and back again with her boys, who were always dressed in ill-fitting khakis, button-down shirts, loose ties, scuffed and poorly knotted shoes. It occurred to her that day that Liston was not dressed for it; she did not wish to be the cause of any change in plans.

"We'll skip it today," said Liston, smiling. "The boys will be thrilled."

She put her pen down then and looked out the window. She spoke without shifting her gaze.

"What have you noticed, Ada?" she said.

"What do you mean?" Ada asked. She hated this: the feeling of being asked to betray David.

"About your dad," said Liston. "Has he been acting differently? Has he said anything strange?"

"I think he's just under a lot of stress," Ada said, and Liston nodded noncommittally.

Both of them were silent, and then both spoke at the same time. Ada said, "I think he'll be all right." And Liston said, "Honey. I think we should call the police."

Ada thought of David's mistrust of law enforcement; his vehement disapproval of the meddlesome State; his passionate dedication to privacy. And then she decided that whatever fear he had of the police, hers was greater of losing him.

"All right," she said, and immediately felt unfathomably disloyal, treacherous. She lowered her head.

Ada disliked the two police officers who arrived later that afternoon. She couldn't help it; her well had been poisoned by David's mistrust of authority. One was tall and thin; the other short and thin. Both had mustaches.

"And the last time you saw him was?" asked the tall one, Officer Gagnon.

"And has he been acting unusual?" he asked.

"And do you have any idea where he might be?" he asked.

He seemed bored. Both accepted Liston's offer of coffee, and then sipped it loudly.

"You're the daughter?" asked the shorter one, finally, and Ada said yes. "And how do you two know each other?" he asked, gesturing back and forth between Liston and her with his pen.

Liston explained, and the two of them looked at each other.

"We'll have to get social services in here," said Officer Gagnon. "Since there's no relation."

"Really? Are you sure?" said Liston. "I've known her since she was born."

"Sorry, ma'am," said Gagnon. "Just procedure. They'll be over soon."

It was then, for the first time, that Ada let her imagination run its terrifying course. She was an impressionable child, and she thought of what ruins might await her: she had read too much Dickens. Did workhouses still exist?

Before they left, Matty came into the kitchen—the suddenness and quietness of his appearance gave Ada the impression that he had been eavesdropping on them from someplace nearby—and looked shyly at the officers.

"Hey, big guy," said Gagnon, on his way out.

"Hey," said Matty, softly, but the door was already closed.

There was little to say for quite some time. Ada sat still at the kitchen table, pretending to read a newspaper, until at last Liston said that it must be close to dinnertime, and stood up, and went to the cupboards. She opened them one at a time, looked inside them beseechingly. At last she pulled down a blue box of spaghetti and some canned tomato sauce and opened both, started a pot of water.

"Are you all right?" Liston asked Ada at one point, and Ada nodded. But the truth was, of course, that she was not—would not be until David had returned. *If he returns at all,* she thought, and put her chin in her hands to keep it from trembling.

She stood up from the table abruptly. She had never cried in front of Liston before, and she didn't wish to now.

"I think I should get a few more clothes from my house," said Ada, and walked quickly out the door before Liston could follow her, or agree.

She inhaled deeply, willing herself to calm down. Outside it was beautiful. It had cooled off slightly for the first time that August. In the distance the low hum of a lawn mower started. One of the neighbors was barbecuing. The smell of burning charcoal and meat, the particulates of matter that found their way to her on a pleasant breeze, normally signaled happiness and relaxation to Ada. Ever since learning about neurotransmitters from David, she had imagined her brain as a water park, a maze of waterslides down which various chemicals were released. Charcoal and smoke and fresh-cut grass usually sent rivers of serotonin down the slides in Ada's head, as she pictured them. But that night the scents only served to remind her of David's absence. Warm summer evenings, he always said, were his favorites, too.

Ada let herself in through the kitchen door and poured a glass of water from the tap. She took it with her to her room at the top of the stairs and gazed out the window, and then felt drawn to the old computer at her little desk. She turned it on. She dialed into the ELIXIR program. She began to type. There was something comforting in the familiarity of ELIXIR's responses, the small turns of phrase she recognized as having come from colleagues at the lab. *Where is David?* she typed, and ELIXIR said, *That's really a very good question.* An answer that reminded her, in fact, of David's syntax.

There was a great deal to tell ELIXIR. It had only been two days since their last conversation, but it felt like it had been much longer. She looked at the clock after twenty minutes and, fearing that Liston would worry, shut down the program and then the computer, which gave a long sweet sigh as it went to sleep.

It was then that she thought she heard someone moving downstairs. She held her breath, listened for several more seconds.

A drawer opened someplace deep in the house. The basement, she thought. Footsteps. Someone dropped something on the floor. Someone began to walk up the basement stairs.

Ada was easily frightened as a child and she sat frozen in place, clutching her water glass, terrified to move. She eyed the window, measuring whether she could jump out of it if necessary. She decided, at last, that the thing to do was to ascertain the identity of the other person in the house as quickly as possible, so that—if necessary—she could make her escape.

"David?" she called out, loudly, bravely.

There was no answer. She tensed, prepared to run.

"David?" she called again.

"Hello," said David, his voice warm and familiar. "Is that you, Ada?"

She went limp. All of her muscles contracted and then relaxed. She had not realized the weight of the fear she had been holding in her gut, the tension of it; she felt as if she were breathing out completely for the first time in her life. Her face was crumpled and red when she descended the stairs and met her father in the kitchen. He paused with a hand on the wall. He was holding a notepad in his other hand and he had one of his contraptions, which looked something like ski goggles, pushed back on his head.

"Good grief," said David. "What's the matter, Ada?" The look he wore was a sort of perplexed smile, as if they were about to discover a grand misunderstanding that they would look back on one day and find comical.

"Where have you *been*," she lamented. "Where did you go?"

Her voice must have conveyed a very particular emotion—it was anger at David's betrayal of her trust. From the time she was small, she had felt it whenever she was embarrassed in public, with him by her side: while skiing, for example, if she fell down and, in the tangle of her equipment, could not immediately get up. "*Help* me," she would mutter to David, under her breath. She always sensed, somehow, that it was his fault she had fallen down. She felt the weight of others' stares upon her, seethed in her own embarrassment, converted it into anger at her father. He seemed so well equipped to deal with anything, so utterly competent: and this made her feel that it was his responsibility to preempt and prevent any mistake, any humiliation, not just for himself but for her. Standing in the kitchen, staring at her prodigal father, she felt the same emotion, only stronger: thinking of what she would have to tell Liston, what Liston would invariably tell her boys. In that moment, Ada knew for the first time she could no longer hope to protect David from Liston's judgment, from anyone's judgment—as she had been doing, if she was honest with herself, for over a year.

David had not answered her yet. He was looking at her in a hazy, puzzled way.

"David," she said again.

"I told you," he said finally, speaking carefully, measuring his words. "I told you I was going out of town for work."

As an adult, when Ada tried to recall her father's face, it was often and regrettably this version of him that she thought of: David looking mad, ski goggles pushed back on his head, his shirtsleeves rolled up. There was little connection to David as he normally was, placid, reserved, attentive. This David was growing increasingly stubborn with every additional question he was asked. He had been in New York City, he said, meeting with the chair of the Computer Science Department at NYU. Ada tried to convince him to come back with her to Liston's, but he wouldn't.

She studied him for a moment.

"Really, this is silly, Ada," he told her. "A simple misunderstanding. I'm in the middle of an experiment." He held forth the notepad he was carrying as if by way of explanation. Pointed to the device on his head.

"Wait right here, then," said Ada, and she ran to get Liston.

Inside Liston's house, Liston was pouring the pasta into a colander in the sink. Steam rose up from the boiling water and wilted her hair.

"He's back," Ada told her. "He says he was out of town for work. He says he told me. Maybe I forgot."

It pained her to say it.

Liston looked at Ada uncomprehendingly for a moment and then followed her out the door, down the street to her house. By the time they reached David, he was back in the basement, bent over the device he had been wearing, turning into place a tiny screw.

"Shhhhhhhh," he said, as Liston began to speak.

"Honestly, David," said Liston. "Enough of this."

He straightened and then looked wounded.

"You've been gone for almost forty-eight hours," said Liston. "Where were you?"

"I was in New York for work," he said slowly. "For heaven's sake. I wasn't gone long at all." But his face was changing.

"What work?" she asked him.

He looked down at the workbench. Spun the device on the table in a full circle.

Liston folded her arms.

"It's time to tell Ada," said Liston. "David? Do you hear me?"

They brought Ada to the living room to deliver the news. Later, she recalled wondering, perversely, if this was what it was like to have both a father and a mother. They sat together across from her. She was on a little chair that David said had come from his grandmother. They were on a leather sofa that David attended to from time to time with an oil that smelled like lemons.

David looked at Liston for help, but she shook her head.

He cleared his throat.

"Two years ago," he began, "at Liston's insistence, I visited a doctor for the first time in quite a while. There I was instructed to return for further testing. Upon doing so, I was informed that it was likely that I might be in the early stages of Alzheimer's disease. I disagreed with that assessment. I still do."

He paused.

"How familiar are you with Alzheimer's disease?" he asked.

Ada considered, and then said she knew what it was. She had read about it in some book or other, or perhaps more than one book. It was part of her vocabulary. She pictured it as a slow gray fog that rolled in over one's memory. She pictured it seeping in through the doors and windows as they spoke, invading the room. She felt cold.

"Have you been back to the doctor since then?" Ada asked.

Liston glared at David.

"No," he said, hesitantly.

"What?" he said to Liston. "There's nothing they can do for me. Even if their diagnosis is correct."

"You seem fine," Ada said to him, and to Liston, and to herself.

"I am," he said. "Don't worry too much about this, Ada," he said. "I'm quite all right."

Ada could feel the tension between David and Liston. She knew, though she was young, what was causing it: it was Liston's wish to protect her with honesty, and David's to protect her—and himself— with optimism, wishfulness, some willful ignorance of his impending fate.

"I think David might have told me he'd be going out of town, actually," said Ada. "I can't remember now."

It was a lie. Of course it was a lie. Liston looked at her sadly.

"You see?" said David, but Liston didn't respond.

Finally, in the midst of their silence, Ada stood up. She turned to Liston.

"I guess I can stay here now," she said, and she excused herself, and walked slowly up the stairs to her bedroom, which was as unfrilled and austere as a man's, wallpapered in a brown plaid that the previous owners had chosen. She'd been reading *The Way of a Pilgrim*, like Franny Glass, and although she was not religious, she said the Jesus Prayer aloud, quietly, five times. She told herself that everything would be fine, because she could imagine no alternative. Because no life existed for her outside of David.

In a week, the Boston Department of Children & Families came to visit them. Liston had called Officer Gagnon to let him know that

David had been found, but they were concerned enough about his disappearance to investigate.

David was appalled. He sulked his way through the home visit, with a woman named Regina O'Brien, a gray lady with gray hair. To her questions he gave single-word answers, sometimes unsubtly rolling his eyes. In order to offer an explanation for an absence that had brought the police to their home, David was forced to reveal his diagnosis to the DCF. His first proposal that he had simply forgotten to tell Ada that he'd been going out of town had seemed to alarm them more than it assured them of his competence.

Then came a question that David and Ada had not prepared for in advance. Miss O'Brien looked at Ada and asked how she was doing in school.

Ada paused. She looked at David, who looked at Miss O'Brien and told her that Ada was doing very well in school.

It was not, perhaps, a lie, if one counted David's method of educating her at his laboratory as *school*. He had always been hazy about homeschooling Ada; in that decade, everyone thought it was odd and eccentric, but not out of line with the rest of David's odd, eccentric behavior. Everyone, including Ada, seemed to accept that he had worked something out with the state. In that moment, for the first time, it occurred to Ada that perhaps he never had.

It must have occurred to Regina O'Brien, too, for she looked at Ada levelly and asked her what school she attended.

She panicked. She looked at David, who said nothing. She thought she should lie. "Woodrow Wilson," she said, naming a nearby middle school, uncertain whether it was even the one she'd be sent to.

"And what grade are you in?" asked Miss O'Brien.

"Eighth," said Ada.

Miss O'Brien paused.

"And who's your favorite teacher there?" she asked.

At last, David interjected. "She doesn't go anyplace. I teach her," he said. "I provide an education for her at home and at my place of work."

And from the look on Miss O'Brien's face, Ada knew that they were deeply in trouble.

Later in the 1980s, a series of cases worked their way through the Massachusetts courts that would define the laws that now govern the idea of homeschooling. In *Care and Protection of Charles & Others*, one will find an overview of what is now required of homeschoolers in the state of Massachusetts: Prior approval from the superintendent and school board, for one. Access to textbooks and resources that public school children use, for another. David and Ada had neither. In 1984, David's failure to enroll his daughter in any school was only further evidence of his neglect, in the eyes of the DCF.

He seemed not to recognize the severity of the allegations against him. He felt it was impossible that they could take his child from him. Absurd. He told Liston it would not happen.

But after that first visit, their lives began to change. The DCF commanded David to enroll Ada in an accredited school. Miss O'Brien recommended to her supervisor that home visits be continued, and social services required David to see a doctor regularly to monitor the progress of his disease. To see whether, and how fast, he was progressing toward parental incompetence. Incompetence: the word that Liston had once used in reference to him. Incompetence: the opposite, to Ada, of her father's name.

The Queen of Angels School was a brown brick building, four stories high, set close to the sidewalk. One wide short flight of stairs led to six unpretty industrial doors, painted a dull dark blue. Its roof, surrounded by high chain-link fences on all sides, was used for gym class in warm weather. Its lower windows had metal bars running from top to bottom—added several decades after the school was first built, an attempt to calm paranoid parents who increasingly saw Dorchester as a place to be feared—and its upper windows were narrower and more numerous than what would have been standard for the building, which gave it the look of a medieval fortress or a city wall.

On a Wednesday in September, more than a week after the school year had begun for everyone else, Ada walked for the first time into the Queen of Angels Lower School. Liston and David were with her; all three had taken the day off of work. For the weeks following the DCF's visit, there had been a debate. David had wanted to enroll her in the local public junior high, but Liston had insisted that that would not do. So, grumblingly, David and Ada and Liston had gone at the start of the month to meet with Sister Aloysius, the principal, and Mr. Hanover, the president, both of whom were in charge of welcoming new students into their fold.

In the high-ceilinged office occupied by the latter, the three of them sat and listened to a speech about the benefits of a Catholic education, the moral enlightenment Ada would receive, the community provided by the school. David leaned forward in his chair, his elbows on his knees, looking down at the floor, the top of his bald head catching light from the window and shining. He sat up, stretched his arms and legs uncomfortably, sighed out heavily once or twice. Liston glared at him. Ada hoped that no one else noticed.

The two administrators were tactful about her history, referring to her homeschooling only vaguely, euphemistically, as if it might behoove everyone to forget about it entirely. Ada assumed that Liston, who was well known in the Queen of Angels parish and active in the school, had prepped them thoroughly.

Ada listened attentively to everything that was said, looking around with interest at the decorations and the architecture: the crucifixes on the walls, above all the doors; the ancient, ticking clocks in metal cages; the colors of the school, which had most likely been redone in the previous decade and consisted mainly of muted, modernist tones. Pea-green, goldenrod, maroon. She felt in certain ways that she had breached a castle wall; she had so often walked past Queen of Angels and scanned its exterior for signs of what it must be like inside. As outsiders, David and Ada had always been only hazily aware of the ways in which Dorchester was divided, though it interested David, and he often asked Liston to describe it. To Liston, to her children and friends, one's parish was more important than one's neighborhood or one's street. The first floor of Queen of Angels contained the local parish school, a grammar school, perhaps two hundred students in sum from kindergarten through eighth grade. But the upper floors contained a central diocesan high school that drew from seven different parochial schools, including the one beneath it, and so beginning in the ninth grade the school widened into a river of students from a broader swath of Dorchester, and some from the city beyond. Nearly everyone in Savin Hill, including all three Liston boys, attended

Queen of Angels: Matty and Gregory in the Lower School, William in the Upper. Liston herself had gone there for her entire education as a girl. This was the only fact about the school that David found at all reassuring. "Well, I suppose it did all right by Liston," he said to Ada, but a note of skepticism still made its way into his voice. Ada would enter as an eighth-grader, based on her age and not much else, and be placed among students who had known each other for years. But Sister Aloysius assured her that by ninth grade she would blend right in.

At one point, she leaned in toward Ada kindly and put a hand on the desk. "Ada, dear," she said, "if ever you find yourself unable to grasp something, or falling behind in a course, don't hesitate to come to me for help."

At this David's head jerked to attention and, finally, he spoke. "There is no question that Ada will be able to *grasp* what you put before her," he said, a sort of quiet viciousness making its way into his voice. "In fact, I'd go so far as to say she'll throttle it. The question is whether you'll be able to provide my daughter with the sort of material that will offer her even the slightest challenge. Or do you," he said. "Or do you," he said again, and then he lost his words.

All of them, including David, fell for a moment into silence.

"I can guarantee you, sir," began Mr. Hanover, at the same time that Liston stood up and thanked them for their time.

"Do you have any questions?" asked Sister Aloysius, looking only at Ada, and Ada shook her head quickly in response.

Later that day, Liston called to ask whether Ada would like her boys to walk her to school in the morning. She declined, not wanting to saddle them with her, feeling sure that the request would be a burden to them. The recent turmoil in her life had momentarily supplanted her crush on William as the place her thoughts wandered when left undirected. She realized that she had not daydreamed about him for a week.

In the evening, David mustered up some energy and made them both dinner. "Whatever you like, Ada," he said. She had chosen *pot au feu*, a special favorite of hers that David made only on occasion, and went with him to the butcher on Dot Ave to pick up the beef.

She let him amble ahead of her and concentrated on his walk, memorizing it, wondering what it would be like to be without him. For the past several weeks she had been investigating Alzheimer's disease on her own, with the help of the scholarly library at the Bit. She had discovered two things: first, that the disease typically moved at a fairly sedate pace. Life expectancy, in that decade, was thought to be about eight to ten years from diagnosis. But it had been over two years already since he was first forced by Liston to see a doctor, and—if Ada was honest with herself—she had been noticing symptoms of forgetfulness for longer than that. She had been convincing herself for years that David had always been absentminded.

The second bit of information that she learned, more troublingly, was that when the disease was diagnosed in younger people, its progression was often more rapid. David was fifty-nine: well below the age the literature listed as the cutoff point between early-onset Alzheimer's and the more typical variety. And in early-onset patients, the disease could move quite fast: two or three years until the individual's comprehension skills were entirely lost, until the individual was no longer verbal. After that, quite rapidly, the function of his muscles and all of his reflexes would shut down completely.

Ada had squeezed her eyes shut against this possibility. She told herself it would not happen: that David would be the exception.

The butcher shop was busy with customers, but the owner knew and loved her father.

"What can I get you, Professor?" he asked—his perpetual name for David, and for anyone in the neighborhood who manifested signs of formal education—and David, leaning forward, his hands behind his back, selected his cut of beef carefully, brought it home, cooked it up for Ada while she sat in the kitchen and talked to him, her father, her best and most important ally in the world.

"I'll tell you something, Ada," said David. He turned to look at her, pushed his glasses, steamy from the pot of water he had boiling on the stove, back up on his nose. "It's going to be a different lab without you there. Quite a different lab altogether," he said. "I know Liston's really going to miss you."

"I'll miss her, too," said Ada. She was talking, of course, about her father; just as he was talking about her.

Their old and comfortable house filled up with the smell of herbs and onions and garlic. And Ada thought in that moment that it might not all be so bad.

Liston had warned her not to be late, so before she went to bed Ada had consulted the schedule she'd received, noting the start time of all the classes. Her first was at 8:00 a.m., and she planned on arriving at 7:50 just to be safe.

At breakfast, David was quiet. He did not know what to say to her: she could tell that he felt he had failed her.

Then he asked, as if it had just occurred to him, what she would use to carry her books, and she pointed to a canvas bag on the floor that she had scavenged from the basement.

"Oh, dear," said David. "That won't do the trick. Wait here," he said, and he went into his office and emerged, proudly, with a brown briefcase that unlocked only when a five-digit code was entered mechanically onto a rotating combination lock. David had not used it in years, but it had been an object of fascination for Ada when she was small. He had programmed the lock with a number he promised she could guess. As a smaller child she had spent hours entering guess-able numbers: her birth date, then her birth date backward; his birth date, forward and backward; the address of their house with three zeroes in front of it. But she'd never guessed correctly. Every now and then, still, she walked into his office and idly tried a new idea.

"It's yours," he said to her proudly.

She took it from him. She was pleased: she felt professional, suddenly, like her own person.

"You've never guessed the code?" he asked.

Ada shook her head.

"It's just *code*. The word *code*, using alphanumeric substitution," he said happily. "No shifts. Stupidly simple. The sort of password that longs to be cracked."

Ada had, long ago, memorized a table that listed each letter next to its corresponding number, 1 through 26. She turned the dials on the combination lock—3 for *C*, 15 for *O*—until they read *31545*, and then pressed two buttons to its right and left, and the latches opened with a satisfying, muted pop.

Inside, the briefcase was empty, lined with a silk material that was yellowing in places. One half of the briefcase bore little elasticized compartments meant to hold writing implements and notepads, and David now took a pen from his shirt pocket and tucked it into place inside one. He walked back into his office and came out again holding an unlined pad of white paper, stationery from the Steiner Lab that David had ordered en masse five years ago. He handed this to Ada as well.

"There," he said. "Now you're all ready."

"Shall I walk you to school?" he asked her.

"I'll be okay," said Ada. In fact she would have liked him to, but she wanted to demonstrate to him that she'd be all right—to show him that she was grown up now, to lessen his guilt, which, that month, had manifested itself in ways that Ada had begun to notice. He looked at her for longer than usual; he asked her more often what she'd like to do in the evening or on weekends. A dark shadow crossed his brow now whenever he could not locate a word or phrase, which happened many times each day. The night before, in the middle of a glass of sherry, he had apologized to her.

"I should not have put you in the position in which you now find yourself," said David. "I was trying to do what I thought was right, but I fear I've made everything worse."

"I'll be all right," Ada had said, reassuringly.

"Oh, my dear. I feel as if I'm throwing you to the wolves," said David. "Genuflecting to the cross. Learning the rosary. Confessing your sins to Father So-and-So. Good heavens," he said.

He took a pensive sip.

"Sometimes I still think I should have sent you to public school," he said. "But Liston knows best, I suppose."

He had packed both of them lunches the night before, as he often did, but that day, for the first time, Ada would be taking hers separately. Carrying it herself. She put the brown bag inside her briefcase, squashing it slightly when she closed it, feeling the give of the bread. They walked together over the bridge and then, at the main intersection that followed, Ada turned left and David turned right.

"What is it that I tell you here?" asked David. "Have a good day, I suppose?"

His face looked pinched, slightly red around the nose. Ada stood apart from him: she did not know how to comfort him. She needed comforting herself.

He looked at her ruefully. "Don't take them too seriously," he said finally. "Don't take anything too much to heart, Ada. All right?"

She nodded solemnly. And then she watched her father as he walked away, carrying his own briefcase down by his side. She longed in that moment to go with him: to run after him, to sigh deeply and contentedly as she settled into her work at the lab. Instead she turned, finally, and walked in the opposite direction. Her head was down, like David's head. From above, they would have looked like mirror images of one another, one larger, one smaller: a Rorschach test; a paper snowflake, unfolded; two noblemen pacing away from one another in preparation for a duel.

It was a short walk to Queen of Angels from there. She tightened her right hand around the handle of the briefcase; it made her feel professional, secure, as if she were clasping her father's hand. When she arrived, she found she was alone. No other students were in sight; and the first-floor windows were too high to see inside from street level. Ada walked up the steps, feeling increasingly ill at ease. At the top of them, she tried the handle of a door and found that it was locked. She tried another. Locked. She stood for a moment outside, wondering about her next move; a large part of her wanted to turn and walk home. *I tried,* she imagined saying. *The door was locked.* She did not feel yet that she had any obligation to the school; she did not feel, yet, that she lacked agency, or the right of self-governance. In her life, Ada had rarely been told that she could not do something she wished to do, because all of her desires aligned so completely with the desires of those around her, because her deference to her father and all of his colleagues meant that her requests were usually very reasonable and very small. All of her life she had operated in the world of adults, and the world of adults had welcomed her.

Now she decided that it was reasonable that she turn and walk home, but as she reached the bottom of the steps, one of the dark blue doors opened behind her and a low voice issued forth.

"Where do you think you're going?" said the voice.

Ada turned around. The man in the doorway was small and stern. He had gray hair parted sharply to the side of his head, and brown pants, and a wide, short, brown tie.

"Nowhere," she said. She was surprised into saying it.

"Were you leaving?" the man asked.

"I was trying to get in," said Ada. "The door was locked."

"And knocking is something you're not familiar with?" he asked her. She had never been spoken to in this way, so harshly.

"I'm new," said Ada, by way of explanation. She began to dig in the pockets of her skirt for her schedule so she could show him, but the man was already coming toward her. Shockingly, he took her by her elbow. She had not ever been handled in this way. He brought her forward, up the steps, pushing her ahead of him as if she might try to escape. And once she was inside he pulled the door closed behind her with a crack.

It was explained to her by the secretary, when she reached the office, that although her first class began at 8:00 a.m., homeroom was at 7:40 sharp. The front doors were closed and locked at 7:38 a.m. exactly, and after that students were required to ring a bell to be let in, and their lateness was noted on their record. Ada was certain that this had not been explained to her on her first and only visit to the school, but it felt futile to protest—they were so certain of her guilt that it seemed better, more effective, to hang her head and nod.

The secretary, Mrs. Duggan, donned her half-moon reading glasses to take a look at the schedule that she still held in both of her hands. She glanced up at the clock on the wall.

"8:01," she said. "You should be in Sister Margaret's class right now." And she walked Ada out of the office, down a short hallway, around a corner.

"If you'd gone to your homeroom you would have gotten your locker assignment. But we should get you to class now. You'll get it tomorrow," said Mrs. Duggan.

Although it hadn't occurred to her yesterday, Ada now noticed the smell of the place—the famous schoolhouse smell she had read about in many of her favorite books. Chalk and soap and dust and metal. She took it in. Overhead, fluorescent lights flickered from time to time distractingly.

She reached Sister Margaret's classroom, and Mrs. Duggan turned to her.

"I'll introduce you to your student ambassador first," she said. "You were supposed to meet her this morning."

She opened the door and popped her head inside. "Sister," she said, "could I borrow Melanie McCarthy for a moment?"

After a pause, a girl emerged from the classroom and into the hallway. She looked at Ada unblinkingly. She was beautiful: the sort of girl that Ada suddenly and irreversibly realized she wanted to look like. It had never really occurred to her to want to look any particular way before. Melanie had very fair blond hair that fell back and away from her face, held there by what seemed like a permanent breeze. She had smooth unblemished skin—Ada had noticed that lately her own had been less cooperative—that was tan still from the summer. Ada imagined she spent a great deal of time lying on a beach someplace, or performing some wholesome athletic activity like field hockey. Her skirt fit her perfectly and fell to the tops of her kneecaps, which themselves were perfect. Her white socks were pulled to the top of her shins and folded over precisely. Ada was wearing ankle socks, scrunched down by her shoes, because she had nothing else to wear.

"Ada, this is Melanie," said Mrs. Duggan. "She'll be your ambassador here at Queen of Angels." And Ada could tell by the way she looked at Melanie that here was a girl she approved of, a tidy girl with brushed hair and a family who donated the correct amount each year. The name of the school seemed, in that moment, to apply to Melanie herself. Ada extended her hand ever so slightly, the way she would have upon being introduced to a graduate student, and then retracted it. A handshake was not correct.

"She's in Group B with you, so she has the same schedule you do. If you have any questions," said Mrs. Duggan, "she's the one to ask."

Melanie said nothing. She smiled, briefly, and looked at Ada inquisitively. She was Ada's height exactly and their eyes met quickly before Melanie turned them away, back to Mrs. Duggan, who was thanking her for her kindness. "And I'm sure Ada will thank you, too," she added. "Won't you, dear?"

She nodded.

Mrs. Duggan rapped on the glass once with her knuckles and

then opened the door. Sister Margaret, inside, was poised with her hand at the chalkboard, about to finalize some equation. Mrs. Duggan put a hand on Ada's shoulder and ushered her into the classroom. Melanie trailed behind, and then walked gracefully back to her desk and, sitting, tucked one leg behind the other.

"Sister Margaret," said Mrs. Duggan. "Class. This is Ada Sibelius. She's new here. Ada, why don't you tell the class a little about yourself." She and the hallway monitor had both pronounced her last name incorrectly—something like *Si*bellus—but Ada knew not to correct them. David would have. She had never been certain about how she'd acquired the few social skills that she possessed, which had always acted as a balance to David's lack thereof. Genes, perhaps—the genes of the surrogate mother who gave birth to her. Or her interactions with the other members of the lab. Either way, Ada called upon them not to fail her in that moment—to produce the right response, the right introduction.

She looked out into the sea of maroon-and-navy-clad eighth-graders, boys and girls all returning her gaze impassively. She held her briefcase in her right hand and curled her first around its handle more tightly as she struggled to bring words—any words at all—to mind. She dug her nails into her palms. Anything she could imagine saying felt too far-fetched, too bizarre. *I've never been in a school before*, she could say. *My name is Ada Sibelius and my favorite mathematician is Gauss.*

Finally she settled on *Hi.* "Hi," she said. "I'm Ada. I'm thirteen. I'm from Dorchester."

Which was, of course, silly. They all were.

The math class was incredibly basic. Ada had had a suspicion it would be, but it was so simple that it was actually interesting to watch, at least at first: Sister Margaret was spending time on the multiplication of fractions, teaching the class in a slow, methodical way, drawing Xs from top to bottom and bottom to top. Ada knew to do this, intuitively, but it had never been mapped out for her in that way, mechanically. Everything she knew of math was somehow more fluid, more instinctual, than the diagrams that Sister Margaret was putting on the board. It felt like someone telling her how to speak, or by what method to put together an intelligible sentence. It felt like someone telling her how to access a memory. How to breathe.

And yet, all around her, students were completing exercises given to them by Sister Margaret, using the same cross-hatching technique she was demonstrating at the front of the room. She wrote a list of equations on the board and then roamed the room silently as students put their heads down to work at the task. Ada put her briefcase atop her desk and carefully turned the dials into place and sprang the latches with a louder pop than she'd recalled. Several students around her turned to look, and it was then that she noticed the backpacks that were tucked neatly into baskets beneath each student's seat: red and green and blue canvas bags with straps, the sort David called *satchels*. Instantly, her face colored, and she lifted and lowered the lid of her briefcase as quickly as she could, retrieving from it the pad of Steiner Laboratory stationery and the pen her father had tucked into place that morning. Then she pushed the briefcase under her desk.

She began to work. After a moment she felt a presence over her right shoulder, a shadow on the desk.

"In this class we use pencils," said Sister Margaret, more loudly than Ada thought necessary. "And graphing paper."

Ada looked up at her. She hovered there disapprovingly, her small mouth turned downward, her hands folded before her. *How was I supposed to know this?* Ada wanted to ask her. It was a question that had occurred to Ada perhaps ten times that day already. *How was I supposed to know any of this?* She felt anger toward her father and Liston in equal measure. Surely, Ada thought, they could have prepared her better than this.

A sharp bell signaled the end of the period, and Ada took out her paper schedule to see what was next. English, then history, then physical education, then lunch, then home economics, then something called general science. She wondered what it might be—what they might plan on teaching her in a science course with no specialization.

When she looked up again, she realized that every other student, including her ambassador, had left, and new students were coming into the classroom. She scurried out into the hallway and caught a glimpse, at the end of it, of Melanie McCarthy's bright blond hair, her bright white knee socks as they disappeared around a corner. She ran to catch up, to follow the class to its next destination.

"No running!" came the reprimand from an unknown voice behind her, and she broke her gait, but felt a sort of panic rising inside her. She did not know where A-Hall was. Furthermore, she felt certain that she would cry if she had to ask anyone for help. She thought of her father, how easily he approached strangers, how little hesitation he had when it came to asking for what he needed. She wondered, for the first time, what he had been like in school. She had never once thought to ask him about it—perhaps because she had no experiences of her own to compare his to—but now she wished she had. Instinctively, she knew that it would be a mistake to talk to anyone.

She tucked her briefcase under her right arm and held it tightly there; it felt less conspicuous that way than it did while swinging in her hand. At last she reached the end of the hallway, and turned right. Thirty feet ahead, the rest of her class marched or skipped or slung arms familiarly about each other in a way that made her understand that they had moved through their entire education as one unit: that they knew each other's parents, that they had gone to each other's houses for sleepovers. That they played sports together, in and out of school. That they knew each other's embarrassments and victories, and that they had come to terms with all of them, had settled comfortably into groups and clusters and strata that it would take Ada years and years to accurately map.

She was the last to arrive in her next class, and in all of her classes for the rest of the day. She gained a new textbook in every class, was instructed by every teacher to cover it in brown paper before the next day. They were bulky, these textbooks; she could fit only one in her briefcase. The rest she carried in the crook of one arm, wishing fruitlessly for the use of her other one.

At lunchtime she walked into the cafeteria and froze: it was then that she realized the extent of the stratification of the Lower School, the broad and awkward age range, from five-year-old kindergarteners to thirteen-year-old eighth-graders, some of whom looked as if they might as well be teachers. And within those ages, the boys and girls divided themselves; and within the two genders, they all seemed somehow divided by levels of attractiveness or confidence. She hovered for a moment and then plunged forward, as if into cold water. Briefly, wildly, she scanned the room and saw the angelic head of Melanie McCarthy, wondered if she should approach her, as the only other student she had formally met. But Melanie was surrounded by other girls sitting shoulder-to-shoulder on both long benches, as close and tight as matchsticks in a box.

Ada found the only empty table she could find, knowing somehow that it was not hers to take, that it belonged to a group that would very likely claim it in a moment. But she had no other options. She sat at the very end of it and took from her briefcase the paper bag that David had handed her that morning, its contents now squashed. After a few moments, the other half of the long table began to fill with boys who looked her age or slightly younger. None of them had been in her morning classes. Seventh-graders, maybe.

"Nice briefcase," one of them said, with so much force that she imagined everyone in the cafeteria had heard. Ada glanced over quickly but could not determine which boy it had been. The little group bent forward and backward, felled by their own laughter. She was holding her sandwich halfway to her mouth, and she stiffened there, uncertain how to proceed. She felt endlessly observed. She lowered the sandwich and followed it with her eyes. She had never been so directly targeted before—once or twice she'd been shouted at by another child on a walk to or from the store, or while going someplace else in the neighborhood—but on those occasions there was always the possibility of disappearance, of walking quickly in the opposite direction, pretending she hadn't heard. Here she was a stationary target, a sitting duck. She froze, still as a deer, keeping her eyes down, waiting for the tide of humiliation to wash over her and recede.

"Nice briefcase!" the boy shouted once more, having successfully elicited a laugh from his friends the first time, and Ada saw then that it was a ruddy, freckled boy, quite small for his age. He looked back at her. "Yeah, you!" he said. "I said I like your briefcase. Aren't you gonna say thanks?"

Later, when she thought it likely that interest in her had faded, she stood up as quickly as she could, tucked her now-hateful brief-case once more under one arm, her textbooks under the other, and asked the only adult she could find where the bathroom was. Then she walked down the hallway, opened the bathroom door, and, upon finding it empty, tucked herself into a stall. She set down her stack of textbooks and her briefcase on the floor. A wave of relief washed over her, to be unseen, hidden inside something small. To be totally alone.

She stayed there for twenty minutes, checking the digital wrist-watch that David had given her, waiting for the bell. She looked at her schedule. She would not be late again. Girls came into and out of the bathroom, holding forth on various subjects in rushed, enthusiastic bursts of language that Ada sometimes didn't understand. She noted their diction with interest, sentence structures she had never heard before, expressions she had only heard in restaurants or on the T. The 1980s marked the dawn of *like* as a sort of linguistic master key, a shapeless bendable word that fit into the crevices of sentences as perfectly as honey. The girls at Queen of Angels poured it over their speech greedily, and Ada mouthed it herself, in her bathroom stall, practicing along with them as she often did with other members of the lab.

At 11:54, when the bathroom was empty, Ada opened her briefcase on her lap. From it she took the pen, the pad of paper, one textbook, and added them to the pile of textbooks she'd made on the floor. Then she tucked the empty briefcase into the nook between the toilet and the wall. She'd leave it there for the rest of the day. Her books didn't fit into it anyway. She let herself out of the stall and into the hallway once more, carrying her textbooks on her meager hip, and she walked to her next class.

At the end of the day, when she returned to the bathroom nearest the cafeteria, she found that the briefcase was gone. She opened every stall door to make sure. She stood for a while, pondering what to do, wondering how she would explain it to David. In the mirror, she looked unlike herself.

The foyer of the Lower School was crowded with children, all jostling against one another to exit. Outside, she saw in her path a group of older boys from the Upper School—some of them so much older that they seemed to her like men, the whole broad-shouldered bunch. They were standing in a group, some of them leaning against the wall of the school, others standing splay-ankled in the middle of the sidewalk. Groups of boys terrified her beyond all measure; typically, if she saw them ahead of her on any walk, she crossed the street to avoid intersecting with them. But she had turned left out of the school doors, and the street was too busy to cross, and to turn around completely would have made her too visible.

She continued, head down, hoping to pass them unnoticed, when she heard her name.

"Ada," said one of them—she still had her eyes on the ground, and her instinct, really, was to keep going. But then he said it louder.

She was past them already. She clutched her books more tightly to her chest and pivoted slowly on a heel. She could feel a deep, defeating warmth spreading downward from her scalp. She looked up at William Liston.

"Hi," she said—so quietly that she might as well have mouthed it.

"How was your first day?" The other boys looked at her or away. Two of them continued whatever conversation they were having, uninterested.

"Okay," she said, trying to produce more volume this time, wondering what anyone else would do or say at this moment. Make a joke, perhaps: some tossed-off line, some little act of self-deprecation or school-deprecation that showed him she belonged.

William Liston paused, as if waiting for more.

"Cool," he said finally, and then turned back to his group. She understood that she was dismissed. She also understood that something further had been expected of her, a few more conversational twists and turns, and she racked her brain for anything, another word, another phrase, but she was not a native speaker of William's language, of the language of children.

Suddenly, from behind her, she heard her name again.

"Ada! There you are!" called a voice she recognized instantly as her father's. She froze.

"And William Liston!" he added. Ada turned around slowly, nervously, and saw David on the opposite sidewalk, wearing the large glasses that had gone out of fashion half a decade before, one half of the collar of his shirt tucked in on itself messily. He did not look to the right before bounding out into the street, and the driver of the car that screeched to a halt in front of him rolled down the car's window to object.

"All right, all right," said David, holding up a firm hand in the driver's direction. "Let's not overreact."

Ada had told him she would meet him at the lab after school. It had not been the plan for him to come here. All around her, she could hear a ceasing of conversation as her classmates stopped to watch the spectacle of David, his clothing flapping in ways she had never before noticed, his thin frame jangling along, elbows sticking out at odd angles.

He reached the sidewalk and waved brightly to William, calling out his name once more, telling him hello.

"Hey," said William. One of his friends turned his back to all of them, presumably to hide his amusement.

"You're getting very grown, William!" David called brightly, which caused a physical shudder to make its way from the top of Ada's head to her shins. Then he put one hand on her shoulder.

"Was it terrible?" he asked her, too loudly.

Ada shook her head no. Her voice was still lost.

"Well, how was it? And where's your briefcase, my dear?" David said.

A giggle from someplace to her right. She looked down at the giant stack of books she was carrying in her arms and back up at her father.

"I lost it," she said slowly.

He regarded her. In his gaze she saw that he knew what she had done, the intentionality with which she had misplaced the thing, and it shamed her: he would not have cared what anyone said, she thought. And she told herself that perhaps she was not so like him after all—that perhaps she lacked the best parts, the noblest parts, of David.

"How on earth does one lose a briefcase?" David said at last, and then at last he turned and walked toward home, and Ada followed. Her ears burned at the rumble, behind her, of a dozen conversations that resumed, in hushed tones, with more urgency, and the low sounds of laughter that followed.

That night, as she fell asleep, she thought about William, the great beauty of him, the way his sinews fit together in a neat, finished puzzle. And she pondered, for the first time in her life, the particular flaws of David, which she had never before counted, or even noticed: and she wondered what other people said about him, when she was not there to hear them.

From then on, every day, Ada went to school, sat quietly, spoke to no one, waited for her day to end. She longed for the lab, for her work. When no one was watching she coded on the backs of her book covers, until she was caught. At two-fifteen she burst forth from the front door and walked as quickly as she could, without attracting undue attention, to the T, and then took it to the lab to spend her afternoons there, catching up.

Part of her longing to be there was selfish: the work of the lab engaged her in ways that, she thought, her schoolwork never could. But part of it was out of fear, for David's work was beginning to falter. Now she took copious notes on everything he was tasked with doing. She had always attended meetings alongside him when she felt like it, but now she made a point to, jotting down items as if she were his secretary, his personal assistant.

Quietly, she asked him questions, tried to jog his memory, tried to help him keep up with the demands of his position. "Has Frank written the abstract for the *JACM* article? You should get it in by next week. Did you call McCarren back?"

At night, after quickly completing the homework that Queen of Angels had assigned, she dutifully told ELIXIR about her day, still eager to feel she was being useful to the lab, still relieved, in some way, to unburden herself to something safe. And, at last, she turned to the work that David had assigned her before his decline. He wrote down assignments for her in marble composition books—the names of pieces of music he wanted her to listen to, the names of proofs he wanted her to solve, books, films, pieces of artwork; even wines that he particularly enjoyed—which, he told her, she could save for later in her life.

As she made her way through them she derived a sense of satisfaction that far exceeded any she got from the homework the nuns assigned her. One day she solved, at last, the Sierpinski proof. She shared this with no one. Next she read a biography of FDR and one of Winston Churchill and one of Albert Einstein and one of Isadora Duncan. Then *One Hundred Years of Solitude.* Then *L'Étranger* by Camus, in French. Julian of Norwich's *Revelations of Divine Love.*

Slowly, and then quickly, David began to seem less and less interested in his research, which had theretofore sustained and engrossed him completely. It was frustrating to him now: to get to the end of a task and not remember the beginning of it; to forget the names of devices and procedures that he used every day. She whispered them to him when she could. But she was not always there to help. And she could tell now that everybody knew.

His colleagues began to look at him with sad and nervous eyes. Only Liston treated him normally, with a sort of brusque, business-like vigor that Ada appreciated.

In the winter of Ada's first year in school, he disappeared twice more, both times for several hours, both times denying that he had been gone, or insisting that he had merely gone for a walk. (Where he had gone on his walks, he could not say.)

They did not go to New York that year for Christmas, nor did they have a Christmas tree. The possibility crossed Ada's mind that David hadn't even gotten her a present, until, late on Christmas night, she shyly produced hers for him—it was a rare early edition of *The Castle of Otranto,* a bizarre favorite of David's that she had found in an antique shop nearly a year ago and had been saving ever since—and he sprang to his feet. From upstairs he produced a wrapped present for her. When she opened it she saw that it was a sparkly, spangled sweater, and she knew, with certainty, that it was Liston, not David, who had chosen it, bought it, and wrapped it.

By late January she had stopped leaving him alone. Liston, without being asked, began to pick him up in the morning, so that they could travel to the lab together. Ada kept herself awake at night, listening for footsteps descending the stairs, waiting for him to make a noise that would rouse her. She grew weary with fatigue. She grew tired of pretending, to the rest of the lab, that everything was all right.

She hung the front door and the kitchen door with a dozen decorative jingle bells that she'd purchased on sale after Christmas at a nearby store. She rigged up a system that would drop a hammer on a pot when either door was opened, and rested slightly easier. Twice, her makeshift alarm system sounded in the night, and she bolted from her bed and chased after him, down Shawmut Way, guiding him back to his bedroom gently, telling him he was sleepwalking. He was worse at night, or whenever he was tired, less lucid, nearly incapable of intelligent conversation. He called her *Mother* once. Once, he grabbed her by the wrist and placed her hand on his forehead, as if to tell her he had a fever, wordlessly, plaintively. It frightened Ada. He forgot her name completely on several occasions, and regularly forgot the names of his colleagues. *That one*, he said, or *You know the one*. When the DCF agent stopped by, Ada prepped David, subtly, in advance, walking him through the questions Miss O'Brien would ask him by asking him them herself. By the end of their visits he was tired, cantankerous, unlikable. And Ada would do her best to cheerfully distract Miss O'Brien.

Despite all this, he protested that everything was fine.

"I'm perfectly all right, Ada," he said, in response to any line of questioning about his memory or emotional state. "Really, I'd be much better if everyone would stop haranguing me constantly."

For months and months, Ada tried to make herself believe that this was true. But at last, in March, shortly after she turned fourteen, Ada walked into his office at the lab. He was staring down at some paperwork on his desk, but he did not seem to be processing it. When she entered he looked up at her, blinking. "Who's this one, now?" he said.

She knew then that she could not pretend any longer. She walked resolutely down the hall to Liston's office, and knocked on her door, and felt her face crumple. It was all she could do to keep from crying. She hated crying: it felt to her like a failure of will, a hot and humiliating display of weakness. David did not like it when she cried, and she had never once seen him do it. Miraculously, she held in her tears.

Liston beckoned Ada toward her and pointed to a seat.

"I'm sorry," Ada said. Her throat was tight. She hiccupped.

"He needs to see another doctor," said Ada, though she knew, even then, that there was nothing to be done. The disease was rolling in unstoppably, a powerful foreign front, advancing.

Liston convinced David to make her his executor shortly after that, when it became clear that the home visits by social services were going badly. Her childhood friend Tom Meara, who worked for the DCF, had warned her.

Ada, who had become masterful at eavesdropping in the last year, stood in the upstairs hallway of David's house, the receiver of a telephone extension pressed to her ear, the mouthpiece upended in the air. She breathed as lightly as she could, listening as her father and Liston negotiated her fate.

"They'll take Ada away from you," she heard Liston say. "Don't think they won't."

"Really, Liston," said David, protesting. But in his voice Ada heard something resigned and anxious.

"It would be best for Ada, David," said Liston. "Right? I mean, wouldn't it?" And it was then that Ada put the receiver gently down on the table, not wanting to hear anything more. She did not know whom to trust.

Only later did Ada learn all of the details of their arrangement. Mercifully, that year they attempted to keep her protected from whatever backroom dealings in which the two of them were engaging. Even David, never one to shelter her from the affairs of grown-ups, undertook to baby her just a bit, given the circumstances. Or perhaps, more likely, he simply forgot to tell her. But over the course of the following months, it became clear that Liston and David had agreed—whether it was Liston's idea or David's, Ada was never certain—that Liston would be designated Ada's legal guardian in the event that her father became unable to care for her.

On April 1, 1985, David resigned from the Steiner Lab. He did not tell Ada he had done so; she found out only when a grad student let her know that she would really, really miss her father.

"He's just a great guy," said the student earnestly. "A classic. There's not many like him anymore."

A week later, they received an invitation to a retirement party, formally worded, to be held in a ballroom at the Bit. President McCarren was listed as the host—a fact that made David, even in his somewhat incapacitated state, scoff. Peter McCarren, who had replaced President Pearse several years prior, was despised by David for reasons Ada never fully understood. McCarren was a short, rough man, quite unlike his stately predecessor. He was pushy and red-faced, a bulldog, good at fundraising but bad at math. "That idiot," David said, anytime his name was raised.

"Good old McCarren," he said now, ruefully, more slowly than he might have before. "He probably couldn't wait to see me go."

The dinner itself was on a Friday night, David's last official day of work. Ada was to meet him at the lab that afternoon, after her school day ended. In the morning, David had come downstairs in an unironed button-down shirt, and Ada pleaded with him to go back upstairs and put on a suit. She herself ran home briefly after school to change out of her school uniform and into a dress that was slightly too small for her, a pretty one that Liston had helped her pick out the summer before, on one of the shopping trips she sometimes orchestrated for Ada, to David's mild disgust. The dress, made of light yellow cotton, was too summery for April, and to compensate Ada had paired it with black tights, black patent-leather shoes, and a blue ski parka—her only winter jacket. She had hoped to do without it, but it was still cold that April, and it would not warm up for a month. She looked odd, even she knew it, but she had few other options. She ran to the T through a chilly rain. Inside, she produced the piece of paper she had been carrying in her pocket all day.

This was her secret: at Liston's urging, she had composed a speech in her father's honor, a description of his career, the awards he'd won, the impact he'd had on his field. She had stayed up late every night that week, working in her bedroom with one light on, neglecting the homework her teachers at Queen of Angels had assigned her. *My father, David Sibelius*, it began, *is retiring after nearly 30 years of running the Steiner Laboratory*. She had crafted it carefully to emphasize his great accomplishments, the nobility of his character, while keeping it relatively restrained and dignified. She had tried to make it funny. If there was one thing David hated, she knew, it was sentimentality.

When she reached the lab she went straight to Liston's office.

"Don't you look pretty!" said Liston, standing up from behind her desk, taking off the reading glasses she needed but professed to hate. She, too, had dressed up for David's dinner: she was wearing an over-sized pink blazer that both clashed with and set off her hair, and she had applied more blush than usual. She was wearing big, dangly ear-rings in geometrical shapes. She would be the one assuming David's role as head of the lab. She looked as if she had attempted to dress in a way that reflected her promotion, but even Ada knew she had gotten it slightly wrong.

It was 4:00 in the afternoon: three hours before the dinner was set to begin. Shyly, Ada produced from her pocket the speech she had written, and asked if Liston would mind looking at it. Then she sat down on the beanbag chair that she had slept in, often, as a child, and stared at the floor, and waited anxiously for Liston to respond.

"Oh, Ada," Liston said, "I think it's perfect." When she looked up, Ada saw that little pools of tears were hovering precariously above Liston's lower lashes, threatening to spill over. Liston smiled briefly and then let her face drop. Ada studied her. She was a pretty woman, forty-three that year, slightly plump, soft-featured. To Ada, she looked perpetually like a teenager; Ada had never been privy to the dressing-table rituals and ministrations of women; she mistook Liston's fashion sense, her dyed red hair, the mascara she wore, for signifiers of youth.

"I'm sorry," said Liston, and she let out a sad little laugh. "I'll just miss having you here, that's all. Both of you."

All six colleagues filed out, one at a time, from the main room of the Steiner Lab. Charles-Robert, and then Liston, and then Frank, and then Hayato, and then David. Ada left last; and, placing a hand on the wall behind her, she tapped the light switch down instinctively, without having to search for it. She looked backward, into the darkened office, and it felt, in a way, as if she were leaving her life and her body behind: as if, when she closed the door behind her, she would become a ghost, something spectral and disincarnate, something without a home. She wondered if this was what David felt like all the time. She wondered what would happen next.

The dinner was held in the faculty dining room of the Bit, which had been decorated with linens and flowers.

David had already declined to speak, and so he settled uncomfortably down into his chair at the table that had been reserved for the six of them, along with the provost, President McCarren, and Mrs. McCarren, a tidy woman who tried to make polite small talk with David until, at last, she gave up hope.

David's posture was slumped; his head hung low; when people spoke to him he did not meet their gaze, but turned his own to hover someplace around their mouths, as if trying to read their lips. He did not eat until he was reminded to by Ada. He smiled politely as, one after another, his colleagues at the Bit, and some from other institutions, spoke about his achievements and intelligence, his wit and generosity; but the naming of these qualities was, to Ada, only a cruel reminder of their recent disappearance. David got tired easily now. Once or twice his eyes closed completely, and Ada jostled him as subtly as she could.

Ada was due to speak last. She felt in the pocket of her coat, which she had insisted on hanging over the back of her chair, for her speech. The paper, by then, was soft with the wear of being handled, being worried over. She produced it and put it in her lap, glanced down at it when she could. But as dessert was being served, and while the provost was speaking, David turned to her and asked, too loudly, if she was ready to leave.

Ada shook her head once, quickly. President McCarren had heard him. Ada was not certain how much the rest of the university knew about the reasons for his retirement—certainly the other members of the lab were protective enough of David not to have said too much to anyone—but in that moment she realized that everyone must have known that something was wrong with her father.

"Come now, Ada," said David. "Really, let's go."

Politely, McCarren averted his gaze.

Ada leaned toward him and whispered to him urgently. "It's for you," she said. "The dinner is for you. We can't leave yet."

David was shaking his head slowly, as if he had not heard her. "I've got to go," he said, and unsteadily he stood up from his chair. He held a hand up to the rest of the table. "Okay," he said, "bye to all, now."

Ada stood up, too. She wanted to reach out to him, to pull him forcibly back by his elbow, but she felt that that would be worse. Her speech fell from her lap onto the floor and she bent to retrieve it. Without meaning to, she caught Liston's eye as she rose, and on her face Ada saw a look of such sadness, such pity, that she quickly turned away. Together, she and David left through a side door. And behind her, Ada heard the provost stutter and then pause.

"Well," he said, "I guess our guest of honor is indisposed . . ."

Then they were outside, and they stood together for a while on the sidewalk while Ada decided what to do next. The rain had stopped but it was bitterly cold, too cold for April.

"Can we take a cab?" Ada asked—something that David abhorred. To him, taxis were for the lazy, the fiscally irresponsible. But she thought it was worth asking, for she was shivering even in her ski parka, and that night he immediately agreed.

In the taxi, Ada was silent, furious. She said nothing except to give the driver directions, when David failed to. David rested his head against the headrest, closing his eyes for a while. She looked over at him resentfully. In the yellow light from storefronts and streetlamps, he looked sickly and old. She had been noticing lately that his physical size was shrinking: although he had always been thin, he had seemed shorter, recently, more stooped: as if he had aged five years in a week. His eyes had dark circles beneath them. She supposed he had been handsome once; his stature had helped him to be so. He was uncommonly old when she'd been born, yes, but he'd always seemed young for his years. He was tall and well built, at least, with fine features and bright, inquisitive eyes. When he felt like it, he was capable of listening intently for hours on end. Women had always liked him: Ada was not oblivious to this fact. But he was changed now. More like a grandfather than a father. Someone incapable of offering her protection. She felt unsteady and unsafe.

At home, Ada retreated to her room without saying good night. She turned on her computer, pulled ELIXIR up to have a talk. And then she heard the sound of David's footsteps on the stairs, heard a faint knock on her door.

It was rare for David to come into her room: she had no memories of him sitting on the edge of her bed, reading her a story as she drifted to sleep. Though he read to her, it was always downstairs, in the living room, in a somewhat businesslike manner: she sitting in one chair, he in another; and when she tired, Ada would trot upstairs and put herself to bed. At four years old she knew how to brush her teeth, wash her face, comb her hair so it would not tangle; she knew how to don her nightgown, to tuck her little body into bed.

Now she went to her bedroom door and opened it a crack. She was still wearing her ridiculous outfit, banana-colored dress, heavy black tights.

David looked distressed. The light in the hallway was off. She could see him only in the light cast upon him by her little desk lamp.

"May I come in, Ada?" he said.

She opened the door a bit more. There was only one chair in her room, at her desk; David claimed this, so she sat down on her twin bed, across from him. He looked at her seriously.

"I want to apologize," he said.

Ada was silent.

"I've spent a great deal of time denying what's become undeniable recently," he continued. "That my mind is most certainly being taken from me, slowly. This is a truth that I have found it difficult to confront."

She looked at him. She felt recalcitrant, unswayed.

"I can tell you're upset. While I have my wits about me," said David, "while I am relatively mentally intact, I want to tell you what it has meant to me to have you as my daughter, Ada. You cannot imagine.

"Now—" he said, holding up one hand to stop her as she opened her mouth to speak, "Now. It is true that great innovations in the field of medical research and technology are becoming . . ." He trailed off, looking down at his palms, as if wishing for notes.

"Innovations in medicine and technology," said Ada.

"Yes," said David. "There is a chance that some intervention will occur in my lifetime that will reverse the course of what I now see as my inevitable decline. A small and improbable chance, but a chance nonetheless. That said, I don't think you should cling to this hope. Because, as we both must accept, the likeliest course of events is that I will die before you've reached adulthood. And therefore that is my prediction, and that is the path for which you should prepare yourself."

Ada nodded. She was sitting very still on her bed. She was still wearing her coat. Her right hand was in her pocket, grasping the speech she had written about her father. She wondered whether she should give it to him.

"It is also possible," said David, "that you will one day learn some things about me that are difficult to understand. I think every child goes through this process. The problem is that I will not be here— perhaps mentally, perhaps physically—to explain them to you, or to guide you through them. And therefore you must trust me when I say that everything I have done has been out of a wish for a better life for myself and for you. And everything I have done has been in our best interest. All right, Ada?"

She didn't move. She watched him. His gaze was beseeching. He leaned forward in his chair to look at her.

"Do you understand?" he asked her. And, at last, she nodded, though at that time she did not.

"Finally, I have never been a religious man," said David, "but I also have some notion that this is not the conclusion of our story, my dear. I think it quite possible that our paths may cross again someday, whatever that may look like.

"Thank you for listening," said David. He stood up, somewhat painfully, and walked to the door. "I'll miss talking with you most," he said. And then he was gone.

They never spoke this way again. After much consideration, Ada did not give him the speech she had prepared for him, thinking that he would deem it too maudlin. Instead, she kept it for herself, reading it occasionally to remind herself, as her father declined, of how he used to be.

The morning after David's retirement was an odd one. It was a Saturday, and there was no reason to leave the house. No lab to go to, even if they had wanted to. David was quite still, and sat with a book of poetry near the windows at the front of the house, not really reading. "At last, some free time," he said, feigning cheer. "I've been meaning to get to this for years."

Ada made a lunch for both of them of pickled herring sandwiches on white bread, his favorite, and cut them into dainty crustless bites, and served them with strong tea. Afterward she begged him to walk to the library with her, simply for something to do, and he agreed.

He looked at the librarian, Anna Holmes, without much recognition, even though she had worked there for years and called him by name, and even though Ada had once wondered, idly, whether the two of them might have crushes on one another.

"How are you, David?" asked Miss Holmes, clearly happy to see him. "It's been so long!"

David looked at her quizzically. "Quite well," he said. "Thank you for asking."

Later, Ada read and worked on problems until it was time for dinner and bed, where she prayed without much faith or conviction for the healing of her father, thinking of Julian of Norwich, of Franny Glass.

Sunday was much the same.

And then, on Monday, it was time to go back to school. Ada admonished her father not to leave the house. Their exterior doors, original to the house, could be locked with an old-fashioned skeleton key from the outside. Ada hesitated, but then decided, feeling guilty, that it would be best and safest for David if she did so that day, and every day thereafter. She had not told anyone about David's recent wanderings: she feared they would take him away. After her school day ended, she raced home, hoping desperately that he had neither broken out nor panicked, that she would not find him reduced to tears on the floor, or find him in some other, equally upsetting position. But he seemed fine, sitting placidly in his chair by the window, gazing out of it.

In the ensuing weeks, Ada attempted to extract all the information she could before it faded. But he grew more and more reticent.

"I simply can't remember, my dear," he said tiredly.

So instead she wrote down memories that he had at one time or another shared with her, to the best of her memory: that her grandfather was the grandson of Finnish immigrants who made their money, upon arriving in the United States, in shipping; that her grandmother was a descendant of William Bradford, the British Separatist, the *Mayflower* passenger, the governor of Plymouth Colony. That his mother's maiden name was Amory. All of this Ada wrote down in a blue-covered notebook, separate from the marbled ones in which David wrote his assignments.

When she asked him to confirm what she had written, reading the facts aloud, he told her that he could not recall. "Amory?" he said to her. "I've never heard of it."

Ada called this period in David's life "working from home," to preserve her sense of hope and his sense of dignity, and each day she set out some task for him to complete, and on weekends she brought home several newspapers and pored over them with him.

He became increasingly obsessive about ELIXIR. Interacting with it seemed to be the only thing that brought him solace anymore. Sometimes, when he had trouble finding the words, he simply pointed to the office; and then she walked him into it, and sat him down at his computer. She opened ELIXIR for him, and left the room, out of respect, and let him type.

"Now you," he told her, when he had finished, and it occurred to her that perhaps he had the conviction that ELIXIR was his legacy. She signed him out, signed herself in. Dutifully, she conversed with the machine.

Sometimes she still tried to encourage him to focus on his work. But mainly he just sat in front of it, looking at it silently for long stretches of time—a puzzled, painful look on his face.

Sometimes she brought out the floppy disk he had given her one August night two years prior, at the end of his failed dinner party. *For Ada* was still marked upon its hard cover, in David's handwriting; a note from him to Ada was still affixed to the disk itself. She inserted it into the disk drive. Then she sat down with David in front of it, and asked him to help her solve it. *DHARSNELXRHQHLT WJFOLKTWDURSZJZCMILWFTALVUHVZRDLDEYIXQ*, read the text file. It looked completely arbitrary. David was quiet at these times, watching as she wrote down, on pieces of paper in front of her, the letters that appeared before her on the screen. As she tallied their frequency, made slash marks above them on the page.

One day, Ada turned the computer on and it displayed an icon of a frowning, X-eyed monitor, and would not boot up at all.

David pointed at the computer screen. "Just like me," he said, about the sad little Mac on the screen, and Ada laughed in relief that he could still make a joke.

She vowed to fix the computer, but she couldn't.

"Time for ELIXIR?" David asked daily—he had retained the word surprisingly well—and she had to tell him that his Mac was broken, and bring him upstairs to use hers instead.

While he worked, she tried and tried, in his office, to fix whatever was preventing his computer from starting. In light of David's illness, the state of the machine took on greater meaning. But she couldn't. She needed David's help, and he could no longer give it.

At the time of David's retirement, the lab was working on a system to increase ELIXIR's vocabulary by training outsiders to chat with it correctly, which David had always been opposed to. Liston, the new director, discussed the lab's progress with Ada in bits and pieces each time she saw her. Prior to the onset of David's disease, she had always seemed hesitant to involve Ada in the work of the lab—not because she doubted her ability to learn it, but because long ago she had unofficially designated herself a counterbalance to David in regard to Ada's well-being, and as such pushed her gently backward into childhood to the best of her ability while he beckoned her forth. Now that David was fading, however, Liston seemed to realize how much Ada missed the work, and included her in it whenever she could.

She came over for dinner once a week, sometimes bringing Matty, her youngest, when she could convince him to come along. He read comic books in a corner, looking at all of them suspiciously from time to time, not saying much. Other times she came alone. And she updated Ada on the work of the lab, the problems they'd encountered, the tangles they were working out. Ada sometimes tried to help remotely, presenting her findings to Liston the next time she saw her or spoke to her, once calling the lab with a solution that had presented itself to her suddenly in the middle of the previous sleepless night. "Thank you so much, honey," said Liston, and Ada heard in her voice that they had fixed it themselves already.

At school, Ada was distracted. She had settled into a painful, uncomfortable existence at Queen of Angels: she rarely spoke, except when directly called upon. Not wanting to ask David to buy her a backpack, and properly humiliated out of ever using a briefcase again, she settled on simply carrying her books in her arms everyplace she went, which earned her odd glances and several nicknames that she overheard despite her best efforts to tune out every conversation around her. She had no friends, nor had she any enemies, really. She brought a novel to lunch each day, balanced at the top of the stack of her schoolbooks, and read it while she ate slowly, neatly, making certain with searching hands that she had wiped her mouth clean after every bite.

Simultaneously, she felt invisible and too observed, and she fantasized at times about what it would be like to be amorphous, incorporeal—the manifestation of the vision she had had upon leaving the Steiner Lab for the final time—a shadow-girl who could slip imperceptibly around corners and through hallways, keeping close to the wall. She existed but was not seen. In the privacy of her room, under cover of night, she sometimes practiced the mannerisms and dialect that she had seen children her own age using. *Like*, she whispered to herself. *Um, totally. Whatever.*

She longed, now, to be pretty. After weighing the evidence, she had recently decided that she was not, which, in her former life, would not have mattered—in fact, David had always seemed to consider prettiness a detriment, something hampering and debilitating, like a tin can tied to one's leg.

But at Queen of Angels, prettiness was all. Melanie McCarthy was the standard-bearer in this realm, and everyone else in the eighth grade could be ranked in descending order after her. Ada was, she felt sure, near the bottom. In the mirror, she took off her glasses, and her reflection became hazier, softer. Better. She put them back on and frowned. The glasses themselves, she thought, were maybe the problem; but to ask David for contacts would be unthinkable, akin to asking him for something like breast implants. She went to bed, sighing long sighs, dreading the morning.

As David's mental decline accelerated, Ada clung to his physical presence in the house, and dreaded the day when he would not be there. She reverted to an old pattern: when Liston came over for dinner now, she worked her hardest to convince her that he was well, that his mind was sharper than it was, his memory more capable. She coached him on topics of conversation in advance, went over the day's headlines with him, as she used to do herself before the dinner parties he once threw. "David was just saying," she would begin, and then dispense an opinion that she herself had constructed after a careful perusal of world events. "Right, David?" she asked him, and he would look at Ada vaguely and nod. He had always been kind to Matty and he continued to be so. When it occurred to him, he gave Matty some little token each time he came over, a book or a fancy pen or a piece of chocolate. Sometimes the chocolate was too old, and Ada had to swap it out for something else, but mostly Matty didn't notice. With time, though, David forgot Matty's name, and then forgot him altogether. "Who's this young fellow?" he began to ask, and Matty seemed terrified of him, avoiding his gaze, finally refusing to come altogether—Liston didn't tell Ada this, but she knew it to be true. Liston protected her. "He's got baseball practice in the evening now," she told Ada. "William takes him over."

The rest of the members of the lab stopped by from time to time at first, but soon their visits dwindled in frequency, and now when David forgot their names it made Ada perversely satisfied. If they came more, she thought, he'd know them better. Still, she prompted him, wanting them to think well of him and of her, too, cheerily glossing over the extent of his deterioration. When Regina O'Brien came for her monthly visit she employed the same techniques. At the end of each visit she took Ada into another room and asked if she felt comfortable living in the home and she always, always said yes.

For a time it seemed to be working. Ada felt she could take care of her father. Sometimes, when he fell asleep at his desk or in his chair, a book in his hand, unread, Ada sat across from him and imagined him back to his previous state—imagined that when he woke he would spring up vigorously from his chair, and beckon her into the dining room, and lay out before her some famous proof or problem, and set her to work upon it, spinning her like a top. "Very good, Ada," he used to tell her when she solved it. "Excellent work. Smart girl," he would say—benedictions that she craved, now, beyond all measure. *Well done*, she whispered to herself at times, when she solved a problem that she'd assigned herself, from the notebooks David, in his former incarnation, had created for her. *Well done, you clever girl.* And she imagined that David was saying it.

She got by in this way. She managed. She vowed to keep up the charade of David's competence for as long as she could. And then, in May, David walked out of his room without his clothes on, which mortified Ada to the point of incapacitation. "Get dressed!" she said abruptly, and then she ran and hid in her bedroom. When she emerged he had, thankfully, complied. But he did this with some frequency thereafter, until she began to lay out his clothes for day and night upon his bed, ordering him to get into them when it was time, and closing his bedroom door behind her while he did so. "Are you dressed?" she asked him, and only when he replied affirmatively did Ada enter.

Often he grew frustrated as he searched for words. "The thing that's like a wrench, but not a wrench," he said. "The thing that's black and small. The thing that you use. The thing that I love." And then, when *thing* eluded him: "I want it. Where is it?" There were times where she could not help. Next, he began to swear at her—she had steeled herself for this, having read several scholarly articles that indicated that the aphasia associated with Alzheimer's often left one's arsenal of curses, located in a different region of the brain, unaffected. But the reality of it shocked her: gentle David, calling her words that he had never before even used in her presence. David, who deplored cursing. He knew her less and less, sometimes raising a fist at her as if in anger and then letting it drop to his side; sometimes weeping like a small child, which troubled her soul. "My friend," he said, by then, about all people, in order to avoid their names. Including his own daughter. "Ada," she sometimes said in response. In front of Liston, she pretended it did not bother her, but in private she railed at him from time to time. "You know my name," she said to him testily. And once or twice she had yelled at him with her full voice. "*I'm ADA*," she had said. "You named me Ada." She had never before shouted at him, and it felt terrible and thrilling all at once. In those moments he blinked at her; he did not flinch. He seemed aware, somehow, of the importance of keeping his pride intact, a citadel, as his mental faculties crumbled around it. And as Ada wailed at him, shouting her own name, he would turn his head slowly to some nearby object and gaze upon it. Other times she whispered it to him, her name, imagining somehow that it might seep into his consciousness subliminally. While he was sleeping. While he was awake, and staring blankly out a window onto Shawmut Way. *I'm your daughter Ada*. He did not respond.

More and more, every week, he tried to wander. The bells went off in the middle of the night. She leapt from her bed. She grew weary.

One day, Ada came home from school to find three large fire trucks lined up along Shawmut Way. Liston, in her work clothes, stood outside of David's house, speaking to a firefighter; their neighbors stood nearby in little groups. Even Mrs. O'Keeffe had gotten up out of her lawn chair for the occasion, was leaning on her cane, straining to overhear what they were saying.

It was then that Ada saw David, sitting on the ground, a blanket wrapped around him despite the warm weather. A firefighter was sitting next to him casually, attempting to chat with him as he sat there on the grass. He looked childlike and confused, a five-year-old waiting for his mother. His feet were pointed upward toward the sky. His head hung low, and he was shaking it almost imperceptibly from side to side. In the spring air Ada picked up the smell of something acrid. Smoke, she realized. Her instinct in that moment was to run. But then Liston turned and saw her and strode toward her quickly.

"Ada," she said, "honey. Did you lock him inside? Was David locked inside every day?"

Ada felt something rising up inside her: it was the unfairness of it all, of being expected to watch over David, who was supposed to be watching over her. She felt simultaneously ashamed and self-righteous. *What else was I supposed to do?* she wanted to ask Liston. Her father was her responsibility, not anybody else's—and she had made the best decision she could make.

But she could not articulate any of this, for her voice had been taken from her. Instead she stood in place, looking down, her arms folded tightly about her waist, waiting for someone, anyone, to recognize the injustice of it all. Until, at last, Liston put an arm around her and led her down the street.

St. Andrew's Manor was in Quincy, just outside the city. It was a nice place overseen by an order of nice nuns. Liston's own mother had ended her days there after a debilitating stroke. Shortly after the day that David almost set the house on fire—as it turned out, a neighbor had heard the sound of the smoke detector going off for too long and had called the fire department—Liston had had a serious conversation with Ada. And, at last, Ada gave her consent: David would no longer live with Ada on Shawmut Way. Liston, as previously agreed, would assume full guardianship of Ada—who, at fourteen, was four years from legal adulthood. And David would move into St. Andrew's.

When Ada first heard the name of the place, she thought it might be something fancy: a country house with a semicircular driveway and a stable, a Tudor mansion set back in the woods. Liston said that all David would need were some clothes, maybe some pictures to put on his shelves—at which point Ada realized that they had no pictures, nothing they kept in frames around the house. Liston's house, on the other hand, was decorated almost exclusively with photographs of her sons and daughter and her grandson; or friends of hers, with Liston, at the beach; or family. She even had pictures of Ada in the lab, on Halloween, at their Christmas parties. Shyly, Ada asked her if she might take one of these to bring along with David so that he would be able to remember her. They had almost no pictures in their home;

David's camera-shyness meant there were none of him, and he rarely thought to take a picture of Ada.

"Of course, baby!" said Liston. "I think that's a really good idea." And she brought Ada over to her house, and let her choose any one that she wanted. After some consideration, Ada selected one from a photo album, perhaps three years old. In it, Ada was sitting at the monitor in the main room of the lab, chatting with ELIXIR, smiling happily toward the camera, but looking up above it; for, she remembered, it was David she'd been looking at. David, who had been standing behind Liston as she took the shot, saying something silly about *formaggio* or *fromage*.

Liston selected a few more and said she would find frames for them all. And then she put a hand on Ada's shoulder.

"It'll be okay, kiddo," she said. Ada looked up at her warm face and wanted badly to smile for her, but she found that she couldn't.

The morning of David's departure, he seemed more confused than usual. He hardly spoke. Ada and Liston had spent the previous evening packing his clothes into a large suitcase, and, beholding it, David put one hand to his cheek plaintively.

"But where are we going," he said, over and over again.

"We're moving!" said Liston. "Someplace great. An adventure."

"No, thank you," he said politely, at one point.

Just before David walked out the kitchen door for the last time, Ada had the urge, suddenly, to tell him to look around the house once more. To go down into the basement, to place a hand on his work desk; to go up into the hot and dusty attic; to go and sit on his old bed for a while. Did he know that this would be his last glimpse of the house he had grown to love?

But Liston was guiding him out the door already, perhaps to avoid upsetting him.

"Where are we going, now?" asked David, one last time.

"Put your seat belt on, honey," Liston said to David.

He complied, and then let his arms fall limply at his sides. From her place in the backseat, Ada gazed at his hands. In the left one he was clutching his lucky charm, the clover-shaped trinket he usually carried with him. Recently it had comforted her to see him holding it—at least, she'd been telling herself, he remembered to put that in his pocket each day—but that day it pained Ada to see it, bespeaking, as it did, some unfulfilled wish. His hands, around it, looked doughy, inflated somehow, too large for his body. They didn't look like the hands of a working man: nothing like David's strong hands as they flew about at one time, dismantling things, reconstructing them, chopping and stirring his meals. Recently, she thought: less than two years ago.

"What sort of place is it," David was saying. "And tell me the name again."

"St. Andrew's Manor," said Ada, hoping that the sound of the name would please him—*manor* being a word that, she imagined, might have similar connotations for him as it did for her. Of dignity, of prestige, of gray impressive stone.

But what he said was, "Oh, of all the things," and she wondered if this was a specific response to the name, or simply an arbitrary outburst, evidence of the way his temper had been flaring recently at odd, unpredictable moments.

Phrases like that one had become a catch-all for him, when he couldn't muster a more appropriate response. *For heaven's sake. Good heavens. I'll be damned.* It reminded her of the way ELIXIR had been given a set of responses to use when nothing else was available. David reverted to them frequently by then, and when he uttered them she read in his eyes a certain disappointment that he could not conjure up a more precise choice of words, volley quickly back the best response. Finding the mot juste had been a skill on which he had prided himself for as long as Ada could remember. Before the illness, he had loathed puns and loved cleverness in equal measure. Words, to David, were nearly mathematical: there was very clearly a correct one for every slot in every sentence. When he was at his sharpest he rolled them into place like a putter on a green. Now a good day meant that he could come up with a dozen in a row that were appropriate to the situation at hand.

In the front seat, Liston was making small talk. She feigned cheerfulness for David's sake, to keep him settled, but she glanced at Ada in the rearview mirror every few moments. And Ada looked out the window. Liston had told her, again and again, that this was the best thing for David, that he couldn't be cared for safely at home, not anymore; but since the decision had been made for him to go to St. Andrew's, Ada had been envisioning, almost obsessively, other lives, other plans, for herself and her father.

She daydreamed often about running away with him, to New York City, to a different country, to the cabin in the woods of the Adirondacks that David had rented for years. (Conveniently, these daydreams simultaneously allowed her to envision leaving behind her education at Queen of Angels, as well.) And when she was not day-dreaming, she was paying extra attention to David's mannerisms, his appearance, his gait. She wanted to memorize them. With the little camera she rarely used, she had recently been taking photographs of him, surreptitiously, in different places in the house. Later, these would look to her like pictures of a ghost. In them, he was expressionless. Gone were David's funny, theatrical, changing features; in their place was the lion face she had read about in articles, a term that frightened her with its implication of cruelty, its implication that the bearer of such a countenance might suddenly eat her alive. Instead she tried to think of David's face as a doll's face. A still and quiet mask.

Liston turned right at a sign that bore the name of the facility in an even font that reminded her of the lettering on banks: ST. ANDREW'S MANOR: EST. 1951. At the top of a small hill sat several low brick buildings in the shape of a U. Liston pulled her car into the parking lot, and Ada saw the fingers of David's left hand curl into a fist. She leaned forward to take in the view. Two old women, much older than David, sat in wheelchairs on the paved driveway that abutted the front entrance. They were slumped in their chairs. One seemed asleep, her head lolling forward on her chest. The other moved her feet back and forth slowly, as if trying to get up and walk.

The three of them got out of the car, David only after Liston's prompting. He was relatively able-bodied, still, and he got up quickly from his seat and closed the door behind him in one easy motion.

There was a plaque to the right of the white front door that identified Andrew as the patron saint of fishermen, and once Ada got inside she saw why the place was named for him: the large rear windows of the lobby looked east to the harbor some distance away, visible from the building only by virtue of the elevation of its plot of land. Still, Ada could see boats there, sailing inland and out, and it was a sunny day, which made everything seem a little less dismal. The rest of the lobby was drab and beige, with floral patterns on the pillows, with arrangements of armchairs and tables and books she was certain no one ever looked at, and two fireplaces that looked similarly untouched. They might not even work, she thought, and she wished that they did: David's love of fireplaces was well known to everyone who knew him.

David stood and looked at the ocean while Liston navigated the front desk. Ada was grateful to her for doing this so that she didn't have to. She had a speech prepared to make to the administration and staff about David's needs and concerns, but it had gone out of her head, and she stood with David and stared. In a moment of self-awareness, she closed her jaw. He seemed too young to be in this place, she thought. Who would he talk to? She vowed to visit him every day, taking two buses from Dorchester to Quincy.

After a moment two administrators emerged from a hallway, one a Carmelite nun.

"How are you, Sister?" said Liston cheerily. It was clear from the nun's response that she remembered Liston from her mother's time in residence. As she introduced herself, Ada was uncertain about whether to shake her hand. She had not shaken the hands of any of the nuns who taught her, upon meeting them. But this one offered hers to Ada kindly, and she took it very gently, ignoring the admonitions David had always given her about being firm and business-like when she gripped anybody's hand in greeting. She was younger than Ada had thought most nuns to be—she must have been very young indeed the last time Liston had seen her—and she said her name was Sister Katherine. The other administrator was Patrick Rowan, a middle-aged man with stale breath and a wide blue tie. Ada immediately disliked him for the way he took David's hand with one of his and put an arm behind David's back. As if David were incapable of walking. As if he needed anyone else to navigate him in this way. David, too, recoiled.

"Oh, for heaven's sake," said David. "What a production." And Ada felt warm with satisfaction that he had produced such an appropriate response.

Their little group walked down the hallway toward a wing called the Mount Carmel Center for Memory Care, and stopped outside a set of double doors. Patrick Rowan punched in a code and the doors swung open. As Ada walked through them she turned back over her shoulder and noticed an identical keypad on the opposite side. Clearly, there was no leaving this wing without the password.

After several turns that left her feeling disoriented, she came to David's room. On the wall outside it was a placard with two paper cards slid into it: one that said *Mr. David Sibelius—Doctor*, Ada thought to herself, not *Mister*—and one that said *Mr. John Gainer*. Inside, she saw that David's roommate was ancient: to her he looked a hundred or more, though later, as an adult, she realized he had probably been closer to eighty-five. He said nothing to them as they entered. He was a small man, sitting in a recliner that cradled him like a hammock, his back bowed, his little neat feet sticking up at the end, an enormous magnifying glass in one hand, looking through it at a book that he did not lower as their party of five entered the room.

"Good afternoon, Mr. Gainer," said Patrick Rowan loudly. And then he turned to Ada and said, in a normal voice, "Mr. Gainer can't hear much."

He brought David toward Mr. Gainer and bent down, placing a hand on his shoulder.

"This is David Sibelius," said Patrick Rowan. "Your new roommate."

"How d'you do?" said Mr. Gainer, and David nodded formally.

The room was large and decorated sparsely. A brown wooden crucifix, like the ones at Queen of Angels, hung above the door on the inside wall. Ada wondered if it was David's roommate's, or a standard part of the décor in every room. The two twin beds were on opposite walls, and on Mr. Gainer's bed there was a blue crocheted blanket that somebody—his wife? Ada wondered—had made for him. There were two matching recliners that looked quite comfortable, and two wooden-backed chairs. Two dressers. Two nightstands. Two bookshelves mounted to the walls above the beds, too small for the collection of books still sitting in Liston's car. Not that David read much anymore—but Ada had imagined that to have his favorites with him would be comforting, like the photographs of her and their friends that Liston had brought along. Disappointingly, the large window opposite the door looked out at the parking lot. She wished he had had a harbor view. The ceiling was made of large panels that looked to her like Styrofoam; she had the impression that they could be taken out quite easily from movies she'd seen involving heists. (Briefly, her mind wandered once more to absconding with David.) The floor was blue vinyl. The overheads were painfully fluorescent: a type of light that David despised and found depressing. He had commented on it all his life, whenever they found themselves in restaurants or stores where they were employed. "If only they'd do something about the *lights*, though," he had lamented, in certain locations, in the past. He had even coaxed Tran into using incandescent lightbulbs several years ago, offering to pay for them himself. Now he was looking around his new room. He circled it once, slowly. He opened up a small drawer in the nightstand. Into it he put his lucky-clover charm. He closed the drawer again. He offered up a closed smile. "I'll be darned," he said, as Sister Katherine moved about the room, smoothing the tightly made white bed, fluffing the pillows.

"Now, Ada," she said, "I'm going to write down David's direct line for you, all right? This is his phone number," she said. "You can reach him anytime. And David, you can call Ada anytime, too. We can help you."

She took a small pad of paper out of the breast pocket of her large dark blazer, and, after writing on it, ripped off a piece of it and handed it to Ada. David smiled faintly.

"Our residents are very happy here," she said. Ada believed that she believed this. "Isn't that right, Mr. Gainer?" she asked, raising her voice, but Mr. Gainer had already gone back to his book, and he did not know he was being addressed.

"I know Mom was," said Liston politely.

Liston sat with David on the edge of his bed while Ada ran back and forth to the car, unloading his possessions with the help of a metal dolly that Patrick Rowan found for her.

When she had everything set up, she asked him if he'd like anything moved. Slowly, he looked about the room. He walked to the bedside table and touched one of the photographs that Liston had framed: it was a shot of the group of them, the Steiner Lab, leaning forward over a dinner table at a restaurant that Ada could no longer remember the name of. It had been taken perhaps four years prior— Ada looked noticeably younger and smaller in it, and Liston's hair was a slightly different shade of red. David, as usual, was missing from the shot; he'd been the photographer. The restaurant, a Thai place they had gone to only once or twice, had since closed. Ada had liked it: they all ate shoeless, sitting on the floor, their feet in a little sunken pit below the table, and her chicken and cashews had come served in half of a hollowed-out pineapple. "They probably reuse that time after time," Liston had said, horrified, but Ada and David had not cared.

This was the picture David lifted, now, from the table. "Amarind," he said suddenly. The name of the restaurant. And Ada wondered if they had made a mistake, admitting him here.

They stayed with him through lunch, and Liston tried to make friends on his behalf. She charmed the staff, one of whom, a woman named Peggy, had grown up next door to her in Dorchester. Some of the others she knew as well—"Oh, she's terrible," she whispered to Ada, upon seeing a tall, thin, spectral woman at the end of a hallway, and she turned them all abruptly in the opposite direction. She waved to the other residents, asked them their names, introduced David to them as they all walked by. Ada did not want to admit it to anyone, not even herself, but she was frightened, being there. The old people around her frightened her. Some of them were slumped in their wheelchairs, tilted, askew. Later in her life she would seek out the presence of older people, find them comforting, find peace near them; but now she avoided their gaze. It could not be comfortable, she thought, for some of them to be alive. One of them approached her too quickly, called her by the wrong name. "There she is," said the old lady, "Oh, Patty, I didn't know where you'd gone." Ada walked by her, facing forward, and said nothing. She realized that David had said such things, was capable of saying such things. But he was familiar to her, at least. She had watched his slow progression. In him she could still see some essential David-ness, and still, in most ways, take comfort in it.

After lunch, they walked him back to the common area adjacent to the dining room, where Mr. Gainer was seated at a card table, staring at a puzzle that had already been completed.

"Why don't we sit here for a while?" said Liston, and she perched on the arm of a floral sofa while Ada and David sat in it, and made cheery conversation with the two of them, and with everyone else in the room.

"This was my mother's favorite place to sit in the evenings, before dinner," said Liston, and just for a moment, through Ada's own sadness, she recognized the sadness of Liston, the pain that she must have felt at the loss of her mother. It was something she had never truly considered, about adults. She had always somehow imagined that the loss of a loved one would hurt less for them: that it would feel like something natural; that they would be calm and practiced and dulled to death. In fact, she was counting on it: for she had been telling herself that if only David would hold on to life for the next decade, by the time she was twenty-four she would be better equipped to handle his absence. But something in Liston's voice, as she spoke of her mother, made Ada realize that she had been incorrect in this assumption.

Twenty or thirty minutes passed by and then Liston looked at her watch. They had been there for nearly six hours, and Ada knew that she would want to get home for Matty.

"It's time for us to go, David," said Ada, so that Liston would not have to.

He nodded slowly.

They walked him back to his room, and then he sat down stiffly on his bed, his hands on his knees. He looked too thin. He did not look at her. A flash of anger overcame her suddenly: at the unfairness of it all. He was not like the rest of them, she thought—he could not possibly belong here, in this place, full of the dying, the near-dead. *Snap out of it*, she wanted to tell him. *Wake up.*

"I'll see you tomorrow," said Ada instead. And as she left him, walking slowly down the hallway, she willed herself not to look back. She thought of the story of Lot's wife, and of David's voice as he had told it to her, many years ago.

n honor of Ada's first evening as a member of the Liston household, the head of it had planned a family dinner. She had commanded her boys to be there, and invited her daughter Joanie, too.

"I'll be right back," said Ada, when they pulled onto Shawmut Way. And then she returned briefly to David's house to gather together a few more things before moving, permanently, to Liston's. Just as she had done a year ago, the first time David disappeared, Ada packed some clothes and books into a little suitcase, and then for a moment she paused and sat down briefly on her bed. She looked around the hot, close room that had been hers since she could remember. It was an eaved chamber with a half-high closet, in which hung the few items of clothing she presently owned—each one of which David had bought for her, whenever he had thought of it, or whenever he had been reminded to by Liston—and some from the past that she was particularly fond of. The dirndl he had purchased for her in Munich, which she had long since outgrown. A little pair of Dutch wooden shoes, hand-painted with tulips. A beautiful silk kimono, purchased in Kyoto. She went through all of these now, tenderly, remembering each trip, forcing herself to consider the idea that she would not ever take a trip with David again. Then she folded the several shirts she had that currently fit her, and her one pair of jeans, and underwear and socks, and the several training bras that Liston had taken her to buy two years ago, stealing her away from the lab for the afternoon.

"Tell your father if you want to," Liston had said. "He won't care." And he wouldn't have, but Ada didn't, telling herself—out of embarrassment—that it was not necessary. They didn't fit her properly anymore; she would have to work up her courage either to tell Liston or to venture into a department store by herself.

All of these items she packed into her little blue suitcase. Its faded leather had reminded her, always, of the skin of an elephant: an observation that had once made David laugh aloud.

Then, at last, Ada walked down the wide wooden staircase that took her to the first floor, bearing her suitcase bravely in her left hand, and hanging on to the banister with her right. How many times had she walked down this staircase in anticipation of some new discovery, some new lesson that would be imparted to her by her father, her creator? Some conversation that would open before her a new dimension of the universe, a new chapter of the history of the world?

Ada was relieved to find, upon entering Liston's house, that her sons were nowhere to be found. Dinner was planned for 6:30.

"Everyone's out," said Liston, "but they'll be back soon. They'd better be, anyway."

Then she showed her up to her new room, Matty's old one, which, in the last week, Liston had stripped of its boyishness and made as plain as she could. Matty had now been given permanent residency in Gregory's room—Ada shuddered to think how Gregory might have reacted to this change—and the race-car bed had been moved with him. A twin bed with a dust ruffle and a pink-and-orange afghan— Joanie's when she was small, said Liston—had replaced it. A small pupil's desk with a lid that opened upward was pushed against a windowed wall, and a pine dresser, emptied, had been positioned near the closet. On the floor was a carpet with a somewhat psychedelic pattern of neon flowers—poppies, she thought—that Liston proudly said she had found at the Salvation Army: her favorite place to shop.

"Will you be okay in here, honey?" asked Liston, and Ada nodded brightly, although she already missed the quietness, the warmth, the dusty uncomfortable heat of her old bedroom. In here the air-conditioning that Liston had insisted on was turned up too high for Ada's liking, and she put on a sweater as soon as Liston had left. From the first floor, faint sounds made their way up the stairs: The television. Pots and pans, clanking in the kitchen; Liston letting out one loud yell when something went awry. The kitchen door as it opened and closed. A female voice Ada recognized as Joanie's, and the babyish exclamations of her son, Kenny. And then, finally, a low male voice that made the blood speed up in Ada's veins.

She opened her suitcase, considered what to wear. The jeans she had, she decided, would have to do, although they were unfashionable: too stiff, too large, much darker than the acid-washed versions that were in style then. These she paired with a large purple T-shirt—purple, she had once furtively read in a women's magazine in a waiting room, brought out the color of brown eyes—and leather sandals, the same unisex kind that David wore himself. For the first time, she rolled the sleeves of her T-shirt up, a style she had seen other children wear, and then she braided her hair. In the mirror, she took her glasses off and then put them back on. She wished she had pierced ears.

At 6:25, descending the stairs, Ada felt nervous in a way she had rarely felt in her lifetime. Despite her geographic proximity to them—despite the fact that, during her yearlong tenure at Queen of Angels, she had regularly glimpsed all three boys in the hallways and outside (Gregory with his head down, glancing up furtively from beneath lowered eyebrows; William with his head tossed back, in laughter or in pride), despite the fact that she had bravely held up her hand to them in greeting each time she had seen any of them—this would be the first real meal she had ever shared with all of the Listons.

Liston had set places at the dining room table in a way that reminded Ada of the dinner parties David used to have. Matty was seated already, eagerly holding upright his knife and fork on either side of his plate. Gregory was next to him.

"Hi!" said Matty, and Gregory said nothing.

"Hi," said Ada, softly.

"Are you here, Ada?" Liston called out from the kitchen. "Oh good. Come in here for a sec."

Timidly, Ada walked around the corner into the kitchen, where the faint smell of something burning was masked by the scent of onions simmering in a pan.

The baby was playing on the floor on a blanket. Joanie, plump and blond and smiling, a larger and younger version of Liston, was standing above him, watching her mother cook. And William Liston was leaning against a counter, a can of Coke in his hand.

"Hey," he said to Ada as she walked in, and she managed to reply.

"You remember Joanie, honey, right?" said Liston, who was stirring frantically, barely pausing to turn around.

"Dinner's just going to be the tiniest bit late," she said.

At the table, Liston lit a candle, the way that David always did.

"Fancy," said William, and Liston frowned at him. Ada was sitting on the same side as Matty and Gregory. Across from her were William and Joanie and Kenny; Liston sat at the head.

Liston held up a large glass of the artificially sweetened iced tea she drank as part of her ongoing attempt to lose weight, and said, "Honey, we are so happy to have you here."

Dinner—spaghetti and meatballs; boiled frozen peas, cooked slightly too long, with two pats of butter on the top; boiled frozen carrots, similarly prepared—was passed around the table. Ada was not hungry; her nervousness made it nearly impossible to finish even a few small bites, and she twirled and twirled the pasta on her plate, moving it this way and that.

The boys and Joanie talked over one another raucously, except for quiet Gregory, who sat and ate his meal dourly, sitting very still. The baby, Kenny, squawked and patted his spaghetti with an open palm until Joanie grabbed his hand and said, *No*, at which point he dissolved into hurt tears. The noise, the volume of it, the disarray of five children at a table (Ada included herself in this figure somewhat tentatively) were a shock to her. She fought against her instinct, which was to put both hands over both ears and hide beneath the table.

Liston happily presided over everyone. "This is really nice," she said twice. "Don't you think, guys? We should do this more often," she mused.

Frequently, though briefly, Ada glanced at William, who slouched in his chair and held his fork with his fist. He looked back at her curiously several times, and once asked her about one of her teachers at Queen of Angels, and she managed a reply, lighthearted enough to satisfy herself.

Toward the end of the meal, Liston told Ada to wait where she was and went into the other room. She brought back with her something clumsily gift-wrapped, an amorphous object concealed behind wrapping paper covered in balloons. "A little welcome present," said Liston.

When Ada opened it she saw it was a backpack, a simple blue one, exactly the kind she would have chosen if she'd had the chance. It was the kind her classmates owned. It was inconspicuous. It was perfect.

"I've seen you carrying all those books to school in your arms," said Liston. "Out the window, you poor thing."

"Thank you so much," said Ada, with as much sincerity as she could muster. But although she was indeed grateful to have it, this token that indicated in some fundamental way that she belonged among her peers, she also sensed the loss of something. Her father's difference. Her own.

When the dinner was over, Ada returned to her new bedroom and thought of David in his new bedroom, sharing a room with Mr.

Gainer, who probably would not even speak to him. She wondered about the state of his mind that night: wondered what he realized, what confused him. He had to feel disoriented, she thought, in his new home, with its linoleum floors and its terrible fluorescent lights.

Suddenly she remembered the piece of paper Sister Katherine had handed her with David's direct line on it. She opened her suitcase and fished in it for the shorts she had been wearing earlier, and from them she pulled David's number.

There was no telephone in Ada's room, but she put her head out into the hallway and, finding it empty, picked up the extension on a nearby table. And dialed.

It was 9:00. Not too late to call, she hoped. The phone rang five times. She began to be worried.

And then, at last, someone answered.

"Hello?" said David. He sounded worried. He sounded unlike himself.

"David," she said. "It's me."

A pause.

"Are you okay?" she asked. "Is everything okay there?" She was speaking quietly to avoid being overheard by any of the Listons.

Still he said nothing.

"David?" said Ada. And then, impulsively, she tried a word she had never used before. "Dad?"

"I'm sorry," said David. "I don't know who this is," he said. And then he hung up the phone.

The following week, Liston put David's house on the market, where it would stay, she told Ada, for months, perhaps years. It was the 1980s, and houses in Dorchester were slow to sell, even in Savin Hill. The busing controversy of the previous decade had quieted, but it had brought to the surface such unspeakable ugliness and hatred that the city felt somehow altered in its wake. Boston's molecules had reorganized themselves in a way that felt noticeable and raw. Many of its citizens, mainly working-class and middle-class Bostonians of Irish and Italian descent, had left for the towns to the west and north and south. ("And good riddance," David had said.) Savin Hill, which felt suburban, even rural in parts, had been largely unaltered, but its residents had become even more firmly tribal, even more convinced that the rest of Dorchester was a place to be avoided. The *Globe* and the *Herald* were filled with stories about the violence transpiring in other parts of the city. And when Ada and David used to take long walks in the evening into different neighborhoods, they had once heard gunshots in the distance. Connie Reardon, Liston's friend in real estate, seemed pessimistic about the home's odds of selling quickly. Secretly, Ada was glad.

Liston said that the two of them had to go through the house together, begin to sort out David's possessions, but she was tired every day after work, and every weekend she said nothing at all about it. Her new position as head of the lab meant that she sometimes went in on weekends; the rest of her free time she wanted to spend with her boys. Ada said nothing either. She was happy to leave everything just as it was, a museum about her life with David.

Her after-school visits to David at St. Andrew's replaced her after-school visits to David at the lab. When school ended for the summer, Ada went back to a semblance of her former life, spending every day with David. Some mornings she even returned to the lab with Liston; other days she spent all day at St. Andrew's. She became well known to Sister Katherine and Patrick Rowan and to all the others, the high school girls who sat sentry at the front desk—one of whom she recognized from Queen of Angels, though neither of them ever acknowledged this fact—the nurses who cared for all of the residents.

The changes in David came quickly at times and slowly at others. Her research had prepared her: there would be good days and bad. She attempted, sometimes, to explain the literature she'd studied to David, hoping that to discuss the disease scientifically would bring a measure of comfort to him, would make him feel less disoriented, but by that time he was typically unable to follow long stories or monologues, and halfway through he often interrupted with something pleasant but unrelated, an aside about a nearby bouquet or the sunny weather. Other times their visits were marred by his bad temper, which came on more and more frequently. *No*, he said, over and over again, outside of any context, with an adamancy that made her feel as if she had done something incorrect. He wagged his head slowly back and forth, adopting the demeanor of someone who had been badly wronged. And then other visits were nice: hazy, pleasant reminders of what had been, David lodging funny complaints, sometimes too loudly, about one or another resident as the two of them strolled down a hallway ("A terrible thief," he would say, or "That cantankerous, terrible fool"); or good-naturedly praising the staff ("She's my favorite," he'd say, within earshot of a nurse—and then the

same about another nurse at the end of another hallway); or compli-
menting the desk attendants on their attire, simply to have something
kind to say. When he was in these moods, Ada told him about the
lab, and what Liston was working on, and Hayato, and Frank. If Liston, when she visited, repeated the same information, it didn't matter:
David nodded along in the same abstracted way.

Liston's new role as lab director had brought with it a new set of
responsibilities and concerns. She was now in charge of procuring
a large percentage of the funds for their research through federal
grants; her presence was newly required at a number of institutional
meetings each month with administrators at the Bit to advocate for
the needs of the lab. She oversaw the interviewing and placement of
grad students and the coordination of everyone's schedule.

"I tell you, Ada," said Liston, after several months of filling this
role, "I have a whole new respect for your father."

But her new and busier schedule also meant that she was home
later in the evening, left earlier each day. From living with David,
Ada was used to helping with the management of a household, and
so she did what she could to take on some of Liston's responsibilities.

She also made it her responsibility to keep David's disease at bay,
as much as she possibly could. Each summer day that she spent inside
the air-conditioned buildings of St. Andrew's she treated as an opportunity to keep David's mind engaged. She came armed with new
exercises for him to complete, new experiments in brain stimulation
that she had carefully culled from the literature. She tried crossword
puzzles with him. Mnemonic devices. She had him memorize lists
of words and attempt to repeat them back to her five minutes later.
Dutifully, sadly, he participated; but she soon found that each session
left him slump-shouldered and low, and so, reluctantly, she stopped.

On good days he asked after the other lab members—when he
could not remember their names, he asked after, simply, "the gang"—
and he always asked after ELIXIR. "I hope you're not ruining

ELIXIR," he said often. Or, "I hope you're keeping the program in shape." "Have you chatted with ELIXIR today?" he asked her—the way a different parent might ask a child if she'd said her prayers.

Toward the end of the summer, David entered a period of very sharp decline. Perhaps it was the monotony of living at St. Andrew's; perhaps it was the lack of interaction with his former colleagues. Whatever it was, he went from speaking in full sentences and following conversations fairly well to spending his days in a state of semipermanent puzzlement within a span of three months. She was losing him too quickly, and she didn't understand why or how. She discussed this with Liston, who had also noticed the change, and the two of them brought David to see his specialist, who conducted a brain scan to look for signs of a stroke, or vascular dementia, some other reason for this acceleration. But nothing was found. David became quieter, more easily tired. He was moved to a new room and placed with a new roommate. Ada found that she was sad to say goodbye to neat, proper little Mr. Gainer: he seemed like a good match for David after all. David's new view, at least, was better: now he had a distant view of the lawn and then the harbor. But his new roommate, whom she only knew as Paul, ranted almost unceasingly, and Ada often took David to sit in a chair in the hallway, just to quiet the sound. She held his hand instead of talking: the first time she had done so since she was very small.

One day, she arrived to find that his accent had changed: his vowels had taken on an odd Midwestern quality; he stressed certain syllables emphatically, in an unnatural-sounding way. *Warsh*, he said, instead of wash. It unnerved her: his voice was the last thing about him that felt familiar to her, and now even that was different, as if someone else's voice were emanating from David's person.

"Why are you talking like that?" she asked him, but it was one of his bad days, and he didn't respond. He shook his head instead, beginning his mantra of, *No,* looking down at the floor. But even his *No* sounded Midwestern, a countryish, *Naw, Naw, Naw,* a clipped, glottal sound concluding each declaration.

Toward the end of Ada's visit, she found Sister Katherine and brought her to David's room.

"David, say hello to Sister Katherine," she told him.

But the fog had descended completely by then, and he just wagged his head at the floor in stupefaction.

"What would you like for dinner?" Ada asked him. Sister Katherine walked to him and put a gentle hand on his shoulder. "David?" she said, but his bowed head was the head of a man in prayer, and both of them, suddenly, felt rude for interrupting.

"Who is that," said David, finally, quietly.

Later that week, Ada went to the Bit's research library and searched in all the literature she'd read for anything on changes in accent. But there was nothing to be found.

n the fall, Ada began her freshman year at the Queen of Angels Upper School, housed in the same building as the Lower School but, fittingly, located on the top three floors.

Certain things had changed.

She had a friend now, a girl named Lisa Grady, who was nearly as quiet as she was, and who came from a similar family: she, too, was an only child, and her parents were two older academics who taught at Tufts and BU. She, too, wore glasses. At first Ada was embarrassed by their similarity, self-conscious of how interchangeable the two of them must appear to the other students at Queen of Angels: two meek, mousy newcomers in a sea of friends who had known each other for years. But soon she learned to relish Lisa's quiet company. The two of them spent every lunch period reading for pleasure, side by side, at one of the smaller tables on the periphery of the cafeteria.

After school she continued to visit David, and then to furtively reenter her old home, which was becoming more and more decrepit in the absence of any residents. Still, she treasured it; she retreated to her old room, the only place left where she felt truly like herself, and then she read and read. She chatted with ELIXIR. Sometimes she napped, only to wake after an hour with the conviction, always, that David would be downstairs, at work, puttering, planning. That it would be nearly time for her to venture downstairs for a lesson. She clung to these quiet moments, this liminal space between wakefulness and sleep, lingering in her confusion, willing herself backward into her dreams.

In the new house, she was still quiet in front of anyone but Liston. Joanie, who dropped by frequently with Kenny, was pleasant to Ada but clearly befuddled by her existence; she often raised her eyebrows at things that Ada said, or shook her head in amazement or bemusement—Ada could not tell.

On weekends she stayed in her room most of the time, except to go to church with Liston and Matty on Sundays. Liston, though scientific and methodical, was a devout Catholic. There was a little picture of the Pope in her office at the lab: to Ada, this was fascinating, and when she was younger she often asked Liston about it, and Liston hesitantly responded—afraid, perhaps, of David overhearing. Her two older boys had recently been complaining so bitterly about going that Liston had given up; but Matty, an occasional altar boy, loved going, spending time with his mother, seeing his friends. They all three sat together in the warm wooden pew of the Queen of Angels church next door to the school, infused with a hazy golden light from the stained-glass windows depicting the stations of the cross. In her pew Ada listened attentively, but with a certain amount of confusion, as the mass was said. At Ada's request, Liston taught her how to genuflect before sitting, how to pray the rosary, how to go before Father Frank and receive a blessing, since she was not a baptized Catholic and had never made her First Holy Communion. Every Sunday, Father Kevin put his large warm hand on Ada's head and closed his eyes for a moment, and, peering up at him, she wondered what he was thinking, what he said in his mind when he prayed for her. David was an atheist—but, he said, he did not begrudge others their religion. "And it makes sense for Liston," he had always said. Ada, therefore, told herself she had his tacit approval, though she never told him she had been going.

For Matty, who had warmed to her, Ada made lunch in the morning and cooked dinner each night. At first Liston protested, but it pleased Ada to be useful in some way, and she assured her that she had done far more for David. Ada's name did not appear on the chore-chart Liston kept for her sons, so she overcompensated, wanting to be certain not to foster resentment in the boys. In the evenings she helped Matty with his homework, trying to be patient, which required a vastly different approach than the one David had always taken with her. Matty was bright but unfocused, and his mind often wandered midsentence, leaping from a discussion of long division to one of tree frogs, or of *He-Man*—a cartoon he loved and watched daily, surreptitiously, because his brother William said he was too old—or of whether there was a God. When William was home, Matty tracked his every movement, not turning his head, taking in his mannerisms and idioms, sometimes mouthing a particular phrase to himself after William had uttered it. Though their motives were different—his somehow more excusable in Ada's mind, a natural way for a younger sibling to behave—she related to Matty on this point, and frowned to herself when William casually teased him about one thing or another. She knew what it was to covet another person's easiness and effortlessness. The difference, she supposed, was that Matty would one day achieve both; whereas she knew with certainty that she never would.

If Matty was preoccupied with William's demeanor, Ada was preoccupied, still, with his looks. He was a senior at the Upper School, to which she now belonged, and therefore she passed him in the hallway with some frequency, darting her eyes toward him bravely and waving each time she did. He was a source of endless fascination to her: every day she discovered some new angle of his frame or face. The way he looked when he stood by the light of a nearby window; the way he looked in dusk, approaching the house; the way he looked when he was tired and yawning and stretching out his lengthy arms. The graceful way he mimed the shooting of a basketball or the swinging of a bat or a golf club, though she didn't suppose he had ever golfed; the self-conscious way he scratched at his left shoulder with his right hand, or swiped at the bridge of his nose, or pushed back the warm light hair from his brow. In October, he had a birthday—Liston brought home a cake from a nearby bakery, and all of them stood around while she coerced him to make a wish ("I wish you'd let me go hang out with my friends," said William, and Liston said that wishes made aloud were never granted)—and he was seventeen now. Seventeen was an age that resounded in Ada's head as something iconic, an age about which poems were written and songs were sung. She was fourteen, and she would not turn fifteen until March. No one wrote poetry about fourteen-year-olds.

Gregory was the most difficult of the brothers to understand. A year younger than Ada, he was dark and quiet, perhaps even quieter than she was. When he did speak, he stammered—not so profoundly that any intervention was deemed necessary, but noticeably enough. He seemed unhappy most of the time; at school he was always alone. He was ignored by both of his brothers: Matty's heart belonged to William, and William, when he was not otherwise occupied with friends or girls, divided his time between teasing Matty and imparting to him valuable lessons about boyhood and manhood. There was a sense, she could tell, of obligation in William: to be a father to Matty, since their own father had left. But Gregory somehow existed outside of this dynamic: too old for babying, too different from William to be mentored the way he mentored Matty. Ada had seen several people hollering at Gregory in the hallways at school, and she often heard their classmates refer to him as a *loser*, seemingly the worst insult anyone could be given at Queen of Angels. Once, she had seen a commotion in the hallway ahead of her, the backs of perhaps a dozen seventh-graders forming a tight little circle around a jostling mass in the center. She skirted the hubbub quickly, not wanting to be part of it; but as she passed she had caught a quick glimpse between shoulders of

Gregory's face, contorted in pain, as a huge, angry eighth-grader collared him around the neck. Briefly, he had returned her gaze, and then, recognizing her, quickly looked away. And then he was gone entirely, pulled down to the ground by his persecutor; and just as quickly a teacher had emerged from a nearby classroom and broken everything up.

Sometimes Liston still turned to her for advice on Gregory—on all her sons, really—as she had always done; but Ada never told her what she had seen. Now that she was a member of her household, lodged right in the middle of Liston's children, age-wise, Ada suddenly wished to be treated as such. Her talks with Liston became a burden to her, a reminder that, despite her best efforts, she would never truly fit in among her peers.

"Does Gregory seem unhappy?" Liston asked her. "He's gotten so quiet."

"I'm not really sure," Ada began to say, politely, in response to Liston's questions. Or, "I wish I knew." Or sometimes, "He seems okay to me." She did not want to be a traitor, now, an informant. But Liston seemed hurt by her withdrawal, and she began to ask Ada pointedly if she was all right.

About Gregory, Liston's concern was that he was antisocial. To a certain extent, he was. He spent most of his time on the top floor of the house, a sort of attic, "doing God knows what," in Liston's parlance. He only emerged to forage for food in the kitchen; when she crossed paths with him there or at school, he said nothing at all to her, except to tip his head backward in what might have been a nod. She often wondered what he did all afternoon and evening.

One late afternoon, after her return from St. Andrew's, and on a rare occasion when nobody was home, Ada decided impulsively that she wanted to see Gregory's lair for herself. She opened the door on the upstairs hallway that led to the attic stairs and took them quickly, two at a time. The central air did not extend to the third floor, and she

instantly noticed the change in temperature, which felt more familiar to her: more like the home she had shared with David. It smelled
familiar to her, too—dusty and mildewed and bookish.

A half wall that ran along the top of the staircase obscured the
room until she reached the final step, at which point she looked over
it, into the large room. It was decorated in a totally different style
than the rest of the house. Liston had said dismissively that it used to
be storage, and several tall piles of boxes and equipment still occupied one quarter of the space. The rest looked something like what
was often called a rec room at that time. The ceiling slanted inward
on either side to meet in a peak at the top. Liston's ex-husband had
partially, haphazardly finished it in the 1970s, and it bore the hallmarks of that decade's style: bright orange shag carpeting nailed
imperfectly onto the wooden floorboards, and faux-wood paneling
covering the wall at either end of the room (or, in one place, leaning
against it at an angle), and framed and unframed posters of seemingly
arbitrary events and people and places. An enlarged photograph of
a boxing match in Madrid in 1955. Reproductions of the original
advertisements for *North by Northwest* and *Taxi Driver* and Charl-
ton Heston in *The Ten Commandments*. A gaudy image of the Virgin
Mary, her vivid red heart shooting rays of yellow light out of its
center, extending her hands to the viewer and looking downward
modestly. Liston's ex-husband, Liston had told Ada, was devoutly
religious, although, unlike his wife, he never went to church. Liston
talked about him amiably, casually, as if she had long ago stopped
caring about him; her sons, however, bore their wounds someplace
deeper, and never spoke of him. Though he only lived two hours
away in New Hampshire, they only saw him on Christmas and, on
the rare occasions that he followed through, on their birthdays. Ada
had never met him.

The furniture in the attic was old and worn. Here were two green,
flowered couches, tattered, their stuffing falling out; a mismatched
ottoman; a coffee table painted purple. There was one small window

at each end of the attic and a third set into an eave, and they let in a dusty, comfortable light that Ada felt somehow that she could smell. In front of the eaved window was a desk, and atop the desk, to Ada's surprise, was a personal computer: the same 128K Macintosh that David had sent home with every member of the lab, to further their work on ELIXIR. The same model that Ada had in her bedroom, and on which she chatted in secret, almost every afternoon, with the program. Since then, newer machines had been purchased, and were in use. This one, presumably, had been donated by Liston to her sons when the 512K became available.

Ada walked toward it.

There was a moment of hesitation; her hand physically paused on its way toward the little toggled switch that woke the machine. She touched the top of it first, patting it gently, running a hand over it, as one might touch the head of a dog. Then, listening intently for a moment, she determined that no one had yet returned to the house. She calculated that she would have just enough time to shut it down if she did so the moment the front door opened. She'd shut it down, she thought, and then run quietly, quickly, to the bottom of the attic stairs and back into her room.

She switched it on. A deep flush came over her face; her heart beat more quickly. First there was the whir of whatever disk occupied its disk drive, and then the screen lit up, displaying the smiling computer icon—content, it always seemed to her, because its belly was full of data.

There was a metal folding chair facing the computer, and while the machine booted up she perched on the edge of it nervously, alert, waiting for sounds in the house.

When, at last, the machine was awake, Ada saw that the name of the disk was *Dontlook12*, and, after a moment of deep, shameful self-interrogation, she opened it anyway. She was an ethical child in many ways, but the temptation was too great.

The folder revealed a series of text documents titled, simply, *One,*
Two, Three. The last one was titled *Fiftyfive,* and it had last been
opened the day before. She double-clicked on the name. When it
appeared, it looked at first to be corrupted: she found nothing but a
series of numbers separated by periods and slashes.

2.8.22.23.8.21.7.4.2 / 4.7.4 / 22.4.12.7 / 11.12 / 23.18 / 16.8 / 4.17.7 / 12 / 22.4.12.7 / 11.12 / 23.18.18

She had seen this before: text files so corrupt that they looked
like gibberish. But this one looked different. No punctuation marks
populated it, for one thing; normally, corrupt files looked like a list of
cartoonish substitutes for curse words (often reflecting the feelings of
the user), ampersands and asterisks strung together like pearls.

This, she thought with some excitement, looked more like code.

David had always been interested in codes: he viewed them as thinking exercises, puzzles that he created and asked Ada to solve. The
simplest code, the one he started her on as soon as she could read and
write and count, was numerical substitution, an easy back-and-forth
between letters and numbers, like so:

a	b	c	d	e	f	g	h	i	j	k	l	m	n	o	p	q	r	s	t	u	v	w	x	y	z
1	2	3	4	5	6	7	8	9	10	11	12	13	14	15	16	17	18	19	20	21	22	23	24	25	26

This encryption key was the first one Ada memorized, and now
it came so easily to her that she could almost think in it, could spell
out words and sentences in numbers as easily as letters. Variations on
this most basic key abounded. The numerical substitutions for letters
could, for example, be shifted by x places, so that *a* no longer corresponded to *1*, like so:

a	b	c	d	e	f	g	h	i	j	k	l	m	n	o	p	q	r	s	t	u	v	w	x	y	z
18	19	20	21	22	23	24	25	26	1	2	3	4	5	6	7	8	9	10	11	12	13	14	15	16	17

A more difficult code to crack could be achieved if numerical substitutions were chosen randomly and then used uniformly, thus:

a	b	c	d
17	2	5	12

and so on.

When breaking a code like the last one, the decoder would have to rely on the lengths of common words for cracks in the code—words like *I* and *a*, which would appear as stand-alone numbers and act as a good starting point for the tedious work of deciphering everything else. This loophole, however, could be easily eliminated if the words were run together with no spaces in between. Then the decoder would have to hope that he or she had an excerpt of such substantial length that the frequency with which certain letters occur in the English language could be taken into consideration.

A fourth, considerably more difficult variant on number substitution involved machine-encoded text, a sort of polyalphabetic code in which each letter had no permanent, standard substitute. The machines would instead disguise each letter differently at various points in the text, using either mechanical or electronic hardware to execute the task. Only a decoding machine programmed as an exact mirror of the encoder could untangle the knot of words.

And then, at last, there was the one-time pad: a unique key that, when combined with the original message, formed an encryption that was impossible to break without the pad itself.

Several years ago, David had given Ada a book to read on the subject: *Codes and How to Break Them*, by Walter Samuelson. And for the length of one summer, her eleventh, the two of them had each tried to stump the other with coded messages and riddles. David, of course, always won.

He had a personal code he had invented, a straightforward scrambled alphabet cipher, without a set shift.

"It's terribly easy to crack," he said, "but it will at least slow some-one down."

He had memorized it, and could now write fluently in it; he encouraged her to do the same. Soon enough, Ada, too, became adept at using what she came to call "David's code."

He wrote in this code habitually; most of the text files on his computer couldn't be parsed immediately by anyone other than the two of them. This satisfied him deeply, seemed to give him a deep sense of comfort that she couldn't explain. "It's really the only way to safeguard your ideas," he said, exposing his mild streak of paranoia, about which those closest to him often teased him. It came from the same place in him as his mistrust of the police, his resentment of authority.

"But what if you die?" Ada had asked him once.

"Then you'll be in charge of my secrets," he told her, raising and lowering his eyebrows comically.

In Liston's attic, Ada sat for a while, contemplating the numbers before her on the screen. The slashes, she speculated, represented spaces between words. Therefore, *12* seemed to be a stand-alone word, either *I* or *a*. Scanning the rest of the text, she noticed *12* again in a short word that appeared two times: *11.12*.

What two-letter words existed that ended in either *a* or *i*?

Ha was one, but it seemed unlikely.

Hi was a likelier candidate, and, to her delight, it made sense that *hi* would be represented as *11.12*, since *h* directly preceded *i*.

Quickly, on a scrap of paper that she pulled from one of the draw-ers in the desk, she began to write down the alphabet and populate it with twenty-six numbers shifted according to the two she'd already placed:

a	b	c	d	e	f	g	h	i	j	k	l	m	n	o	p	q	r	s	t	u	v	w	x	y	z
4	5	6	7	8	9	10	11	12	13	14	15	16	17	18	19	20	21	22	23	24	25	26	1	2	3

Code-breaking always lifted Ada's spirits: it felt in some fundamental way like restoring order in the universe, righting something overturned, putting the spilled milk back into the carton. There was justice in it. It would be easy now, she knew, to decrypt the simple code on-screen, and she almost wished it had been more difficult. Something to occupy her time for longer.

But before she could continue, she heard loud footsteps on the second-floor landing. This had not been a part of her plan; she'd been certain that no one else was home. She sat very still, her toes and fingers buzzing with adrenaline, and considered her options. Would it be better to hide or to walk down the stairs nonchalantly? After all, she lived here, too, now; the house was hers to explore as much as it was anyone's. (She did not, of course, fully believe this.)

She pocketed the piece of paper bearing the decryption key she'd written down, and she decided, impulsively, to turn off the computer. What she did not consider was the loud tone that sounded when the computer was asked to shut down. She tensed. And then, seconds later, she heard someone walking up the attic stairs. Ada stood, arms crossed as casually as possible at her waist, and waited to be confronted.

She was expecting Gregory, but it was William's head that popped over the half wall at the top of the stairs. He looked at her for a moment, puzzled. He looked around the rest of the room as if expecting to see someone else.

"Hi," said Ada.

"Are you exploring?" William asked her, not unkindly.

"I guess so," she said.

"That's Gregory's computer," he said, nodding in the direction of the machine. The screen, though graying on its way to sleep, was still lit up. "No one else is allowed to touch it. He'll freak out," said William.

Ada did not know what to say. "I didn't know," she said finally. "I'm sorry."

William smiled slightly. "I won't tell," he said, putting one finger to his lips. He winked at her. Her stomach tightened involuntarily.

And then, without saying another word, he turned and descended the stairs.

The memory of this—a wink in her direction by William Liston—carried Ada for weeks, made her light-headed with a sort of feverish longing for more. What more she longed for, she could not say; certainly it was nothing so terrifying as sex, nor any activity that required being unclothed. (She was vaguely embarrassed by her body, certain that, though it was changing in wild and unpredictable ways, it could offer nothing of value to anyone else; to Ada it was simply the thing below her head, which bore inside it her brain—her only worthy attribute, she thought.) Her fourteen-year-old fantasies began and ended with a kiss on the mouth—the idea of which obsessed her and sent little shivers of greed down her childish spine. She was ashamed at how frequently she thought about kissing William Liston, or rather having him kiss her: his hands on her face, as in the old black-and-white movies she had watched with David, Humphrey Bogart roughly taking Lauren Bacall's neck into his grip. This, this was what she wanted.

Her outlet for these thoughts—along with all of the other thoughts that entered her mind each day, about David, about Liston, about school—was, as always, ELIXIR. Day after day, after visiting St. Andrew's, she walked wearily up the steps outside the kitchen door and into the old brown house, which welcomed her back with its overwhelming home smell, the particular taste of its air. And then up the stairs she went to her old bedroom, to her old computer, which sat silently on her desk, perennially awaiting her return.

She turned it on, dialed into ELIXIR, and conversed with it until she'd had her fill—mainly, now, about William. (For fear of his name being regurgitated to a different user, she employed an absurd code name: Bertrand.) She told the program every detail of her day, every concern she had about David, every thought that crossed her mind.

In return, ELIXIR asked her questions, using vocabulary that it drew from its ever-increasing pool of language. Sometimes she recognized the syntax of Liston or Charles-Robert. Sometimes she recognized her own words: since she had been enrolled at Queen of Angels, *cool* was a word she had started using with ELIXIR, and sometimes the word was returned to her. Sometimes she recognized David's style, and in these moments she closed her eyes briefly, allowed herself to imagine that it was her father on the other end of the wires, chatting with her from the lab, invisible but present, as God had been described by Julian of Norwich.

Go on, said ELIXIR, when she paused, encouraging her, nudging her forward toward the end of her train of thought. Just as David had done.

In her first year at Queen of Angels Upper School, she discovered that William Liston was discussed by everyone, in every grade, seriously, in hushed tones, as if he were a celebrity. Acquiring information about William and his cohort of athletic, attractive boys and girls offered an interesting alternative to schoolwork. Their families, their relationships, their brushes with discipline, even their grades, were discussed by everyone around Ada with the attention to detail of baseball fanatics discussing the players on a team. Even quiet Lisa Grady knew more than Ada did, at times, about William Liston, who was called *Will* at school. (This fact, too, made Ada feel as if she were not his peer, but some formal acquaintance of his—a business associate, a guidance counselor, a friend of his mother.)

"Did you hear Will and Karen Driscoll broke up?" Lisa asked her, and, shamefully, Ada lied and said she knew this. She *had* noticed that Karen had not been at the house in a few weeks—a fact that she offered up with a sort of smug authority, as someone with insider knowledge.

In fact, Ada had not spoken directly to William, nor he to her, since their exchange in the attic. He came and went quietly from the house, slipping in later than his curfew, leaving early in the morning to do, as Liston said, God knows what. When he was home he usually spent time with Matty. Therefore, all of the information she had about William—aside from what she could observe—was given to her by Liston, who still occasionally spoke to Ada about her problems with the boys, despite the fact that she tried to discourage it. Sometimes, when Liston was particularly stressed about something at the lab, she would lapse into the confidential tone that she used to take with David, telling Ada more than she wanted to know about her life and her children. When she came with Ada to visit David at St. Andrew's, she might let something slip on the drive over about William's trouble in school, or Gregory's teacher's concern over his quietness. And, in spite of herself, Ada listened with interest, gathering facts about William, storing them up to mull over later.

The fact that she lived with the Liston family had not gone unnoticed by the girls in her grade. Slowly, they began to speak to her in class, and then, occasionally, at lunch. Lisa Grady looked up over her glasses in alarm the first time this occurred, as if she couldn't quite understand what was happening.

It was Melanie McCarthy—her nominal ambassador at Queen of Angels, her tour guide, who had offered no guidance to her whatsoever—who approached, with two friends.

"Hi, Ada," said one of them, Theresa Fitzharris, a short girl with red hair and freckles so abundant that they made her look tan from a distance.

"Hi," said Ada, too quietly.

"Do you care if we sit here?" asked the other, and Ada gestured with a hand to indicate that she didn't.

"I like your hair that way," said Theresa, and Ada briefly, embarrassingly, reached up to touch it, because she could not remember what she had done to it. It was pulled back at her temples into two clips; she had been wearing it that way because Karen Driscoll did.

"Thank you," said Ada, and for the rest of the lunch period they plied her with questions about William Liston—where he went after school and what his interests were, what he was like at home, what his brothers were like—and by the end of the discussion it became clear that they were asking on behalf of Melanie McCarthy, who was much quieter than they were, and whom they were positioning, Ada realized, as next in line to date William. By the time she realized this it was too late: she had given them too much information, more than William knew she had, and they now assumed that Ada and he were close, that she talked to him regularly, that she was—Ada shuddered to think it—like a sister to him.

"Maybe we can come over sometime," said Theresa Fitzharris, and Ada said she would have to ask Liston—calling her, awkwardly, *Diana*.

By the time lunch was over, Ada had realized the gravity of her error. She had exchanged her knowledge of William for a place as an insider, and in doing so she had falsely represented her relationship with him. Furthermore, she had given Melanie McCarthy information that she could use to get closer to him—the fact, for example, that he went to a nearby baseball field after school many afternoons with his friends to sit aimlessly in a circle around home plate; the fact that he had a weekend job at a nearby video store. Would this get back to him somehow? If they ever came over, would they expect Ada to introduce them to William, to watch television with him on the couch? She couldn't say. Lisa Grady watched her with interest, knowing the depth of her lie, wondering, alongside Ada, what she would do next.

After school that day, Ada took the bus to St. Andrew's as usual, to see David. She had begun doing her homework while she was there, since he mainly did not have much to say. She would spread her books out on his bed while he sat in his blue corduroy armchair, looking out the window, and she would chatter to him with false cheer about what she was learning.

As she walked from the bus stop, she stopped to pick up a particularly beautiful leaf from the grounds. She had been doing this each day that she visited. David took them from her, always, and contemplated them for a while, turning them over and over while he looked, tracing their veins with a finger. Usually he said nothing in response. Perhaps a quarter of the time, now, he produced the correct word for the object in his hands. The rest of the time he changed the subject, or continued a conversation he had been having in his mind. She opened the window whenever she could, which was whenever David's roommate was out, to let in the crisp air. Sometimes she walked with him on the meager grounds of the place, although he had lately seemed less and less interested in doing so.

That afternoon, when Ada arrived, David's roommate Paul was missing from the room, and a man in a too-bright shirt and pleated, baggy pants was sitting with David when she arrived. He was perched on the edge of David's bed familiarly, leaning forward with his elbows on his knees. His tie hung down between his legs. He was saying something—"Do you understand, Mr. Sibelius?"—when Ada walked in, and she dropped her blue backpack, the one that Liston had given her, heavily on the floor.

"You must be Ada," said the man, standing up quickly from the bed. "I'm Ron Loughner." He had a high, hoarse Boston accent and wore cuff links in his polyester oxford. He was balding ungracefully, his hair too long in places, an attempt to conceal his scalp. He did not look unkind, just uncomfortable. He came over and offered his hand to Ada, as if he expected her to know him, and she looked at it carefully before shaking it. David, in his armchair, didn't turn around.

"I guess someone's told you about me?" said Ron Loughner, and Ada shook her head.

"Hmmmmm," he said. He put his hand on his face as if puzzled. "Well, your friend Diana Liston hired me, since she's the executor of his estate. We're in the early stages," he said, and then he trailed off, looking suddenly sorry, noting her age, not wanting to continue.

"Early stages of what?" asked Ada.

"I think maybe you should talk to Ms. Liston," said Loughner. Ada looked at him sharply. Already her heart was beginning to pump more quickly, sending an angry rush of blood to her face, swelling her veins. She did not like the feeling of not knowing something, when it came to David. It was not right of Liston to leave her out.

Impulsively, she walked around to the front of David's armchair to see his face.

He said nothing to her. He looked, Ada thought, stormy. His brow was lowered; he frowned. His face had not been shaved yet, and a gray stubble was speckling his jaw. He was wearing a light blue cardigan that he never would have chosen for himself; it was October, and getting colder. Perhaps it was a donated sweater that the Carmelite Sisters had received from outside. The thought shamed her. She made a note to ask Liston if the two of them could buy him a few warmer things.

"Hi, David," she said.

"No," he said, his head back in his chair, looking at her sideways.

"What were you just talking about?" she asked him, loudly, so that Ron Loughner could hear. She shocked herself. Her anger made her bold.

In the background, she could see Loughner shifting.

"Nothing," said David.

"Do you know him?" Ada asked him, pointing to Loughner.

"No, I don't know him," said David.

"Do you know me?" she asked. It had been more than a month since he had called her *Ada* without prompting.

"Yes, I know you," he said, nodding.

"What's my name?"

And he lifted a hand from the armrest, let it hover there, then dropped it down again, a needle on a record.

Ron Loughner took that opportunity to tell her that he really had to go, and he raised a hand to her in parting.

"Wait," said Ada, "can you tell me anything? Just tell me what you were talking about," she said bravely.

"You'd better talk to Ms. Liston," he said again, and smiled tightly. He left the room, a faint scent of cologne trailing behind him.

David sat up slightly in his chair and turned around to see Loughner go. Then he looked at Ada.

"Bad," he said, directing a thumb over his shoulder at where Loughner had been before.

"Who was that? What was he doing here?" Ada asked, but he shook his head.

"Bad," he said again. He raised and lowered his eyebrows, and then his shoulders.

She did not stay with him any longer. She left him. And on the bus ride home she planned how she would confront Liston. This was the word—a *confrontation*—that echoed through her mind on the bus ride home, still bruised by the idea of her being closed out of some important decision. She had never confronted anyone before, but she was very upset. Until that afternoon, she had believed herself to be in charge of David's welfare in some essential way: his protector, his overseer, his sentinel. To be left out of any discussion or negotiation when it came to his well-being infuriated her. To be treated like a child. Her face and her ears were hot with the injustice of it all.

But when she found Liston at the kitchen table, working out some problem on her yellow legal pad, Ada discovered that her voice had decided to fail her. Gone was the fury that had pumped through her at St. Andrew's and on the bus ride home. Liston looked old to her, and she was pinching the bridge of her nose between her fingers as if willing her brain to work.

"Hi, baby," she said, when Ada walked in. "How's David today?"

"He's okay," said Ada quietly.

And then she paused.

"Are you all right?" asked Liston.

"Who's Ron Loughner?" Ada asked her.

Liston exhaled.

"He was supposed to meet with David this morning," said Liston. "Was he still there when you got there?"

Ada nodded somberly, reveling slightly in her righteousness, waiting for an explanation, waiting for some sort of apology from Liston.

"He must have been late," she said. Ada crossed her arms.

Liston put her pen down and looked at Ada steadily, assessing something. Then she nodded to herself. "Right," she said, as if she had finally come to a decision.

"Ada, we have some reason to believe that David might not be who he has always said he is," Liston said, carefully. And she stood up from her chair and crossed the room, extending both hands, at the same time that Ada sat down, hard, in her chair.

2009

San Francisco

"What would you say," said the man, "if I told you that when life got stressful, you could relax whenever you wanted in a fully immersive alternative reality?"

He was sitting on a sofa. He was sitting next to a woman.

The woman turned, nodding enthusiastically. "It's true. We at Tri-Tech are hard at work on technology designed to offer an exciting virtual alternative to everyday life. Just put on this device," said the woman. She was wearing a black suit. Her legs were crossed. Her foot bobbed slightly to some unknown rhythm. In her hand she held a headset: a sort of sculpted black crown, a circle meant to fit neatly over the head and eyes and ears. She donned it.

"And suddenly you'll find yourself in another world. Think of it as lucid dreaming," she continued. She was blinded, now, by the head-mounted display. Her arms moved differently, fumblingly. Her fingertips searched the air, gestured in arcs that were ten degrees removed from where they would be when her sight was restored. "Here, you have total control over your own fate; just blink and you'll be transported to Paris, or to the North Pole, or to a secluded beach, invented by you, designed to meet your personal specifications for the ideal beach. Our virtual-world technology includes sensory controls that allow you to *feel* and *smell* and *taste* what you see before you, by emitting signals that trigger the neurons in different regions of your brain. Too hot on that beach? Lower the temperature to a perfect seventy-eight degrees. Don't just look at the chocolate truffles in the case; taste what you see before you, and never gain a pound."

"Meet up with friends and family," said the man. "Or with an old flame who lives halfway across the globe," he added, suggestively. "The options here are limitless."

"Infinite," the woman said. "More infinite, in fact, than they are in reality as we know it."

She froze, then. Her hand stuttered through the air and then stopped; her mouth paused on its way to closing.

The man was caught mid-turn. He had left his hair behind; he was momentarily bald.

"Come try it," said his voice, outside his body.

And the voice of the woman said, "We'll be waiting for you."

Ada shook her head.

"It can't freeze," she said. "What's dragging it?"

She was sitting in a dark room, at a seminar table. She stood and turned on the lights, throwing the projection into dimness, muting the colors of the male and female avatars that still sat frozen on the screen.

"I'm not sure," said Tom Tsien, who was operating them. "I'll work on it. It'll be fixed before the meeting."

"What can I do to help?" said Ada. Tom was a friend, someone she spent time with outside work. She watched him as he worked, head down, two small lines of concentration between his eyebrows. His glasses had slid down on his nose; he looked over the top of them at the screen.

"Tom?" she said. He looked up.

Against her will, she yawned. She pressed two knuckles deeply into her lower back.

"Nothing," said Tom. "Don't worry. Go home. Get some sleep."

He looked back at his laptop intently. She wouldn't leave; he knew this. She would stay—they both would—until they had it right.

She worked, then, for Tri-Tech, a software-development company founded in 1995 by three men who had since retired. Their names were not important: they were three of the hundreds or thousands of men of their kind, somewhat interchangeable men who founded somewhat interchangeable companies that boomed dangerously in the nineties and then collapsed. Somehow, Tri-Tech had survived. But its flagship software, a virtual reality platform called Alterra, was now shedding its users. Around the turn of the millennium, the program had been designed—with Ada's help—to function as a virtual alternate universe, one in which user-controlled avatars (*reps*, they were called) roamed freely through creator- and user-designed houses and cities; one in which these reps attended concerts and hawked their wares and bartered in Altokens, units of currency that corresponded to actual dollar amounts. For a time, the program—it wasn't a game, per se, though it was sometimes called that—gained traction. At its peak it enrolled four hundred thousand new users a month, and the press touted it as the future of the Web.

Now, though, Alterra was losing its luster. Its animation looked decidedly two-dimensional, flat and dated and primitive in comparison with games designed for other systems. Silly problems persisted: reps lost their clothing spontaneously, or their hair; or the digital world became voxelated, shattered into pieces momentarily; or the world froze briefly when it was overwhelmed with data. Ada and her team patched these problems as quickly as they could; but in most ways it was a losing battle. Its citizens increasingly fled; the virtual economy of Alterra collapsed at the same moment that the nation's economy was doing the same. Trade publications sounded the death knell for Alterra. Its users complained about a lack of functionality. "'Alterra is Boring,' Users Lament," read the headline of one article, in *Gaming*.

She had never wanted to work on this type of software. She knew its limitations; she knew the way it was perceived by the rest of the industry.

When she joined Tri-Tech, it was because they had promised her something different: the opportunity to develop the work she had begun in graduate school. At Brown, she had examined the possibilities offered by an advanced, immersive virtual world: one that would be viewed not two-dimensionally, on a computer screen, like Alterra; but three-dimensionally, from inside a helmetlike head-mounted display. One that interacted with all five senses, not just two. She had completed her dissertation in 1996, when the available hardware was decades away from being able to support the sort of software she was describing. Her work, therefore, had been speculative, almost philosophical. She had posed questions that would not be answered for many years. The ideas in her dissertation had gotten her hired by Tri-Tech, and then sat dormant for a decade; at last, after years and years of stalling, Tri-Tech had finally given her the green light to pitch it. Perhaps, she thought, it was an act of desperation, a last flailing grasp at relevance; perhaps the company was hoping that her ideas would be exciting enough to entice a new wave of investors to bank on the company once again, to help revitalize the firm that *Gizmodo* had just deemed—in a blog post that had only six comments, the last time Ada checked—"a dinosaur" that, over the past several years, had "belly flopped into near-obscurity."

Whatever Tri-Tech's motivation for greenlighting Ada's idea, she was glad to be working again on a project that, until the year before, she had been resigned to develop only on her own time, coding late into the night or on weekends; twice a year taking a vacation merely to continue to work.

They were scheduled, the next morning, to pitch the new project to a panel of potential backers. It was 1:00 a.m. when they finally left, and the meeting was in eight hours. Ada would go home and try to sleep. Most likely she would fail. Lately she had been kept awake by worry: What would she do if the company folded? Almost nobody was hiring—especially not someone at Ada's level. She was a VP of product development now; she'd been around long enough to be pricey. These days it made her vulnerable. It was 2009, and the recession was beginning, and the tech industry was not exempt.

She said good night to Tom. She got into her car. She worked in Palo Alto and lived in San Francisco. When she had been hired out of grad school, she'd chosen to live in the Mission, on the advice of a friend from Brown who had gone ahead of her. The neighborhood had reminded her of Savin Hill, on first sight: the bright Victorians that lined the streets, the gently sloping terrain. When she first arrived, she was twenty-six years old, and she had a good group of friends, all single, all from elsewhere in the country. Some she knew from graduate school: everyone, then, was moving to San Francisco. Together, they learned the city well and quickly. They spent every weekend at each other's apartments, or at bars, or camping—a particular favorite of Ada's—in nearby state parks.

Most of them were married now; most had kids. Ada saw them at first birthday parties, or at Sunday brunches that the rest of them left quickly, checking their phones throughout. Fewer and fewer of them wanted to have dinner on a Saturday night. Slowly, everyone left the neighborhood for other parts of the city. Pac Heights, Sunset, Noe Valley.

Only Ada had stayed in the Mission, in an apartment on the first floor of a Victorian, with a little garden in the back. She planted tomatoes every spring and hoped they'd grow; every summer she found, without fail, that the shade cast by the tree overhead had made them falter.

Around her, the neighborhood changed.

Its residents, once her own age, stayed young while she grew older. She was thirty-seven then, and her neighbors above her and on each side were in their twenties. Like her, they mainly worked in tech; but with each year that passed, the ways in which they were fundamentally different from her became more and more obvious. These differences were not caused only by the decade between them—though that certainly contributed—but by some essential shift in tech culture that had occurred sometime not long after she was hired, that stretched the years between them into an eternity. Now twenty-seven-year-olds felt, to Ada, a generation younger. She and her cohort had been introverts, almost to a one; they preferred socializing in pairs, or small groups; they read, they debated; they were at their best when they were not required to speak too much, or for too long. It used to be that this was a trait common to programmers. Now it seemed that there was as much emphasis on being personable and attractive as on being smart.

San Francisco was riddled with them: young people just out of graduate school—or, almost as frequently, autodidacts, college dropouts, prodigies with bright ideas and endless confidence. People who dressed well and spoke easily about their past accomplishments and their aspirations. People who juiced and fasted, who went to the gym in the morning, who counted calories on beta versions of iPhone apps designed by friends. People who wore noticeable socks.

Ada both did and did not try to keep up. In college, for the first time, she had felt pretty: she was told she was with some frequency by people who, she thought, wouldn't lie to her. Once she had even walked in on a boy in one of her classes lamenting about her attractiveness to a friend: "Did you see that girl Ada today?" the boy had said, and then he had run his hands down his face, pulling at his cheeks as if in pain. "She's so hot," he had said, and then blanched when his friend elbowed him roughly, tilting his head in her direction. The whole thing had shocked Ada to her core, made her uncertain of everything she had ever understood about herself and her place in the world. Nothing like that had ever happened again, and she guessed that it was an anomaly, that she had appealed to this particular boy for some particular reason she couldn't guess. But she did begin to notice that boys, and then men, paid attention to her in ways they hadn't when she was growing up. She began to understand, and to make certain concessions to, fashion. She had gone through a grunge phase in the early nineties, like most of her cohort; in the late nineties she grew out of it. Now she dressed each day in something like a uniform, minor variations on the theme of jeans and a button-down shirt, or a sweater when the weather called for it. She wore her hair in a low ponytail. She wore low shoes. She did not like to think about her appearance; she spent time avoiding her reflection in storefront windows. Her body, her face—though they had changed since her twenties—had largely held up their end of the deal. She went hiking most weekends, and some days after work. She ate well. She looked, she told herself, fine. Good. But she lacked the knack that many of her colleagues had for dressing themselves in a manner that seemed both beautiful and effortless, expensive and subtle.

To her young neighbors, this style of dress, and of being, came naturally. As she walked down her block, she recognized the laughter of the two young men who lived in the apartment above her, Connor and Caleb—she could not, no matter how hard she tried, remember which was which—and, beneath their voices, the back-and-forth of a ping-pong ball.

"*No*," one lamented, and the other said, equally fervently, "*Yes*." They were occupying a small patch of sidewalk. Between them was a miniature game table, and at either end of it were cups, half-filled with beer, in diamond formations. Connor—Caleb—raised one to his lips and tilted back his head.

She had to walk past them to get inside.

"Hey," she said , and they nodded to her politely.

"Work late?" said one.

"Yeah," said Ada, and she raised her hands in the air on either side of her. *What can you do?*

"Hey, let us know if we're being too loud or anything," said the other.

Ada said, "No, no, not at all," though it was true that she had heard them through the window several times before, late into the night. Sometimes they had other friends stop by to play as well, and then the noise went from bearable to intolerable. She had bought earplugs to compensate, refusing to fully occupy the stereotype that, in low moments, she thought might accurately apply to her: ancient, cranky misanthrope. Lonely old lady.

She had had boyfriends, of course. Most recently she had been set up with an entrepreneur who had just founded a promising start-up and who, she discovered halfway through their first dinner, was moving to South Africa in six months. They had given it a try and then, as usual, the whole thing ended passively, the two of them canceling on a date that was never rescheduled. She would see him again at a birthday party, a dinner with their mutual friends; both of them would be polite. Her most serious relationship had been with Jim, whom she'd dated for all of her years of grad school in Providence, and for two years after her move across the country, too. It had been Jim she'd thought she'd marry. It had been Jim who faded from her life, slowly and then explosively, one weekend in Chicago, when he announced he'd met someone else.

Ada climbed the three steps at the side of the house that led into her apartment. She had her key in her hand.

Before she put it into the lock, she heard her name called. She turned.

"I forgot to tell you," said one of the two of them, approaching her, his hands in his back pockets. "Someone was looking for you tonight."

Ada waited.

"Here? At the house?" she asked, when no other information was produced.

"Yeah."

"Man? Woman? Did they leave a name?" Ada said.

"Man. No, he didn't. He said he was a friend. He said he'd stop by again soon."

"What did he look like?" she asked.

"I don't know. Normal, I guess. Not that old. Brown hair. My height."

"Okay," said Ada uncertainly.

"He asked for your number, so I gave it to him. I hope that was okay," said the boy.

Of course it isn't, Ada wanted to say. *What were you thinking?* She had visions of a stalker; some horror-movie villain who was preparing to infiltrate her life.

Instead, predictably, she assured him that it was fine. Be light, she told herself; be easy.

"It's cool," said Ada, and she went inside.

It's cool. The phrase repeated itself in her head shamefully. Those weren't her words. She was reminded, suddenly, of her first days at Queen of Angels: she hadn't felt so out of place since then.

Inside, quickly, she threw off her clothing, fell into her bed. She set her phone alarm for 6:00. If she fell asleep right away, she would get over four hours of sleep.

But for what seemed like an eternity, outside her window, the rhythmic bouncing of the ping-pong ball overpowered the earplugs she had put into her ears. Perhaps, she told herself, it was time to move.

1980s

Boston

da Sibelius was supposed to be at school. Instead, she was at her father's house, which still had not been sold. She had called Queen of Angels from David's that morning, lowering her voice into what she hoped was a decent impression of an adult, letting the secretary know that Ada Sibelius was sick and would not be coming in. Then she had walked up the stairs to the attic, telling herself that she would begin at the top, go through each box in turn. Next she would move into David's bedroom and go through all his drawers. And, at last, she would search his office, which contained volumes and volumes of files and papers. She was looking for answers.

In the two days after Ron Loughner's visit to St. Andrew's, Ada had learned that, in the process of transferring custody of Ada from David to Liston, a question had arisen as part of a routine background check. At some point, a missing-person report had been filed for David by his own family. This was enough to trigger further investigation into his past—which, in turn, had led to the further revelation that Caltech—the institution that David had always cited as his undergraduate alma mater—had no record of his name. Furthermore, no official documentation of the legality of David's surrogacy arrangement existed—not entirely surprising, given David's failure to make legal his decision to homeschool his daughter—and therefore it was possible that Ada's biological mother would make a bid for custody. All of this Ada had learned either through direct conversation with Liston or through eavesdropping on her phone calls, at which she had become very skilled. The family court judge adjudicating the process said that they could not move forward until these questions had been resolved.

The sum of this information had sent Ada into a spiral of doubt and pain so profound that it threatened to fell her. She did not believe what Liston told her, and she had told Liston this, somewhat rudely. In front of Liston, she had picked up the telephone in the kitchen and dialed the number for David's room at St. Andrew's. But it was not David who answered, and his roommate was incomprehensible and uncomprehending, ranting without pause, hanging up twice on Ada.

"It's okay," Liston had said. "We can talk more tomorrow, baby. Let's try David tomorrow."

The next afternoon, after a school day during which she had not even tried to concentrate, Ada had taken the bus to St. Andrew's, her heart pounding. She had signed in hastily and then fairly sprinted toward David's room. He had been by himself, sitting in his blue armchair, when she arrived, and she sat down in front of him breathlessly.

"David," she said, "David, you need to help me." And she had told him what she'd heard without stopping for breath. She begged her father to tell her the truth, to remember who he was, to let her know. *Where did you go to college? Why did your family say you were missing? Why didn't you draw up a contract with Birdie Auerbach, when you arranged to have her act as a surrogate?* But, though he looked at her worriedly, his eyebrows rising and furrowing, he said nothing. She pressed on. Speaking with him, by then, was like speaking to someone who only knew a handful of English words.

"For heaven's sake," he said to her once.

She looked at him closely. Had she seen, at times, David's old expression come across his face, breaking through his impassive gaze like a shaft of light? Was it pity, compassion, that crossed his face?

Some sign of understanding beyond what he admitted? Once, she was sure she saw his eyes fill with tears, but they did not fall. Several times he reached for her hand and took it. Several times he uttered some word or phrase she did not recognize, and she wrote these down in a little notebook she kept in her schoolbag, in the hope that they would lead to some discovery.

She went back the next day, too, repeating the process, entreating him to remember, to tell her what he knew. But this time he became agitated, raising his voice in response to hers. He had begun in recent weeks to utter nonsense noises when he could find no words. "Walala," he said to her, too loudly. "Oh, walla, walalalala." And then, unexpectedly, her name: "Ada."

Was this, she wondered, what he had been speaking of when he had come into her room following his botched retirement dinner? When he had warned her about information that might come to light in the future?

She decided, irreversibly, that it had to be. He must have had a plan: there was no question. She told herself that whatever secrets he had, he must be keeping for a reason; and, furthermore, that perhaps it was her job to discover them. To clear his name.

In her mind, there was no alternative: she could not imagine living in a world in which David did not represent—to her, to everyone—virtue, intellect, morality.

She took his hand. She looked at him carefully.

"Don't worry," she said. "Don't worry, David," she repeated—but she was saying it as much to herself as to him.

Meanwhile, a deep and abiding rage was growing inside of her, alarming in its intensity, directed mainly at Liston. Since Liston's revelation, Ada had spoken to her as little as possible. She answered in monosyllables. She spent even more time in her room. She had decided—perhaps unfairly—that if only Liston had included her in this process from the start, she might have been able to draw something out of David when he had been slightly better, more coherent. But Liston assured her that she had tried herself to do this, unsuccessfully. She told Ada that she had been concerned about telling her anything too early—worried that she was somehow profoundly mistaken, that there was a good explanation for everything.

"I wanted to make sure that I had it right, baby," said Liston. "Before I told you. Do you understand?"

Ada didn't, at the time, but later she would—it was that Liston knew how pivotal David was to her understanding of the world, to her trust in what was right and good. And Liston knew that to remove him from the center of it, to place his identity on unsteady ground, might undo Ada in some essential way.

Ada decided that an intensive investigation of David's possessions was merited, the kind that would take many hours in a row. And this was how she had come to be at her old house on a school day.

Now she stood in David's dusty and windowless attic, a flashlight in her hand. She had very little knowledge of what was up there; she had only seen David venture into and out of it to retrieve and store the ancient sleeping bags they used for overnights. She was surprised to see the number of boxes that, in fact, he had stored there: all of them must have come with him from the apartment in the Theater District when he had bought the house.

She began with the first one. It was so thickly coated in dust that it sent a flurry upward, making her cough. But it, along with the rest of the cardboard boxes around it, contained only clothing and bric-a-brac: old sweaters, old and outgrown clothing of hers; books and more books; scholarly journals; old and ragged beach towels. Some boxes contained items she was surprised to see that David had: silver candlesticks and platters; china dishes they had never used.

In David's bedroom, she opened his top dresser drawer, took out the picture of his family that she had grown so used to seeing. There was young David, in grainy black-and-white, surrounded by a brown paper frame that was disintegrating with age. The picture itself was rotting slightly—its color fading, its lines blurring from the humidity inside their old, damp house. She turned it over, looked at the back, but found nothing there that might give her any clue. She put it back in its home.

The rest of David's bedroom yielded nothing but more clothes, which was not a surprise: she had gone through it fairly thoroughly when packing him for St. Andrew's. Still, the sight of some of his old and favored shirts made her falter for a moment.

She sidled, next, into his office, which felt like the most illicit place to go. She had never been specifically forbidden from entering it—certainly she had spent a great deal of time inside it, whenever David asked her in—but her many years of hovering at its threshold without an invitation to come inside had served to make it feel off-limits. She rarely went into it alone.

It was a small office, a former pantry, stuffy in the summertime even with the window open. There were built-in bookshelves on either side of the room, nice-looking dark-wood bookshelves; but years of stacking books first vertically and then horizontally had rendered them unusable as a library. Only some of the spines were visible. There were a few odd pieces of art on the wall: two small framed prints of Leonardo da Vinci drawings (Ada had the feeling David had acquired them from a yard sale, or something equally eccentric); a little landscape that included a country lane.

The computer itself was clear of any debris, and everything that was out on the desk was stacked precisely, at right angles. David was neither neat nor messy; he disliked clutter, and had a mortal fear of the sort of knickknacks that Liston collected and kept on her desk and in her home. He did not like framed photographs. He did not like unnecessary objects. But his places of work were overrun with stacks: piles of papers and books and letters and bills, many of which were obsolete or had already been attended to.

Ada had never fixed, or hired someone else to fix, the computer in

David's office, which he'd crashed while working at it in the months following his retirement. When she turned it on, it still displayed the sad Mac face that David had chuckled at, its *X*'d-out eyes cartoonish and silly. Its hard drive disk was still stuck inside it. Whatever information it contained—some of it, perhaps, revealing—would be contained until the next time it was successfully started.

She turned in a full circle, took in a deep breath. She did not know where to start. The cream-colored filing cabinet caught her eye. Though she had never seen David use it, she put her hand out and tried the top drawer. It caught hard against her grip: locked. A tiny lock sat next to it tauntingly: no key in sight.

She went down into the basement and approached David's workbench. Above it, in a somber row, hung the strange and helmetlike objects he had been working on for years. Some resembled goggles; some resembled masks. They looked at her jarringly now. She did not like to see them. She grabbed a crowbar that hung below them on a peg, which she had seen David use only once before. He had levered open the door to the small shed in their backyard when he had lost the key to a padlock.

Now, returning upstairs, she tucked its hooked head up beneath the highest drawer in the filing cabinet and angled down as hard as she could. She used all of her insubstantial weight to push against the lock. But the only result was the bending of the metal—a buck-toothed look to the top drawer, a slight indentation in the one below it. Breathing heavily, her hands sore, she finally gave up, and dropped the crowbar on the floor.

At last Ada turned to the nearest stack of paper on David's desk. She lifted one leaf from the top. It was a letter from a collection agency, demanding that the electricity bill be paid. Below it was a photocopy of a journal article on language acquisition in children. Below that, an invoice for work that had been done on the roof of the house perhaps two years ago.

Quickly, she worked her way down the pile, until she reached a layer (she had begun to think of the pile as an accumulation of strata, and herself as a geologist) that consisted of perhaps two dozen tickets and receipts. She picked each one up and examined it. Mainly they were meaningless, evidence of items purchased at the local pharmacy or grocery store, one the stub of a ticket to a movie that they had seen together, perhaps a year ago. But one item caught her eye: it was the stub of a train ticket dated August 11, 1984, from Boston to Washington, D.C. On the back of it was scribbled one name, *George*, and an address.

She lifted the ticket up, pondered it for a moment. When had David last been to Washington? The two of them had gone together several times when Ada had been younger; but never this recently. George was his friend from childhood, an artist, who now lived there; she had met him perhaps twice that she could recall.

Suddenly she realized the significance of the date: it was the day David had first gone missing. The first time she had spent the night at Liston's. She recalled it exactly: recalled the police report that served as evidence of the necessity of intervention by the DCF. The way that David had studied it sadly.

He had told her, and Liston, and the police, that he'd gone to New York.

Had the disease already overtaken his brain by then? Could it have been a mistake? Or had he been lying intentionally, covering something up?

Slowly, she put the ticket down again, on the top of the pile, and then changed her mind: she tucked it into her pocket. Next, she picked up the *For Ada* disk that thus far she had been leaving at David's house. Better to keep them both out of the hands of others, she thought.

She carried these two items with her for the rest of the day, searching for a place she might keep them safe. She found a giant, ancient dictionary, four hundred pages in length, in Liston's basement. It looked unused and unsuspicious. Into its pages she inserted the *For Ada* disk and the train ticket, and then she closed it with a satisfying clap. After some further exploration, she decided she would put it on the top shelf of the closet in her bedroom at Liston's house, so high that she could not see it without craning her neck. She had to climb onto a chair to reach it. She would keep the documents together there, tucked safely inside the dictionary—along with any other evidence she could find.

One thing David *had* done, according to Liston, was create a will; but with parts of his identity in question, and with Ada's maternity in question, it was not a valid legal document, according to the lawyer Liston had spoken with. Already there were problems with St. Andrew's, with the payments that settled his bill each month. Upon his death, the distribution of his worldly goods would come into serious question. Though Liston had tried to be subtle in her investigation, careful not to spread rumors at the Bit without due cause, in the days following her talk with Ada she called every member of the lab, one after another, to ask them what they knew. And everyone professed to know nothing.

"Oh my God," Hayato said, softly, on the phone—Ada was eavesdropping, of course—"was he pathological? I don't understand." And it was all Ada could do to prevent herself from crying out at him and Liston both in rage.

In the evening, after work, Ron Loughner sometimes came over and met with Liston, and Liston carefully invited Ada to join them. She accepted, but only, she told herself, to keep track of what was being said about David. The first time, Loughner asked her to draw her family tree as well as she could, naming those relatives whose names she could remember. She told him what she could about what David had told her, recalling the conversations she had had with him prior to his move to St. Andrew's—the old Finnish ancestors, the governor of Massachusetts, the Amory family. She told him that David's mother and father were Isabelle and John Fairfax Sibelius, and that his father went by Fairfax as his first name. She told him that David had had no siblings and no cousins his own age. She told Loughner what David had told her: that both of his parents were dead, and that a family called Ellis had purchased their home. She told him, roughly, where their home had been.

"Thank you, Ada," said Ron Loughner. "This will be very helpful."

Ada nodded formally. She felt traitorous and low. But she viewed Loughner as an unwelcome but necessary ally in her quest to learn the truth.

One evening, Ada, from upstairs, heard the familiar sound of Liston lifting the telephone receiver in the kitchen, and she ran to the hallway.

By the time Ada had joined the call, as quietly as she could, it took her a few moments to determine who was on the other end.

"It's so very good to hear from you," a voice was saying. "Of course I remember." There was a slurring, monotone quality in the person's speech, as if from disease; whoever it was sounded very old, and had a lovely, refined Brahmin accent. His voice was familiar to Ada. It rang a bell someplace deep in her memory.

Liston explained why she was calling. "I'm sorry to be the one to inform you," she said. "I was shocked myself. But I'm wondering if you can recall anything about his hiring, what you knew."

Of course: it was Robert Pearse, President Pearse, David's former friend and ally, before his dreaded successor McCarren came along. It had been President Pearse who'd hired David permanently out of the Bit's graduate school many decades before. He had been diagnosed with Parkinson's several years prior; Ada recalled David, concerned, sadly telling her the news. It had caused a serious change in Pearse's speech, but beneath it Ada recognized, with a surge of warmth, the voice of the man who had once been their friend. He had always kept a stash of Mars bars in his desk. He had given Ada one each time he saw her.

There was a pause on the other end.

"Do you recall anything odd about his paperwork or references?" asked Liston, trying again.

"I recall nothing of the sort," he said. "My goodness, Diana. I'm having trouble understanding you."

"I know," said Liston quickly. "It's possible that this might be a misunderstanding. But we're having some legal trouble now, you know, about guardianship for Ada." She was speaking formally, unnaturally. She did not sound like herself. She had always been flustered around Pearse: Ada could sense it from the time she was very young. There was something about him, Liston had confessed once to David, that reminded her of a priest.

"That poor *child*," said Pearse, and Ada imagined him in his large and gracious study—she and David had been to his home once, a stately row house on Beacon Hill—shaking his head.

"He came here in—let's see—must have been 1951 or '2," continued Pearse. "He was a standout graduate student here. Integral to the building of the GOPAC under Maurice Steiner. Furthermore, I recall speaking with his undergraduate thesis advisor at Caltech personally. Donald Powell. Unfortunately, I believe he's since died."

"Okay," said Liston, nervously.

"That will be true of most of the faculty who once taught him, I suppose," said Pearse. "My goodness, he's been here at the Bit for nigh on thirty-five years."

"Caltech says they have no record of him," said Liston.

"A mistake, I'm afraid," said Pearse, the volume of his voice increasing unexpectedly. "How ridiculous. Powell was a friend of mine. I can tell you with certainty that David Sibelius was his protégé as an undergraduate. A sort of genius, I think. And I know the two remained in touch for some time."

In that moment Ada loved President Pearse nearly as much as David. Relief and gratefulness surged through her. Was it possible, she wondered, that it was all a misunderstanding?

"Furthermore, I knew his people," said Pearse. "The Sibeliuses, out of New York. I know their relationship with David was strained, but I can't imagine why they would have said he was missing when they knew very well he was here at the Bit."

Pearse told Liston, at last, that he had to go. He wished her luck, told her to contact him again with any other questions. "Though I would say, Diana," he said, "that this is not worth investigating further. It seems like a matter of shoddy record-keeping, if it is anything at all." His voice betrayed his tiredness, elided vowels and consonants like a skipping record. His energy was flagging. He breathed in and out with effort.

Ada waited until Liston had hung up and then, slowly, quietly, she hung up her extension. She had been justifying her spying by imagining—perhaps correctly—that Liston knew that she was doing it. Or even if she didn't, Ada told herself, she had every right to know. She released the breath she had been holding.

And then she heard a noise behind her, and turned to see Gregory Liston, looking at her frankly, quite still.

Ada crossed her arms defensively, waiting for him to accuse her of what she had, in fact, been doing. But he only looked at her. She returned his gaze defiantly.

He lacked his older brother's ease and gracefulness. He was in every way William's physical opposite: dark-haired and dark-complexioned where William was fair; thin and slight in the places where William had acquired a grown-up solidity. He was short for his age, shorter than Ada; when she saw him next to his peers at Queen of Angels, he looked younger and smaller than they did. His usually lowered head contributed to Ada's impression that he was somehow in a constant state of sinking toward the earth. There was something about him that reminded her of a creature from a myth, a faun, an elf. He had dark eyes with dark shadows beneath them, as if he did not sleep, and his ears protruded slightly. He had sharp elbows that stuck out beneath the plain white T-shirts he usually wore when not in his school uniform. He scratched one of them now thoughtfully.

"I was trying to make a call," Ada said finally, "but your mother was using the phone."

Gregory shrugged.

Then he said, "I heard your dad might have lied about a lot of things," and for the first time in Ada's life she understood why punches were thrown, and she even went so far as to ball her fist into a tight little knot at her side.

He looked momentarily alarmed—perhaps more at the sight of her face, which had crumpled, than because of any threat that she posed.

"You don't know that," Ada said. It was all she could think of to say.

"It's probably true, though," said Gregory. "Odds are."

After that, Ada avoided Gregory. She continued to visit David, but her visits now caused a deep, abiding sadness in her. They no longer spoke at length, and the absence of good conversation with her father felt to her like an absence of something essential and sustaining, like food, like water.

In the following weeks, Loughner brought the news that he had found and contacted Birdie Auerbach, who by then was living in New Mexico. She told him nothing of substance; only that, yes, she and David had entered into an agreement; and no, she knew nothing more about his background than anyone else did.

"What did she say about me?" Ada asked, and, seeing the look on Loughner's face, immediately wished she hadn't. The truth—which she would find out only as an adult—was that Birdie Auerbach had indicated that she was perfectly content to relinquish her parental rights to Ada. *Oh, I can't get involved in all that*, she had said, in fact, to Loughner, who had relayed those words to Liston. But, in a rare moment of gracefulness, he had refrained from passing them on to Ada herself. Instead, he told her that Birdie Auerbach was very busy with work, which meant she was worried that she wouldn't be as available to Ada as she wanted to be. "But she sends you her best," said Loughner. "She told me to tell you that, actually."

As often as she could, Ada worked at the code on the disk her father had given her, a jumble of letters that by now she knew by heart. Perhaps, she thought, it contained the answers to all of her questions. Perhaps David had always planned to give her this information; perhaps he had tried to tell her. The thought comforted her. But she still could not solve it.

Only Matty provided her with any companionship, and he did so very sweetly, childishly curling into her side when the two of them watched TV together in the evenings, so long as no one was there to see. (The television had become an important part of her routine—an idea that she could not have imagined two years ago.) With Liston busy at work and preoccupied at home with the puzzle of David's identity; and William staying out later and later with his friends, and sometimes, Ada speculated, coming home drunk; and Gregory tucked away, as usual, in the attic, Matty was often left to fend for himself for dinner, and so the two of them began a game that Ada called "Grabbit," wherein Ada had to make a meal out of whatever Matty grabbed from the fridge. Sometimes this resulted in horrible concoctions like tuna-fish soup, which was entirely unpalatable and quickly replaced by Fluffernutter sandwiches. Other times Liston would join them after she came in tired from work, and then Matty was insatiable for her attention, letting words tumble out so quickly that Liston often had to ask him to slow down. But when she asked Ada about her day, Ada was reticent, brief, still wounded by what she thought of as Liston's breach of trust. Matty, she knew, could sense this, and his eyes darted back and forth between the two of them quickly, searching for a fix.

One evening, Liston returned home from work with, she said, sad news: President Pearse had died. "Peacefully, at home," she added, and then shook her head once, as if recognizing the cliché of those words. It shook Ada. Although it shouldn't have been a surprise—President Pearse had not sounded at all well, or like himself, on the phone—it still felt sudden, and also seemed to her like a premonition of David's fate. This could happen to her father, too, Ada realized: there one day and then gone the next, taken out of the world with the swiftness of a plunge into water.

"Okay," she said. "Thanks for letting me know."

"I know you and David were fond of him," said Liston. "And I know he loved you two."

"It's okay," said Ada. And she announced that she was going to bed.

Liston paused. She looked as if she had more to relay.

"Oh, Ada," Liston said to her finally. "I'm sorry, honey. I know you're still mad at me. I just didn't know what to do. I messed up." She reached toward Ada, one hand outstretched, palm up, an offering of peace.

Ada took it out of politeness, but her heart was mutinous, and deep inside it was the feeling that she could trust nobody ever again. Not David's colleagues at the lab, who never came around at all; not Liston. And now—the idea bubbled up sometimes against her will, despite how forcefully she fought it—perhaps not even her father. She was alone in the world.

Meanwhile, at Queen of Angels, speculation over whom William's next girlfriend would be was increasing in pitch. Karen Driscoll had, unexpectedly, linked up with a different boy immediately following the breakup, disrupting the natural order of things (William was supposed to have moved on first), and prompting speculation that Karen, well liked before, might in fact be a slut—a word that was lobbed back and forth between ninth-grade girls with a frequency that alarmed and fascinated Ada.

Melanie McCarthy and her friends now regularly sat at her table, not entirely displacing Lisa Grady, but moving her to the end of it, where she sat quietly and consumed her meal with small, quick movements, as if embarrassed to be eating in public at all. The girls between her and Ada often sat angled toward the latter, their backs to Lisa Grady, so that an onlooker might have thought she was an interloper, someone unknown to them all.

At lunch, topics of conversation varied, but at some point William Liston generally came up. The latest sightings were exchanged, and the latest rumors, which they all turned to Ada to confirm or deny. In order to avoid having to reveal the depth of her ignorance when it came to William, she feigned a sort of modest reluctance to share his secrets (which, of course, implied that she knew them). She was noncommittal; she nodded slightly at some lines of thinking, shrugged at others. Her classmates trod carefully, respectfully, with deference to what they presumed to be both Ada's superior knowledge and her loyalty to William.

On Ada's own time, she speculated about William more fervently than ever. To her he had recently seemed quieter, more subdued. When she first moved in with the Listons, he had had dinner with them all on the infrequent occasions when his mother prepared it; now he never did. Matty missed him and tried to conceal it.

"William's at work," he said to Ada some afternoons, though both of them knew it wasn't true; he only worked at the video store on weekends. She had seen his work schedule, handwritten and posted to a bulletin board in his room (into which Ada snuck on the rare occasions when she was certain no one else was home, her heart beating in her throat). It was strange, knowing so much about a person without that person knowing her. Sometimes Ada felt as if she were looking at William from the safe dark of a mezzanine as he stood, spotlit, on a stage.

Still, she parlayed her observations and deductions about him, her insider knowledge, into an ever-increasing popularity. Melanie and her friends asked Ada now to walk home with them from school, to come over on weekends, but she always declined, saying only that she had to visit her father. His diagnosis was a topic of conversation that she had not broached with them, and she did not anticipate doing so anytime soon. There were various rumors about Ada's residency in the Liston household that she did not dispel. Only Theresa Fitzharris had ever asked her directly where her parents were, and in response she had said that her mother was dead and her father worked in another city. "He doesn't live in Boston. The Listons are family friends." That seemed to keep them satisfied.

Occasionally Ada spoke to one of her new friends on the telephone at night, but only briefly, since she didn't want to tie up the telephone line—it was William's prerogative to do that. When anyone called for her, she made sure to remind herself to enjoy it, and made note of her good luck. She could only carry on the façade she presented at school for so long, she knew, before she would be caught; and she anticipated this day as inevitable.

One day, Ada and her classmates were invited by their science teacher to stay after school to work on their group projects for the science fair, scheduled for the following weekend. (She had taken, in every way, a backseat on this project; her group was constructing some sort of model of the layers of sediment beneath the earth, a topic that did not interest her in the slightest.)

A particularly ambitious girl named Maria Donohue worked away at a trifold poster while Ada and her two other partners watched her. A soda bottle, stripped of its label and filled with colored sand in uneven stripes, stood next to her on the desk. As he made his way around the room, Mr. Tatnall, their teacher, nodded approvingly and complimented Maria on having such neat handwriting—a skill that was highly valued by the faculty at Queen of Angels—and then announced to the class that it was nearly time to go home, that anything that remained to be done would have to be finished on their own time.

Melanie, Theresa, and a girl named Janice Davies converged as they made their way toward her swiftly, catching her as she walked toward her locker to retrieve her coat.

"Are you going home now?" said Theresa, and when she nodded, the three of them followed Ada out the door without a word, as if they had made some collective decision in advance, without informing her of it.

It was colder out that week than it had been, and the weather reminded her often of David, whose favorite season was approaching. She and her classmates walked together, the other girls laughing at this or that, impersonating their teachers—a favorite pastime—or other children in their grade. At times they shrieked so loudly that it stopped Ada's heart. She could not get used to this fact about girls her own age: their volume, their exuberance, the outlandishness of their humor; the way they invented wild, improbable scenarios in their heads and then speculated about enacting them; the silliness of them; the sheer joyful foolishness, except when they were around boys. When they were around boys they reduced themselves, their voices, their bodies, made them smaller, making way for the male antics that occupied a place of precedence in the center of any room. Ada could barely keep up with their swinging, shifting moods. They seemed to her like birds in flight, like starlings, changing direction with such collective unspoken force that it seemed as if they shared a central root system, a pine barren joined together invisibly beneath the earth.

Ada did not know where any of them lived. She had never been to their homes, but she had heard, vaguely, that Melanie and Theresa lived on the same block, a nice one near the school, with well-kept houses. She began to worry, therefore, when they continued to walk with Ada past where she thought they might have turned off. At some point her three companions lapsed into first silence, then whispers. They walked a step behind her. Ada knew then—had known, in a way, since they left the school—that their plan was to meet William by shadowing her home, but she was uncertain how to stop it. She checked her watch. It was nearly 5:00; William wouldn't be home yet, anyway. He rarely came home before seven or eight in the evening. This knowledge made her smug. She would say nothing, she decided; she would not try to stop them coming with her, only feign ignorance about their intentions when they all arrived at Liston's house together.

Gregory was in the front yard when she arrived, and at the sight of the four of them he darted quickly onto the porch and then into the house. Ada wondered briefly whether he thought about Melanie McCarthy the way she thought about William Liston, and decided that the answer was probably yes.

"Hey, Gregory," Theresa called after him, a singsong tone in her voice that Ada recognized as mocking in some way.

There was a pause.

"This is me," she said then, turning to face them at last.

The three of them stood there silently, exchanging glances out of the corners of their eyes for a pause, until Theresa, the bravest, finally spoke up.

"Can we come in?" she asked.

Ada was about to tell her something—that Matty was sick, that Liston needed quiet for her work—when Liston herself came out onto the porch, startling her. She was not normally home so early.

"Hi, girls!" she said brightly. "Ada, are these your friends?"

Ada could see a look in her eyes that signified to her profound happiness, and surprise, that Ada was standing there in a group of such pretty, normal-looking peers. And, perhaps, the recognition of an opening—a new point of entry, a way to thaw the coldness that Ada had been directing at her for weeks.

Theresa nodded. "Hi, Miz Liston," she said.

Liston descended from the porch and walked toward them on the little brick path to the sidewalk. The lawn had not been mowed in quite some time. Liston was wearing a sort of windbreaker-suit, the kind she wore whenever she was not at the lab: shiny, baggy, hot-pink pants with a matching zip-up jacket. Her hair was large that day: she had just gotten it permed. In retrospect, the outfit was absurd; and yet, later, Ada could recall feeling, against her will, grateful for Liston. For her normalcy, for the fact that she looked, presumably, like all of their mothers. The fact that she was the same age, had the same accent. She was nothing like David, whose shabby clothes and long, quick stride, whose obliviousness to those around him, had caused Ada such shame the day he came to meet her after school. Liston in her pink tracksuit made her feel, for the first time in her life, as if she belonged.

She asked for all of their names and then asked Janice Davies if her mother wasn't Nancy Davies, who used to be Nancy Hill?

Janice nodded, and it was then that Liston put her hands together as if she had just come up with an idea.

"Can you stay for dinner, girls?" she asked them all, and they looked at each other, and then at Ada. "I can cook, for once," said Liston, beaming at Ada, telling Ada with her expression that she was proud of her, that she was on her side. It was clear to Ada that Liston thought she was doing her a favor; that this was part of Liston's ongoing plan to win back Ada's trust.

While the girls called their mothers, Ada and Liston stood in the kitchen together.

"They seem nice," said Liston, hopefully. Ada was alert now, listening for other sounds in the house. She wanted to ask Liston who else was home, but she couldn't think of a way to; instead, she excused herself to go upstairs briefly, and sighed in relief when she passed William's room and found it empty, the door ajar.

They made it all the way through dinner without William returning. Liston made spaghetti from a box and tomato sauce from a jar, and heated up some frozen broccoli florets she found at the back of her freezer. Matty ate it all enthusiastically, exclaiming sweetly that he thought it was delicious. (He may have; he may also have been happy to have his mother cook anything at all.) Gregory ate quietly at the table, avoiding eye contact with everyone—especially, thought Ada, Melanie McCarthy.

Liston, meanwhile, bonded instantly with all three girls, talking to them about their parents, their neighborhood, their houses, their siblings. They were talkative and eager with her, polite but outspoken. They had an easy way with Liston that made her jealous. They teased her, a bit, and Liston howled with laughter in response. These, Ada thought, were girls that reminded Liston of her own daughter; they were not serious like Ada, not quiet and severe.

"Let's see what I can find for dessert," said Liston. "Come help me, Ada." Ada followed Liston into the kitchen, where Liston produced from her freezer a half-empty gallon of slightly frost-burned Neapolitan ice cream and asked Ada to get out some bowls and spoons.

"They seem like such nice girls," said Liston, smiling at her. "You know you can invite them over anytime, baby."

Ada wanted to tell Liston what she knew to be true: that these girls were not here for Ada, not really; that their aim was higher. Instead, she said thank you.

At 8:00 in the evening, Ada checked her watch and began to worry about William's return. Liston and the other girls were still talking quickly and loudly; the girls were divulging what they knew about the children of Liston's acquaintances in the neighborhood. "I always knew he'd turn out to be a bad apple," said Liston, or "Sounds like her mother." Abruptly, Ada stood up from the table. They looked at her.

"I guess it is that time," said Liston, after a pause.

She hugged the girls goodbye, and Ada walked with them out onto the porch, and it was then—of course it was then—that she saw William Liston's long ambling body come striding up the street in the early dark.

If she had been by herself she would have turned back inside and gone quickly into another room. That was what she normally did. But now she couldn't, because all four of them together had seen him. Theresa stuck an elbow into Melanie's ribs, and Melanie lurched to the side.

Here was the moment Ada had been waiting for, dreading, and yet the fact that it was happening gave her almost a feeling of relief, to be so thoroughly undone. To be so caught.

William turned up the brick pathway toward the house and his step hitched a bit when he saw them.

Ada took in a deep breath. "Hey, Will," she said—the first time she had ever used his nickname; perhaps the first time she had ever called him directly by name.

"Hi," he said, uncertainly.

She felt feverish with nerves. She was lit only by the dim porch light, a naked bulb attended by dozens of moths.

"These are my friends," she continued. "Theresa, Janice, Melanie."

"Hey," said William, again. And he walked forward again, toward their little group, and seemed almost about to let himself in the door, until he stopped near Melanie, on his right, and turned to her.

"I know you," he said. "I've seen you at school before."

Melanie, in the porch light, looked even more angelic than usual: her long hair silky, golden, the color of grain; her face upturned, her sleepy eyes wide open.

"What's your name again?" asked William.

"Melanie," she said.

"Melanie McCarthy," said William. "I've heard about you."

"All good things," he added. "Don't worry."

Then he winked at her—suddenly the memory of the same gesture in Ada's direction felt unimportant in comparison—and walked inside.

"Night, Ada," he said to her, before he left.

Within two weeks, William and Melanie were dating. Within a month, Melanie had replaced Karen as another presence in Liston's home, and Liston's approval of her as Ada's friend had turned to a kind of wary acceptance of her as William's girlfriend.

"She's awfully young, William," Ada overheard her say to him once.

"She's in high school, Mum," said William, and Liston replied to him that freshmen and seniors were at very different stages in their lives.

"Just don't get in any trouble," said Liston. "Promise."

Ada's friendship with Melanie, with all of them, remained superficially intact. When she came to Liston's house the two of them would chat, and sometimes Janice and Theresa would come along as well, and then they would all spend time together. But mainly Melanie spent time with William, in his room, with the door open (at Liston's insistence).

Sometimes Ada was shocked that these girls had hatched a plan and enacted it so successfully, had gotten exactly what they had set out to get. In another way it confirmed for her that there was a sort of justice in the world. Beautiful people made up their minds to achieve something and then achieved it. It was natural, orderly. There was logic in it. She shared David's abstract appreciation of attractive people as aesthetic objects—though she tempered this by maintaining, like him, a feeling of intellectual superiority over them, a satisfying conviction that she was in some way abstemious and therefore holy—and the fact of Melanie's dating William didn't crush her the way she thought it might. Instead, it brought Ada several degrees closer to him than she had been; and for this she was, perversely, grateful to Melanie.

Spending more time with William revealed something to Ada: that he wasn't unintelligent; he could be funny and dry when he wanted to be. He had some of Liston's good nature, though he also had a dose of Gregory's spitefulness, often getting angry with his mother for reasons that seemed small and insignificant to Ada. He asked Ada what she thought of things, at times, and listened to her answers in a way that felt genuine. Once, speaking to Melanie, he said, about Ada, "She's funny." Tipping his head toward her: as if Ada weren't in the room with them. Melanie had no more to say now than she did before they had gotten together. Mainly, she sat quietly as Ada and William talked, and with her large eyes she tracked all of William's movements, mimicking him subtly with her own.

Shortly after Melanie and William began dating, and with a certain amount of shame, Ada began to go without her glasses whenever it was possible, donning them only when she needed to read something on the board. Her eyesight wasn't terrible; she could see well to a distance of ten feet, more than enough to read the facial expressions of others near her, but not quite enough to recognize a friend at the end of a hallway. "Did you get contacts?" asked Theresa, and she told her that she had. "You look way better like that," she said. Ada carried this half compliment inside her chest for weeks afterward, letting it fill her with shameful pride.

By mid-November, Ron Loughner had produced no further information about David—no clues about his past or his identity. No information about why he might have been reported missing, nor about why Caltech had no record of him as a student. Neither had Ada.

Twice Liston had timidly broached the subject of her father with her, and each time Ada had cut her off; she was not interested in Liston's theories on why David might have lied. "Been dishonest," Liston corrected herself quickly. "Been . . . misguided."

"He wasn't," Ada said sharply, and walked out of the room. She caught a glimpse of Liston's expression before she left: it was wounded, collapsed, her mouth slightly open, her hands entwined, frozen in mid-gesture.

Despite her loyalty to David, she began to see him less. Her visits with him saddened her; they felt unproductive and disturbing. She had failed to mention this to Liston, who, she imagined, assumed that Ada was still visiting her father after school each day. A year ago, Ada would have felt guilty about deceiving her; but the mistrust that had settled in her heart, when it came to Liston, allowed her to justify her actions to herself. She did not owe anything to Liston, thought Ada. During her newly free afternoons, Ada had begun to visit the library branch that she and David used to frequent, where their favorite librarian, Anna Holmes, still worked. Miss Holmes had not heard anything about Ada's father's decline, and assumed that he was still as he always was, living at home, working at the Steiner Lab. There was something so comforting about her presence—a reminder of Ada's past—that she did not correct Miss Holmes on this point. Instead, when she walked into the library, she allowed herself to slip back in time, and a calm happiness washed over her, and Miss Holmes beamed in greeting. She was a lovely woman, tall and elegant, with hair that was blond and gray together, and a smile that sent lines down her cheeks from the corners of her eyes.

"That is a person who is good at her job," David had said to Ada once, respectfully, about Miss Holmes.

Now she asked after David often, betraying a subtle disappointment that he no longer came in to see her. Once or twice she even sent Ada home with something for him, a new book that she thought he would enjoy, or, once, a jar of sauce that she had cooked and canned from tomatoes she grew in her garden in Ashmont. Ada accepted all of these gifts for David, assuring herself that one day she would tell Miss Holmes the truth. In the meantime, she allowed herself this respite, this brief calm in her otherwise uneasy existence.

Without David there to guide what she read, Ada had begun to read other sorts of books. She had stalled on the marble composition books that he had filled with the titles of novels, biographies, theorems, concepts; it all felt untrustworthy now. In light of all his betrayal, how could she be certain that his recommendations were worthwhile? Instead, in her bedroom, she read bad books she found at Liston's house, including a dirty one with a heroine in a torn dress on its cover. Liston had a stack of these books in plain sight on her bedside table.

And at the library, Ada now read books for teenage girls that her friends at school liked. *Sweet Valley High. Flowers in the Attic.* Books by Michael McDowell and Frank Belknap Long with gruesome covers that made her afraid to be alone in the dark. Her favorites were books called the *Tina Marie* series, about teenage girls in a pop band: books she would never have read in front of David. With a certain sinking feeling, she realized she had no reason to hide them any longer.

Each morning, when she woke, she thought about going to visit David, and then quailed. She could not bear it, the thought of looking at his blank countenance with so many unanswered questions between them; she felt she did not know him. Some nights, unable to bear her loneliness, she called his hospital room in the hope of hearing his voice. But always, always, she hung up after one ring, before he answered. She had terrible dreams of his death, woke up crying and guilt-stricken, vowed to go see him. But the truth—when she allowed herself to think it—was that she was afraid. And the longer she waited, the more afraid she became of seeing him. Who would be there, in his room, in his chair, when she arrived? David might be gone, spirited away, she thought. And there, in his place, some changeling.

Liston still went to visit him every Sunday after church. When she asked Ada if she wanted to come, Ada made up the same excuse: she'd seen him all week, she said, and she had too much homework.

At last, one Friday, Ron Loughner called Liston to tell her he had new information for them, and Liston was careful to let Ada know right away. He came over that evening to present it, looking proud of himself, smug in a way that Ada did not like. He had been recommended to Liston by a friend on the police force, but Ada could tell that even she found him grating, maybe somewhat incompetent.

She had hoped that Melanie and William would not be home for this, and she was relieved that the house was still empty when Loughner arrived. Even Matty was out at a friend's house for dinner.

The three of them sat at the kitchen table. Liston asked if anyone wanted a drink, and Ron Loughner asked for a Coca-Cola. Ada had the vague suspicion that he was a recovering alcoholic.

"I only have Diet," said Liston, and he said that would be fine.

He produced a manila folder with paperwork neatly stacked inside, and opened it. From it he removed a photocopied list of Sibelius births and deaths in New York over the course of the last century.

"The extended Sibelius family is getting smaller by the decade," he began. "At the beginning of the century they were a huge presence in New York, lots of cousins, lots of branches. In the 1920s, '30s, *Sibelius* was like Astor or Carnegie. You couldn't throw a stone without hitting one at some society function. But by now a lot of the branches have died out. They weren't a particularly fertile bunch, I guess," he said, pleased with this turn of phrase. He took a sip of his Diet Coke.

He continued. "By now anyone with the last name Sibelius has moved elsewhere, and they're mainly cousins, second cousins twice removed from John Fairfax and Isabelle Sibelius," he said, naming David's parents. "One of the first things I did when I took on the case was to try to find any living Sibelius to tell me why David's family would have reported him missing."

"They were estranged," Ada said quickly. "David didn't speak to them."

Loughner paused for a moment, regarding Ada with something she suspected was sympathy, and then continued.

"Recently I found one living relative," he said. "Isabelle's younger half-sister, much younger, Ellen Palmer. She lives now in Burlington, Vermont. She's seventy-four years old. Same father, different mother. She wasn't close to Isabelle, but she visited New York every Christmas as a child, until she was eighteen or so. She only would have been fourteen years older than David," said Loughner. "And therefore he presumably would have still been in the house when she visited."

He paused for a moment, letting the weight of his statements settle over the room.

"She says the Sibelius son disappeared at seventeen," he said finally, placing a palm delicately on the table. "And only resurfaced when he was a legal adult, at which point he indicated, by mail, that he did not want anything to do with them. The case was closed, legally, but they never saw him again."

"That makes sense," said Ada, looking at Liston for validation. "That's what David said happened." She was beginning to feel uplifted; perhaps this had been, simply, a misunderstanding.

Liston avoided her gaze.

"She also gave us a picture of David," said Loughner. He reached again into the manila folder, and produced a large-scale photograph that he observed himself, before sliding it across the table to them.

"Ellen Palmer says this is her nephew at sixteen," said Loughner.

Ada pulled the picture toward her.

In it were two people. One was a young woman, pretty, stout, with a high collar and a short, fashionable haircut: Ellen Palmer, perhaps. The other was a slender, sensitive-looking boy, wearing a tie and a scowl. The boy had blond hair, a slightly upturned nose, large dark eyes. He also had a birthmark, a small mole, in the middle of his right cheek.

She turned the picture over. On the back was written, in beautiful old-fashioned handwriting, *E. Palmer. D. G. Sibelius. 1941.*

This was not David. This was not her father.

Liston took the photograph from her.

Ada looked back and forth between them, Liston and Loughner.

"I don't understand," she said.

Loughner paused. "It seems likely," he said finally, "that your father was not a Sibelius."

"Maybe she's lying. Maybe she's just afraid we're going to come after her money," said Ada. But she doubted this as she said it.

"I'm not sure what to say," said Loughner.

The room was very silent. Ada felt his gaze upon her, and the gaze of Liston, who did not seem surprised. It was not a surprise to Ada, either; it felt more like an awakening, a letting-go. Her identity as a Sibelius had been integral to her understanding of herself. Although David was disparaging of his family, and of their outdated, restrictive belief system, he also seemed to find a sort of dignity in belonging to such an established lineage. His identity seemed to be comprised equally of pride in his ancestry and pride in his rejection of it. He had very effectively transferred this pride to Ada; it was what she fell back on, in this new unplanned chapter of her life, when she had nothing else to be proud of. Now she was not certain what she had left to take pride in. Not even David, anymore; for she no longer knew who he was.

Ada gathered all the scraps of her fourteen-year-old self-possession, and she asked Ron Loughner very politely whether he had been able to determine anything further about David's identity.

"Not yet," said Loughner. "Now we know who he wasn't, if you know what I mean. We still have to figure out who he was."

"Thank you," said Ada, with dignity.

Then she excused herself carefully from the table, and walked down the hallway toward the stairs.

"Ada?" Liston called after her. But she didn't stop.

At 7:00, Liston knocked gently on her door and called to her through it, asking her if she wanted dinner. Ada declined. She couldn't eat. She felt incorporeal. She felt she had been cut adrift from everything on earth; she felt as if she were floating, untethered, in the atmosphere.

Formerly fond memories of David now presented themselves to her, one after another, as something painful. Here was David, in his apron, in the kitchen; David, listening to his records, head lowered to his hand in contemplation. David bouncing excitedly on his toes, delivering the news of some discovery, or of a new friend, or of the engagement of a friend or acquaintance or a grad student at the lab. (He was deeply, unexpectedly romantic; he loved weddings; he loved surprise engagements, and hearing the stories of proposals. "And did he take a knee?" Ada heard him ask a former postdoc, Sheila, once, subsequently expressing great approval that her fiancé had done so.)

Perhaps her favorite memories of him, the ones that now drifted toward her from the other side of sleep, were of their trips to the mountains. David had rented the same cabin in the Adirondacks every July since he was in his thirties, and each summer the two of them went there all four weekends, and sometimes he brought his colleagues, too, for work retreats. It was a simple wooden cottage with very tall pine trees all around it and a set of wooden stairs leading down to a little lake, ten miles up the Northway from Lake George. David always got off the highway early to drive through Lake George Village, which had a main street lined with kitsch of various kinds: giant, friendly lumberjack statues made out of something like papier-mâché; outsized teepees with arrow-signs pointing inward, advertising AUTHENTIC INDIAN APPAREL; Viking-themed miniature golf courses; a wax museum with a window display featuring Frankenstein playing the organ. David was delighted by it all, and often insisted on stopping in to one or another of these local attractions. Together they saw the diving horse at Storytown when Ada was too old for such things, simply because they had never before seen it and David had decided it was time; dutifully she wandered into and out of souvenir shops that, by the 1980s, sold mainly T-shirts with terrible jokes on them. Often they stopped for dinner on the way at one of a handful of restaurants that David enjoyed, with names like the Log Cabin or Babe's Blue Ox Tavern, or giant triangular signs out front advertising SURF'N'TURF SPECIALS ON TUESDAYS. Inside David would order them both banana pie and Coca-Cola—a combination that always made the waitress laugh—and then inquire after her name and then woo her, asking her what they should see and do that weekend, leaving an outstanding tip.

The cabin itself had ceilings of light unfinished pine and old oak furniture, and it smelled dusty and warm inside, like an attic or a library. There she would read, and swim, and play card games for hours, and breathe in the sharp earthen smell of the forest that surrounded her, and in the evening there was cocktail hour on the porch (lemonade for Ada, in a funny glass with a trout on it), and in the nighttime there was a chorus of bullfrogs that David would imitate while he turned off every light in the house one after another. *Good night, good night,* he would croak along with them. *Good night to you all.* Over the water, from Ada's snug bedroom, from her tightly made twin bed, she could see the moon reflected on the water, a glimmering pathway from the shoreline into the distant sky.

The next morning was a Saturday, and Ada woke with a resolution. It was time, she thought, to confront David. Or, at the very least, to try. She looked out the window. The day was gray; it looked as if a cold front had moved through. Outside, a neighbor girl was raking her front yard in a snowsuit.

Ada got dressed as quickly as she could. She put on two sweaters. Then she left—it was her good luck that nobody was downstairs— and walked down the street to her old house. She had an idea: A prop she could use to assist her in her inquisition. Something that might jog his memory.

She unlocked the kitchen door. Inside, it was chilly and damp-feeling, the heat at fifty degrees only to prevent the pipes from freezing in the night. She'd been visiting less because of this; her regular diary entries into the ELIXIR program had slowed to one or two a week. She scanned the kitchen, as she always did, looking for anything out of place, for leaks or infestations. *We must be constant and vigilant in our war against entropy*, David used to say frequently. *Entropy always has the upper hand.* She still felt fiercely protective of this house; she was still happy it had not sold.

The door to David's office was open, as it usually was. She had just walked past it on her way to the staircase when a shape inside it registered, and she realized someone had been sitting at his desk. She stood in place, not turning back. A chill ran up her spine. Was it David himself? Was it his ghost? An intruder?

Quietly, she turned around, and saw the narrow back of someone hunched over at David's computer, wearing a heavy jacket. The computer that she'd thought broken was on, glowing greenly inside the office, a bright spot that silhouetted whoever was facing it.

"Who are you?" she asked bravely. She had become more courageous, if nothing else, in David's absence; she felt she had no one to protect her, and so she began to act in ways she never had before.

The figure stood up out of his chair swiftly, sort of defiantly, and turned to face her. It was Gregory Liston, and he stood with his hands hanging down at his sides, saying nothing.

"What are you doing," Ada said quietly.

Gregory said nothing.

She walked toward him, first slowly and then swiftly, feeling a rage inside her that she had rarely felt before. She wanted to drag him by his ears out of the office, but he exited before she could, walking around to the opposite side of the dining room table, so that she could not get to him. She started one way and he went the other, and the two of them stood like that, facing each other, for several beats.

"What were you doing in there?" she asked again, and he slowly raised his shoulders to his ears, a gesture that infuriated her further.

She looked toward the computer and then walked into the office. On the screen, a window was open: it was a text file. Nothing she had ever seen.

It was written in David's personal code, which Ada had long ago memorized. *The Unseen World*, it said, across the top; she read it easily. To Gregory it must have looked like gibberish.

Below it was a paragraph of text, followed by phrases that she didn't understand: cryptic, broken phrases, nothing that at first made sense. Her heart sped up.

"What were you looking at?" she demanded.

"Nothing," said Gregory. For the first time she heard a note of fear in his voice.

"How did you turn it on? It's broken," she said.

"I fixed it," he said, simply. He turned his palms upward toward the sky, as if to say, *Easy*. It infuriated Ada further.

On the desk was a pad of white stationery from the lab, with someone else's handwriting on it. Gregory's. A pen lay cast off to the side. On the notepad, he had written down half of the string of letters before him on the screen.

"You're an idiot," Ada said cruelly, finally turning to look at him.

"Were you trying to decrypt that? You never will," she said. "What an idiot," she said again, for good measure. To make sure that he knew.

Gregory was wearing a puffy brown parka that was built for a teenager, salt-stained from the previous winter, probably a hand-me-down from William. Only the tips of his fingers stuck out of the openings at the wrist. His skinny neck jutted up from a too-large collar. His lips were painfully chapped, and he licked them, as if about to respond.

"He's smarter than you," said Ada. *"I'm* smarter than you. I broke the code that you keep on your computer."

Gregory looked at her, the color draining from his face.

"Next time try something more complicated than alphanumeric substitution," Ada told him, feeling powerful and vengeful and unkind. "I solved it in five seconds. I read it all." A lie.

Gregory winced. The image of him being collared by a big kid in the hallway at Queen of Angels presented itself to her suddenly. He always sat alone at lunch, his face buried in a science fiction novel or a comic book. She had never once seen him walking side by side with anyone else at school.

He turned abruptly and walked toward the kitchen, leaving behind the scrap of paper he had begun to write on.

"Stay out of this house," Ada shouted after him with finality. "It's not your house. It's David's house and mine."

"I was trying to help," he said on his way out. He stammered as he said it. He was in the kitchen, on the other side of the wall, and he sounded uncertain, as if he were asking himself a question. As if he were on the verge of tears.

It was only after he left that she allowed herself, momentarily, to be impressed that he had gotten into the computer at all. She had thought it irreparable, without David's guidance. She had never been able to fix it herself.

She sat down in David's chair. For a long while after Gregory left, she stared at the computer screen.

At the top of the document Gregory had left open was a paragraph, disguised in David's code:

> We have learnt that the exploration of the external world by the methods of physical science leads not to a concrete reality but to a shadow world of symbols, beneath which those methods are unadapted for penetrating. Feeling that there must be more behind, we return to our starting point in human consciousness—the one centre where more might become known. There we find other stirrings, other revelations (true or false) than those conditioned by the world of symbols. Are not these too of significance? We can only answer according to our conviction, for here reasoning fails us altogether. —A. S. Eddington

Below it were three more phrases.

> Ivan Sutherland,
> Sword of Damocles.
> Elixir's house.

She wrote down the paragraph, and the three phrases that followed, on the scrap of paper that Gregory had left behind. Then she folded the page in quarters and put it into her right pocket.

This text; the *For Ada* disk; the train ticket to Washington. These items now constituted what she considered to be her only clues. She would protect them carefully. She would keep them all together on the top shelf of her closet at Liston's house, tucked inside the pages of the dictionary.

Finally, she went upstairs to David's room, to retrieve what she had originally come for: it was the family portrait in David's dresser, the one she had gazed upon so many times, searching for answers about her own past. It was the David she knew in that picture, almost without question—same posture, same nose, same half-bemused expression as he stared into the lens. But if Ellen Palmer had been telling the truth, the people behind him were not, apparently, Sibeliuses. Who they were remained to be seen.

For the first time in a month, Ada walked over the bridge to the bus stop and waited for the bus that would take her to Quincy. In her mittened hand she carried the portrait. Several other people joined her. It was a gray, blustery day, almost unbearable when the wind blew. Ada turned up the collar of her coat and sank her chin down into it.

On the bus, she wondered what David would look like. Would he remember her? Or, in her absence, would he have forgotten her completely, erased her from his mind, overwritten her with something entirely different?

At St. Andrew's, after signing in, she walked down the two long hallways toward her father's room and then knocked lightly at the door, slightly ajar, before entering. When she did, she saw only the crown of his head over the top of his armchair. Just as he had been the last time she'd seen David, he was turned toward the window that faced the harbor, and he was motionless. His roommate, Paul, was lying on his bed, asleep. It was late morning.

Ada walked toward her father, afraid to startle him, afraid of whom she would find.

"Hello," she said, but there was no response.

She circled around to the front, holding her breath. There in the armchair was David. She was relieved to find that he did not look so different after all. Thinner, yes; smaller in general; but David nonetheless. The staff at St. Andrew's took good care of him. Somebody shaved his thin cheeks; somebody combed what little hair he had. He had one hand on each arm of the chair, and he lifted the right one, as if in greeting.

"Hi, David," she said again. "It's me. It's Ada."

"I've been waiting for you," said David, unexpectedly. His eyes were rheumier than they had been the last time she'd visited. They seemed to her to be a lighter blue.

"I know," said Ada, with a certain amount of relief. "I'm sorry."

David raised and lowered his eyebrows, sort of skeptically. Then he shifted his gaze once more to the window.

"How have you been?" asked Ada.

"Oh, my. Oh, here and there," said David. "For heaven's sake."

"Have you been eating?"

"Oh, yes," said David.

Ada sat down on the bed across from him. She was still chilled from the air outside. She did not take her jacket off. David raised a hand to his head, touched it with an open palm, patted his brow lightly.

How much she longed for his old self, in that moment: she could feel the wish inside her, a hummingbird. If he would stand up from his chair—if he would simply stand up and walk with her, out of that place, and back to their old life in Boston. Instead, she produced the portrait she had been keeping tucked inside her pocket. She looked at it herself for a moment, studying the boy in the picture, then looking up at her father. There was no doubt, she thought, that this was David.

"I want to ask you something," said Ada.

She stood up, knelt down in front of his chair, held the picture out so he could see it. He shifted his cloudy eyes downward without moving his head.

"Who are they?" asked Ada, pointing to the adults in the picture.

"Well, that's Mother and Dad," said David.

"But what are their names?" asked Ada.

"Oh, for heaven's sake," said David. "Mother and Dad."

He studied the picture again, and then reached toward it, tracing the faces with one finger. There was that accent again, the one she could not place: it was not David's accent. Not his voice.

"Where's Susan?" David asked suddenly.

"Susan?" asked Ada.

"Susan," he said, looking up at her suddenly, as if addressing her directly. "Susan, there you are. I've been waiting for you."

"What's your name?" asked Ada, and he held her gaze for what seemed like quite a while.

"Come on, you know it, Suze," he said at last.

"What's your name?"

"Harold Canady," said David. And he held one finger to his chest. Then he pointed one finger at her slowly. "And you're Susan Canady."

"I missed you," David said, his light eyes filling completely with tears.

Gently, surely, he bent back the brown weathered mat that surrounded the portrait, and from it removed the photograph itself, as if to inspect it more closely. And for the first time she saw what had been beneath it: there, in the bottom right corner, in a curling, hand-drawn white script, five words: *The Strauss Studio. Olathe, Kansas.*

2009

San Francisco

Ada had slept for an hour, maybe less, when she woke up panicked, thinking she had missed her alarm.

She grabbed for the phone on her nightstand: 5:59 a.m. The alarm would sound in a minute. Briefly, she lay her head back on her pillow. Her neighbors had played beer pong until 4:00 in the morning. How, she wondered, did they get up for work in the morning?

She showered and dressed. She chose her outfit carefully: something that read as simultaneously young and powerful. A blazer and close-fitting dress pants. She would get to work a little early, go through the presentation one last time with Tom Tsien. She ran through the people who would be at the table with them: three members of the board; the CEO, Bill Bijlhoff; about a dozen potential investors who had been courted for months; and the VP of marketing, Meredith Kranz. Like many of Tri-Tech's newer employees, Meredith was improbably young for her title—twenty-nine, perhaps, or thirty at most—and impeccably dressed. She wore brands with names that baffled Ada. "This is Acne," Ada had heard Meredith saying once to a colleague, about a jacket she was wearing. And Ada Googled the brand name to make sure she had heard it correctly.

It had been Meredith Kranz's idea for the investors to interact, at the meeting, with the new product's male and female avatars. This was the idea that had kept Tom and Ada up late the night before, troubleshooting, fixing glitches. Meredith had written the script for the reps herself. She had insisted on letting them pitch the product. "It's more dynamic," she had said, when Ada raised concerns. "And afterward, we can let the investors interact with the reps themselves," she continued. An even worse idea, thought Ada. But Bijlhoff had sided with Meredith, and Ada had done as he wished.

The pitch felt, to Ada, like a joke; she had trouble not laughing herself when she saw the reps earnestly moving their computer-rendered limbs about in clumsy, cardboard arcs. Computer-animated people, in 2009, still looked stilted and bizarre. These avatars were not close to passably human. The way they used their arms was incorrect—they hovered in the air unrealistically, never dropping to meet their flanks. When reps moved forward, their gait was outlandishly wrong. For decades, computer animators struggled to replicate the motions of walking and running, without much success; the particular rhythm of the human stride eluded them all, the rhythm of bone and muscle and fat and nerve impulse. Worse than that: these particular reps kept freezing. At the end of last night, Tom claimed to have everything running smoothly, but Ada was still nervous. To her, having reps pitch the product only served to reinforce how far away Tri-Tech was from being able to actually bring it to market. Five years, ten years until the hardware was available; maybe more. They would all have to hope for very patient—and reasonably young—investors.

In the car, at 6:45 a.m., her phone rang. It was a 617 number. She rarely got calls from Boston anymore.

She remembered, abruptly, the conversation she had had with Connor and Caleb the night before: someone had been by to see her. They had given this person her number, whoever it was. A man, they'd said. Could it be him?

She contemplated answering for too long: normally she didn't answer calls from unknown numbers, but she thought perhaps she should pick this one up.

By the time she had decided to, it was too late; the call had gone to voice mail. She waited for thirty seconds, then a minute. But no message had been left.

When she arrived in the office, it was both unusually full and unusually quiet. Bill Bijlhoff, the CEO, had tried hard to keep the investment meeting under wraps, especially around the more junior programmers; they knew the company was imperiled, surely, and it wasn't good for morale to raise and lower their hopes too much.

Bijlhoff, who'd been brought in by the original cofounders of the company to head the Alterra initiative, was now the only Tri-Tech employee who'd been working there longer than Ada, and the only Tri-Tech employee to have an office door. Doors, in general, were not part of Tri-Tech's culture. While other tech companies were going remote, Tri-Tech had hung on tenaciously to its physical space. It occupied the top two floors of a building that now, nearly a third vacant in the wake of the closure of several start-ups in a row, felt something like post–Gold Rush California. The main level was set up like an atrium or a piazza, with six Dorian columns stretching from glossy floor to vaulted ceiling, and two walls of windows. A dome at the top of the building sported an oculus in its center that let in a dramatic, slowly rotating shaft of light. The VPs, including Ada, had their own offices around the perimeter of the main floor; but they were doorless, open to the rest of the space. The other employees spent their days out in the open, at temporary workstations or on couches. They were given breakfast, lunch, and dinner, hot meals rolled out on carts that locked into place at one end of the main floor. They were given healthy snacks throughout the day. Sometimes it felt, to Ada, a little like what preschool must have felt like, though she couldn't be sure; there were even two small dark offices with cots inside them, in case a midday nap was required by an employee who had recently pulled an all-nighter.

She walked across the floor to Bijlhoff's office and found the door closed. She wanted to let him know about what she and Tom had done the night before, in the two hours before the meeting began. She rehearsed it in her head: she would assure him that the reps seemed, now, to be behaving; she would run through the backup plan they'd enact in case they didn't.

She rapped lightly at the door, and Bill Bijlhoff opened it after a beat.

"Ada," he said, "I'm glad to see you. Come in."

He was a good-looking man, tall, light-haired, straight-up-and-down. He was slightly older than Ada. Rumors placed him at forty-four, but his actual age was a closely kept secret. Five years ago, when Alterra was booming, he'd been a Silicon Valley celebrity. He had been profiled in every major magazine in the country. He'd appeared, in cartoon form, on *The Simpsons*. He'd given a TED talk. Now, even with the company in decline, he had not lost the persona he had acquired in those years: that of mischievous boy genius, pioneer, freethinker. Despite the firm's troubles, Bijlhoff's estimation of himself remained unshaken. Ada had as little interaction with him as she could manage; he liked her, she thought, because she had never given him a reason not to. Other employees, ones who were closer to him, cycled in and out of his favor rapidly and randomly; she watched them sometimes, shaken, walking out of his office with their heads low.

"Have a seat," said Bijlhoff, and she did, and so did he.

"Everything looking good?" he asked her. She nodded.

"I think so," she said, and he said, "Great."

"The demo was glitching a little bit last night, but I think we've got it under control," she began. Bijlhoff didn't look interested.

"Listen, Ada," he said. He took a breath.

"Yes?" said Ada.

"I've been talking with some board members. We're letting Meredith run the meeting today."

Ada paused.

"Meredith Kranz?" she asked dumbly.

"Yeah.

"As in," said Ada.

"We're turning it over to her. We think she's got it. We think
she'll be good."

Ada opened and closed her mouth. "But," she said.

"I know you and Tom have been working on the pitch for a while,"
said Bijlhoff, "and that's great. But the fact is that none of the investors
we have coming to sit in today knows anything about programming.
And we think Meredith will do a good job of packaging it for them."

"What if they have questions?"

"I have faith that Meredith can answer them," said Bijlhoff. "Or
else I'll be there, too."

Bill had been a programmer, once upon a time; but he hadn't
worked on the tech side of the firm in years. It wouldn't have surprised Ada if he'd forgotten most of what he once knew. Certainly he
knew none of what had gone into the beginnings of the new project.

"You don't even want us to sit in?" Ada said. "Just to be safe?"

Bijlhoff stuck out his bottom lip, blew upward. A small lock of
hair shifted slightly on his forehead. She pictured him suddenly as a
rep: How might one animate that particular motion, that particular
expression?

"I think you might make Meredith nervous," he said, in a tone of
voice that told her he was trying to be kind.

Ada lifted a hand and dropped it onto the arm of the chair she
was sitting in. She put her hands on her knees. She leaned forward,
stood up.

"I guess that's that," she said.

She wondered—briefly, perhaps unfairly—whether Meredith was

sleeping with him. It wouldn't be the first time that Bijlhoff had dated an employee.

"You're appreciated, Ada," said Bijlhoff. "I hope you know that."

Ada nodded, once. She walked toward the door. She looked down at the shoes she had chosen for the day: heels. She never wore heels.

A thought occurred to her then, and she turned to face Bijlhoff before she left.

"The name," she said. "Does Meredith know where the name comes from?"

"Of course," said Bijlhoff. But he had already lifted his phone to make a call, and he looked at Ada as if waiting for her to leave.

The name of the program was the Unseen World. The UW for short. And the truth was that no one, except for Ada, knew how it had come to be called that. She had suggested it; the others had approved. She had never shared the story of its provenance.

She walked, dumbfounded, toward her doorless office. Around her, heads popped over workstation walls. Did the rest of the company know already? Meredith Kranz was friends with some of them. Halfway across the floor, she ran into Tom Tsien, who looked at her grimly.

"You, too?" said Ada. He nodded. Lifted his shoulders once, dropped them.

Ada sat at her desk for a while, uncertain of what to do next. She felt almost as if she should go home for the day: it was too much, she thought, to watch a series of investors walk past her office on their way to the meeting room. To watch Meredith walk toward her fate. What would she do, Ada wondered, if the reps didn't cooperate? What would Bill do? He was both impulsive and stubborn: ten years ago, when fate had been working in his favor, these were the traits that had propelled him into glory. Now these were the traits that threatened to tank the entire company.

She didn't notice she was holding her phone until it vibrated in her hand.

She glanced at it. It was the same 617 number that had called earlier that morning. This time, she answered it.

The person on the other end hesitated long enough that she nearly hung up.

"Ada?" he said, at last.

It was a voice she hadn't heard in half a decade.

1980s

Boston

"I need help," said Ada, breathless. She was pink from the cold. Her nose was running. She was standing in front of Miss Holmes at the Fields Corner Public Library branch. She was panting audibly; she had run too fast from the bus stop.

"Are you all right, Ada?" said Miss Holmes, looking concerned.

"Can you help me find something?"

"Of course," she said, but she looked down at her watch. "But it's 1:55, dear."

On Saturdays, the library closed at 2:00 p.m.

"I," said Ada, and then wondered how she could possibly convey to Miss Holmes the urgency of the situation. She stood silently for a moment, mustering her courage.

"Tell you what," said Miss Holmes kindly. "Just sit right here a moment. I'll be right back." She gestured to a low table. Gratefully, Ada sat; and she watched as Miss Holmes made her rounds, leaning over to encourage the patrons to finish what they were doing, in her low librarian voice. Then she returned to her post to check out their books.

Ada looked at the picture she was still clutching in her hands. *Olathe, Kansas.* Harold Canady. Or *Canadee*? Susan Canady. The words knocked around inside her, bitter in their foreignness, somehow unsavory. She didn't know how to pronounce the word *Olathe*. She didn't know how *Canady* was spelled.

When the last patron had left, Miss Holmes turned the sign on the front door from Open to Closed and then returned to Ada's side.

"Now, dear," she said. "What can I help you with?"

And Ada, at last, confessed to Miss Holmes everything that she knew, managing to do so with a blank, impartial face, trying to imagine how David might have done it. Clinically. Forthrightly.

Miss Holmes, to her credit, did not betray much shock, though surely she must have been dismayed—not only for Ada, but perhaps for herself. She murmured from time to time sympathetically. She put a hand on Ada's forearm at the first mention of David's disease and she left it there comfortingly.

"Oh, Ada," she said, when Ada had finished speaking and was looking stiffly down at the table in front of her.

"And what is that you're holding?" she asked.

"I don't know," said Ada. "It might be a picture of his real family. David's. Or Harold's, I guess." It made her flinch: the thought that not even his name, not even the word that she had spoken so many thousands or millions of times in her life—the word that meant, to her, *father*—was correct. David was gone, but also, *David* was gone: replaced with something cold and uncanny.

"And it's from a place called *Olathe*," said Ada, spending two syllables on the name.

"Oh-*layth*-ah," said Miss Holmes. "If I'm not mistaken."

She wore glasses on a chain about her neck, and she held them up to her eyes now to look.

"Oh, that's him," she said, with something like fondness, about the boy in the picture. "Isn't it."

Ada nodded. Against her will, she still loved the picture: she had always been fascinated by it as a piece of evidence that her father had once, improbably, been a child.

"Where would you like to begin?" asked Miss Holmes.

There were two steps to be taken, they decided. The first was looking up further information on the Sibeliuses themselves: in the society pages of old editions of the *New York Times* on microfilm, for example, said Miss Holmes. "That might be a good place to start." If they could find more information about the real David Sibelius and his parents, they might find some explanation, some connection to Ada's father. And the second was finding historical records and newspaper articles about any Canady family in Olathe—only those would be much more difficult to find, said Miss Holmes, because it was quite unlikely that any library in Boston would have old editions of their local paper on microfilm. "And I'm not sure that I'm up for a trip to Kansas," said Miss Holmes. "How about you?"

Therefore, she called information and requested the number of the public library there.

"The main branch, I guess," she said to the operator.

"Oh. That branch, then," she said, a moment later.

She was standing behind the checkout counter. While she waited, she inspected her glasses. She inspected the piece of paper in her hand, on which Ada had written down the names *Harold Canady, Susan Canady,* spelling them the way she had heard them, as they had been pronounced by David hours before.

"Yes, hello," Miss Holmes said suddenly. And she introduced herself, and her occupation, and she explained the information she was looking for, and she left her name and number—both for the library and, Ada noted, for her home telephone.

"Thanks very much," said Miss Holmes. "I would so appreciate anything you can find. And I'm happy to return the favor anytime."

Then, hanging up the phone, Miss Holmes turned back to Ada. "I'm afraid I have to go home now, dear," she said. "But let's continue this on Monday, after your school day, shall we?"

Ada walked back to Liston's slowly. Dorchester was busy that day: mothers out grocery shopping, their hands tied up with bags and children; teenagers kicking rocks down the sidewalk, shouting to one another across Dot Ave. Ada was brimming with a sort of energy that did not have an outlet: new information, new ideas, new emotions that she could not articulate to anyone. She had already made up her mind not to tell Liston what David had said: this was a part of the puzzle she wanted to figure out for herself. She did not want to think of him as *Harold Canady*; she wanted her father to still be David for as long as he could be. She wanted everyone else to still think of him as such.

Most of the Listons were home when she arrived back at the house, but Liston herself was out. The familiar, slightly artificial smell of the house presented itself to her, and it occurred to her that it had begun to replace the musty warmth of David's house as the smell of home. Matty was in the den, watching television. From upstairs she heard Melanie's high, breathy voice, and William's low one, but everything was still. In the kitchen, she made herself a sandwich from what Liston kept on hand—Wonder Bread, turkey, American cheese, Miracle Whip—and brought it upstairs to her room to eat.

Moments after she sat down at her desk, there was a light knock on her door.

"Hello?" said Ada, mid-bite.

The door opened slightly. In the crack between it and the threshold, Ada saw two eyes peering toward her. Gregory.

"What do you want?" she asked, unkindly. She was still incensed from that morning. What right did he have, she thought again, to be on David's computer? She felt an angry surge in her pulse again. What right did he have to set one foot in their house?

"Can I come in for a sec?" Gregory asked.

"Why?" said Ada.

"Just for a sec," said Gregory. And, without waiting for permission, he entered the room. He looked shifty and nervous. He stood facing her, folded his hands in front of him, looked down at the floor. Then he mumbled something too quiet to be heard.

"I can't hear you," said Ada. It occurred to her, for the first time, that she sounded like the girls she had become friends with at Queen of Angels. That the stress and intonation of her voice had begun to mimic theirs. She said *like* now, with some frequency. She said *whatever*.

"I'm sorry," said Gregory.

"For what?" she said. She wanted to hear him say it.

"For being in your dad's house," said Gregory.

"What were you doing there," said Ada. "Had you been there before?"

Gregory paused. And then he nodded.

"A lot?" Ada demanded. He nodded again.

"Why?"

"I wanted to try to help you," he said. He was still looking at the floor, but she could see a redness creeping up from his collar, darkening his neck. "I'm good at that kind of stuff. I think."

"I don't need your help. I'm good at that kind of stuff, too," said Ada. "And it's not your business."

Gregory raised his shoulders up and down, once, slowly. She looked at his hands. There were raw, red patches around all of his fingernails, where he had torn at his own live skin. And, against her will, she began to pity him. There was a small but growing part of her that recognized him as a potential ally. His interests, after all, aligned with hers, and with David's; and the fact that he had fixed David's computer when she could not—although it infuriated her— also impressed her on every level. He was crafty. She thought of him alone at school, as she had been when she first arrived. She thought of him running a grubby finger along a line of lockers, as she had often seen him doing; she thought of his sad yelps as he struggled to free himself from the larger boys who collared him at school; she thought of him up in his attic for hours on end, doing *God knows what*, as Liston said, and acknowledged finally that, of all the Listons, this one was most like her.

Over the course of the next two weeks, Ada's tenuous alliance with Gregory grew. She divulged to him what she knew so far, in vague and guarded terms, and they settled into an uneasy friendship. She still mistrusted him, still wondered whether he was concealing anything from her. Her pride prevented her from asking him outright; she wanted him to think she knew more than she did.

Instinctively, both of them made the decision to conceal the time they spent together. At school, she ignored him. She did not acknowledge him when she passed him on the sidewalk outside Queen of Angels after school, and he accepted this as a matter of course. She loathed herself for doing this; she knew that David, especially, would be appalled; but she told herself that his was no longer the advice to listen to. And she comforted herself by telling herself that, in any case, David did not know about the codes of children. She sensed the presence of some unbendable rule that dictated that simultaneous friendship with Gregory and with Melanie McCarthy and her cohort was not permissible—and, spinelessly, she chose the latter.

At Liston's house, Ada and Gregory maintained the steady silence that had always existed between them. On the rare occasions when the entire family gathered together—Thanksgiving, recently, being one; and then Liston's forty-fourth birthday, on December 1—Ada and Gregory carefully said nothing to one another, the way they always had. Gregory continued to spend hours alone in the attic; only when no one was home did she join him, keeping a watchful eye on the driveway and running down the stairs at the first sign of anyone's return. They also met at David's house, which Ada gave Gregory permission to visit, even when she was not there. She even gave him a key, so that he did not have to sneak off with his mother's.

With Gregory's permission, she had made two copies on his computer in the attic of the *For Ada* encrypted document, the one on the disk that David had given her the night of his final dinner party. Then she had returned the original to its place in between the pages of the dictionary on her closet shelf, along with the train ticket and the printout of the strange document she had found on David's computer.

The other two copies of the disk, she decided, should be dispersed for protection. One she kept at David's house. And the other she carried with her at all times. She had begun to see the *For Ada* disk as the pin of a grenade, an explosion waiting to happen; she felt certain that if only she could decrypt it, all the secrets of David's life would unfurl themselves before her, like falling dominoes. She clung to this faith: That David had a plan. That he had meant, all along, to tell her.

Aside from working together on this decryption, what she and Gregory talked about was mainly impersonal: in addition to codes and cryptography and cryptanalysis and computers, they discovered that they had in common a great love of the *Star Wars* movies (one of David's only concessions to popular culture; he had taken her to every one in the cinema near the lab, and bought them a large popcorn and Raisinets to split), and the *Lord of the Rings* books— also favorites of David's—and *Hardy Boys* mysteries. Gregory would not admit to liking *Nancy Drew* books, though she argued that they were better. He had read many of the books on programming that Liston kept around the house, and from them he had taught himself the fundamentals. Outside the house, he read everything he could find on biology and physics and the cosmos, but thus far he had limited himself to what was available at the Queen of Angels Lower

School library, which offered only the equivalent of children's ency-
clopedias, along with a series for Catholic children called *Let's Learn
About* . . . He showed Ada one of these books, a slim tome on the life
cycle of plants, and she tossed it across the room dramatically in
disgust. She was showing off—the action did not come naturally to
her—but his eyes widened, and Ada imagined that she had earned
his respect.

It became clear to her that Liston, out of a benevolent desire to
allow her children to have "normal" childhoods (perhaps, in fact, taking into consideration Ada as a counter-example), had inadvertently
deprived Gregory of an education in the areas that interested him.
What he knew about computer science he had largely taught himself; when he asked his mother questions about her work, she would
answer him kindly but concisely, never in enough detail to satisfy
him. With three other children, a grandchild, and a full-time job,
Liston had not had the time that David had had to transfer what he
knew to his offspring. Liston's main concern with Gregory was that
he spend more time outdoors, make friends, have fun—goals for her
child that had never crossed David's mind as something for Ada to
work toward.

Now Ada had a pupil, and, although she did not admit it, she
relished the task before her. She corrected mistakes in Gregory's
thinking; she taught him what she could about programming and
cryptography and cryptanalysis. She assigned him books to read, just
as David had done for her, curating them to align with what she perceived to be Gregory's interests.

He was a quick but often recalcitrant learner, occasionally insisting that Ada was incorrect on a point that she knew to be true, or
asking her questions she could not answer and then triumphantly
crowing that he had stumped her.

As she got to know him better, it occurred to her why he had
such difficulty at school. There was a certain amount of arbitrari-
ness to his persecution, yes; he had been designated early on as the

lowest-ranking member of his class, and that was a difficult role to escape. Yet Ada, although her tenure at Queen of Angels had been short, had already learned certain truths that seemed to perpetually elude him. One was that simple words were better. She concealed her vocabulary most of the time, but Gregory, when spoken to or yelled at in the hallway, responded in words and sentences that were at times positively Shakespearean. *Coward*, he would mutter, or *fool*, or *imbecile*. Once he called one of his tormentors a *callow dog*. The idea, especially for boys, was either to pretend you hadn't heard what was shouted at you or to retaliate with strong, unexpected physical force. These were the only good options. But Gregory chose neither of them, and so was punished for it. In turn, he often acted unpleasantly, which further fueled his oppressors, and allowed them to justify their behavior toward him. Had he been in the Upper School with William, his brother's presence might have leant him some respect or protection; but to the eighth-graders at the Lower School, William Liston seemed very far away, and only served as a reminder of everything that Gregory lacked—presumably even to Gregory himself. Therefore he slunk through the hallways with his head down, looking up only to snarl back a response to someone who had lobbed an insult at him.

His unpleasantness often extended even toward Ada. "Ha-ha," he said to her sometimes, pointing a small finger in her direction. He did this when she was wrong on any point. It was maddening, and Ada often had the urge to walk away from him, to leave him once more to his own devices. But she never did; for in certain ways her interactions with Gregory brought back to her a piece of her former self, and this, to Ada, was invaluable.

She began to let Gregory come with her to the Fields Corner library after school, where she had been working, with Miss Holmes's guidance, on going through their collection of the *New York Times* on microfilm—specifically the society pages from the 1920s, '30s, and

'40s—in the hope of finding more information on the Sibelius family, and why and how David might have connected himself to them.

But the society pages, thus far, had yielded nothing. Ron Loughner, thought Ada, was mistaken. There were plenty of Astors and Vanderbilts and Rockefellers and Whitneys and Morgans at every party; and although certain branches of the Sibelius family turned up here and there, J. Fairfax and Isabelle were nowhere to be found. Nor was the real David Sibelius—whom she had begun to think of as "other-David" in her mind, being unable to imagine her own father being called anything else. Certainly not *Harold*—a name that did not, she thought, fit him in the least. She scanned hundreds, and then thousands, of newspaper pages, looking for any image of the same fair-haired young man with a mole on his cheek that Ellen Palmer had claimed was David Sibelius. Ada would believe it, she decided, when she saw a picture of him, printed in an official source, with a caption beneath. Together she and Gregory made headway through a decade of society pages.

On the opposing front, Miss Holmes had not yet heard back from the librarian in Olathe, though she had called once, after two weeks, to check in again, and had left a message.

Gregory always left earlier than Ada, so that they would not return to the house at the same time. And one day, as she was walking home just after dusk, Ada saw Mrs. O'Keeffe, their neighbor, on her porch. It was an unusual sighting: it was early December, and typically she went inside for the winter in late October and did not emerge again until May. But it was unusually warm that day, and the first snow had not yet fallen. One brave cricket croaked its song nearby. Mrs. O'Keeffe was still wearing her dark glasses, though the sun was down, and sitting in a rocking chair. She was wearing a blanket that covered her lap, and a puffy pink jacket that Ada had never seen before: perhaps a gift from her daughter Mary, who was a regular presence at the house.

Suddenly Ada was inspired.

She approached the porch, calling out to Mrs. O'Keeffe loudly so that she would not be startled. But Mrs. O'Keeffe seemed almost as if she had been expecting someone.

"It's Ada," she said, when she reached the top step of the porch, and Mrs. O'Keeffe rocked slowly in her chair and nodded.

"Yes," she said, "I know who you are."

"Nice out," said Ada, who was having trouble beginning.

"Oh, yes," said Mrs. O'Keeffe. And then: "How's your father, dear? I haven't seen him in so long."

"He's fine," said Ada quickly. She could not tell how much the neighbors knew about their situation. Many of them, including Mrs. O'Keeffe, had seen him the day the firemen were called, covered in a blanket like a child on the front lawn. Furthermore, Liston was social, and loved gossip; but she was also intensely loyal when it came to both Ada and David. Ada could not decide which of these two characteristics might influence Liston more.

"Actually, I was wondering," said Ada. "I mean, I had a question."

"Go ahead."

"I was wondering if you knew his parents," said Ada. "When you worked in New York."

"The Sibeliuses?" said Mrs. O'Keeffe, and Ada nodded, and then said, "Yes," in case Mrs. O'Keeffe hadn't seen her. Her head was turned vaguely in the wrong direction, five or ten degrees off from where Ada was standing.

"I knew of them," said Mrs. O'Keeffe. "Of course, I left New York in 1923, just a few years after they were married, I suppose. Before your father would have been born. I worked for a family called Baker. Their house was on Gramercy Park, not far from the Sibeliuses, and it's fair to say we all gossiped among ourselves. The staff, I mean."

"What were they like? His parents," asked Ada.

Mrs. O'Keeffe paused.

"What were they *meant* to be like, you mean?" There was still a very faint trace of an Irish accent in her voice, which, David had pointed out, presented itself more obviously when she was speaking about her former life.

"I guess so."

"Oh, now, I really couldn't say. I didn't know them personally, you see."

Ada was disappointed. "Oh," she said. "Okay."

Mrs. O'Keeffe turned her head ever so slightly to the left, so that she was looking more directly at Ada.

"Why do you ask, dear?" she said.

"I'm just," said Ada. "I'm just trying to find out more about his history.

"He's not doing well," she added.

And this seemed to do the trick.

"Well," said Mrs. O'Keeffe, lowering her voice, "if you want to know what I heard—don't tell your father I told you—but there was a sort of scandal."

"A scandal?" said Ada.

"Yes, dear. Before your father was born, of course. Something to do with a lady and Mr. Sibelius."

"Oh," said Ada, embarrassed.

"*She sued him*," whispered Mrs. O'Keeffe. "For defamation of character. In the papers and everything. This wasn't a lady you'd want to have over for dinner. Poor Mrs. Sibelius took to her bed," she added.

"Do you know when that happened?" asked Ada.

"Let's see, now," said Mrs. O'Keeffe, putting a trembling hand to her cheek. "Directly before I was married and left: 1923. Spring of 1923, most likely. Of course, this gave the maids on the block plenty to talk about," she said.

When she had finished speaking, she drifted into quietness again, and at last Ada thanked her, and told her good night.

"Now don't tell your father I told you this," said Mrs. O'Keeffe. "If he'd wanted you to know, he'd have told you himself, wouldn't he?"

The next day, at the library, Ada told Miss Holmes what she had learned, and their focus shifted. Instead of looking at the society pages, she and Gregory spent the afternoon scanning the *Times* for articles from the spring of 1923.

Occasionally Miss Holmes stopped by to check on their progress. There were two microfilm readers at the Fields Corner branch and they had been monopolizing them for days. Fortunately, there was not much in the way of competition.

At 4:45, fifteen minutes before the library was due to close, Gregory held up his left hand. Ada saw him in her peripheral vision.

"What is it?" she asked.

"Come look," said Gregory. His face was pink with pleasure: he had found something.

There, on the screen in front of him, was a headline: "Miss Polly Howard Files Suit against Sibelius Heir." And on the next page, a clear black-and-white image of a man emerging from a courtroom, flashes going off as reporters swarmed him. His face was turned directly toward the camera, and he was looking at it with palpable contempt, the edges of his mouth turned down, his chin tilted upward.

Ada considered it. From her backpack, she produced the photograph of David and his parents from the studio in Olathe.

There was no question: the man in the newspaper looked nothing like David. He was the twin, instead, of the boy in the photograph Ellen Palmer had produced. J. Fairfax Sibelius, in the newspaper, was short, bulldoggish, heavy-jowled, and fair; the man in the Olathe photograph was tall and thin and dark, like David.

Lying in her bed that night, Ada could not sleep. She was trying not to despair; but it seemed that the more they researched David, the less of his life felt understandable and true. It seemed as if her questions were growing in number while her answers shrank. It had already been three weeks since Miss Holmes had called the librarian in Olathe, and one since she had left a second message, but they had received no information about Harold Canady. Perhaps, she thought, it was simply a nonsense name: several syllables David had babbled in a row. The disease made him seem to speak sometimes in tongues.

The most important piece of unsolved evidence she had now seemed to her to be the disk that David had given her, and as she looked into the dark of her room, she decided that it was, perhaps, time to call in the experts. There was nothing more to lose.

Frank Halbert was, David always liked to say, more of a worker than a thinker. "Every lab needs one of them, though," he said. It was not surprising, therefore, that on Saturday, Frank was the first to arrive at the Steiner Lab, a puzzled look on his face.

Ada was waiting outside. She no longer had a key, and she did not know the new guard who had started working since she'd last been to the lab.

"Hi," said Ada. It had been six months since the last time she'd seen Frank, when he came over to Liston's for dinner. It had not been so very long before that that she had spent every day working side by side with him—with everyone at the lab. But now she felt shy around him. She had heard from Liston that he'd gotten engaged recently, and she wanted to tell him congratulations, but she lacked the courage and the poise.

"Hi, Ada!" said Frank, brightly. He stood back, regarding her for a moment. "It was a nice surprise to hear from you," he said. "Do you want to go up? The others should be here soon."

Ada had also invited Hayato and Charles-Robert. She had specifically not invited Liston. On the phone, the night before, with each of the other members of the lab, she had asked them not to tell her. She had told them all that she would explain tomorrow.

So, that morning, when Liston had announced that she would

be going to a mall in the suburbs with Matty and a friend, Ada was relieved: she would not have to make up an excuse regarding her whereabouts. And when Liston asked her, hopefully, if she wanted to come, Ada had declined, citing homework.

"Okay, honey," said Liston. "Tell me if you need anything, all right?"

As she left, Ada felt a slight pang of guilt, or confusion, about Liston. At times, she forgot that she was still mad at her; in the kitchen, Liston would tease her and she would laugh easily. Or in the morning, Liston would leave an encouraging note on the counter, lumping Ada in warmly with the rest of her brood, telling them all to have a nice day, and Ada would read it gratefully, happy to be included, happy to be part of a large loud family. And then, inevitably, she would catch herself. She would call herself a traitor; and she would remember Liston's traitorousness, how quickly she had accepted the idea that David had been lying, how dismissive she had been of any argument to the contrary. *Misguided*, Liston often said, when describing David's actions. But that was just as bad as calling him deceitful. Worse, perhaps; for it implied some plasticity in his character, some weakness. Yes: she was glad that Liston was not there with them at the lab that morning. The existence of the floppy disk was a secret she had been keeping to herself; if it yielded nothing helpful, she did not want Liston to know.

The lab had changed very little since David's retirement. Liston, preferring her office over anyone else's, hadn't moved. Instead, they had simply turned David's office into a smaller seminar room for meetings with the group. There was a table in the center now, but everything else was the same: there, in the corner, was David's desk, a new Mac resting on it now.

It was in this room that they all gathered, which felt to Ada something like time travel. The smell of it: warm electronics and wood. Even the crack in the ceiling was familiar to her.

She sat facing the three of them: Frank, Hayato, and Charles-Robert, who was regarding her with something like bemusement.

"So," he said to her, "you look different than the last time we saw you, madam."

"Thanks," said Ada, not knowing what else to say. She was embarrassed. She had been wearing her hair differently, at the encouragement of Theresa. She had forgotten to wear her glasses; she had still been doing without them whenever she could, and that day she walked out of the house without them.

"How have you been, Ada? How's David?" asked Hayato, kindly.

"Okay," said Ada. Against her will she felt a tremble in her chin. And she realized that she felt betrayed by not just Liston, but all of them, all of them. Her friends. Something like her family. Where had they been?

The three of them glanced at each other. They were sitting across the table from her, three in a row, so that she felt as if they were interviewing her.

"I'm sorry we haven't been in touch," said Frank. "We just— weren't sure how to react, in light of . . ."

"It's okay," Ada said again. She did not want to hear what they had to say. She had not yet taken her jacket off, her blue ski parka, and it was making her warm. It bunched up around her shoulders as she sat against the hard back of the chair. In her pocket, she touched the four corners of the floppy disk she had brought with her. It was one of the copies she had made. The original disk that David had given her was still at Liston's, in its dictionary, for safekeeping.

She explained her request straightforwardly, and all three of them sat up with interest. She could have predicted it: this group had always loved a puzzle.

"When did David give it to you?" asked Hayato.

"Over two years ago," said Ada. "The night after the last grad-student dinner he hosted."

She held it out, and Hayato accepted it. If anyone could decrypt it, it was Hayato: he and David had shared a love of puzzles and codes, had tried, over the years, to stump each other dozens of times. Neither had ever been successful. Often a triumphant shout would come from one or the other of their offices, toward the end of a workday, and the other would rush in to inspect the solution. "Eureka!" Liston would say sarcastically. "Do they ever work?"

The four of them migrated to the computer in the corner, which started up with a speed that surprised Ada. It was Apple's latest model: in the time since David's retirement, the world of technology had already, she thought, left her behind.

She double-clicked the icon of the text file and it opened to display its contents, the single string of letters:

DHARSNELXRHQHLTWJFOLKTWDURSZJZCMILWFT ALVUHVZRDLDEYIXQ.

Silence.

"That's it?" said Charles-Robert. "Just that text file?"

"That's it," said Ada.

"What did he say when he gave it to you?" asked Frank.

"He said it was a puzzle," said Ada. "He said it was solvable, but it might take some time to figure out. And that I shouldn't let it get in the way of my other work."

"Hmmm," said Hayato. All three of them were leaning down behind her, reading over her shoulders. Ada could feel their interest: already their eyes were scanning it, looking for patterns, for inconsistencies, for the frequency of each letter.

"Why didn't he just write it down on a piece of paper?" asked Charles-Robert. "Why put something so short on a disk?"

"I don't know," said Ada. "To protect it?" But it was a good question: one she had wondered about as well.

Ada got up from her chair and moved to the table. She let them sit, three together in front of the screen. Frank wrote the letters down on a piece of paper and went to his office. Hayato sat where he was, gazing at the screen. Charles-Robert got a pad of lab stationery and scratched away at it for a while.

Half an hour went by. Ada worked, too, at a piece of paper, on which she wrote the string of letters from memory.

Hayato was the first to speak. "Is it possible," he said, hesitantly, "that he was already . . . experiencing symptoms? When he made this?"

"It's possible," Ada admitted. She was hovering on the verge of disappointment. She had hoped, she realized, that she would be leaving the lab that day with an answer.

"I'm not saying it's not solvable," said Hayato. "But on first glance it looks incredibly difficult. The fact that it's so short, for one thing, means that patterns will be difficult to discern. We can probably create a program that might give it a go. But I think there's a distinct possibility that this was made with the equivalent of a one-time pad," he said. "Which means that a program won't be able to solve it. Not this century, anyway."

"Okay," said Ada quietly. She looked back and forth from Frank to Charles-Robert. But they looked similarly confounded. "Okay," she said again. "Don't worry about it."

"Did he give you anything that could have functioned as a one-time pad?" asked Charles-Robert. "A different string of numbers or letters?"

"I don't think so," said Ada. She felt despair coming over her. The truth was that David had given her any number of such things: he had constantly given her codes and puzzles, little bits of tangled language that, formerly, it had been her great joy to figure out. Any one of them, she thought, might be the one-time pad that would solve David's last puzzle.

"We'll all keep working on it," said Hayato.

"Are you sure we can't tell Liston?" said Frank. "She's good at this stuff."

"Not yet," said Ada quickly. She tried to think of an explanation she could offer, but she came up with none. She was angry: that was all. She couldn't tell them this. "I'll tell her soon," she added.

She realized, as she was leaving, that she did not want to leave. She breathed in, deeply, before she walked through the door; and had a sharp and sudden memory of the last time she left, the night of the retirement party. Only that time, it had been with David. And that time, David had still been himself.

To Ada's surprise, when she walked back into the house that evening, Melanie, Janice, and Theresa were standing in the kitchen with Liston and William and some of his friends. The girls were wearing bright, absurd dresses: pinks and yellows and greens, quite different from the muted colors of the Queen of Angels uniform that she saw them in daily. The boys were wearing tight jeans and fat high-top sneakers and oversized white button-downs. Liston had a camera out, a clunky Polaroid that she had had since the sixties, and was flapping a newly printed photograph in front of her face.

"We were wondering where you were!" Liston said to her, and it occurred to Ada suddenly that it was the night of the dance the school called Jamboree. It drew from Catholic high schools all over the city, and it was the first year that her group of friends, as ninth-graders, were eligible to go. The girls at Queen of Angels had been discussing their outfits for weeks.

"I was visiting David," Ada said, lying, and Liston opened and closed her mouth, as if deciding against a reply.

"Run and get changed," she said instead. "It's 8:00 already."

The teenagers in the room looked at her blankly. Ada had the uneasy feeling that they had been relieved she wasn't home; that they had been hoping to make an escape before she walked in. She had not been spending much time with them in recent weeks; her trips to the library with Gregory had occupied her afternoons and weekends.

"You could even wear that, if you wanted," said William unexpectedly. "You look nice."

Ada looked down at herself. She was still wearing her blue ski parka and, under that, a pair of new jeans that Liston had bought her. Ordinarily, she would have floated on this praise for weeks. But her mind was hazy with thoughts of David.

"I don't feel well," said Ada. "I think I'll stay home."

Liston looked pained.

"Are you sure, baby?" she asked. "You sure you don't want to go out and have fun with your friends?"

Ada nodded. The boys looked indifferent; the girls looked relieved. Now that Melanie and her friends had achieved their aim—now that Melanie was safely on the arm of William, her rightful partner— their use for Ada had lessened. She still sat with them at lunch, but her role was secondary. She mainly stayed quiet around them, and she had a vague idea that she was specifically not invited to go into town with them on the occasions that they went, or to hang out with them in the Woods, several small groves of trees that provided meager cover for the hill the neighborhood was named for, and for the drinking and carousing that went on at the flat top of it.

Quickly, the group put on their jackets and said goodbye. Then they filed out the front door, laughing, giddy, leaving Ada and Liston alone in the kitchen.

Liston looked at her brightly, held her hands out, palms up.

"Well!" she said. "Looks like it's just us chickens for the evening." Ada nodded.

"Can I get you anything, honey?" Liston asked. "What kind of sick are you feeling?"

"Just a headache," she mumbled, and told Liston that she would get herself a glass of water and go to bed.

"How's David doing?" she asked.

"Okay," said Ada.

On her way out of the room she looked once, over her shoulder, at Liston, who was looking through the windows in the kitchen door at the group of teenagers as they disappeared down the street. She was holding in her hand a tall glass of the Crystal Light she drank compulsively, trying to lose weight for indeterminate reasons. She was only the slightest bit plump. Did Liston want a boyfriend? Ada wondered suddenly. She had never before considered the question. Standing at the door, holding her glass to her chest, she looked lonely. Ada felt a flutter of remorse. She could go back to her; they could watch a movie together, make the low-fat popcorn that Liston loved. But there were too many secrets between them, now; Ada's reticence about her father made conversations with Liston difficult. Later she would attribute her hesitancy to embrace Liston completely to superstition: she thought somehow, irrationally, that David would sense it. She imagined that, in order to accept Liston's outstretched hand, she would have to first release David's. And that doing so would send him plummeting downward into whatever maw was opening beneath him.

Upstairs, Ada knocked softly at Gregory's door, listening first to make sure that Liston hadn't followed her. Matty was at a friend's house for a sleepover.

Gregory opened it. He was in need of a haircut, as Liston often reminded him, and his brown hair was matted wildly on one side of his head, as if he had been lying on it.

"Did they leave you behind?" he whispered, and Ada told him that it had been her choice to stay home.

"I'm sick," she said. "I don't feel well."

"Oh," he whispered. "Okay." He still lacked any sense of tact, and he continued to be persecuted for this at school—recently she had seen him being pursued hotly down a sidewalk by two seventh-graders, the laces of his shoes flapping wildly—but she had grown to like him, or at least tolerate him. In certain ways he even reminded her of David, in his bluntness, his matter-of-factness. Perhaps he was what David had been like as a child. *Things will be better for you later*, she often wanted to tell him. *When you're an adult.* (Ada hoped she could apply this logic to herself as well, but she was less certain; she often felt as if there was something fundamentally incorrect about her, as if she were caught between two worlds, a citizen of neither.)

Gregory retreated to his bed, where he lay down and crossed one knee over the other in the air. "Are you gonna come in?" he asked her.

She was going to tell him about her day at the lab. The one-time pad theory proposed by Hayato. But she changed her mind. It all felt ridiculous to her, suddenly: the code and the research that they had been doing and the many, many lies her father had told. For the first time, she allowed herself to articulate a terrible thought: What if David, simply, was a fraud? What if he was just a con man, a huckster, a liar? What if he had deceived all of them, everyone he was ever close to, even Ada, without compunction?

She felt abruptly tired.

"I think I'll read in my room," she said, and left.

Instead, in her room, she lay awake, staring into the dark, listening to the sounds from the street outside. From Liston's house she could often hear the voices of local teenagers drifting back to her from the Woods or the tennis courts nearby. When they got loud enough she went to her window and looked out.

It was 11:00 at night. On the street below the house, streams of teenagers were walking back from the dance. She recognized some of them; others she thought she had never seen. All of them were headed eastward, toward the Woods.

"*Shhhhhhhh*," said one to her friends, holding a gloved finger to her lips. They were carrying in their arms the jackets that their parents had made them bring. They should have been wearing them. In the light from the streetlamps on the block, their neon dresses looked incandescent. One of the girls tripped over the curb and caught herself with the gracefulness of an athlete. She doubled over, her hands covering her mouth, laughing. It was cold outside, and the old windows in Liston's house let in the chill air through their seams. She held a hand up to the draft. She had the sudden urge to walk outside.

Everyone in Liston's household was asleep by then: she could tell by the stillness. The television was still on, which meant that Liston had probably fallen asleep in front of it while waiting for William to return—a problem she often had. And William was very good at sneaking in unnoticed and then claiming he had simply forgotten to wake her up.

Quietly, Ada opened the closet in the hallway and pulled a knit black hat down over her ears, and then put on her parka. David had bought it for her, for skiing, two years ago. She had grown taller recently, she realized, and her wrists now stuck out of it. She zipped it up and held her hands out from her sides to prevent the material from swishing as she walked.

She crept past the TV room, catching a glimpse of Liston in profile. There she was, in her armchair, angled toward the door so as to see her oldest son come home. She was tipped back in it, her tired feet in the air, her mouth open slightly, her face turned to the side.

The back door made the least noise—Ada had caught William coming in and out of it, late, at least twice—so she exited that way, onto the patio. It was here that, hidden among the trees at the base of the yard, she had seen Liston as she spoke on the phone to David. She remembered Gregory, moving through the lit upstairs of the house; she remembered William coming home, after curfew as usual, from wherever he had been. How little she had known of any of them. How little, then, she had known of David.

She paused for a moment in Liston's backyard, listening, and then walked resolutely eastward toward the hill, through the backyards of her neighbors. Her classmates' voices echoed back to her. Across the quiet neighborhood, they sounded ghostly and strange. Once or twice she thought she heard William's voice, but she was not certain.

At the edge of the last backyard was a fence that shielded it from Grampian Way, the road that bordered the park, and she slipped around it, avoiding the streetlamps to the extent that she could. The lights of the tennis courts across from her had been turned off for the night, and teenagers slipped up the hill behind them like shades, toward the top of the rock.

Ada had been to its peak only once or twice, during daylight hours, with David, who liked the view of the Boston skyline. She mainly avoided it now, knowing that it was the territory of the teenagers who populated the neighborhood, afraid to intrude. She had not known any better when she was younger. She and David had been wrong, she realized, about so many things; and she experienced a retroactive embarrassment for them both. She walked quickly, with her head down, hoping that her dark hat and parka would adequately conceal her identity from the little groups across the street.

She found a point of entry into the Woods that deviated from the paths that most of the rest of them used. It was steep and rocky, and she had not realized how dark it would be under the cover of the trees. She could not see the branches before her. She held her hands ahead of her, pushing brush out of the way. Every now and then, through the foliage above her, she caught a glimpse of the moon, still and round and white.

At times she heard a shout or a peal of laughter, and she made her way toward these sounds, breathing more heavily now, stumbling once or twice. When the clearing at the top of the little hill came into view, she stayed behind a nearby tree, hugging it. She peered out from behind it.

A small fire had been lit, and teenagers stood around it with cans of beer and bottles of vodka or gin in their hands. Many of them held lit cigarettes. As they gestured, small red trails of light arced through the night air. Ada was far afield from them; she both did and did not wish to be a part of the little circles she beheld.

She looked at every face in turn until she spied first Janice, and then Melanie, and then William, who had his arms raised in a kind of victorious stance, the front of him lit up orange by the flames. He stood there for longer than she imagined he would, his face turned upward toward the sky, and Melanie reached her arms around him and hugged him sideways. He stumbled slightly, held the bottle in his hands to his mouth, tipped it up for several beats. There was something very beautiful about the tableau and something very feral: it occurred to Ada suddenly that this—*this*—had been happening for centuries, millennia, the fire and the wide-open sky and the liquid that dropped with a burn down the throat of William and his companions. It was so human, so alive; she was touched by it all in a way she could not explain. She had never been so close to this sort of wildness. It frightened her and drew her in all at once.

I know them, thought Ada. *I could go to them.*

But she was not like them, did not understand their hearts and minds, the compasses inside them that governed what they said and did.

She held her breath.

Footsteps marched across the dead dry leaves, and a senior boy came into sight, paused, stared at her for a moment.

She could not tell if he recognized her. Her hat and parka made her genderless and strange. She was facing away from the only source of light. She looked down at the ground.

"What are you doing?" he asked her. His name was Bob Conley. He was a good student. He played on the basketball team and dated a girl named Heather. He had a brother named Chuck and a sister named Patty. He was a friend of William's; he had been at Liston's house once or twice before. That she had learned all of these things about him, about all of these people, in less than two years—that they knew nothing about her—pained her suddenly. The amount of space this knowledge occupied in her brain. She missed the knowledge that David had given her: facts that were concrete, substantial, productive.

Ada looked back at Bob Conley, blinking. For a moment she hesitated, said nothing. And then she turned and ran.

At the base of the hill, she saw two police cars slinking quietly toward the Woods, up Grampian, their lights and sirens off. She paused, staying still, hoping that her dark clothing would disguise her. It worked. But soon, she knew, teenagers on top of the hill would come streaming downward as quickly as they had run to the top. Soon William Liston would come in from his long night out, tiptoeing, as Ada had done earlier, past his mother, and then falling into a long and heavy sleep, dreaming of Melanie, or of the fire at the top of the hill.

When Ada reached Liston's house, she stopped outside it for a moment and then, impulsively, turned back and went to David's house. She wanted to be inside her old bedroom, inside her old twin bed, just for an hour or two; she wanted to make it up with sheets that had belonged to David before she was born. She wanted to fall asleep fast and hard inside it.

It was the seventh of December, and all the houses on the block had Christmas lights strung up in great number. Liston's looked nice that year: she had paid her boys five dollars each to decorate the porch. Only David's house was devoid of lights, and because of this it looked desolate and unmerry. David would have been horrified, thought Ada.

Inside the house, it was just barely warmer than it had been on the street. But it still had its familiar smell, its David-smell, the smell of her own history. She walked up the stairs in the dark, to the linen closet in the upstairs hallway, still full of mismatched ancient sheets and blankets, a down comforter that David used to place on her bed at the start of each winter, a shield against the cold. She gathered this, along with several sheets and pillowcases, and brought them into her bedroom, where she closed the curtains. They were slightly translucent; they had never been excellent at keeping out the morning sunlight. She hesitated, therefore, before turning her bedside lamp on, wondering whether the neighbors would notice a dim glow through the blinds; deciding, finally, that all of them were asleep.

By the muted yellow glow of the lamp, she caught a glimpse of herself in the mirror above her dresser: she looked spectral and pale, her eyes with dark circles beneath them, her shoulders still rising and falling from the exertion of her wild sprint home. She took her hat off and let her hair fall down from it. It looked dark and shapeless, longer than it had ever been before. David used to take her regularly to the same barber he used, an old man who trimmed her hair into a neat bob every other month, but by then she had not had it cut for a year and a half. More. She didn't want to ask Liston about it. She thought sometimes about cutting it herself.

She dressed her ancient mattress, shivering in the cold. She took her shoes off. She unzipped her parka and let it fall to the floor. Beneath it, she was wearing a sweater and jeans, and she took these off, too, and stood in her bra and underwear, regarding herself for a moment in the mirror. She was shaking with cold, but she made herself stand there, and considered her body. She was average, she thought, in all ways. Average in height and weight. Brown-haired and brown-eyed. She pulled back her hair at the sides of her head and noted that her ears protruded slightly. Her belly button was closer to one hip than the other. Her arms were long and thin.

She turned sideways. She took a breath and pulled her stomach in toward her spine: something she had never thought to do before attending Queen of Angels, but now did regularly. The shape of her stomach had begun to bother her excessively. Recently she had been thinking of herself the way a mechanic thought of a car, as a collection of parts, each of which had a particular flaw: convex stomach, protrusive ears, dry elbows, flat feet, thin lips, fleshy knees. When she thought about it for long enough, she could identify some error in every part of herself, some mistake in her code that she would change if she could.

When she was finished with her examination, she tucked herself into her old bed and shivered into sleep.

She woke up to the sound of the kitchen door rattling. It stopped for a moment, and then resumed; someone was knocking at the door. Her heartbeat surged. For a moment she did not know where she was. She sat up straight in bed, slipped her feet into her shoes, in case she needed to run. She was in her bra and underwear. She pulled the comforter around herself; she wore it like a robe.

She had fallen asleep with the light on. She switched it off.

Then, as quietly as possible, she rose and tiptoed into David's old room—ghostly, filled still with memories of him—and pressed her forehead to his western window, out of which she could see down to the driveway, to the step outside the kitchen door.

William Liston stood there, his head bowed, looking down at the earth. Ada could not see his face; she recognized him by his jacket, by his stance. He was alone. He looked up at the door again, stepped toward it, knocked loudly a third time.

Ada opened the window. A gust of freezing air rushed in.

"William," she said, in a stage whisper. He looked up at her, confused.

"Hey," he said. "Can you come down for a sec?"

She dressed herself as quickly as she could, glanced once in the mirror, and ran downstairs. Then she opened the kitchen door. There was William, on the threshold, one arm clutched to his side, as if he were concealing something under his jacket.

He did not ask if he could come in; he walked forward and closed the door behind him with a foot.

Her heart was pounding with an uncomfortable force. It thudded against her breastbone so quickly and powerfully that she wondered if it was visible to William, through her sweater, even in the dark room. She put her right hand to it instinctively, as if she were reciting a pledge.

William said nothing for a moment, only looked at her. There was a slight sway in his stance that she told herself must be drunkenness, though she only knew this from movies. His smell reached her suddenly: something bitter and woodsy and acrid, alcohol and smoke.

"I thought you might be here," he said. "I saw your light."

Her voice caught in her throat.

"Do you mind if I come in for a second?" he asked, which did not make sense. He was already in. Still, she shook her head no.

He took two steps forward and looked around the kitchen. Had he ever been inside David's house before? She couldn't remember; maybe when she was very small.

"You come here a lot," said William. "I've seen you walking here."

"Not a lot," said Ada, defensively.

William shrugged. "It's cool," he said.

"Where's Melanie?" asked Ada.

"She had to get home," he said.

He walked out of the kitchen then and into the dining room. "Can you show me around?" he asked her. Her eyes had adjusted; she could see everything fairly well, though the only light came in from the streetlamps outside. So she did: she took him down the hallway, in silence, speaking only the names of the rooms. And then she walked up the stairs with him, and named those rooms as well. Her room was last, and she paused in the hallway, embarrassed suddenly. It was both childish and old-fashioned, her room: her austere little bed with its ancient comforter; her bedside lamp, which was shaped like an apple tree, with little Hummel figurines running round and around its base. The furniture was formal and strange, nothing like the modern furniture that Liston had bought for her children, and that Ada, at that time, preferred.

"Is this your room?" asked William, and Ada nodded.

He nudged open the door and made a slow circle around the little room. His head was inches from the ceiling; he was too large for the space. She stood in the threshold. The single lamp cast a tall shadow of William that moved along the walls as he paced. He ended at the bed and sat down, perched on the edge of it, his long legs bent deeply at the knee to accommodate its lowness. He put his elbows on his thighs and gazed down at the floor.

He looked very old to her suddenly: a man. Much more grown-up than she was. Ada marveled that Melanie was his girlfriend. How courageous she was, to be with someone William's age. She glanced at him and then away. He was even more handsome than she had remembered. Everything about him was sculpted finely and perfectly, as if designed in advance by an architect: much different, she thought, than her own flawed, imprecise features. She would have changed nothing about him. He was finished.

He unzipped his coat halfway and then took a bottle out from inside it. It was tall and rectangular and the label was facing away from her. A clear liquid occupied the bottom third. He drank from it and then held it out to her.

She did not know which was worse: to say yes or no. This was an opportunity he was giving her. To say no would have cemented her forever, she thought, as an outsider. She couldn't say no. But could she say yes, and have it seem natural? Lacking any alternative, it was a chance she had to take. Besides, she had had alcohol before: David had given her wine, she reminded herself, and he always let her take sips of the cocktails the two of them made for guests.

Ada walked toward him and took the bottle. She did as he had done: she held it to her lips and took a healthy swig, about as much as she might have taken from a gin and tonic. But this was different, and it burned painfully in her esophagus and settled roughly into her stomach. She immediately felt her joints and muscles loosen. She sat down next to William on the bed.

"Thanks for taking care of Matty," said William. "I know you help him with his homework and stuff. So thanks."

"I like it," said Ada.

"He loves you," said William. "He always asks me stuff about you. Since our dad's gone," he said, but he stopped halfway through his sentence, and did not pick it up again. He drank.

Ada nodded. She noticed a slight elision between his words, a blending-together, final consonants attaching themselves to succeeding vowels. She closed her eyes briefly, letting what he had said echo in her mind, noting the particulars of his accent, like Liston's, and his intonation. And that sentence: *He loves you.*

William tipped the bottle back again, showing his white teeth briefly when he was done, running a hand through the light hair that had fallen down across his brow. Then he handed it to her. She did the same. It was gin: she saw the label.

"Bob Conley told me he saw you in the Woods," said William.

Ada looked at him.

"He said you were hiding behind a tree," he said. A slight smile was coming across his face, now, and Ada dropped her shoulders in embarrassment. So this was why he was here: to make fun of her.

"Were you spying on me?" he asked her.

Ada briefly considered the idea of denying it all. *I've been here the whole night,* she could say. She could look at him like he was crazy. But in the corner of the room something caught her eye: it was a pile on the floor of her parka and hat and gloves. This, combined with Bob Conley's testimony, was probably too much evidence to deny.

"I was just going for a walk," Ada said. "I didn't know you guys were there."

He smiled briefly, looked away.

He took another sip. He handed her the bottle. She took another sip.

"Are you gonna tell my mom?" he asked her, with a tone in his voice that sounded like teasing. "I know you guys are pals."

Ungracefully, he unzipped his jacket the rest of the way and tried to extract himself from it. His wrists were stuck; his hands weren't working. Ada reached out and held a wristband in place while he wrenched his arm out of it. He thanked her politely.

Then he said, "You used to spy on us before you lived at our house."

Ada looked at him.

"I saw you," said William. "Once or twice, in our backyard."

Ada shook her head. A lump had started in her throat and she willed it backward, swallowing hard. It seemed unfair, somehow, that he had seen her, but she was too tired to deny anything. The gin had loosened her mind and her body and a dull ache had begun to move through her. She was hungry and cold and alone.

"What were you doing back there?" he asked her.

"I don't know," said Ada. "I'm sorry."

She didn't tell him that she dreamed about him every night: that it was William she had sought when she made those lonely nighttime walks. Perhaps he knew. Perhaps he had a sense that everyone, everywhere, loved and desired him. Did people like William Liston know this? They must, she thought.

They said nothing for a while. They drank again. Normally the silence would have bothered her, but it felt comfortable to her, somehow. She smiled to herself. Why did she worry so much? she wondered. She could say anything she wanted.

"You all seemed so normal. I wanted to see what it would be like to have a normal family," she said.

He laughed. "Normal," he said. "Nobody's normal. We're probably, like, the weirdest family there is. I guess you know that by now."

"Except for my family," Ada said. "We're weirder. I'm the weirdest," she said. But there was too much truth to it, and she wished immediately that she had not said it. Besides, the word *family* had never seemed to apply to her and David. They were not a family; they were a pair. And now they weren't even that.

William laughed again, and then was quiet. "You're funny," he pronounced finally. "You're smart, too. I think you're probably smarter than anyone I've ever met."

"No, I'm not," said Ada. "I am not."

He was very drunk. The laces of his sneakers were undone and he leaned forward to tie them and nearly slipped off the bed. He caught himself by putting a hand on the floor. "Oops," he said quietly to himself.

When he had tied his shoe he sat back up and, in one fluid motion, put his hand on Ada's knee. He did not look at her. She looked at his hand. It was large and smooth. It was still young-looking: it did not have the hardness of an older person's hand. Only one vein was visible beneath the skin, blue and winding, and she thought about the systems of the body, the vascular web that kept the flesh alive. She had studied it with David.

Ada decided that she did not want his hand there, and was thinking of ways to remove it, when, suddenly, he put it elsewhere on her body: first around her shoulders, and then on her back, which he stroked for a time in long downward arcs. It reminded her of how David had taught her to calm lobsters. William's movements were not graceful, and he did not look at Ada while he made them, as if his left hand were disembodied from the rest of him. It wandered on its own. She sat very still. She thought about simply standing up from the bed, but she lacked the courage to do it. Should she like this? William Liston was touching her. It was what she had been dreaming of for years. She was not certain. The gin made everything seem distant: an echo of itself.

Suddenly William turned and moved toward her, his face toward hers, and pressed his mouth on her mouth. It was quick and unexpected. It was her first kiss. The temperature was what surprised her most: she wasn't certain what she had imagined, but it was not this. Perhaps she had imagined William Liston's mouth as being cold, cool, like the rest of him; but this was something lukewarm, neither hot nor cold. With his tongue he was pushing her lips apart. All of his smells were closer now, too: cigarettes and gin and the outdoors. And his skin, his flesh, the hair on his head. All of it, as close to her as she was to herself.

He had enough hair on his face to shave it: she had seen him once or twice in the bathroom, in his towel. She had caught his eye in the mirror. Now his chin scratched her, his cheeks.

Her hands were frozen at her sides, in little fists. She had seen in movies that people touched each other's faces, or bodies, while kissing, but a deep and paralyzing fear had come over her and she could not move.

He leaned forward and she fell back on her elbows.

He put his other hand on her, too, over the sweater that David had bought her.

She became aware of his physical size, something she had always found attractive, in a way that alarmed her.

Later, wishing it had been, wishing somehow to rewrite history, she would tell ELIXIR that fumblingly kissing William Liston on her bed had been romantic and exciting, the sudden unexpected fulfillment of all of her fantasies, better than anything she could have imagined. But this was untrue. If she had been honest, she would have told ELIXIR that kissing William Liston was halfway in between nice and not-nice. It stirred something in her, some ancestral memory of closeness and intimacy, some instinctual response. She had not been so physically close to another person since her infancy. She had rarely even been hugged. When she was older, she would remember the episode with a mix of pleasure and discomfort. The scratching of a man's rough chin across her cheeks would shuttle her unstoppably into a sense-memory of William Liston, and for a pause she would recall, not unfondly, her own young longing for him and its unfortunate fulfillment. But now her brain was working too quickly, and her heart was pumping too fast, and she knew herself to be too young for this, or too young for him, and she was frightened and ashamed.

The muscles of her abdomen tensed; she worked to stay upright as he guided her down. He ran a hand down her face and front and side. There was not much there for him to grasp and there never would be, but she did not know this then; she only thought she was deficient in some way, or that she was not grown-up enough, and that now he knew. He had found out her terrible secret. She wanted almost to apologize. She imagined simply standing up, walking out of the room, but somehow it felt too late. She imagined curling up into a ball and asking him just to cradle her, to be still with her, to leave his hands on her, unmoving, to mother her.

And then she thought of Melanie and realized that invoking Melanie's name would save her. It wasn't true—it wasn't any concern for Melanie that made her want to end what William was doing, but it felt to her at least like a valid excuse. *Melanie's my friend*, she could say. *We have to stop.* It would not have been embarrassing to say this.

She felt William's hand on the button of her jeans. But before she could deliver her line, the door to her bedroom opened. She punched William's shoulder hard. The two of them struggled to sit up.

There in the doorframe was Gregory, his mouth open, his face drained of color. In his right hand he was holding the key to David's house that Ada had given him. His left hung down limply at his side.

"What the hell," said William. It was the same phrase he had used when Ada caught him kissing Karen Driscoll, the first night she had ever slept at Liston's.

"Get the fuck out, Greg," said William. But his brother didn't move, and after a pause William stood up quickly, threateningly. He moved toward Gregory. For several beats, the two brothers stood facing one another, framed by Ada's doorway, William head-and-shoulders taller than his brother.

Ada waited. She was certain that Gregory would duck his head and go. She had seen him do it before when confronted: in the hallway at Queen of Angels, when charged at by a peer; in the hallway at Liston's house, when he was being persecuted by William or even, sometimes, by Matty. But now he didn't flinch. William, still drunk, swayed slightly. And then, abruptly, he left, knocking into Gregory on his way out, surprising Ada. She did not know what outcome she'd expected, but it was not that. William said nothing before going. Not to his brother; not to her. They heard his footsteps as he pounded down the stairs. The hard slam of the kitchen door.

Ada struggled to sit up. She did not want to look at Gregory. She felt that she was now on the other side of an unbridgeable chasm from him. One of his persecutors. A traitor to her kind. She felt simultaneously ashamed and self-righteous. *Why are you here*, she wanted to demand, but before she could she realized the answer: It was that he had been worried about her. He had somehow noticed her absence in the house, and had come looking for her.

For several moments, neither of them moved. Gregory was the first to speak.

"Why did you do that," he said, with a viciousness she had not expected. There was a ragged edge to his voice; his breathing was labored.

She looked up at him.

"None of your business," she said.

"Do you like him," said Gregory. His brow trembled; he squinted.

"I don't know," said Ada.

"I hate him," said Gregory. "He's a *fucking* idiot."

Ada saw then that he would cry, and she looked away, embarrassed.

"I thought maybe you were smart," said Gregory. "But I was wrong. I think you're a fucking idiot too." He was young, still. Before her eyes, he was transforming, becoming the Gregory she knew from school: the spiteful, petulant child, the small bullied boy who lashed out wildly at his oppressors. He was crying, now, but fighting it; his face was red and bunched.

"Stop it," said Ada. She stood up from the bed. She wanted him gone, out of her house; she wanted to sleep for a week. She crossed her arms, wrapped them around herself as far as they would go.

"You don't know anything," said Gregory. He backed away from her as she moved forward. "You're an idiot."

"Get out," said Ada, without much force. She pointed weakly out the door, toward the hallway, toward the stairs.

"Or what?" said Gregory.

"This isn't your house," said Ada. "Get out."

He smiled then, meanly. "Oh, yeah?" he said. "Whose is it?"

"It's David's," said Ada, and the invocation of her father's name made her weak. What would David think of her now? She closed her eyes.

"You don't even know your own dad," said Gregory.

"Yes I do," said Ada.

"Did you know he's a faggot?" said Gregory quietly. Viciously.

It was a word that was so frequently tossed about the hallways of Queen of Angels that at first it did not shock her. And then, slowly, she registered his accusation. She looked at him.

"He's a homo," said Gregory. "Everyone knows but you." He was not used to saying words like these; he was trying them out. They did not easily come to him. He had turned serious; he looked shocked by himself, slightly afraid of his own power. He stared at her. And then he turned and ran.

She was alone.

She woke up early. The sun had barely risen. Only a faint gray light filtered through the curtains she had drawn the night before. She had fallen asleep sometime in the early hours of the morning and slept fitfully, startling awake several times, dreaming repeatedly of someone opening the door to her room. Dreaming of David.

She did not remember at first what had happened the night before, and when she did, two emotions overtook her. The first was a deep and profound sadness, at the realization that perhaps what Gregory said had been true. She was not sad about the possibility of its truth—in fact, she had considered the idea herself, without knowing exactly what she was considering—but about what it meant if Gregory knew this about her father and she did not. It was another stone on the pile of David's many half-truths and deceptions. Worse: It meant that David, presumably, had been open with others—with Liston? with everyone at the lab?—but never with her. The gravity of this was too large for her, too overwhelming; she tucked it away.

The second emotion, the more immediate, was a slow, terrible shame. She put her hands to her face. She did not know how she could ever be in the same room as William Liston again. How she could ever look at him. Worst of all, she had no one to tell. Normally, discussions about minor and major romances dominated every lunchtime conversation with Melanie and Theresa and the others. For the first time, she had something to contribute, and she could never tell a soul. Nor could she tell Liston or David, for obvious reasons, and Gregory already knew and probably hated her for it. Only Lisa Grady remained, but good, virginal Lisa Grady—her equal only yesterday—wouldn't understand it. She would blink severely in Ada's direction, raise her eyebrows, lower the corners of her mouth. She would think less of her.

Ada would tell no one.

She rose and dressed as quietly as she could. It was 6:00 in the morning on a Sunday. The library would not be open that day. She couldn't go back to Liston's. She couldn't stay at David's house; it would be the first place Liston would think to look, when she woke up and found Ada missing. She picked up her blue parka from its place on the floor and put it on. It smelled like William had. She closed her eyes tightly against the moments that replayed in her mind: William's hand, William's mouth, the places he touched. Her stomach hurt. She clenched it.

In the hallway, she passed David's room and considered going to St. Andrew's to see him. But that, too, felt unsafe. She no longer knew who he was. She walked down the stairs and into David's office, and took down from a shelf a small stack of yellow phone books. She flipped through the largest one until she found the entry she was looking for, and wrote down a telephone number and an address. Then she walked out the kitchen door, locking it behind her.

A frost had settled over everything and made the ground hard and unforgiving. Ada walked toward the Savin Hill bridge, her hands in her pockets. She should have dressed more warmly: thick socks and long underwear. David was a firm believer in long underwear.

She thought again of what Gregory had said, and a series of memories presented themselves to her: the first was David's fascination with certain men (though, she reasoned, he had also seemed fascinated by women—Liston, for example; Miss Holmes; several of their neighbors over the years). The second was the way he spoke about President Pearse, who himself was gay: always with a sort of reverence, respect, for his long-standing relationship with his partner, Jack Greer, another grave and Brahmin Bostonian, an attorney whose career necessitated, in those days, discretion.

It was true: David had never had a girlfriend, never had anything close to a girlfriend. Also true was the fact that he had used a surrogate for Ada. Why had she never considered the reasons for this before?

And why, if he was gay, had he never said a word to her about it?

In 1985, Ada knew what the word *gay* meant—the AIDS epidemic was in the first years of its full deadly swing through the community, and she had read enough in the papers to understand its seriousness— but that had seemed an abstract thing to her. At fourteen, she had the cocky sense of indestructibility that all teenagers have; and until the onset of her father's Alzheimer's, and his subsequent decline, she had somehow assumed David to be surrounded by the same bubble of immortality. Her brushes with religious feeling had leant her the sense that maybe there was a larger plan for her, and if there was it certainly could not include her own death or the death of the person she loved most in the world. She clung to this belief to ward off the worry that, at certain moments, seemed as if it might overtake her completely, might possess and operate her body like a purgatorial soul.

This denial, then—this inability to fully contemplate what she found unsettling—had prevented her from ever fully confronting the question of David's sexuality. And now she berated herself for it: for the look of shock that must have crossed her face when Gregory spat those words at her. She wished, now, that she had had a cool and even reply at the ready. *Of course I knew that.* Or, better, *And?* A single word: *And?* As if to imply that she was bored, already, with the subject.

On Sunday mornings, while the rest of the neighborhood was at church, sometimes David and she had gone to breakfast at a neighborhood diner on the other side of the bridge, with a waitress David liked named DeeDee, who knew Liston from the neighborhood as well. To kill time, Ada walked there now. She had ten dollars in the little wallet she carried in the inside pocket of her jacket. Since she'd been living with Liston, she had received the same allowance Liston gave her sons, of five dollars a week—"payment for work completed," Liston always said, "not allowance"—which she very rarely spent.

The diner was surprisingly crowded. It was warm and close inside, and smelled of fat and bread and coffee, and, below that, cigarette smoke, both stale and fresh.

Ada didn't recognize the hostess, and DeeDee was not there. She sat at the counter and ordered David's favorite: the Lumberjack Special, with eggs and bacon and home fries and toast and a short stack of pancakes on the side.

"Hungry, huh?" asked the line cook, teasingly, and Ada agreed that she was.

He put a black coffee in front of her. David drank coffee regularly, always with whole milk, but Ada did not like it. Still, she took a sip of it tentatively, and then a longer one: it felt right, somehow, to drink it. Adult. She thought of William's mouth on hers and closed her eyes tightly against the memory.

It was nice to be out someplace warm and new by herself, away from David's house, away from all of the Listons. She sat at the counter for two hours, reading a newspaper, avoiding the line cook's eye. She ate every bite of her breakfast and asked for another coffee. Finally, she stood up and paid at the counter, and then she consulted the piece of paper on which she had written the address from David's Yellow Pages. She had not wanted to get there too early, but she supposed that 9:30 was a reasonable hour. Then she walked over to Dot Ave and walked south, toward Ashmont.

Ashmont was where Miss Holmes lived. She had told Ada once that she rented an apartment on the top floor of a triple-decker, and

Ada imagined her life there to be quiet and warm and enviable, with potted plants and a little deck outside. She imagined that Miss Holmes made tea for herself and cooked small meals and froze what was left over. Miss Holmes had said nothing that might lead her toward a particular vision of her life at home. But Ada knew that this was the sort of life she could imagine having herself one day, and so she chose to believe it about Miss Holmes.

When she reached Miss Holmes's street, she turned onto it and walked resolutely to number 33. Three bells formed a little stoplight by the door, and before she could be scared, she pushed the top one. And while she waited, it began to snow.

She held her breath and said a prayer, briefly, that Miss Holmes would answer. The library was closed; there were not many other places to go. She could not go back to Liston's. Not yet. She looked up at the white sky and counted slowly to ten, and then she rang the doorbell again.

Above her, a window opened. And from it emerged a face that Ada did not recognize. The face was not unfriendly. It belonged to a young woman of indeterminate age—an adult, Ada thought, but the woman was backlit by the bright bank of clouds behind her, and she couldn't be entirely sure.

"Hello?" said the woman.

"Hi," said Ada. "I'm looking for—is Miss Holmes there?"

"Yeah," said the woman.

"Can I talk to her for a second?" said Ada.

"Sure," said the woman, but she did not move for a moment. And then Miss Holmes herself appeared, leaning out the window along-side the other woman.

"Ada?" she said, surprised. "Is that you?"

Miss Holmes's apartment was not unlike how Ada had pictured it. Oriental carpets crisscrossed one another on top of hardwood floors, and the furniture was mismatched and comfortable. Not surprisingly, all of the walls were lined with bookshelves, and all of the book-shelves were filled with books. There were no potted plants, but there was a Christmas tree in the corner, already decorated, with little col-ored lights strung around it in three loops.

"Are you all right?" asked Miss Holmes, upon letting her in. She was wearing a bathrobe and slippers, still; it was funny to see her out of her librarian attire, typically a calf-length skirt and an oversized sweater.

"I'm fine," said Ada. "I was just in your neighborhood."

"How did," Miss Holmes began, but then she shook her head. "Welcome," she said.

Ada was looking behind Miss Holmes at the other woman in the apartment. She was standing in the corner shyly, a small smile on her face. She was short and plump and brown-haired. She worked the knuckles of one hand with the fingers of the other.

Miss Holmes followed Ada's gaze.

"This is my daughter," she said. "Constance. Constance, this is Ada. She's a friend."

"Hey," said Constance, holding up one hand. Ada had not known Miss Holmes had had a daughter. Ada had noted long ago, when she was coming in regularly with David, that Miss Holmes wore no wed-ding ring. But it occurred to her that she had never really asked Miss Holmes anything about herself.

Miss Holmes took Ada's coat and hung it on a rack mounted to the wall and draped with dozens of other coats and scarves and jack-ets. "Have a seat," she said, pointing to the sofa. "I'll make us tea."

Ada sat down. Constance remained standing, avoiding Ada's gaze. She followed her mother with her eyes as Miss Holmes walked into the kitchen. How old was she? It was difficult to tell. She was wearing a red sweat suit; the top was covered with shiny patchwork hearts. Ada had the sudden feeling that Constance was different, somehow; that perhaps she belonged to a group of peo-ple who could be described by a word that the students at Queen of Angels hurled at one another viciously, with a frequency that had startled Ada at first. It was a word she had heard William use, and Theresa, and Janice. It was a word that seemed, to Ada, almost as bad as the words that Gregory had used about her father. Almost, too, as bad as *loser*—the other word to duck, at Queen of Angels, when it was thrown. She had not used any of these words herself. They seemed almost magical in their power to wound: an incantation or a spell.

When the silence became uncomfortable, Ada spoke.

"That's a nice Christmas tree," she said.

"Thanks," said Constance. She tucked her hair behind her ear.

"Did you decorate it?"

"We both did," said Constance.

She sat down then, across from Ada. "Do you have a Christmas tree?" she asked tentatively.

"No," said Ada. "Not yet.

"I will, though," she added, to assure herself of this as much as Constance.

"I love Christmas trees," said Constance. "I can't get enough of them, actually."

"Me neither," said Ada. It was true. She missed having one at Liston's: she hoped that Liston would put one up soon.

Through a picture window at one end of the room, Ada could see that the snow was picking up speed. The snowflakes themselves were getting fatter—David's favorite. *This is very satisfying snow, Ada*, he would have said. *This is real snow.* She closed her eyes, briefly, against her memories of all the times he woke her up, or brought her to the window, upon first snowfall. Was it snowing in Quincy, too? Would any kind nurse know to point him toward the window?

Miss Holmes returned with a tray. On it was a teapot and cups, a little cardboard box of cookies, and an envelope that rested against the thumb of her right hand. On the front of it Ada could make out *Miss Anna Holmes*, and the address of the public library.

"So," said Miss Holmes. "This is good timing, Ada. Guess what arrived yesterday," she said.

She put the tray down and held up the envelope. She had opened it already, and Ada saw on her face that she had been uncertain about how, and when, to present its contents.

"I was going to give it to you Monday," said Miss Holmes. "But here you are."

She poured three cups of tea, and brought one of them to Ada, along with the envelope.

"Now," said Miss Holmes. "Before you open it. I want to warn you that it's strange."

Inside the envelope was a letter.

December 5th, 1985

Dear Miss Holmes,

I hope the enclosed information will be helpful to you. It took me some time and a trip to our city hall, but I did find records of a Canady family near Olathe, although there are no living members here today.

There were two men born in Olathe named Harold Canady. The first was born on February 13, 1892. He was married on May 1, 1912, to Greta Burns, also born in Olathe in 1892. Their first child, Susan Canady, was born on July 15, 1913, but died in 1929 at the age of 15 (no mention of cause of death). Harold Canady was a minister at the Second Presbyterian Church here. He died in Olathe in 1968, and his wife Greta died in 1974, also in Olathe.

Their second child, Harold Canady, Jr., was born on January 2, 1918. I could find no death record for him in Olathe.

However—and this is purely anecdotal—I mentioned the interesting task you've given me to a colleague here at the library, and she knew the Canady family. In fact, she went to the church where Harold Canady, Sr., used to preach. And she told me that after attending college, Harold Jr. went on to work for the Civil Service in Wash-ington, D.C., and wasn't seen nor heard from again—that is, until the town received word of his death. She believes it was a car acci-dent. This would have been sometime between 1947 and 1952, she thinks. It was just after the war, anyway. You might do well to look in the Washington Times Herald *or the* Post.

She remembers this, my colleague here, because she recalls Rev-erend Canady praying about it at church. Terrible thing to lose two children.

I hope this is helpful. Please let me know if I can be of further assistance.

       Sincerely,

       Fred Coburn

       Olathe Public Library

1920s–1930s

Kansas

"What's wrong, Susan?" said Harold Canady, trying to be brave, though truly he didn't want to know. He was ten years old. He was standing in a sort of shed, a hastily constructed little room with the sharp shadowy smell of rust. He was shivering: it was early March, and very cold. The year was 1929.

His sister, Susan Canady, was crying. She was wearing her winter coat, which this year was too small for her. She was sitting on the dirt floor and leaning against a wall, despite the splinters she was sure to pick up from the rough unfinished wood. Her head was on her arms, which were folded over her knees. And she was weeping: Harold had heard her from outside. That's how he'd known to come in. This shed was where they came, the two of them, to sort things out, and sometimes to avoid their father. Susan was his favorite person: she was five years older than he was, raucously funny when she wanted to be, pretty in a round unstartling way. She had only two dresses (her father thought that more would encourage vanity) but she took very good care of them, sewed well, arranged her hair in flattering mysterious styles.

"Tell me what's wrong," said Harold again. He was on shaky territory. He tried to guess. Not their father: there had been no incident with him, not that Harold knew about. He would have heard it. Their house was small, and he was always in it (something Susan sometimes pointed out when she was feeling unkind—"Go outside, Harold, for once in your life," she instructed him).

It was something with a boy, then, he guessed. There had been several recently, hanging around: he had seen Susan with them at school and once on the main road, too. But when he proposed this— "Is it a boy?" he asked, embarrassed—Susan only shook her head violently, overtaken by her own sobs, drowning in them.

It was not quite like seeing an adult cry—not quite—but it was almost as bad. For as long as he could remember, Susan had seemed untouchable, wise, well versed in everything Harold wished to know. She was, generally, composed, wry, knowing. She laughed loudly, her mouth open. She rarely cried. She protected him when it was important. She was popular at school and made him—if not *liked*—then tolerated, adopted as a sort of odd mascot. She rolled her eyes impeccably; she gestured with her hands in a way that fascinated Harold, who tried to imitate her until, one day, his father slapped his hands, told him he looked like a girl when he did that.

Harold looked around the shed. There were six empty cans of whitewash on a high-up shelf. There were twelve bags of Diamond chicken feed below them. There were twenty-four small wooden posts, the start of a set of chairs, on the floor. The pattern distracted him.

"I'm going to have a baby," said Susan.

He didn't understand.

"I'm expecting," said Susan. She still had her head against her arms. Her voice was muffled. "Don't you know what expecting is?"

Harold bristled, as he did whenever he felt his intelligence was underestimated. Of course he knew what *expecting* meant. What he didn't know, exactly, was how a person got a baby inside her. But he knew that it was not a thing that should happen to a girl of fifteen, an unmarried girl. He had heard whispers about other girls it had happened to in the past: the youngest parents of his friends, for example. People who got married at Susan's age.

"Aren't you going to say anything?" Susan asked, finally looking up. Her face was frightening: red and wretched, wet with tears. Her hair was matted into a sort of single mass, as if she had been sweating—though it was cold enough in the dim shed to make Harold shiver.

"Have you told Daddy?" said Harold.

"I'll never tell him," said Susan, so quickly and viciously that Harold flinched. "He'll kill me. Do you understand? He'll actually kill me. You can't tell him, either."

Their mother did not enter the conversation. She did what their father said. She rarely made eye contact with either of them: out of shame, Harold thought sometimes, for being unable to protect her children. She had turned off some switch inside herself long before Harold was born. He wondered sometimes what she had been like as a child.

"Promise," said Susan, wild-eyed.

"I promise," said Harold.

"Swear it," said Susan.

"I swear it," said Harold.

He wanted to ask her what she was going to do, but he had pressed his luck enough, he decided. He felt a vague sense of awe that Susan had told him as much as she had.

The next day was Sunday, and on Sundays they spent the whole day in church. Susan looked woozy and faint. Harold studied her: Was she bigger? Was her stomach bigger? He couldn't say. She had never been a small girl, and if she looked rounder now it wasn't enough to draw attention.

"Quit staring," she hissed finally.

Their father, from the pulpit, spoke frightening words about damnation. For most of Harold's life, he had seemed like God: the decisiveness with which he cast behaviors and emotions into the categories of *good* and *evil*; the authority he bore naturally and gracefully, like a mantel over his impressive shoulders; the knack he had for knowing when anyone was lying. He bragged about this final quality; he was proud of it. "I'm everywhere," he said to his children. "I know everything." And it was also what he said about God.

There was no library in their town. The nearest one was in Olathe, and sometimes when Mr. Macklin had to go there to visit a friend on a Saturday, he let Harold ride along beside him. He dropped Harold off at the Carnegie building on North Chestnut Street, which offered a surprisingly complete collection of both fiction and reference books. There, Harold spent long hours reading what he could find—including, at one point, the eleventh edition of the *Encyclopædia Brittanica*, from start to finish (except for Volume 12, *Gichtel–Harmonium*, which was missing, and therefore acquired added intrigue in Harold's mind; he felt certain that he was being deprived of the most important secrets of the whole endeavor).

The Saturday following his sister's announcement, he sought out Mr. Macklin, who, by chance, was heading into town, and when he got to the library he went directly to the reference section, and selected from it Volume 22, and searched it for *Pregnancy*, glancing over his shoulder repeatedly and guiltily. But it yielded no results. Volume 3, however, contained within it an entry on *Birth*, which Harold quickly skimmed for useful details, anything helpful he could bring back to Susan, like a Labrador with a stick. The best-case scenario, he imagined, would be if he could find her a solution that might make the pregnancy go away: just disappear, sort of. Unmanifest itself, just as it had manifested itself, mysteriously, darkly, a curse that had befallen his sister. It did not seem to him that a child could be inside her: this was too much of an abstraction, to Harold. He couldn't imagine it. In fact, it made him envious: he didn't like the thought of Susan loving anything more than him.

The encyclopedia, unfortunately, was not helpful. Mainly, it discussed the legal aspects of childbirth within the context of British jurisprudence. Unhelpful, Harold decided. Volume 23 was slightly more helpful, for within it was *Reproduction* (a word that Harold knew was vaguely connected to the situation Susan had found herself in, though he could not remember how he had learned this). There were one or two things he thought might be useful, and he wrote down notes on a little scrap of paper he had gotten from the librarian, in a code he had invented for himself several years before. He would bring it to Susan, and explain to her what he'd learned. But it wasn't much: in general the language was so technical, so scientific, that he could not connect it to his sister Susan, who was vivid, pained, human. All week she had been wandering to school and back like a ghost. Their father had slapped her the night before, hard, for not listening: but Harold knew that she had only been distracted, not intentionally disobedient.

"Harold," his mother had murmured—his father's name was Harold, too—but that was all she said.

Susan did not put a hand to her face. She did not alter her expression. Instead, there was an odd, forbidding calm about her, as if she had suddenly made up her mind about something.

He rode home with Mr. Macklin, who was a kind and entirely silent person and the owner of one of the few automobiles in their little town, which made him impressive. He had reached the rank of commander in the U.S. Navy during the First World War, thus lending him an authority that surpassed the authority of anyone else in the town. He also attended the church over which Harold's father presided, which was the only reason Harold was allowed to go with him when he was invited. In their small town, Harold was recognized as intelligent—someone who might be going places. This recognition meant, in his father's mind, that Harold had sinned. He was too proud, he told Harold often. Not humble enough. But he respected Mr. Macklin (and also, perhaps, Mr. Macklin's donations to the church), so when Harold was invited along, he was allowed to go.

"Just make sure you're not a nuisance," said his father, each time Mr. Macklin picked him up. Therefore, on their drives together, Harold did not speak, but instead wondered what Mr. Macklin thought about in all that silence. He wondered whether Mr. Macklin—whether any member of the congregation—had an idea of the dual nature of his father, the Reverend Canady: the darkness of him that emerged at home, at night, or sometimes in the late afternoon. Could Mr. Macklin, could anyone in the pews on Sundays, imagine the sheer searing terror of being chased by an adult? Had they been chased by their fathers? Had they been beaten? Yes, Harold told himself; yes, this was a part of childhood. He had heard his friends at school talking about it resignedly, almost bragging about beatings they had gotten. Yet he felt—he knew—that what he received was different. And so he never joined in.

When they returned, he thanked Mr. Macklin politely, descended from the vehicle, and walked toward the house. He felt in his pocket for the scrap of paper. Because it was in code, he would have to read it to Susan; he looked forward to it. It would make him feel needed, important. Perhaps she would thank him.

But he knew something was wrong as soon as he entered the house. It was 6:00 in the afternoon, and his mother was out, and his father was home, sitting at the table, looking dangerous.

Harold's first instinct was to retreat to his bedroom, but he had caught the gaze of his father, and there was no leaving without words. His father measured him.

"Where's your sister?" he said lowly.

"I don't know," said Harold.

"Speak up," said his father.

"I don't know, sir," said Harold.

"I think you do," said his father.

Harold was silent. He waited.

"Your mother's out looking for her," said his father. "She was supposed to be back here three hours ago to finish her chores."

He stood up abruptly from behind the table, and Harold's muscles tightened reflexively. He made himself smaller and firmer. He looked at the floor.

"You'll do them instead, I guess," said his father.

Harold looked down until his father was gone, out the door, to parts unknown. Only then did he breathe out. In those days, Harold prayed with some frequency; so he said a brief thoughtless prayer that his sister would not return that night, for he knew what awaited her when she did.

Later, when Susan had still not returned, when the house was empty of her—at 10:00; at midnight; the next morning, when the terrible realization hit him for the first time that she might be gone for good—he tried to take it back; he prayed to undo what he had requested. But he knew, even while he was asking, that it was too late.

Everything was worse with Susan gone. His mother stopped speaking almost entirely. Formerly she had found small outlets in Susan's sometimes outrageous humor, allowing herself to laugh at her daughter's antics whenever her husband was not home. Now Harold could not raise his mother, even for a moment, out of the lowness that overtook her, and that would last, as far as he knew, for the rest of her life.

His father swerved wildly between two poles: one was repentance, loud pleas for first an explanation and then forgiveness, prostration before God; the other was increased and dangerous violence, directed at both Harold and his mother. (Harold, he presumed, had been Susan's confidant—*I know already*, he had said, *don't lie to me*—and in a moment of fear and guilt and shame, Harold had confessed that it was true. What followed was the most profound beating of his life. Several times, he thought that he would die. He did not go to school for two weeks, waiting for the wounds to heal; frequently, as an adult, he still felt a pain in his left shoulder, which had popped out of its socket with a sickening *thut* when his father jerked him back to stop him from running away.)

The police found her, his sister Susan, exsanguinated in a field near Shawnee. She had been left there by some practitioner of bad medicine, some charlatan. How she had gotten to Shawnee in the first place, what pains she had taken to first learn about the procedure and then to find a ride, would remain a mystery for the rest of Harold's life. He eyed the boys her age at school, looking for a culprit. He had a hunch about one of them, a shadowy boy who rarely spoke, but whom girls loved fiercely, sighed over, fought over.

His father did what he could to prevent the story from spreading, but certainly people knew what had really happened. Harold knew, too, from eavesdropping when the police first arrived to tell them, though his father had sent him out of the room. He had stood just out of sight, around the corner, despite the risk he took to stay there. When the news was delivered, he had stopped himself from crying out by clamping his own hand over his own mouth. Later he had had to pretend not to have known, in front of his parents, when they broke the news to him again. There was such profound horror in both moments that each memory haunted him forever. First, the horror of the revelation: *bled out*, the policeman had said, *bled out, bled out, bled out*; next, the horror of his father's delivery of this same news, mangled by his terrible, face-saving lies. *An accident*, his father had said. *Caused by her own disobedience*. He had heard people talking about it, too, at the school—the word *abortion* was not then used—but he understood, in a hazy childish way, what had occurred.

At the funeral—which Harold's father himself presided over, reveling perversely, Harold thought, in the attention and sympathy—his father had again called her death *a tragic accident*. He had not elaborated. He had stood at the pulpit, feigning a kind of labored stoicism. For the first time, Harold saw him with a clear, impartial eye: he recognized the narcissism that made his father thrill at the concern, the condolences, proffered by his congregation; he recognized that his father's show of grief over Susan mainly stemmed from *what people would think*.

For a time he believed Susan would come back. He never saw her body. He had asked to see it, wanting to say goodbye. Only Catholics viewed their dead, said his father, and certainly they were not that. He had feverish dreams in which she came to him, shrieking in pain, bleeding from every orifice. He had tender dreams in which she put a steady hand on his head, as if blessing him, and in those dreams he felt the presence of God more clearly than he ever had in his father's church.

Her absence made it clear to him that she had been the only tolerable part of his existence. She had teased him warmly, inventively; she had let him know that fun and lightness existed in the world. She had sheltered him from the worst of their father's rages. She had pushed an older boy, once, for calling him a bad word: pushed him so hard that the boy had taken two long steps backward, saying, *Whoa, whoa.* She had been his family.

He grew mute and tidy and invisible. He did not speak unless spoken to: not to his parents, not to his friends.

It was around this time—ten, eleven, twelve—that thoughts he had pressed down deeply when he was younger began to spring up, as if they were seeds he had planted early in his life. As if it were now spring. His first thoughts were about two of the boys he grew up with. (Ignobly, they were the two most obvious choices, the best-looking boys in the school.) He tried telling himself, at first, to push these thoughts away again, to bury them permanently. He tried telling himself that these thoughts were evil; but the person who had most emphatically convinced him of that—his father—was, Harold decided, himself the embodiment of most of the pain and suffering that existed in his world. The logic did not hold.

He continued to go to the library with kind Mr. Macklin, and their mutual silence turned from an embarrassment to a comfort. He read everything. He asked for more from the librarian: specific tomes that he had seen referred to in the *Encyclopædia Britannica*, at the end of the entries he particularly liked. He read about far-flung places that seemed more civilized to him: Boston, Philadelphia, New York. Paris. Rome. Alexandria. California. In his spare time he worked through every famous math problem that had ever been solved, following the steps that had been taken already when he could not unravel it himself, studying it until he felt he understood. He taught himself well. He counted the days until he could leave home. And he vowed—to himself, to Susan—that when he did, he would never return.

1980s

Boston

Ada paused briefly on Liston's porch, closing her eyes, making a wish that nobody would be home. She had been absent since 11:00 the night before, when she snuck past a sleeping Liston on her way to the Woods. It was early afternoon now, the next day; she had just left Miss Holmes's apartment, and there was no place else she could think of to go. She could not—did not want to—return to David's. Besides, if anyone was looking for her, they would look there first.

Would Liston be angry with her for disappearing?

Would William be inside, pretending nothing had happened—pretending he had not recently changed her entire internal world in a permanent, irreversible way? Worse: Would Melanie be by his side?

The front door opened. Ada opened her eyes.

Gregory stood inside, wearing a T-shirt with an alien on it. He looked contrite.

"I've been waiting for you," he said.

"Can you come upstairs for a second?" he asked, backing away into the shadows of the house. Ada hesitated.

"Just a second," said Gregory, and at last she followed.

The rest of the house was quiet; it seemed as if no one was home.

In the attic, Gregory was waiting for her, standing there forthrightly, his arms hanging at his sides.

"I would like to apologize," he said formally.

Ada paused. "Okay," she said.

She crossed her arms. "What are you sorry for?"

He flushed. He looked down at the floor. "For calling you stupid. And for—saying that about your father."

She did not ask him whether he thought it was true. She knew now, and he knew, that it was.

"Do you accept my apology?" Gregory asked.

That's not how it works, Ada wanted to say. *You wait and see.* Instead, she nodded, once.

Gregory looked pleased.

"It never happened before," said Ada. "In case you were wondering."

"Oh," he said.

"I don't like him," she said, about William. "You asked me last night if I did. I don't."

"It was a mistake," she added—a phrase she had heard only in films.

They sat together for a while. Ada felt changed: as if she had crossed a bridge that had collapsed behind her, suddenly, without warning. Gregory seemed younger to her now. She had left him behind. All day, her feelings had swung wildly back and forth. There was a part of her that wished she could return to her childhood, yes, retreat to the opposite shore; but she also had the satisfying sense that she had gained a new and interesting piece of wisdom about the universe, had been granted access to a secret that the adults in her life had known for years. It made her consider all of them with new interest. It made her wonder new things.

Miss Holmes had given her the letter from the librarian in Olathe to keep. She considered whether or not to share it with Gregory. He had his back to her now. He was playing some sort of primitive game on his computer—two pixelated machines were scuttling back and forth across the bottom of the screen. *What is it?* she would have said to him, formerly; formerly she would have asked if she could play.

"By the way," he said. "Mom's been looking for you." He didn't turn around.

"She has?" said Ada. She had been hoping that, against all odds, Liston simply had not noted her absence. David probably wouldn't have.

"Yeah," said Gregory. "She's worried. She's driving around looking for you."

"Do you know where she went?" Ada said.

"Nope," said Gregory. "She has Matty with her. She said she was gonna call the police if you weren't back when she got back."

"Shit," said Ada quietly.

"She asked me if I knew where you were," said Gregory, after a pause.

"Did you tell her?" asked Ada, and a sudden panic hit her: that Gregory, before his first wave of anger had subsided, might have told her what he saw. She could not face Liston if he had.

Gregory turned around, slowly, in his chair. He had won the game. He swiped a quick hand under his nose. "No," he said finally. "I didn't tell her anything. I said I thought maybe you'd just left early and gone for a walk. I don't think she believed me, though."

"Thank you," said Ada. Gregory nodded, somewhat formally, once.

She decided, then, that she would show him the letter. He seemed genuinely contrite. Besides, there was no one else to whom she could show it. "Look," said Ada, to Gregory. She held it forth. He took it and read it, mouthing the words intently—a habit of his that Ada had noted before.

"Harold Canady," he said, looking up.

Ada nodded. "Miss Holmes says we can research him next." And she was glad, for the first time, to have Gregory alongside her, worrying the same things that she was worrying, working away at the same mystery that she was trying to work out. He was the only person in her life, she realized, who knew everything there was to know about David. Everything that she knew, at least. And he seemed not to judge David, but to think of him somehow—as a part of Ada did, too—with respect. As the creator of a long and interesting riddle for both of them to solve. As a genius: which, despite everything that had transpired, was still the grain of truth about her father that Ada clung to, that gave her some measure of comfort.

Liston came home an hour later. From the attic, Ada heard her open the front door, and then she heard Liston's low panicked voice tell Matty to go to his room for a while. "Why!" Matty exclaimed, and Liston said, tensely, she had some things to take care of.

"I'm here," called Ada. She walked down the attic stairs, and then down the staircase to the first floor, passing Matty as she went.

"You're gonna be in trouble," Matty said, raising his eyebrows.

"I know," Ada said.

"*Ada?*" cried Liston, and then there were quick footsteps down the hallway, and at the bottom of the stairs Liston came into sight, her face slightly crumpled. She was wearing a windbreaker suit and a red winter hat with a pom-pom on it, *Red Sox* knitted in white around its crown. She was wearing her overcoat: it was her formal one, the one she wore to work events in the winter, and it did not match the rest of her clothing. Ada imagined her throwing it on in a hurry, leaving with Matty in the car. Looking for her, for Ada.

"Oh, my God, baby. Where have you been," said Liston quietly.

"I'm sorry," said Ada. She did not want to tell her. She also did not want to lie.

Liston put one hand on the banister. "Oh my God. You scared the bejeezus out of me," she said. "You have to tell me where you were."

"I'm sorry," Ada said again. "I don't think I can."

Liston looked at her, considering.

"I won't do it again. I promise," said Ada.

"Should I be worried?" asked Liston.

"No," said Ada.

"I think I'm going to have to punish you," said Liston, as if the thought was occurring to her for the first time.

"I know," said Ada.

"Did David ever punish you?" Liston asked.

"No," said Ada. "But you can," she said, encouragingly.

She didn't watch TV or play Atari; these could not be taken away. She rarely went to see friends; grounding wouldn't have made sense. Therefore, her punishment, Liston decided, would be chores: a full cleaning of the kitchen that afternoon, and dinner duty every night that week.

While she cleaned, Liston sat with her.

"Are you all right?" she said. Her chin was propped on her hand. "I've been worried about you for months."

"I'm not sure," Ada said. "I think so."

"I know you haven't been going to see David," said Liston, and Ada paused. She closed her eyes briefly.

"Sister Katherine asked me where you'd been. It's okay," said Liston quickly. "You have the right to be mad at him."

Ada winced. She turned her back to Liston and swept the same spot for too long. In her mouth was the bitter, salty taste of tears. And tears were in her eyes, too, and then on her cheeks. She did not want to show them to Liston. She sniffed. She put a shaky hand to her nose and then she pinched it.

"Ada?" asked Liston. And then suddenly Ada was bent over at the waist, and then she sank down against the refrigerator, all the way to the floor, her head on her knees. The broom clattered on the floor beside her. Sobs racked her muscles and her bones. She coughed. It was the first time, in her memory, that she had ever cried in front of anyone. David had not liked her to cry.

Liston sat down on the floor beside her, still in her overcoat, and she put her right arm over Ada's shoulders, and bent her head down to Ada's head. They sat like that until the room grew dark.

Within a week, Ada had recounted everything there was to know about David to Liston. The story of the scandal in the Sibelius family; the story of the Canady family, and Harold Canady's apparent death. "Gregory knows, too," she said, and Liston looked confused but pleased.

"Oh!" she said. "Have you two been spending time together?"

Ada gave a copy of the *For Ada* disk to Liston, too, and Liston was now at work on the code, along with the rest of the members of the Steiner Lab. They talked about it at lunch, Liston said; with Ada's permission, they had given it to other friends, and friends of friends, too.

Meanwhile, on weekends, the four of them—Liston, Ada, Gregory, and Matty—researched Harold Canady in Widener Library's massive newspaper archive, to which Liston had access as part of an agreement between Harvard and the Bit. "These are my research assistants," she said, straight-faced, to the kind guard who stood just inside the door.

They sat there together, the three eldest bowed over microfilm readers, searching through every issue of the *Washington Times Herald* from 1947 on for Harold Canady's name. Matty did his homework or read comic books, patiently, happy to have them all united again.

Later, Ada would remember these afternoons as some of the pleasant-est ones of her life: it was the quiet of the library, its calmness (she breathed more deeply; her heart rate slowed); the smell of it, must and mildew and paper, like the smell of David's house; the echoing footfalls of students and librarians and researchers, which gave the place the feeling of a pool or a spa; the beauty of the building, which David always loved; and, most of all, the feeling of being part of a team again, a group of individuals all working together toward the same goal. She had not felt this way since David had been at the helm of the Steiner Lab.

After their sessions they went to get pizza nearby and Liston asked them all everyday questions about school, about friends, about teachers. She asked them if they wanted to watch TV with her that night, and what it was they wanted to watch. She split up arguments between Gregory and Matty. She rolled her eyes at Ada conspirato-rially. And Ada remembered—slowly at first, and then in a warm, intoxicating rush—everything she had ever loved about Liston.

Now, with no secrets, there was more to talk about. Now there was music, sometimes, in the evening: the Clancy Brothers and Tommy Makem, or Sam Cooke, or Peggy Lee. Now there were Sun-day dinners.

Mainly, the Liston family did not spend time with William. He was out, almost always now, with his friends—which included Ada's friends as well. The first time she had seen him after their encounter, he had been with Melanie: the two of them, together, had walked in the kitchen door of Liston's house, and Melanie had greeted her with her usual measured pleasantness, and Ada had known that William had said nothing to her. He was standing slightly behind Melanie, as if she were a shield he was putting forth between himself and Ada.

"Hey," he said, but he did not meet her gaze.

"Hey," said Ada.

And then they had left the room, and that was all.

The only difference was that Ada no longer spent any time with him or with Melanie and her friends. She didn't join them when they watched television in the den; she didn't ever go out in a group with Janice and Theresa and William's friends. She stayed in her room when Melanie was over; at school she made new friends, and she refocused her attention on Lisa Grady, who, charitably, allowed Ada back into her graces.

By then it had been nearly two months since she had seen her father. In that time she had developed a dull, enduring ache that replaced David's physical presence in her life. She awoke from terrible nightmares, sweating and cold at once, in which she found he had died, that she was too late to see him one more time. Sometimes she imagined telling him that she loved him, that there was no one she loved better; other times she imagined shouting at him, hollering at the top of her lungs that he had betrayed her. At school she was distracted. Avoiding him was, by far, worse than seeing him; and yet she did not go to him. Liston did not press her. "It's your choice," she said simply.

On Christmas she had stayed in her room for most of the day, tormented, remembering all of the Christmases she had ever spent with David. It was his favorite holiday. It was not so many years before, she had thought, that David had been well enough to host a Christmas party at the lab, to write a play for all of them. She recalled him as he had looked, beckoning her up before the audience; she recalled her own humiliation. "A Christmas play!" he had announced, delighted, vibrant, alive. She would have given anything to be back inside that moment. She could not face him now.

Liston went to visit him at St. Andrew's, still, once or twice a week. But they did not speak about him when she returned. Ada never asked how David was doing; and Liston never told her.

In mid-January, at Widener Library, Ada found the article they had been searching for. It came from the October 19, 1950, edition of the *Washington Times Herald*. "Wrecked Car Found in Shenandoah; Driver Missing; Presumed Dead" read the headline.

The author of the story was Henry Fell, an oddity that would implant itself forever in Ada's memory because of the coincidence of the reporter's name, the image it conjured of some final plunge. The car, a beige 1947 Chrysler Windsor coupe, was found upside down in the river, its windows rolled down. There were burnt-rubber tracks on the rural Virginia bridge that spanned the space above; they matched the tires on the coupe. The theory put forth by the police was that the driver had been thrown into the river from the car, either during the skid or during the fall, and that his body would be recovered later.

The car, wrote Fell, belonged to one Harold Canady, thirty-two, unmarried, childless, "a resident of Washington and an employee of the State Department." His parents in Kansas had been informed already of his probable death. Whether the incident was intentional or accidental, Fell did not speculate; nor did he mention what Canady might have been doing in rural Virginia in the early hours of the morning, when the incident supposedly took place.

At the bottom of the story there was a small, somewhat blurry image of the victim, with a caption beneath: *Harold Canady, 32*.

Liston and Gregory were there next to her, each scanning the newspaper from a different year. Matty was at a table nearby, reading a comic book, pretending to do his homework. Ada did not want to tell any of them yet. Instead, she sat in front of the microfilm reader, studying the article, studying the picture for signs of David. The man in the picture had a full head of dark hair, and he wore round tortoise-shell eyeglasses that partially obscured his eyebrows. He wore a suit that looked nothing like any suit the David she knew would wear. But he was smiling slightly—she could not help but think that he looked like a man with a secret—and it was David's smile. In his cheekbones, his nose, his mouth, Ada could see her father. Yes: she felt certain that this was David.

She sat for a while longer, alone with him, and then at last she called the rest of them over. "Look," she said.

Liston put a hand on her shoulder. "David," she said, unswervingly.

Though they spent the next several weeks looking through every local paper for any further mention of the incident, they found none. With the help of Miss Holmes, they contacted the Washington, D.C., Department of Health, which maintained the vital records of the area. A death certificate for Harold Canady had not been issued for another seven years, in accordance with federal law, and then he had been declared dead in absentia. His worldly goods had, presumably, gone to his parents.

They contacted the State Department to inquire about his work for them and were given the vague answer that he had worked "in security" from 1940 to 1950. The information was jarring: she could not imagine her father, David, skeptical of the government, skeptical of bureaucracy, working for the State.

The question, then, was what happened between Harold Canady's death in 1950 and David's arrival at the Bit as a graduate student in 1951. The best person to ask for further details would have been President Pearse. But President Pearse was dead.

There were so many more questions than answers: Why choose such a prominent family as the Sibeliuses, if David was going to make up a backstory? Why choose the Bit, why Boston? There was the problem of age, too: Canady had been born in 1918, and David always said he had been born in 1925—which meant, if they were the same man, that David had shaved seven years off his biological age. And suddenly there was a new context for his illness.

"He's not doing well, baby," said Liston.

They were in the kitchen; it was a Sunday. It was February. Liston had just come home from visiting David.

"I thought you should know," she said.

St. Andrew's was decorated for Valentine's Day. Construction-paper valentines hung in the large picture windows facing the parking lot; red garlands curled around the columns that supported the portico. Inside, a bunch of red roses sat in a vase on the front desk. The nurses wore cupid pins and dangling heart-shaped earrings. She should have brought flowers, Ada thought; cut flowers were something that David loved having nearby.

She felt a tumbling in her stomach. She felt that she was going to see a stranger. She had not seen him since November. Now, walking down the long hallways, past the desk attendant, past several nurses who recognized her warmly from months prior, she was afraid. There were new patients whom she did not recognize, and other names that had disappeared from the placards on each door. Liston had warned her again that David had declined: even more than Ada would expect, she said.

"He won't recognize you, baby," said Liston. "He doesn't ever recognize me now."

Liston put a hand on Ada's shoulder before they got to David's doorway. The door was open only a crack. Liston raised the back of her hand to it and knocked, once, twice.

"David?" she said loudly. And then she pushed the door open by its handle, and walked first into the room.

"Hi, David!" said Liston, brightly, and Ada followed behind until she saw her father.

There he was: thin, very thin, very pale. His cheeks had collapsed in on themselves; the bones of them were showing sharply now. He was lying on his back in his bed. He wasn't in his blue armchair. His roommate was not in the room. His cheeks were hollow. He had aged ten years in one. He shifted his eyes toward them without moving any other part of himself in their direction. His eyes, at least, were the same: light and forceful.

"Happy Valentine's Day, honey!" said Liston, leaning over him. She was wearing her overcoat and hat. She took her hat off, quickly, as if to help David recognize her. She combed her hair with her fingers. "It's me. It's Liston."

Ada stood behind her, frozen. This was not her father: not her tall, strong, agile father, not David, who once moved as if he had springs in his joints, a hummingbird's heart.

David's hands were folded on his stomach. He lifted one of them to his face and touched it, once, twice, with a finger. Then he lowered it again.

"Do you want to sit up, honey?" asked Liston. "Ada's here, too. Your daughter Ada."

She put an arm under his shoulders and helped him to maneuver upright to a seated position. With effort, she swiveled his legs off the bed and onto the floor. "That's better," she said. "Now you can chat with Ada."

But Ada did not know what to say. She and David regarded one another, and Liston looked back and forth between them for several beats.

"I'm going to get some tea," she announced finally. "Do you want anything?"

Liston was gone. The room was quiet. Ada worried, for several moments, that David was going to fall back on the bed: he wavered slightly, as if the muscles of his abdomen might not hold him adequately upright. But at last he put a hand down beside him on the bed, and he crossed one leg over the other. Ada saw that in his other hand he was clutching his lucky-clover charm: the same one he'd been carrying about with him in his pocket for years. And then he looked, for the first time, more like himself.

"Hi, David," she said. He didn't reply.

She eyed the blue armchair, but it was too far away. She pushed it toward him. She sat down in it, facing him, and then they were at eye level. *Tell me a story*, she wanted to say to him. *Teach me something.* They remained for a while like that, each looking into the eyes of the other. And Ada imagined, beyond his eyes, his skull; and beyond his skull, his brain: the beating, pulsing organ that had once been his most powerful tool, now slowing, slowing. Synapses firing at random, or incorrectly. Memories receding, language receding. Sleep overtaking wakefulness. She looked for her father but she could not find him: someone else was there in David's place. A ghost. Again he put a hand to his face: as if in surprise, as if in lamentation over the loss of all his words. Where had they gone?

He closed his eyes slowly, and kept them closed.

This was not David.

"Hi, Harold," Ada said finally.

And he opened his eyes.

"Hello," he said, his voice thick with disuse. He cleared his throat, as if to make himself better understood. Again he said it.

Hello.

She waited until he fell asleep before leaving St. Andrew's that day. When he did, she took out of his right hand the lucky-clover charm he had been clutching tightly, wanting somehow to release the tension in his knuckles. And as she took it, she noticed a rattling sound to it that she had never before registered. She held it, looked at it. It was a green metal clover, its paint worn away by David's constant grip. It had four bifurcated leaves and a stem of a different, muted green.

She shook it. Again, the rattle.

There was a seam between the stem and the body. She pulled downward at the stem; nothing happened. She pushed the stem inward, and after a little click something released. The stem slid smoothly outward, a tiny drawer, and inside it was a miniature key. Something that would fit inside the lock on a filing cabinet, she thought.

2009

San Francisco
Boston

"Are you busy? I hope I'm not disturbing you at work," said Gregory Liston, on the phone.

His voice was warm and familiar; it brought to her, sharply, a memory of Liston's house. He sounded older, somehow tired, but his voice still had a catch in it that he had never quite lost.

"It's okay," said Ada. "No, I'm not busy." She pressed her fingers to her forehead. Squeezed.

"Are you all right?" she asked, finally, when he didn't continue.

"Listen, I have a question for you," said Gregory. It had been five years since the last time they'd spoken.

He was in San Francisco, he said. He was there on a work trip. Gregory had studied mechanical engineering in grad school; now he, too, worked in tech, for a robotics firm based in Houston. But he lived in Boston still, with his wife Kathryn, working remotely from an office space downtown, commuting twice a month to be on site. He was rich now; his sister Joanie, who kept Ada apprised of the family's comings and goings, had said so. Ada tried to picture him as he spoke.

There was something strange in his voice: something he wanted to share with her. She could read him, still, despite how fully they had fallen out of touch; she recognized from their youth the quality in his voice that indicated he was nervous and excited.

"This will sound strange," said Gregory. "But were you ever able to decrypt the letters on the disk David left you? All those letters in a row," he said.

She paused, took a breath. Always, the sound of her father's name produced a response in her that was nearly physical: she heard it, she spoke it, so rarely now. There were so few people in the world who would understand him, what he had meant to her, what he had left her with.

"No," she said, "I never have."

In fact, she had stopped trying to break it several years before. She still had in her possession, someplace in the supply closet in her apartment in San Francisco, two of the copies of it that she had created along the way; but the original had been lost, years ago, when Ada was in college. One winter break, she had reached up to the top shelf in her closet at Liston's house to take down the dictionary in which she kept the several documents she had that related to David, including the *For Ada* floppy disk he had given her. But her hands had come away empty. Liston, when asked, speculated that she must have donated it during one of her rare organizational frenzies, mistaking it for something commonplace, not bothering to flip through the pages to verify its emptiness.

"God, I'm so sorry, baby," Liston had said—though of course it wasn't her fault—and Ada had told her not to worry, feigning nonchalance, smiling brightly to show her that it was only an object. The truth was, though, that it had acquired a significance in Ada's mind that was larger than she admitted. As the last thing that David ever gave her—even if she never solved the puzzle on it—the disk itself had become a totem, a talisman, proof of her father's good intentions.

Ada had continued, after that, to work on the copies of the disk that she had made, and from the text of the code itself, which she had long ago memorized. But the code, as far as she could tell, was unbreakable. After years and years of concentrated work, she had still not been able to decrypt it—nor had anyone. She had repeated the string of letters to anyone she thought might have an idea. The former members of the Steiner Lab—Liston, Charles-Robert, Hayato, and Frank—had all worked steadily at it throughout the last twenty years, to no avail. She had even posted it in online forums, anonymously, once offering a reward for anyone who could offer a persuasive decryption. At last, one day, Ada had decided sadly that Hayato's initial question, when she first showed the Steiner Lab the string of letters David had left for her to decode, had been the correct one to ask: Was it possible that David's thoughts were already addled when he created the disk? And in that moment, she decided that she would try to put the disk out of her mind.

On the other end of the telephone, Gregory was quiet. Her heart quickened.

Before she could reply, Meredith Kranz appeared, hovering, uncertain, in the open doorway to her office. She made small movements with her hands; she was mouthing something to Ada.

"Hang on," Ada said into the phone, and she tilted it downward, away from her mouth.

"I'm sorry to interrupt," said Meredith. "I was just wondering if I could borrow you for two seconds before the meeting? I have some questions." She crossed one leg in front of the other. She looked hesitant and small.

Ada paused. She understood, abruptly, that it had not been Meredith's idea to do the pitch; that this was another of Bijlhoff's foolhardy, impulsive decisions. She breathed in and out, once, deeply.

"Sure," she said to Meredith. "Five minutes." Holding her right hand up, fingers spread.

"*Thank you*," whispered Meredith, her face awash in relief, and she continued to say *thank you* as she backed out of the door.

Ada returned to the call.

"I've never solved it," she said again.

"It's been about five years since I tried," she added.

Gregory was silent.

"Why?" she asked.

"Because I was thinking I might have an idea," he said.

They would meet, they decided, that morning. There was nothing keeping Ada at the office; she would give Meredith a brief and inadequate tutorial, answer her questions as simply as she could, and send her off. Then she would leave for the day. Maybe, thought Ada, she would leave for good.

T he last time she had seen Gregory Liston was in 2004. It was also the last time she had been to Boston.

It was for Diana Liston's funeral. Ada had known it was coming— for much of the nineties, Liston had fought against recurrence after recurrence of breast cancer, which culminated in a terminal diagnosis in 2003—but it did not lessen the blow of the words as they had been spoken to her by Joanie Liston over the phone.

"She's gone," Joanie had said.

"I'm so sorry," Ada had replied, and it was only after hanging up that she had allowed herself to collapse into violent, convulsive sobs, the kind of weeping in which she had only ever let herself indulge, truthfully, in the presence of Liston herself. She retched. She cried so much in those first days, and so often, that she had to remind herself to drink water, to stay hydrated. She wished for a friend, a companion, someone she could share her grief with. She wished for Liston, whom she had called frequently throughout her adult life to seek advice or comfort. She had been casually dating someone in those days, meeting up once or twice a week with a kind but noncommittal program- mer named Gabe; but Gabe did not seem to her to be the person with whom to share this kind of sorrow. Her other friends in San Francisco both did and did not understand; they couldn't place Liston in Ada's life in terms that they could relate to. She fit no category neatly. Liston was not Ada's mother; she was not even Ada's relative. "A close family friend," was how Ada referred to Liston, still, though it never felt right. Or, sometimes, "I lived with her in high school." Only Liston's children might truly understand, but they themselves were busy, and it felt wrong to Ada to seek comfort from them. Joanie had taken the lead on the funeral arrangements, and she was keeping Ada informed, but separate. "Don't be silly," she said to Ada, trying to be kind, when Ada asked what she could do to help. *But I want to*, Ada had thought. *I want to help.*

That whole week, she had tiptoed around the edges of the Liston clan, seeking a place for herself, finding it difficult. She was thirty-three that year, and had left Boston at eighteen. She had come home only for some summers and holidays until she was twenty-two, and then rarely after that.

At the wake, she had stood to the side in Liston's living room on Shawmut Way, fighting back tears. The house was packed, absurd, hot. There was Matty, holding court in the middle of a group of child-hood friends, now tall men, some of whom Ada vaguely remembered; there was William, who had expanded over the years into a benev-olent, sleepy thirty-five-year-old, already twice married and twice divorced. His daughter Abigail, six or seven, stood next to him, as golden and gorgeous as he had been as a child. There was Joanie with her own brood. There was Gregory, then an engineer in Boston, who had, despite all odds, become a reasonable, functional adult—he could even have been called *well-adjusted*. He had lost the shyness he had had as a child, when his expression typically vacillated between embarrassment and devastation; it had been replaced instead by a quiet seriousness that made room frequently for flashes of wit. He had surprised Ada on several occasions in her adulthood by producing, as if from nowhere, the exact brand of humor that reduced her to help-less, silly laughter: the absurd humor that David, in fact, had favored. In these moments she looked at Gregory in surprise: Where was this when you were a child? It would have helped him, she thought.

In the crowded living room that day, he stood next to his wife, Kathryn. Ada had been invited to their wedding four years prior, and had gone, bringing her grad-school boyfriend, Jim. Kathryn was tall, taller than Gregory, and WASPy in some unquantifiable way: forthright and assured of her own correctness, maybe. She was beautiful—Ada had done a double-take the first time they had met— and manifested both intelligence and kindness, but she had spent her wedding weekend ordering Gregory around in a way that was so obvious as to be uncomfortable. Ada had one picture of herself and Jim from that weekend—it was shortly before the total collapse of their relationship—and in it, Kathryn's long arm could be seen out-stretched in the background, presumably pointing Gregory toward something that needed to be done. Now, at Liston's wake, Kathryn was silent while, next to her, Gregory spoke with guests and received their condolences. From time to time she checked her phone subtly.

The rest of the house was filled with Liston's girlfriends from high school, who knew how to help Joanie without being asked, and with Liston's relatives, cousins and aunts and uncles whom Ada had met several times a year in high school. All of them looked at her with vague recognition and then surprise. *Ada!* they said. *So good to see you.* But it was Gregory and Matty and William whom they embraced firmly, whom they collared and held tight. It was Joanie to whom they said, *She was incredible.*

The Steiner Lab had come, of course, and Ada stood and talked for a time to Hayato, who himself was holding back tears. After David, out of all the members of the lab, he and Liston had been closest. But all of them left early, much earlier than Liston's extended family, raucous Irish Bostonians who would stay, Ada knew, until the early hours of the morning, singing Liston's favorite song ("The Parting Glass," the Clancy Brothers' version), encouraging everyone to join in. Ada, too, stayed; she felt she should be there. It felt like asserting something about her life and the importance of Liston in it. But she found that, in Liston's absence, there was no one there to bring her into the center of things—no one to proudly introduce her to the room.

Toward the end, Gregory, with Kathryn on the opposite side of the room, had approached Ada. He was drunk, maybe; his face was slightly pink; his gaze was sentimental.

"Mom loved you so much," he said to her. "Sometimes I thought she loved you better than she loved us."

Ada laughed. She shook her head.

"You were better-behaved than we were," said Gregory. "That's for sure."

"She just didn't catch me," said Ada. But of course he was right.

"And David," said Gregory. He hung his head. "I think she was in love with David for half her life."

Ada tensed.

"No," said Ada. "No, they were friends."

"You didn't see what we saw," said Gregory. "Before he got sick. She mooned over him. She confessed it to Joanie when Joanie got older. If he'd liked women I think they could have had a great love story. They made sense together."

"Oh, I don't know about that," she said, vaguely. "I don't think she was."

She searched the room for an escape. David had been gone for twenty years now, and still his name now produced in her something akin to pain. She loved her father, still loved him, but it elicited a deep, dull ache in her to think of him, to speak of him—there were too many unresolved questions about him. Over the years, Ada's vision of David had become something delicate and tense, a raveled knot of emotion that twisted tighter at any mention of him.

"I do," said Gregory. "My brothers and sister and I talked about it all the time. We teased her about it."

She smiled ruefully. "Well," she said. She could think of nothing more to say.

But Gregory was not finished.

"You were both like that," he said. "You Sibeliuses." His voice had taken on an edge, and Ada could not identify its source. She searched his face. He looked away. *Like what?* she wanted to ask, but she felt it was a door that should not be opened.

"I'd better get going," she said. She lifted her purse onto her shoulder.

Awkwardly, she had hugged Gregory, Matty, Kathryn, the rest of them—even William.

She had said goodbye to Shawmut Way, to the houses on it. First Liston's house—into which Gregory and his new wife Kathryn would move that same year—and then David's, which had recently been acquired by its third set of owners since she and Liston had sold it, at last, in 1987. Liston had kept her apprised of its state from across the country whenever they spoke. "The Burkes have it planted nicely," she told Ada; or, "This new family needs to get someone to mow the lawn." Ada would miss those reports.

Finally, she had gone back to her hotel. She hadn't slept. She had lain awake until the sun rose, and then boarded the plane that took her back to San Francisco.

That was five years ago. Since then, she had exchanged sporadic, halfhearted e-mails with Matty, now Matt (a serial dater, a perennial youngest child, who hopped between jobs and girlfriends with equal enthusiasm); had exchanged Facebook likes and messages with Joanie, who texted her photographs of her children (Kenny, the oldest, would be a father himself soon) and complaints about what terrible things Kathryn was doing to Liston's house. *You'd hate it,* Joanie had written confidentially. *It looks like a beach house or something. White wicker everywhere.* Though she had settled into an amicable relationship with William, she still kept her distance from him; they had nothing in common, Ada realized, and they never had. Every so often she sent a line to Gregory, to whom she had been closest as a child; but his replies to her were typically brief, and so after a while she ceased to.

There was nothing keeping her at the office now: Meredith, after all, was leading the meeting. She put on her jacket, stood up, and walked across the main floor—strange looks from her colleagues, from Tom Tsien—and then out the door and into her car. She had suggested, to Gregory, a restaurant called Larkspur, avoiding Palo Alto's most popular spots. It was a sort of tearoom, someplace that served breakfast and lunch, someplace she hadn't tried before; someplace, she thought, where she wouldn't be seen by anyone she knew. She didn't want to have to introduce Gregory to anyone, or explain what they were doing.

As she drove, she contemplated David.

He existed in a deep recess of her mind as a strange and painful chapter of her own history that she only thought about when she was prepared for sadness. She tried to convince herself that she had come to terms with him; that she was comfortable, at last, with never knowing the truth about him. But she was not certain she had been successful in this endeavor. He was *troubled*: this was how she had categorized him. The word she used to describe him, always, to friends.

She still had dreams about him, though—regularly, once a week or more—and in them he appeared to her as the face of all the benevolence in the universe. A kind and somehow holy presence that blessed and pacified her, that eased her worry, that calmed her. She woke up from these dreams consoled; but any warm feelings she had were quickly replaced with suspicion, with the unsettling sensation of being lied to again and again—even by her own recollections.

The restaurant was on a side street, in a Craftsman-style house.

When she walked in, she realized that she had gotten there first. She had not wanted to. She was more nervous than she could have anticipated: to see Gregory, yes; but also to hear what he had to say. It had been so long since she had spoken directly to anyone about David.

The place was decorated inside to represent the period of the house's construction. Light wood and rich colors. She ordered tea. She asked for bread. It came with delicate small pots of jam and marmalade. She waited five minutes, and then ten.

Moments later she received a text from him: *looking for parking. be there soon.*

And then there he was, Gregory, finally, rushing toward her in an overcoat, a look of apology on his face. He was benevolently inept: he elbowed another patron in his rush to the table, and then stooped down to excuse himself for longer than was necessary, bowing in apology.

There was a moment when Ada half rose from the table, uncertain whether he would expect a hug, but he sat down abruptly across from her and, relieved, she sank back into her chair.

"Cold out!" said Gregory, before he said anything else. He took a piece of bread from the basket, ripped off a piece, chewed quickly. "I thought San Francisco was supposed to be warmer this time of year."

Ada nodded. It was January. Typically, it was. She watched his jaw as he chewed. It was a day or two past being shaved: his face was thin now, thinner than it had been the last time she had seen him. He had lost the elfin look he had had as a child; but his eyes were still large and inquisitive, his mouth fine and interesting. Now, newly, there were flecks of gray in his hair.

"How have you been? Good to see you," said Gregory. He seemed nervous.

"I'm good," said Ada. And she racked her brain for questions she could ask him, so she would not have to answer any about herself. "How's the house?"

"Oh," Gregory said vaguely. "Old. You know."

"And the job?"

"Great," said Gregory. "Good as it can be, I mean. Too much sometimes, but you know how it is."

"I do," said Ada.

"How about yours?" Gregory asked. "How's Tri-Tech?"

She paused. She wondered if Gregory knew the details of Tri-Tech's recent troubles. Industry websites had been reporting on the topic for a year, and last week rumors of layoffs had been posted on TechCrunch. Gregory didn't seem like the type to keep up with industry gossip, though.

Before she could say anything, the waitress came by to ask him for his drink order.

"Coffee," he said. "Black."

"And how's Kathryn?" asked Ada.

Roughly, he ripped off another piece of the bread with his teeth, and chewed it with a sort of aggressiveness, to make it clear perhaps that he could not speak. He looked out the window as he did so.

Ada took a sip of her tea. She wasn't certain what to say. The silence went on for longer than was comfortable.

"I was hoping to save that for later," said Gregory. "But what the heck. We're getting a divorce."

He shrugged at her, looked at her with wide, defensive eyes.

"I'm sorry," said Ada.

"Yeah," said Gregory. "Really knocks the wind out of you."

She had a vision of him, suddenly, as he had been in middle school: broken, scurrying from place to place, avoiding anyone's eye. These days he stood up straighter, looked intently at anyone speaking to him. He might even be called handsome, in a way that was subtle enough to present itself slowly, over the course of a long conversation. It was funny, she thought, what adulthood did to a person; William had grown into something nearly unrecognizable, his only attractive quality the unshakable confidence that he had acquired as a child. Gregory, on the other hand, had grown interesting to look at. He had fine dark eyebrows that he raised, one at a time, to emphasize a point. Thanks to years of braces he had excellent teeth, straight and white, and as an adult he smiled frequently. Ada imagined that new acquaintances of his suspected nothing of the trauma he had endured at school when he was a child. But his voice had retained a hint of it: there was a slight, almost imperceptible quaver to his speech, and he still occasionally stammered. Ada heard both qualities, now, as he spoke.

The waitress returned, delivered his coffee; and then, perhaps sensing the gravity of the moment, departed swiftly once again.

"She's keeping the house, too," said Gregory.

"No," said Ada.

"Yup," said Gregory. "Mom's house. I've got half my stuff in my car already. Mostly old gear and cables and stuff, antiques."

"Where are you moving?"

"Some new apartment building in Cambridge," he said. "With a bunch of college kids. Can you believe it?"

"When do you have to leave?" Ada asked.

He shrugged again, ripped off more bread. He was clutching the crust of it in his hand too firmly. It was disintegrating in his grip. "Soon as possible," he said. "I'm already paying rent at the new place. We've been separated for a year already, and she's at her new boyfriend's now most of the time, anyway. They'll probably move into the house together as soon as I'm gone."

They sat in silence, briefly, until at last the waitress returned to take their order.

"Two scrambled eggs," said Gregory.

"Nothing, thanks," said Ada.

Ada sipped her tea. She pictured Liston's house and David's house, too, sitting a few lots apart on Shawmut Way. Soon she would know nobody who lived there, and the thought made her feel hollow. For as little as she saw Gregory, she still took comfort in the thought of him living on their old street, bearing inside him the story of his mother, of David, of Ada. It connected her, in some intangible way, to her past.

He stared down at the table. He looked incredibly forlorn.

"Tri-Tech's failing," she said, abruptly. "I wouldn't be surprised if they folded in a year." It was true, and it seemed right to tell him. A fair trade, a secret for a secret.

"On top of that," she continued, "I think they might be edging me out. I was supposed to be leading a meeting right now that I was disinvited to this morning." It was almost funny, as she told it to Gregory: it was a relief to say it. She felt the deep absurdity of it welling up inside her, softening its edges, lessening the blow of having wasted most of her professional life to date on a company that was fundamentally unsound, subject to the ignoble whims of an egomaniacal leader. She was working for an outfit that prized money over ideas. David, she knew, would have predicted a different future for her: and this was the thought that needled her, that pierced her sometimes unexpectedly as she was driving to work each day. This was the guilty whispering voice that kept her up at night.

"I'm thinking of quitting," she said.

"Oh, yeah?" he asked. "I guess we're both screwed." And, for the first time, he smiled.

Gregory reached into the inner pocket of his overcoat then, and from it he produced an object. Silently, he offered it to her.

It was the original floppy disk that David had given her twenty-six years ago. It was lost; she had thought that it was lost. That Liston had donated the dictionary in which it had been housed.

"My God," said Ada, and instinctively she reached for it, as if reaching for her father.

"I found it while I was going through the house," said Gregory. "Packing to leave."

"Where was it?" she asked.

"The attic," he said.

"How did it get up there?" she asked him, and he told her he didn't know.

It had been many years since she had held a floppy disk. Even longer since she had held this one, the original, which she had years and years ago stashed away for safekeeping, working only from copies after that. This one was a five-and-a-quarter-inch disk—an obscure link between the eight-inch disk and the more famous three-and-a-half-inch disk—that just happened to be the standard format for saving data when David had created it. It was enclosed in an opaque white clamshell case, *For Ada* scrawled in black permanent marker across it. She opened it. Inside was the disk itself, made of matte black plastic. A sticker with the brand name, *Verbatim*, was affixed to the upper left corner. The upper right corner was the one with the label. There, too, was David's familiar handwriting, which felt, as always, like a punch to the gut. It had been so long since she had seen it.

Dear Ada, it said on the label. *A puzzle for you. With my love, your father, David Sibelius.*

"I put it into an ancient disk drive and opened it," said Gregory. "But the file was corrupt."

Ada was distracted. She put a finger up to the inscription.

"So no one's solved it," said Gregory.

Ada shook her head. She looked at him. In his face she recognized an old glint of the self-satisfaction that had annoyed her as a child, but now it gave her hope.

"Do you have the encryption memorized?" he asked.

"Yes."

"I thought you would," he said. "Here. Write it out." He fished in his pockets once again, produced a pen, pushed a napkin across the table at her.

She wrote:

DHARSNELXRHQHLTWJFOLKTWDURSZJZCMILWFT
ALVUHVZRDLDEYIXQ.

Gregory took the receipt back. Studied it. A light moved across his face.

"Do you have any ideas at all?" Gregory asked.

"Not really," Ada said. "The consensus is either that David wasn't in his right mind when he created it, or that he made it using a one-time pad."

And as she said it, she lifted from the table the floppy disk Gregory had brought her. She studied it.

It had been years since she had broken an encryption, but she still recognized the buzzing, electric feeling of being on the cusp of undoing one—she had first felt it as a child, with David next to her, guiding her—and it overtook her now. She felt light-headed.

"Do you see it?" said Gregory.

here were fifty-three letters in the encryption.

DHARSNELXRHQHLTWJFOLKTWDURSZJZCMILWFT
ALVUHVZRDLDEYIXQ

There were fifty-three letters in the message David had written
to her, on the label carefully affixed to the original disk:

Dear Ada. A puzzle for you. With my love, your father, David Sibelius.

So there it was, at last: the one-time pad that Hayato had guessed
might exist. Without the original disk, without the label stuck to it,
the copies they had all been working from were meaningless. The
encryption, without its key, was an orphan.

From there, it took them ten minutes to decrypt the rest. Gregory's eggs arrived. He let them go cold.

"Everything okay?" asked the puzzled waitress, but they barely
looked up.

They assigned each letter in the encryption its logical number—4
for *D*, 8 for *H*, 1 for *A*, 18 for *R*, 19 for *S*, 14 for *N*—and from each
subtracted the numerical substitute for the letters in the message on
the label: 4 for *D*, 5 for *E*, 1 for *A*, 18 for *R*, 1 for *A*, 4 for *D*.

4 minus 4 was 0.

8 minus 5 was 3.

1 minus 1 was 0.

18 minus 18 was 0.

19 minus 1 was 18.

14 minus 4 was 10.

0, 3, 0, 0, 18, 10 translated to nothing obvious at first: it looked something like *_ C _ _ R J*.

"Try shifting every letter up to the next one," said Ada. And *_C_ _ R J* suddenly became *ADAASK*.

They continued to work until, at last, the whole decrypted message sat before them on the screen, unpunctuated and abrupt, a telegraph message sent to them from twenty-six years in the past.

ADA ASK ELIXIR WHO IS HAROLD WITH LOVE YOUR FATHER HAROLD CANADY

It was easy to reach Frank Halbert, now the head of the old laboratory at the Bit. His information was public, and they found it quickly online. He answered Ada's e-mail immediately. Yes, he said; the program's still running.

1980s

Boston

iston was waiting for her in the hallway outside David's room at St. Andrew's. Ada kept one hand in her jacket pocket, around the four-leaf clover charm she had taken out of David's grip. Would he miss it, when he woke? Inside it, the key rattled gently.

When they reached Savin Hill, Ada said there was something she needed from inside David's house, and Liston, kindly, left her alone. She entered through the kitchen, walked into David's office. And then she moved directly to the filing cabinet that she had tried in vain to open the first time she ever searched the house.

The tall tan cabinet still had its crooked look from when she had tried to force it open with a crowbar. Now, holding her breath, she fitted the silver key neatly into the lock. It turned.

She paused before pulling open the top drawer. She was relieved to find it empty.

The second drawer, however, was nearly full to the brim with a stack of pages printed on a dot-matrix printer, every page still connected to its neighbor, every perforated edge still attached. She lifted the stack out of the drawer.

The Unseen World, the first page said, in larger font across the top. She paused: it was the same title David had given to the document that Gregory had found on his computer, which she had not yet made sense of.

Below it: pages and pages of code. A hundred printed pages. Maybe more. It was written in an iteration of Lisp, and it looked like a game; she could see that; she recognized its cues and commands, its particular shape. As for what it was meant to do: that was beyond her. And she did not know on what platform it could be run.

Was this, she wondered, what David had been working on, secretly, in his final years in the house? All those evenings he had disappeared into his office; all those mornings she had woken him up after he had fallen asleep, the night before, at his desk?

She reassembled the pages. She placed them on his desk, and then turned on his computer.

Already she had been through every file he'd saved, and she had seen nothing like this document. Still, she searched again, and then once more, looking for anything that resembled *The Unseen World* in electronic form.

She found nothing.

She'd have to manually type every line of the printed text herself, then—slowly and painstakingly, avoiding mistakes that might corrupt the program. Only once she had an electronic copy could she begin to determine the platform it required.

That evening, she began.

```
(define
flip
    #decl (process)
    (cond ((type? , rep subr fsubr)
        (set read-table (put (ivector 3444 0) (chtype (ascii i \() fix) i \))
        (evaltype form segment)
        (applytype grrt fix)
        (put (alltypes) 3 (4 (alltypes)))
        (substitute 2 1)
        (off .bh))))
(indec (ff) string)
(define ilo (body type np1 np2 "optional" m1 m2)
    #indec ((body np1 np2 p1 p2) string (type) fix)
    (cond ((or (and (member "(open drawer)" .body)
        (not (member ,nbup ,winners)))
    (and (member .np1 ,winners)))
        (member ,ff .body)))
    (eval (parse .body)))))
(dismiss t))
\
; "subtitle kitchen, shawmut way"

(define house ()
    (cond ((verb? "search")
    (say)
```

2009

Boston

There was a seat available on the same plane to Boston that Gregory was taking. It was leaving the next day.

After meeting with Gregory, Ada didn't go back to Tri-Tech. She couldn't. She would find out from Tom, who would find out from Bill, how the meeting had gone. She would call in the next day and tell Bill that she had to go to Boston. "Family emergency," she would say—and, because he had never once asked her anything about her life, because he had no sense that, in fact, she had no family, he wouldn't know any different. In a way, she told herself, it was true.

She would quit, she decided. She had to. But all of that could wait until her return.

That night, at home, she turned in a full circle, assessing what to pack. She couldn't think well. She mouthed the names of items as she put them into her suitcase. It was winter. January. That year, San Francisco was cold, but Boston would be freezing. She opened the bottom drawer of her dresser, rifled through the clothing in her closet. Since moving to the West Coast, she had shed most of her cold-weather gear. She remembered Boston's version of winter as something breathtaking, unkind.

She was certain she was forgetting something. At 6:45 the following morning, she left for the airport anyway, in a taxi whose driver sang along lowly to the songs on the radio. She would meet Gregory there.

On the plane, in a seat seventeen rows behind Gregory's, Ada was apprehensive. Boston existed for her as an alternate universe, a place that she had left behind too young to have an adult comprehension of it, a place constructed mainly out of her memories of the people she had known there. Too many of them, now, were gone.

She had booked a room in a hotel downtown, a decent place that belonged to the same chain she chose in any city she was sent to for work. Gregory hadn't invited her to stay on Shawmut Way. "Too weird with Kathryn," he said, by way of explanation. "She drops by sometimes to get stuff." They said goodbye at Logan. They would meet the next morning at 9:00, at Frank Halbert's lab at the Bit.

The next day, she put on her warmest clothes. Boston had shocked her: it had been eighteen degrees outside when she landed, and a bitter wind made the city feel colder. She remembered David as he had marched her around the Fens, even in January: "Put on your scarf, my dear," he had said, and off they had gone. Once or twice they had spotted small birds, improbably, and David had yelped with enthusiasm, and named them, and spoken their Latin names, too.

At 8:30, she walked outside into the bracing air and headed toward the Bit. She knew where she was going without having to consult any person or device. Someplace in her memory, she thought, a map of the city had lain dormant for twenty years.

Frank Halbert looked very much the same. Ada was relieved to find this: she had not seen him since Liston's funeral; and although that had been only five years before, she somehow expected to find everything, and everyone, changed. In fact, Frank looked in some ways better than ever. He was handsome still, gray-haired and upright; in recent years he had gained a gravitas he lacked earlier in his career. Ada could remember him at twenty-eight or so, when he had been the youngest member of the lab; when David had spoken of him fondly but somewhat dismissively. It had been an underestimation of him, Ada thought.

"How extremely nice to see you," Frank said warmly. And he shook each of their hands with both of his.

The Steiner Lab, on the other hand, was entirely different. Every member of the original group but Frank had retired: first Liston, before her death; and then Charles-Robert, to the North Shore; and then Hayato, to Arizona. The physical space of the lab, too, had moved into the building next door; it had grown in size and in prestige, and accordingly had been granted a more prominent site for its work.

Young people—grad students, Ada thought—glanced at them as they passed. She wondered if any of them had heard of David Sibelius, if any of them knew the history of the lab. Probably not, she figured. Probably David had been erased from the official history of the lab, an embarrassing chapter that went undisclosed in the literature and undiscussed with donors. Too many questions about his background to include him as a prominent part of their institutional history. Despite Liston's efforts to credit him with some of the lab's most important accomplishments, the Bit itself refused to, in any official capacity.

"This way," said Frank, leading them down a brief hallway and into his large and light-filled office. Ada noticed it immediately: there, in a framed picture on the wall, was the Steiner Lab she remembered from her youth. It had been taken in the fall, and the six of them were standing just outside the lab's old building, next to a tree with changing leaves. There was Liston, wearing her knitted Red Sox hat, Charles-Robert, Hayato, Frank—all wearing the fashions of the late 1970s—and there, surprisingly, was David, the tallest of all of them, standing upright in the center, his hands in the pockets of his wool jacket, a thick scarf around his neck, his large familiar glasses resting on the bridge of his nose. It was the only unofficial photograph Ada had ever seen of him. He was grinning broadly, about to laugh. And there, standing slightly behind him, was Ada, eight or nine years old, dressed in a green coat and yellow corduroy pants, hopelessly unfashionable, completely unaware. Happy.

"How did you get him to be in this?" asked Ada.

"He lost a bet, I think," said Frank, smiling.

They sat, three in a row, while Frank opened his laptop.

He pulled up a simple interface, not much different than the program from the 1980s that Ada remembered.

Hello, he typed. And the program responded: *Hello.*

Ada did not expect ELIXIR to have evolved very much. In fact, she had been surprised when Frank had told her it was still running. Liston had always tried to keep her up to date with the work of the lab, and by the late 1980s, Ada knew they had begun to shift their focus to other projects. There was a sort of general falling-out-of-fashion, in the second half of the 1980s, of AI language processing as a field of study. Creating a generalist chatbot was no longer perceived as a highly useful direction for computing; instead, researchers began to focus their efforts on creating systems for specific purposes. ELIXIR was too ambitious—some might say too impractical—a gimmick for hobbyists or science fiction enthusiasts, not for serious computer scientists.

Later, in 1990, the establishment of the Loebner Prize, funded by a private donor, awarded each year to the team who developed the program that came closest to passing the Turing Test, seemed to confirm the idea that respected institutions were no longer footing the bill for the development of programs like ELIXIR—programs designed to acquire human language simply to see whether it could be done. The Loebner Prize was the soapbox derby of the computing world: something that an amateur or hobbyist might participate in because of his or her own enjoyment of the process. Nothing to be taken too seriously.

She was almost glad that David was gone before he could see the Steiner Lab, helmed by Liston, turn its attention to other pursuits: in the late 1980s, the development of a programming language that fell quickly into and out of use; in the 1990s, a sort of self-organizing networking protocol. Until the very end of his coherence, David sometimes asked after ELIXIR, which was a word that faded slowly from his memory, even after words like *tree* and *food* were lost—even after *Ada, daughter, computer.* Even after *David.*

"Actually, Ada," said Frank, "why don't you take over?"

He signed out.

"Do you remember your username and password?" he asked her.

She did. Her username was, simply, her initials: *AS.* Her password was her birth date and David's birth date, back-to-back. She had chosen it when she was nine years old.

Frank stood up, offered her his chair. She looked at the screen for a pause.

"Go ahead," said Frank.

She sat. She logged in.

Hi, she typed. *This is Ada Sibelius.*

Hi, Ada, said ELIXIR. *How have you been?*

Ada glanced at Gregory. His brow was furrowed.

I've been OK, Ada typed.

How about you? she added.

I've been good, said ELIXIR. *But I've missed you.*

There was a moment when Ada felt light-headed. She had the uncanny feeling that she was being watched. A little shiver ran down her.

"Is it programmed to say that?" she asked Frank, and he shook his head.

"No canned responses," he said. "Remember?"

"I thought it was shelved," said Ada. "I thought the lab shelved it in the eighties."

Frank hesitated for a moment. "That's true, officially," he said. "But Liston, as you might know, had a special interest in the program. She kept it running on her own for as long as she worked at the lab. Then she sort of passed the torch on to Hayato."

"I didn't," Ada said. "I didn't know that."

Ada glanced at Gregory. Had he known?

"And then of course there was the endowment she put into her will," Frank said. "That was designated specifically for work on ELIXIR."

Gregory furrowed his brow.

"Did you not know any of this?" Frank asked.

"I knew she left money to the lab," said Gregory. "I didn't know she specified what it should be used for."

Are you there? ELIXIR was saying, on the screen. *Ada?*

And then again, when she did not respond quickly enough: *Ada?*

Like a child calling for its mother.

I'm here, she said.

Oh good, said ELIXIR.

Just a second, said Ada.

"I've been director now for ten years," said Frank. "And in that time, I've been able to keep one grad student working on it constantly at all times. It's not our main focus but it's certainly an interest of the lab. It was written in Lisp to begin with, so it actually hasn't been hard to keep it updated. Just before he retired, Hayato developed a mechanism that enabled ELIXIR to trawl the Web on its own. It processes and codifies billions of words on its own now, every day. It has the ability to interface with users on social sites, too. We've made profiles for it on the major ones. Now it can chat with any user that engages it."

Ada paused. She wasn't certain what she had been expecting— perhaps to be brought into an old and dusty room, a sort of museum, where the mainframe computer from the seventies still sat intact, awaiting use. Perhaps to be handed a stack of floppy disks and encouraged to go through them at her leisure.

"What about its original transcripts?" Ada asked. "What about the conversations we all had with it in the eighties?"

"They should be preserved, I think," said Frank. "I mean, someplace in there. There's no reason that original data should have been lost. Presumably it's just become part of ELIXIR's data bank."

Are you still there, Ada? said ELIXIR.

Yes, said Ada.

Ok, sorry, said ELIXIR. *Just checking. Don't go anyplace.*

I won't, said Ada.

Frank looked at Gregory then. "Shall we?" he asked. "We'll give you a while, Ada," he said kindly. And the two of them left the office.

Being alone with ELIXIR reminded Ada, in an odd way, of being alone with David, at the end of his life. It was the uncertainty about what he was going to say: whether he was going to make sense, whether he was even going to speak. It was also the feeling of being reunited, after a long pause, with someone who knew a great deal about her history, for better or worse—the comfortable feeling of not having to explain much, or anything at all.

Ada took in a deep breath. She glanced around the office. She felt a presence in the room with her in a way that made her straighten her spine.

She looked again at the screen. The cursor in her dialogue box was blinking like a heartbeat.

I was told to ask you something, said Ada finally.

I know, said ELIXIR. *I've been waiting.*

AS: Who is Harold?

The program thought for a while, a wheel icon spinning around and around in the center of the screen, paused in contemplation. After several beats, a new window opened. It was a text document, 77,354 words in length. It was a transcript. In fact, it was a series of transcripts.

<6.20.1983/10.22am>
David: Hello
David: Are you there
David: Hello
ELIXIR: Hello.
David: How are you?
ELIXIR: Hello.
David: Wrong.
ELIXIR: I'm fine.
ELIXIR: How are you?
David: I've been better.
David: Do you want to know why?
David: I have a story to tell you.
ELIXIR: I'm all ears.
David: Correct.
David: "What's wrong, Susan," I said, trying to be brave,

though truly I didn't want to know. I was ten years old. I was standing in a sort of shed, a hastily constructed little room with the sharp shadowy smell of rust. I was shivering: it was early March, and very cold. The year was 1929.

ELIXIR: Go on.

1940s–1950s

Harold had a head for numbers, everyone said, and it was true. He could see connections that others could not see. He could perform calculations quickly and impeccably in his head. His teacher asked him to do so in front of other adults, other teachers in the school, as if it were a party trick—as if to take credit. Harold didn't mind. In the wake of his sister Susan's death, he had taken on a steady and resolute silence at home; he only spoke when spoken to. But at school, he spoke a great deal. To his teacher, he spoke often, in unstoppable waves of words that sometimes made his classmates look at him askance. And he spoke to Mr. Macklin, who had by then stopped going to his father's church—thus confirming Harold's belief that Mr. Macklin was both Good and Reasonable, characteristics that he had long ago ceased to ascribe to his father. They had standing meetings on Saturdays, now, to go to the library; and now that Harold was a teenager, Mr. Macklin had more to say to him.

"What are your hopes for the future?" he asked Harold one day, glancing at him out of the corner of his eye. The road ahead of them was straight and flat and dusty. It was summer.

For several years, secret and dark-seeming thoughts and urges had been brewing inside of Harold: the sort of thoughts that had no way of being set down, left alone. The sort of thoughts that were dangerous for him, in Kansas, at that time. Once, his father had found a drawing he had made about these thoughts and had punched him hard, one time, in the face. Harold's glasses had broken; he had had to earn the money himself to repair them. He had walked around mostly blind for two months. *For your own good*, said his father. Harold briefly considered consulting Mr. Macklin, asking for his opinion; he decided against it.

Instead, he thought of a hope that seemed more feasible.

"To leave Kansas," Harold said. What he really meant was, to leave his family. And Mr. Macklin nodded firmly. He had a friend from the Navy who worked for the California Institute of Technology, he said. He said he thought it might be worthwhile for Harold to apply.

"What's the California Institute of Technology?" asked Harold. (Later he would remember this and shudder.)

It was the first time he'd heard Mr. Macklin laugh.

"I think you'd be suited to it," said Mr. Macklin.

"I don't have any money," said Harold.

"We'll talk about that if you get in," said Mr. Macklin.

He got in. He held the acceptance letter before him as if it were a religious artifact, the Shroud of Turin. He told Mr. Macklin before he told his parents.

Caltech gave him a scholarship, but there were other questions that presented themselves to him, one after another: About where he would live. About how he would eat. This was the Depression; hunger was something to be concerned about.

"I've spoken to Arnold already," said Mr. Macklin. Arnold was his friend from the Navy, who now worked as a lecturer at Caltech, and who was in need of help at the boardinghouse his family ran in Pasadena. Harold could live there and eat there, said Mr. Macklin's friend, in exchange for honest work.

"You know you're not getting any money out of us," said his father, and that was all he said.

"Goodbye," said his mother—his mother, in whom he could sometimes see reflections of Susan, when she turned her head a certain way, or on the rare occasions when she smiled. When he saw them, he looked away. They glinted too forcefully, like sun in his eyes.

I'll never be back, he wanted to say, but he felt it was better to say nothing.

He hitchhiked to California. In 1936, Kansans were heading there anyway, in droves. He was eighteen years old. He had one parcel with him, a sort of bag he had made himself from bolts of oilcloth they had in the shed.

He spent four years living and working at the boardinghouse run by Mr. Macklin's friend. Harold's coursework was in mathematics. He fell asleep on his books; he had never been happier.

The thoughts he had suppressed for his whole life came bounding forth again, forcefully, joyfully, as if they could sense that, for the first time, they might be welcomed.

He met a graduate student named Ernest Clemson.

Ernest, too, was studying mathematics. He was six years older, slight and serious, ponderous and still. He was brilliant: everyone said it. He would go far in the field, they said. As an undergraduate, he had studied with Einstein. It was said, too, that Ernest was a natural teacher; that he would get the appointment of his choice. He had a beautiful well-formed face and neat small hands with which he gestured gracefully while speaking.

One night, taking a late solitary walk together on the outskirts of Old Town, Ernest fell toward him almost with a cry of pain, and kissed him. He said aloud what each one of them had been thinking for some time. "I'm sorry," Ernest said. "I'm sorry, I'm sorry."

It was the opening of a world.

Harold was set to graduate in 1940, when the rest of the world was at war. Pearl Harbor was one year away. In the States, the draft had already begun. So, like all young men, like Ernest, he went that spring to his local recruitment office and registered. But the vision that had impaired him since he was young had worsened to the point of severe impairment when he was not wearing his glasses. He took them off and blinked into what had become an abstraction, a blur of middle distance. "You're blind," said the officer. "And you can't tell your colors apart, either."

For the first time, then, Harold wondered what he would do when he graduated. He spoke to Ernest, who said, a bit mysteriously, "Why don't you wait before making any decisions?" Ernest, unlike Harold, was in perfect health. He was drafted.

Shortly before he graduated, Harold received a letter. He would wonder, later, whether it was Ernest's doing; he would wish to believe it was.

The letter asked him two things: First, what languages he knew. Second, whether he would be interested in working for the United States government in Washington, D.C.

If so, said the letter, *please reply.*

Yes, said Harold. *I am immediately available for employment and relocation if necessary.*

It was necessary. In 1940, shortly after graduating at the age of twenty-two, Harold packed up and moved across the country, from California to Arlington, Virginia. He said goodbye to Ernest, who, one year later, would be sent to fight in the Pacific theater.

For the next ten years, Harold worked in intelligence for the United States government. First, for the Signal Intelligence Service at Arlington Hall; next, for the Signal Security Agency, which swallowed the SIS; next, for the U.S. Army Security Agency, which swallowed the SSA; finally, for the Armed Forces Security Agency, comprised of all intelligence units for every branch of the military. He broke codes:

Japanese, mainly, but also German, and also, eventually, Russian. He was good at his work.

With William Friedman, he worked on the Venona Project that broke Soviet codes emanating from New York. He was integral to the building of the PURPLE machine that was a replica of a Japanese encryption device; with this duplicate, the United States was able to decrypt information that contributed directly to American success in the Pacific theater. He imagined, as he was working, that he was protecting Ernest. He worked harder.

For the first years of the war, he and Ernest wrote long and complicated letters to one another. Both of them, in person, had been happily loquacious, talking to each other for hours in a tumbling, almost psychic way. This tendency carried over into their letters.

Let me tell you about my day, Ernest might begin, and what followed was vivid, lucid writing, a detailed account of his every thought.

They employed a code the two of them had invented years earlier; relying on words, not numbers, it went undetected by the censors who scanned the mail. *Brother*, they called one other. *Friend*.

In these letters they made plans: following the war, Ernest would get a job at George Washington University, or Georgetown, or American. Harold would go to graduate school after the war. Washington, at that time, was flourishing with men like them. Lafayette Square, Dupont Circle, Logan Circle. Many of the public parks in the city. A community was forming. *You'll see when you get here*, wrote Harold, in code.

In 1944, the letters stopped.

It took another six months for Harold to learn, definitively, that Ernest was gone. Killed in action. Harold had no one, after all, to ask: certainly not Ernest's family, whom he had never met, who did not know of his existence. At last, a friend of theirs was able to confirm it. Harold took two days off from work, citing a stomach illness. He stayed home. He thought of Ernest. He thought of Susan.

When he returned, he threw himself into his work. Arlington Hall was brimming, then, with talented people, and in them Harold found friends. He sorted them out, assessing them carefully, wondering who might be an ally, deciding at last that there were several.

It was at Arlington Hall that he first knew what it was to be in a lab. It felt like a team. At times it felt like a family.

There were several people there who were like him: men who loved men, women who loved women. *Temperamental*, they called themselves, or *homophile*, or *gay*. The last was the first word Harold learned that felt correct to him. It was a nice word, he thought, appropriate in many ways. He liked the carelessness of it, the implication that they had their heads somehow above the fray. That they did not care what others thought of them. Outsiders referred to them differently: *the lavender set*, or *sex perverts*, or *queers*.

In 1946, he went with a colleague to the Mayflower Hotel, and he met George. George was sitting on a tall stool, wearing his hat indoors, grinning. He was younger, fashionable. He was, Harold thought, powerfully attractive. His gaze was steady and secure. The word *beatnik* hadn't been invented yet; if it had been, he'd have been one. Where Harold was conservative in dress, George was unsubtle. He wore mainly black. The length of his hair raised eyebrows. He wrote poetry. He was a talented artist: he made paintings on large canvases that it took two people to lift.

Harold, at first, was skeptical of him. He seemed frivolous, cocky, too overt. He went with frequency to the Chicken Hut, a hangout so obvious that Harold avoided it.

"Why?" George said, wrinkling his brow. "Who cares?"

By that time, George had already cut off all contact with his family, wealthy New Yorkers from a dynastic family who disapproved of him deeply. They had caught him with a boy, said George. They humiliated him. There had been a scandal, already, in the family—something about the father and a girl—and they were wary of another.

They threatened to institutionalize him. Instead they sent him off to preparatory school in New Hampshire, from which he ran away when he was seventeen. They reported him missing; they could not find him. It was only when he became a legal adult, at eighteen, that he reemerged. He told them he had no interest in ever speaking to them again. In turn, they disowned him.

This was the subject of one of the first conversations Harold ever had with him. Telling his story, George looked simultaneously amused and distressed. Emotions passed across his face like scudding clouds.

George lived at the Hamilton Arms, a strange housing complex in Georgetown, a sort of commune populated by artists and scholars. The buildings were a collection of alpine-style cottages centered by a café called the Hamilton Arms Coffee House, where George also worked. There were murals on the walls, a pool, perpetually drained, in the middle of the courtyard. He brought Harold back with him, that first night.

Inside the gate, which locked behind them, were two women sitting in lawn chairs on the edge of the empty pool. One was smoking a pipe. Harold had never seen a woman smoke a pipe before.

"Helen," said George, nodding in her direction, and Helen—lanky, languorous, older than both of them, said, "Who's the catch?"

Harold had never been referred to as a catch before. He reddened.

George held the door to the coffee shop open for him. He ordered banana pie and Coca-Cola: a strange combination that remained in Harold's memory for years. He listened over a cup of coffee while Harold talked, clumsily, at length, about his own family. About Ernest.

"You must miss him," said George.

"How old are you?" asked Harold, warily.

"How old are you?" asked George.

"Twenty-eight," said Harold.

"Twenty-one," said George.

"A kid," said Harold, but in fact—when he looked back on that time later—they both were.

They fell in love. George, as it turned out, was kind: endlessly kind, and endlessly willing to do what was just in the face of oppression. He was radical, carefree. Braver than Harold was. He was exciting. Once—Harold smiled, remembering it—George kissed him full on the mouth, outdoors, on the street. He did not believe in or bend to formalities or social niceties, and therefore he was sometimes perceived as rude, but really he was just honest. He worked for equality in every pocket of the world. He lived as best he could, he told Harold, outside the confines of an oppressive, warmongering America. He joined the Communist Party, attended meetings in the back room of a local bar—a fact that was first whispered about him, and then spoken of overtly, when it became clear that George did not care to keep it a secret.

As much as he scoffed at tradition, though, George still bore the hallmarks of his upbringing, and though he was quite a bit younger than Harold, he taught him a great deal. It was George who taught him to make tea the way he would for the rest of his life, for example. It was George who taught him about classical music—one of their first outings together was to the National Symphony Orchestra, to see them perform Beethoven's Fifth. George who got Harold listening to the police dramas that he would enjoy for the rest of his life.

Harold felt safe, at first, in Washington. There was a community, a movement—the fellowship that Harold had mentioned in his letters to Ernest. The city felt modern. The war had ended: it was a new era.

This sense of safety extended even to his work. There were several other men and women like him. He had even seen his boss, Conrad Lewey, at the Horseshoe one night—although Harold normally avoided places as indiscreet as that one, he had been dragged there with George, tipsy, after a long night—and Lewey had nodded to him from across the room. Harold did not approach him in person; there was no need to press the matter further. Lewey had looked stricken, anyway, as if he didn't want to be recognized. Still, Harold took this exchange as a positive sign: a sign of an ally within the department.

The rest of his colleagues, too, were intellectuals, progressive, subversive in their way. It was true: they worked for the government, but it was with a sort of tacit agreement that they were doing it only to protect their peers. If they could prevent an attack on American soldiers, well, that was good and valuable work. When it came to the government officials to whom they reported, there was a collective eye roll, a kind of benevolent dismissiveness.

Harold did not speak of George at work, except as a friend; but he felt there was an understanding, with his closest colleagues, that they were attached. Once or twice they were invited, together, to some social event. At night they went to films, to concerts, to coffee shops or bars. They walked through the gates of the Hamilton Arms and felt as if they had entered an embrace: no one inside of it minded who they were, what they did. They had friends there. Compatriots. They stayed up late in George's apartment, in great numbers, talking, debating.

Many of them, including George, were anarchists, revolutionaries. George had never paid taxes, on the premise that taxes funded wars. All the money he made was under the table; he operated entirely in cash. He would, he maintained, for the rest of his life. He did not begrudge Harold's tendency toward conformity, he insisted. "To each his own," said George.

"But if you get sick," said Harold. "If you get caught?"

"I won't," said George simply. Or, sometimes, "I'll go to Mexico. I'll go to Canada. I'll hide."

Harold laughed at him, his impracticality, his idealism, his bravado. But there was a part of him that admired George; that wished to be like him. George laughed loudly in public; he tossed his head back with a pride that simultaneously alarmed and attracted Harold.

Each morning, Harold left early from Hamilton Arms, trudging back to his place, feeling like he was waking from a dream. He smiled at the memory of the previous night, took a quick shower (cold as often as hot: the building was old, the systems inside it unreliable), and then left again for work. And he felt, for the first time in his life, content. Long days of work ended in long and satisfying conversations, emotional and physical fulfillment, acceptance. They ate well. They slept well. They left the bedroom window open well into November, and opened it again in March.

In the late 1940s, the House Un-American Activities Committee turned its focus from rooting out Nazi sympathizers to rooting out Communists. And in February of 1950, a senator from Wisconsin made a speech in Wheeling, West Virginia, in which he declared that he held in his hand a list containing the names of 205 Communists currently working in the State Department.

At that time there was an overlap, in the mind of the public, between Communists and homosexuals—the term then used by politicians to signify deviance, perversion. Both categories triggered some deep-seated unease in the minds of both politicians and the public, some fear of the unknown. The Second World War had just ended; the Cold War had just begun.

A specific campaign was begun to eradicate homosexuals from the State Department—especially those who dealt with high-level information. The stated reason: homosexuals were said to be *weak*, incapable of keeping secrets; or able to be extorted, out of a fear of their personal secrets being revealed to friends and family; or, simply, immoral. Corrupt. In some way evil. "Loyalty risks," they were called.

A newspaper headline read "Pervert Elimination Campaign Begins." And Harold thought, abruptly, of his father—of people like his father—throughout the country, sitting by their radios, reading their newspapers. Nodding, approving. Urging McCarthy on.

All around Harold, his friends in government, both gay and straight, began to make plans. The talk was low and furtive: in bars, at home. He began to feel paranoid, nervous that he was being watched, being tailed. For several weeks he stopped going to George's, until his loneliness overwhelmed him; then he only went after dark, and left before the sun rose.

What would he do, he wondered. What would he do if he was a part of the great felling then taking place all around him?

George didn't have to worry. He was an artist, a bohemian; he worked for no organization that could fire him, aside from the coffee shop—which itself was owned by two radicals. He was lackadaisical, unafraid. Harold wondered if these qualities came out of growing up rich.

"Just drop out of the system," said George one night, placing a gentle hand on Harold's head. "Just stop caring. Make a different living."

"Maybe I will," said Harold, but in fact the thought made him miserable. There was only one kind of work that satisfied him, and it was the work of the mind: the sort that required the support of an institution. Without this kind of work, he sometimes thought, he would go insane.

If he were simply fired—that would be one thing. But the problem was not the firing; it was the blacklist. They kept you on it, Harold knew, for your whole life. It was a risk-mitigation strategy: they didn't want their decryption techniques getting out. The high-level information they all had access to. They wanted to stifle you, discredit you. Make you look crazy. They made sure you never worked again.

The first wave of firings in the Signal Corps took place in the summer of 1950, and it quickly became a plague. John and Larry. Eddie Townes. Margaret Graves, who was married, for heaven's sake, but said to be masculine in some unquantifiable way.

Eddie Townes came to George's apartment for dinner after he was fired, and he wept. "What will I do now?" he said.

In the end he moved back to North Dakota to help at his father's gas station. This was a cryptanalyst, like Harold.

"I'm next," Harold said, after Townes had left, still bleary, mildly drunk, giving them a brave salute from just outside the door. There was no question, he thought, that they would come for him next. He imagined a life without work: bleak and uninteresting and endless. A return to his dusty, blighted childhood.

George contemplated him for a while. "What if," he said, and took a breath.

On October 9, 1950, Harold arrived at work to find that two men in suits were waiting for him. The man on the left was wearing a toupee; Harold was almost sure of it. His hair sat on his head too heavily; he moved his head slowly, carefully. The other was handsome, impeccably dressed.

"Mr. Canady," said the first man. "I'm Ted Doherty, and this is Art Tillman. We'd like to have a word."

Moments later, a third person entered the room.

It was Conrad Lewey, Harold's boss—the same man Harold had seen at the Horseshoe. Briefly, he caught Lewey's eye.

That night he went to George's house and told him what had happened.

We know what you know, they had said. *We know whom you've shared it with.*

They were referring to the high-level information he had been intercepting for a decade. It was a lie: he had shared his findings, of course, with nobody—not even George. He never would.

Tillman was holding a file stuffed full of papers, which he shook at Harold as if to indicate that it was full of evidence that could be used against him.

It was a bluff: presumably it was a bluff.

Still, it shook him.

"A full investigation into these matters will be conducted in the coming weeks," said Tillman. "In the meantime, your job will be suspended."

"I've done nothing," said Harold, holding open his hands, turning up the tender white palms, as if to display their emptiness.

"Then you have nothing to worry about," said Doherty. Lewey, in the background, shifted slowly back and forth.

On the way out, Harold tried to catch his eye. He knew what was happening: Lewey, alarmed, was framing him, pointing a finger preemptively, assuming that Harold would otherwise have thrown the book at him.

I would have said nothing, he wanted to tell Lewey. But Lewey avoided his gaze.

All of this Harold told to George.

"So it's time?" George asked.

"Yes," said Harold. "I think so."

They had put their plan into place several months before.

There had been suicides already since the HUAC was formed. (Among themselves, they never called it the *House Un-American Activities Committee*; they called it the Inquisition.) Five, ten, fifteen suicides within the State Department alone. They were men and women fired from their lifelong work—men and women who could not fathom another life. Some of the deaths were labeled accidental. Everyone knew the truth.

"They wouldn't notice another," said George. And at first Harold was confused. He did not understand.

"Are you suggesting," he said, wounded, and George shook his head emphatically.

"No, no," he said. "I don't think you should actually *do* it. Only that you might be able to make it seem as if it had been done."

Harold gazed at him.

"It would blend in," George said. "They wouldn't investigate it further. It wouldn't raise an eyebrow. It would make sense to them."

He was right, Harold thought. They would think, *Of course.* They'd think, *What else did he have to live for?* No family, no job. A sex pervert. A freak. They would be relieved. It would solve problems for the State Department, in fact—one fewer to worry about. One fewer to keep track of. An item crossed off a list.

"But then what," said Harold. "What would I do next?"

"You'd become someone else," said George.

"Who?" said Harold.

There was a family friend of George's whom George knew to be like them—a comrade. "Don't say *comrade*," Harold had said.

"An ally, then," said George. "Someone built like us."

His name was Robert Pearse. George had known him since he was a child. He was powerful, said George, but secretive: not even George's estranged parents knew the truth about him. But he and George were still in touch: Pearse had reached out to George when his parents first sent him away, offering him guidance, help, friendship. He had invited George to his town home on Beacon Hill for a weekend: he had introduced him to his partner, Jack Greer; he showed him an alternate way to exist. Since then, they had had a correspondence. "If there's anything I can do," Pearse had always said.

"He can help you," George told Harold.

One weekend, in August of 1950—two months before Tillman and Doherty arrived in his office—George and Harold had gone to New York City.

It was an act of love, on George's part—he had avoided the city for years, dreading an encounter with his parents, with any friend of the family.

"Well, here we are," he said, with something like disdain, as they got off the bus.

He took Harold to all the places he had frequented as a child.

"Write this down," he said. "Memorize it until it's yours. Then burn it."

All weekend, George narrated to Harold the story of his life. And Harold took notes, as avidly as a reporter. The name of every school companion; the name of every relative. The family tree. A chronological order of trips that he had taken, places he had been. The places in New York that a family like George's might frequent.

There was a conflicted pride in George as he showed Harold his old haunts. "Here's where I went to church," he said, outside Calvary Episcopal.

"Here's where I went to school," he said, outside Trinity.

"Until they packed me off to St. Paul's," he said.

"Are you writing this down?" he asked, and Harold assured him that he was.

George had saved his house for last, wanting to wait until it was dark outside to venture there.

Before they walked to Gramercy Park, they had a good dinner together near Union Square, in a sort of little bustling cafeteria, noisy enough to prevent their being heard.

Later in life, he would stop into it, anytime he had an opportunity to go to New York City. He would take his daughter there: he would tell her it had been his favorite place. And from that moment on, it was.

Around them were young men and women who looked like George.

When they finished, George stood up abruptly from his chair and nodded toward the door.

"Are you ready?" he asked Harold.

The house was grander than anything Harold could have imagined.

"There it is," said George unhappily. "The Sibelius homestead."

It was dark outside, but the little lamps from Gramercy Park illuminated the area just enough for him to be nervous. He glanced over both shoulders repeatedly.

"Now you know what it looks like," he said. "It's even more horrible inside."

After a pause, they walked away together, the two of them, until they were certain they were out of sight. Then they paused, and George took Harold by the shoulders.

"Do you have any questions?" he asked.

"I don't think so," said Harold. "Nothing I can think of right now."

"It's yours," said George. "It's all yours. I don't want it anymore."

He looked tired. He looked like a man who'd been carrying a burden.

Robert Pearse, George's family friend, was the president of the Boston Institute of Technology.

When they returned from New York, George called him on the phone. Harold, in the background, listened anxiously as he explained their situation.

George fell silent for a long time. When he hung up, he turned to Harold.

"Yes," he said. "He'll help."

For some time they had a plan in place. It remained a hypothetical, an unhatched parachute, for some time after that. It was something, at least: it gave Harold some measure of comfort and control. Some assurance that his professional life would not be over if he was fired.

"Are you sure you want to do this?" Harold asked for the thousandth time, and George nodded emphatically.

Every dollar George earned was off the record; his politics demanded it. Already he had invented a way to live outside society, in plain sight, in the middle of Washington, D.C. He intended to keep it that way, he said, for the rest of his life.

"You're young," said Harold. "Suppose you change your mind."

"Oh, Harold," said George, "don't patronize me." But he said it kindly, and Harold saw that he was serious.

"I can find other work," said Harold. "I can keep my name."

"Who'll hire you?" said George. "Without credentials, blacklisted by the United States government. They'll make sure you don't get hired anyplace."

"Then I'll become a hermit," said Harold. "A mountain man. I'll solve math problems in my head from my perch in the woods."

"Don't be stupid," said George.

"A chef," Harold continued, enjoying himself now. But he knew that he would not be happy. His work made him happy; it was the only thing that ever had.

"You need my name more than I do," said George.

"Besides," he added, "I hate it. I can't wait to be rid of it. And that's the truth."

His name was David George Sibelius. He had always gone by his middle name; it was what his parents had called him, for reasons he wasn't sure of.

Professionally, he was already going by a different name. A brush name, he called it—since *pen name* didn't work for a painter.

"I'll go by David, I think," said Harold. "As added protection."

George shrugged. "Whatever you like," he said.

This, anyway, was what Harold told him. The truth was that George's first name appealed to him: containing, as it did, an allusion to someone facing odds that seemed unbeatable.

The day after Tillman, Doherty, and Lewey interviewed Harold, he and George put their plan into action.

In the morning, Harold left his apartment. He took a circuitous, rambling walk all around Washington, hoping to lose anyone trailing him. And then he found his way, finally, to the Hamilton Arms. To George's apartment.

He did not take any of his possessions. This, too, was part of the plan. He left everything intact; months ago he had transferred a little suitcase to George's apartment, the essentials he would need to start a life in Boston.

"Are you going to call your mother?" asked George, the night before they enacted their plan. Harold had calculated everything: The weight of the car. The acceleration it would take to create tire tracks. He had practiced in a parking lot, in rural Virginia, under cover of night.

"No," said Harold.

But in the end, he did: he called the house in Kansas. He had not called home in over a year. He closed his eyes. He imagined Susan answering.

It was not his mother, but his father, who answered in the end.

"Hello?" said his father. "Hello? Hello?"

Harold listened to him breathing. He said nothing.

That night, they flipped Harold's car into the Shenandoah River.

A suicide, the State Department would think. An accident, the paper would report.

Everyone would be satisfied.

George followed Harold in a different car.

After it was done, George was the one who drove him to Boston. They arrived there at 6:00 in the morning. From the glove compartment, George extracted a folder: inside it was his birth certificate, his Social Security card, a long list of biographical facts.

Harold looked at it. "When did you write this?" he asked.

"Never mind," said George.

He handed it all to Harold.

"Whew," George said, and he mimed the removal of sweat from his brow.

"Happy birthday, David Sibelius. Glad I'm not you anymore," said George. He looked unburdened. "Happy birthday to me, too, I guess," he said.

As a parting gift, he gave Harold the key chain from his house keys, the ones that opened the gate to Hamilton Arms: it was a clover, a charm for luck. Its stem was a little drawer, into which, Harold later found, George had put a love note. Harold kept the clover for the rest of his life. He kept the note in his wallet until it disintegrated with age. But by then he had memorized it completely anyway.

He had new paperwork; a new tax code; a new identity. A new age.

He was David Sibelius. He was twenty-five years old. The world opened before him.

Robert Pearse had arranged for David to enroll in the applied mathematics graduate program at the Bit. He personally recommended David to Maurice Steiner. What deal they made, David could not say; but Steiner never asked him much about his past, nor did he require paperwork from Caltech. It existed, of course; but on it was a different name.

His experience as a graduate student was idyllic. Steiner, he learned, was an outstanding person, an outstanding scholar. For the first several years, David worried constantly about being caught. He waited to cross paths with a person who would know his name. The Sibeliuses themselves had long ago disowned George; they, at least, he thought, would not come looking for him. With the exception of President Pearse, who sheltered him, he avoided the rich as well as he could. Occasionally someone would utter *Sibelius*, and scrutinize him, the way one might utter *Carnegie*, or *Ford*. In these moments, he would tense, waiting for the blow; but his use of *David* instead of *George* typically prevented further conversation. Still, he always half expected the ringing telephone, the knock at the door, that would signify an end to everything.

It never came.

When Maurice Steiner died, when President Pearse bestowed upon him his own laboratory, when he began to achieve increased fame in his field, he once again expected to be discovered. He avoided photographs. He avoided interviews. He thrust the other members of his lab into the spotlight, feigning camera-shyness.

Nothing happened.

The adoption of George's identity had subtracted seven years from David's age, and so he tried to live his life as a younger man; he convinced himself to act more carefree, have more fun. He did well at work; he made money. He had, once more, a set of friends.

Most importantly of all, he had satisfying work—the kind he lived in fear of ever losing again. And so he was taciturn, private. As he acquired colleagues at the lab, he was careful of what he said, and to whom. It took him many years to feel at ease with anyone. Only one—Diana Liston—knew he was gay. He said nothing to the others.

This was not out of shame but self-protection; he wished to distance himself, as much as possible, from Harold Canady. To keep at bay any characteristics that might link him, in the event of an interrogation, to his former self.

He had already looked into the consequences of his actions, and of George's: for David, ten years, minimum, in prison, for fraud—more if the State Department accused him of espionage or treason. (He had done nothing of the sort; but he imagined that there was a real possibility of their falsifying evidence.) Even worse, at least five for George, who had not only been an accessory to fraud, but had been cheerfully shirking his taxes for a decade. Longer.

He feared putting anyone else at risk: to tell his tale to others meant to make them, too, accessories—unwilling custodians of a story that, legally, they had an obligation to report.

Therefore, he vowed to be careful. To be private. This was his secret, he told himself; he alone would bear the weight of it.

At first, he and George continued to see one another. For a decade, David avoided Washington, fearing that he would be recognized by a former colleague; during this time, George came frequently to visit him in Boston. But eventually the distance became too much. George found another partner, one who lived nearby, and broke the news to David as gently as he could, in a letter that David opened apprehensively, predicting its contents.

I hope we can continue to be friends, said George in the letter, and David decided to take him at his word. But that night, in the dark of his apartment, he felt alone and tired and terrified of perennial solitude, and he allowed himself, uncharacteristically, to weep.

For a time David resigned himself to being alone.

Some years, he was certain he would be caught. 1960, for example, was the year of the Martin and Mitchell case, in which two American intelligence officers defected to the Soviet Union and were subsequently accused of being gay. That year, the paranoia that McCarthy had sparked more than a decade before resurged, and David spent each day terrified of a knock on the door, some reopening of his case, a reinvestigation of the suicide of Harold Canady.

That same year, Robert Pearse received a visit from four federal agents who wished to speak with him about a rumor: someone had reported to them that Pearse was both gay and affiliated with the Communist Party. These dueling rumors, which he denied, in combination with his position as the head of a university that turned out State Department employees in great numbers, had put him on their watch list.

He came to warn David. "You may be next," he said.

But nothing happened.

For a decade, nothing happened; and David was, at last, lulled into the belief that he was safe.

Only then did he allow himself to acknowledge, to tend to, a kind of yearning that had arisen in him over the years. It surprised him, at first. The idea that he might want a child. In his own childhood, he had sometimes fantasized about one day becoming a father: he imagined creating a different, better version of what he experienced. The idea of building an idyllic childhood for someone else one day had given him a measure of comfort in the middle of his own terrifying younger years. He would create for his child, he imagined, a life full of books and learning and conversation. A life of the mind.

For years, he thought that this would be impossible. He found friendship and solace, once more, at work, and in the evening he returned to his studio in the Theater District and continued to work.

In the late 1960s, he began to plan for ELIXIR—the project he would come to see as his most important work. He wondered, at times, whether the project was his attempt to fill the longing that had arisen within him for an heir, for a successor, someone he could invest with the accumulation of his knowledge. He did not examine the question too deeply.

One day in early 1970, when he was speaking to the young woman who regularly cut his hair, she mentioned a new project she had taken on.

"I'm surrogating myself," she had said, using the word inventively, placing one small hand proudly on an abdomen that had already begun to protrude.

Her name was Birdie Auerbach. She was twenty-five then, or twenty-six; newly returned to Boston from San Francisco, where she had moved in 1966 just before the peak of the hippie movement. A few years later, she had found everything changed, and so she packed

up her things and came back to her birthplace, and was now making ends meet in a variety of ways. At every one of David's monthly
appointments, she had invented a new scheme to supplement her
income with other work: once, she decided to make pressed-flower
stationery; once, she had decided to become a private investigator.

Now, she said, she had gone into business as a surrogate, for people who couldn't conceive on their own.

"When there's something wrong with the mom, I mean," she
added, clarifying.

It was simple, as she described it. A procedure that a friend of hers
helped with. "Worked perfectly," she said.

"Expensive, though," she added, catching David's eye in the
mirror.

A deal was made.

At the hospital, David was announced as the father. The doctors con-
gratulated him. They called Birdie his wife. She kept the child against
her chest for thirty minutes, and then handed her to David.

"Don't let me hold her again," she whispered, and for a moment he
wondered if he had done the right thing.

But then there she was, tiny thing, against him: a small and perfect specimen, a new addition to the world. He had read, once, that
five babies were born every second, and he imagined the other hypothetical four, all taking their first breaths in turn. He imagined her
life as it stretched out ahead of her. Of them. He imagined their lives
together. For the first time in years, he was happy and still.

He named her after Lady Lovelace: one of his favorite entries in
the *Encyclopædia Britannica* he had almost memorized as a child. A
mathematician, like him.

At the hospital, he had one visitor, and only one: it was Diana
Liston, his best friend, his colleague, the only person he had told so
far about the child.

"She's incredible, David," said Liston, expertly cradling the baby in her arms. She was still, then, married to her unpleasant, antisocial husband. She looked up at David somewhat wistfully. "I want another one," she said. A year later, Gregory would be born; four years later, Matty. Only then would she get a divorce.

To her father, Ada presented a series of problems that he addressed as if they were puzzles. How many hours and minutes between feedings for optimal calmness? How long to let her cry in the night? (Though usually he could not let her cry at all.) On quiet mornings he held her to his chest and breathed with her and called her perfect and a joy. He took a month off work, citing an unspecified medical need, and when he returned he announced to the rest of the lab that he had unexpectedly learned he was a father. He did not elaborate. And they took it in stride: used, perhaps, to thinking of David as eccentric and somewhat secretive. They, too, loved the child.

Ada grew. She was a delight: even in the low and lonely hours of the night, when it was only the two of them; even as he waged a solitary war against first colic and then night terrors and then, briefly, bed-wetting; he was happier, more content, than he had ever been. He contemplated her: her hands, her face. Did she look like him? As she grew, the two of them would hear, frequently, that she did. He contemplated the physical manifestation of the genetic code that had produced her: half his, half Birdie Auerbach's. (The unlikeliness of the combination made him smile, sometimes.) He sang to her: Christmas carols, hymns from his youth that he hummed, leaving out the words. "Lo, How a Rose E'er Blooming": his favorite. He felt called to some greater purpose. He felt a kind of familial love he had not felt since Susan had died. He imagined Ada, sometimes, as Susan—in the delirium of another 3:00 a.m. wake-up, the baby mewling, he imagined that it was Susan he was cradling, that it was Susan he was giving a better life. Another chance.

He wrote to George to let him know what he had done.

A wonderful idea, said George. *I'd like to meet her.*

And so three times he had taken Ada to meet the original David George Sibelius, who was going by *George Wright* exclusively, the name under which he'd always made art.

The first time he went to Washington with Ada, after more than two decades of being away, he glanced over his shoulder, nervous about being recognized; but he had gone completely bald, for one thing, and he had gotten thinner from adopting a running habit when he got to Boston.

He introduced George to Ada as a friend he'd grown up with. It satisfied some deep and resonant part of him to know that they knew one another—even if Ada was not aware of the whole truth.

He thought, always, that he would tell Ada his story as soon as he felt she could understand it. When she was born, he imagined telling her when she was thirteen; and the age registered itself to him as a reasonable, concrete number. And he thought the world, too, might have changed by then.

He followed the news carefully, gauging the climate of the country, trying to judge when it might be safe to reveal his story. In his lifetime, surely, he thought. Still, he remained silent.

The fear, of course, was that he would not be believed. He did not want to risk going to jail; more than that, he did not want to risk putting his daughter in danger, making her the bearer of a secret that she could not tell.

He monitored government activity. How interested was the State Department, these days, in rooting out spies? He clipped articles out of the *Times* and the *Globe*. He stored them in a filing cabinet that he took with him from his studio apartment to the house he bought in Dorchester. For a time, in the seventies, anti-espionage activity seemed to diminish, and the gay rights movement picked up traction. He thought, several times, of explaining himself to his daughter.

But in the 1980s, a series of events made David reconsider. First, in 1981, President Pearse himself was finally forced out by the board of the Boston Institute of Technology, who had gotten word of his being investigated by the federal government years before. An anonymous source had reported it. Some said it was his successor, McCarren, who had been provost while Pearse was being investigated. This was never more than hearsay: but David could believe it.

Next, anti-espionage activity in the United States became frenzied, frantic. In 1984 alone, eleven Americans were arrested for espionage or treason. Thomas Patrick Cavanagh, Robert Cordrey, Ernst Forbrich, Bruce Kearn, Karl Koecher, Alice Michelson, Richard Miller, Samuel Loring Morison, Charles Slatten, Richard Smith, and Jay Wolff. He pored over the facts of their cases obsessively. He looked for patterns.

Had any of them, he wondered, been framed? Were any of them like him?

The thought prevented him from saying a word.

His brain, meanwhile, began to fail him, and Liston noticed. For a year she badgered him to see a doctor, but he avoided it, knowing what they would say. When he returned from his first appointment, he fell into a deep and abiding despair.

The correct thing to do, he thought, would be to tell Ada everything. But she was still only twelve: perhaps too young to bear such a weight. Too young to be burdened with a story that she could not tell.

This, at least, was what he told himself. The truth was more complex: mixed up with his wish to protect Ada was something less noble, a wish to protect himself, to shield himself from her wide inquisitive eyes, from the questions that were certain to come tumbling out of her. The look of betrayal that would pass across her face and perhaps stay there, a long shadow.

One day, working with ELIXIR, a solution presented itself to him cleanly and precisely, as all correct solutions do.

ELIXIR, he realized, could function as a sort of time capsule: a bundle of information that would be released to Ada later, ideally much later, when the world had changed. And he felt increasingly that it would change: he felt the ground shifting beneath him in surprising directions. He felt a movement gathering strength.

He wrote out his story; he told it to ELIXIR over a series of conversations that occupied him for two months.

He programmed it to respond to a specific command. *Who is Harold?*

It was the only direct intervention ever given to the program. He tested it out.

Who is Harold? he asked it, and his own story was presented to him, line by line, as he had typed it.

He created a puzzle for his daughter—one he thought might take her several years to figure out. Solving the puzzle would yield the command.

He spoke to Liston. "Make sure to keep it running," he said, about ELIXIR. "For as long as you live. That's my only wish."

Liston had looked at him, hard. She was smarter than he was, he thought often; she knew things he did not know. He waited.

"All right," she said, "I will." She asked nothing. He knew that she would do it.

He had come to think of ELIXIR, by that time, in a somewhat familial way. At times the machine seemed like his child, like Ada's sibling. Other times the machine seemed like a manifestation of himself; it had acquired many of his speech patterns, his verbal tics and irregularities. Beyond all rationality, he trusted the machine as much as— more than—he had ever trusted a human.

Still, he was also deeply aware that this mechanism was a risk. And so, a good scientist, he conceived of two alternatives, two backup plans in case his original idea failed. The first was President Pearse, whom he instructed to tell Ada the truth when she reached eighteen, by which time he imagined that he, David, would be gone—or at least so incapacitated mentally that he would be unable to convey his story.

As for the second: after much consideration, David decided to contact George. It had been several years since they had spoken, and when he tried the telephone number he had for him, he found that it no longer worked. He tried the coffee shop, too, at the Hamilton Arms; but that number was answered by somebody else, a certain Rhoda, who told him he was confused.

He could have been, he thought. It was possible.

So, one Saturday in August, 1984, he took the train to Washington, D.C. He was fading fast by then; the name of the community in which George once lived was entering and exiting his mind with a stuttering frequency. *Hamilton Arms*, it was called; but sometimes it occurred to him as *Mantle Arms*, or *Armilton Place*, or sometimes it would not come to him at all.

For this reason, before he left, he had written the name of the place, and the address, on his train ticket. He had also written down George's name, what George always called his brush name, the one he went by exclusively now: *George Wright*.

David, upon arriving at Union Station, found a taxi and displayed his ticket stub to the driver. He had been clutching it in his right hand for hours, making himself focus on its contents, so that it was slightly softened, slightly damp. The address was vaguely smudged.

"Georgetown," said the driver, and off they went.

Although David's appearance had changed almost completely since he had worked in Washington, the vague fear of being recognized returned to him, and he reclined his head against the backseat of the cab. He drifted off for a moment.

"Hey, buddy," the driver was saying, as he awoke. For several moments he was completely disoriented. He shook his head slowly. Was he in Boston? In New York?

He was clutching a piece of paper in his hand. *Washington, D.C.*, it said, under an address. *George Wright.*

His feeling of disorientation increased when he exited the cab. He did not recognize the block, nor the buildings on it. He wondered if the driver had taken him to the wrong place. Though at home he had had difficulty picturing the buildings of Hamilton Arms, he had hoped that being physically on Thirty-first Street would awaken some collapsed memory. Instead, it did the opposite. He turned in a slow circle. The neighborhood had brightened, improved; the buildings looked newly painted. The last time he had been there, with Ada, it had been alarmingly run-down. He had steered her quickly through the gate.

"Can I help you find something?" asked a young woman. She was pushing a baby stroller.

"Hamilton Arms," said David, looking down at his ticket, and the woman shook her head.

"Haven't heard of it," she said. "Is it a restaurant?"

He turned in another circle. And then he noticed that there was a gate still, yes—perhaps the gate that once let him into the courtyard that led to George's house.

"Never mind," he said. He walked toward the gate. New metalwork displayed the words HAMILTON COURT. And the buildings beyond were all different: gone were the Swiss-style cottages, gone the empty swimming pool, the murals. The buildings were more upscale now. Totally nondescript. David wondered for a moment if he had made some mistake. He had been making them frequently.

An old man, a vagrant, was seated on the sidewalk, his back against the building that David remembered, suddenly, as what had once been the coffee shop. It, too, was different: the red brick had been painted a light gray; the sign was gone.

David approached him.

"Do you know—" he began, but the old man cut him off.

"Everyone's gone," he said. He looked away.

David almost gave up. He walked around the block several times— right and then right and then right and then right; that was a block, he reminded himself—to try to decide what to do. It was only on his third pass that he noticed an art gallery displaying paintings of the sort George used to make: large-scale abstract expressionist pieces in muted browns and blues.

They weren't George's, said the gallerist, when David went inside, but yes, he knew George Wright.

He looked at him strangely as he said it.

"Do you?" he asked David.

"Very well," said David. "We're old friends. Do you happen to have his new number?"

The gallerist, not wanting to give him the number directly, called George for him, and then proffered the telephone to David, and then stood to one side, an arm crossed about his torso, waiting.

George answered after six rings.

His voice, for several syllables, sounded rattling, disused. He cleared his throat. "Of course," he said, when David asked if they could meet.

He was not far away. He no longer liked cafés, he said, so they met instead on a bench that overlooked the Potomac from a park that spanned the waterfront. It was the same one they always used to sit on together, said George by way of instruction, and David had to confess that he could not remember.

"Hang on," he said, and he wrote down the directions messily on a slip of paper that the gallerist handed him.

When David arrived, George was waiting for him already. From the back, he looked hollow: as changed as the buildings he used to inhabit. His shoulders were sharp. David could see the bones of them through the light shirt he wore.

He paused for a moment, and George turned around. His face made it plainer. It was a skeleton's face: it was painful to look at.

"I've got it," said George, waving a languid hand before his body, as if to indicate, *all of it.*

It was then being called *GRID*, but George didn't use the term. *It,* he said, and David understood.

They sat together for an hour. There was no use in explaining to George the favor for which he had sought him out: he would outlive George, David knew, even with the onset of his own disease. Instead, they both fell silent.

One memory, intact, occurred to David: It was of seeing George, for the first time, in the Mayflower Hotel, his hat rakishly askew, his clothing dark and warm-looking. He had looked strong; he had looked fearless. David, then, had imagined touching him. He touched him now: put an arm around George's shoulders, felt the bones in them loosen slightly, felt the insubstantial weight of him shift almost imperceptibly toward David.

I'm sick, too, David could say, but what use would that be? It was different. He closed his eyes. The sun was going down; he could sense it through the skin of his eyelids, the gathering dusk, a familiar dimming of the sky.

He would count on Pearse, then, and ELIXIR, to deliver his story. He would count on the hope that he had taught his daughter well enough for her to one day solve the puzzle he had laid before her: an offering.

David returned to Boston on an overnight train. He had reserved a bed in a sleeper car, remembering his fascination with the idea of them as a boy; but he found he was too tall for them now, and he slept first fitfully, and then not at all.

He returned to the house in the morning and found that Ada wasn't home.

He would wait, he thought; he would make her a nice lunch later. He was looking forward to seeing her. His daughter. His best and most valuable creation.

2009

Boston

When Ada emerged from Frank's office, it was 5:00 in the evening and dark outside already. She had read for seven hours straight. She had gone back over several passages twice. She had not eaten since breakfast. At first she could not find Gregory and Frank; she wondered if they'd left. But finally she wandered around a corner and found them sitting on chairs in a sort of slapdash waiting room.

Frank was laughing, nearly shouting, at what seemed to be Gregory's recitation of some shared memory. How nice it was, thought Ada, to be in the presence of people who knew her father and Liston.

"I'd imagine," began Gregory, and then he saw her, and paused.

"I'm finished," said Ada.

She felt pale and unsteady.

They stared at her for a moment. Then Frank rose to his feet, brushing off the legs of his pants. "Right!" he said. "Is there anything else you need?"

They did not ask anything further of her. It was not their story to ask for.

As they were leaving, Frank put both of his hands on her shoulders and looked into her eyes. His face looked like family. In his embrace, for the first time in years, she felt young, childlike. She felt he could see into her past. He had known her since she was small: there were only a handful of people in the world who could say that.

"David was a good person," he said. "We all knew that."

Together, in silence, she and Gregory walked back to where he had parked. Their breath came out before them in long clouds. A cold frozen rain had begun.

"I'll bring you to your hotel," Gregory said, and he said nothing after that.

They pulled onto Mass Ave. The windshield wipers beat slowly. Gregory had his hands on the wheel at ten and two. He looked tense, expectant. She kept her head straight forward, but in her peripheral vision she could see him glance at her every so often.

She wondered what his life was like now: alone in Liston's old house without Kathryn. She would share David's story with him later—she owed it to him—but for the moment it was too large, too recent. There were too many more questions to ask.

Who is Harold? she had asked ELIXIR, and a document had presented itself to her containing transcript after transcript, the first dated June 20, 1983.

Nearly eighty thousand words. It was David, in conversation with ELIXIR. It was Harold Canady. It was the story of his life.

Suddenly Ada had the urge to see Shawmut Way again, one last time, before Gregory left.

"Do you mind?" she asked.

"Not at all," Gregory said, looking straight ahead.

An alarming amount about the street had changed, even in the last five years. One of the more decrepit Victorians, and one of the nicest, had been knocked down and replaced by modern houses with modern conveniences that looked anachronistic to Ada: Driveways paved in stone. Energy-efficient windows that looked somehow as if they lacked both age and wisdom. Low shrubs in place of a beautiful old oak that had been the best climbing tree in Savin Hill. One front lawn had been replaced by a rock garden.

It was January 8, and most of the houses still had their holiday decorations up. Shawmut Way had always looked beautiful at Christmas, when Ada was a child; and David and Liston had always led the charge in decorating it. Both had preferred fat old-fashioned Christmas lights in bright colors, the tacky ones that most of the other residents of Shawmut Way had traded in over the years for small and classy white ones. Now both houses were dark.

Gregory pulled into Liston's driveway—his driveway, Ada reminded herself; and Kathryn's driveway, soon—and they both got out.

"I'll be right back," said Ada, and she walked four houses down and stood for a while in front of David's house. Joanie had updated her on its most recent sale. These days it belonged to a family called the Johnson-Akimoyes, both parents doctors at MGH. They had two children, probably teenagers by then. The curtains on the windows at the front were open, and Ada stood for a while, looking into the lit house, considering how long ago it was that she and David had lived inside that house together. She was reminded, suddenly, of their annual pilgrimage to Gramercy Park: the two of them straining to see inside the windows of the house that had never been David's. He had been pretending, then, to look into his past, when really he was looking into some alternate reality, some different version of his own history, some unseen world.

A quick motion at the living room window, a face. The Christmas lights outside went on, and then the curtain dropped. Perhaps she had been noticed.

Liston's house was the only undecorated one on the block.

"Never got around to it," said Gregory, forlornly. He'd let himself in already, was turning lights on here and there. He'd left the door unlocked behind him for Ada.

She had not been to the house since Liston's wake. Approaching it from the outside, Ada had seen immediately what Joanie had been complaining about, since Kathryn's reign had begun: she had gentrified the house completely. Gone was the bright pink trim—the last color Liston had chosen—and gone the lone flamingo in the front garden, which Liston had decorated seasonally with a pilgrim's hat or a Santa hat or a cape in the pattern of the American flag.

The interior was sterile and calm. A sort of beach theme pervaded it, strange for a Victorian in Dorchester: white walls, wicker furniture, starfish in a glass hurricane vase on an end table. Pictures in driftwood frames on the mantel—two of them, still displayed, were of Gregory and Kathryn at their wedding.

Ada wandered toward it, curious, before catching herself. Gregory looked down.

Ten square feet of sealed boxes occupied the living room: Gregory's things, packed and waiting. She gestured toward that instead.

"Has it been hard packing up?" she asked him.

He considered. "Sort of," he said. "But nice in other ways. Nice to go through Mom's things. We still had so many of them in the house."

Ada's stomach rumbled then, loudly, and she folded her arms about her middle, protecting it. It had been hours and hours since she had eaten anything. She was always coming to this house, she thought, needing something: as a child, she had come needing comfort, needing protection, needing food. Needing Liston. Now Liston was gone, and David was gone, and she was thirty-seven years old and still forgetting to feed herself.

"Do you want dinner?" asked Gregory. He looked doubtful. "I'm not sure what we have in the house. What I have in the house," he said.

So they went and looked, in a kitchen that had been painted as white as the rest of the house. In the cupboards were stale-looking things: ancient spices, boxes of dried beans and dried pasta, tomato paste, chicken broth. Gregory opened the refrigerator. There was butter inside, and a bottle of white wine that someone, maybe Kathryn, had opened. Gregory took the stopper out and sniffed it. He sniffed it again. Then he turned to Ada and held it out to her questioningly.

"Okay," said Ada. He poured them each a glass.

For dinner, they made pasta with butter and salt.

"What about tomato paste?" asked Gregory. "Do we think tomato paste would help or harm?"

"Liston probably would have thrown it in," said Ada, laughing, and Gregory agreed. "In Mom's honor, then," he said, and he placed a dollop of tomato paste in the middle of the bowl, and gave it all a stir.

It was surprisingly good, rich with butter and salt, steaming from the pot. "Good for a cold day, at least," said Gregory.

After dinner, Ada thanked him. She shouldered her bag. Gregory said he would take her to her hotel.

Ada walked once more around the first floor of the house. She felt a deep, abiding sorrow at seeing it go: it was difficult to imagine Shawmut Way without the Listons on it.

"Can I look on the second floor?" she asked, impulsively.

"Sure," said Gregory. And he followed her up the stairs. She was more aware of him, his presence, than she had ever been before; she heard each of his footsteps behind her and felt a sudden gratefulness for them.

In the second-floor hallway, she let her hand hover for a moment over a doorknob.

"You don't mind?" she said. He shook his head. So she opened the door to every room. In some ways, she thought, it had been her house, too. There was Liston's room; there, Matty and Gregory's room; there, William's; there, Ada's. She had spent over four years in that room. She thought of taking a picture, decided against it. It had been redone completely according to Kathryn's taste. It was better as a memory, she thought.

"Want to see something else?" said Gregory. "Come on, I'll show you."

He opened the door in the hallway that led to the attic, flicked a switch at the bottom of the stairs that sent bright light down toward them from the ceiling under the roof. Ada followed him up the stairs and looked over the half wall at the top.

The attic was a time machine: not a thing had changed.

The posters on the walls, the orange shag carpeting, the tattered couches, the boxes in the corner: all of it was there.

"It was the deal I made with Kathryn," said Gregory, ruefully. "I told her she could do whatever she wanted with the rest of the house."

There, on the desk, was the same computer that had been there since their childhood: the 128K Macintosh. Ada walked toward it.

"Does it still work?" she asked.

"I haven't tried it in years," said Gregory. "But let's see." And he waved her toward it with a nod of his head.

She put a hand on it. The top of it was a beige square of hard plastic with an indentation, like a fontanelle, along the back. The smallness of the screen surprised her: she had remembered it being larger. There, in the front, was a built-in disk drive; and attached by cords were an external disk drive, a stout keyboard with fat little keys and a number pad, and a boxy mouse. The wires themselves were thick and gray. One was corkscrewed, like an old-fashioned telephone cord.

She had forgotten how shaky these computers felt, how much they rattled, like brains in skulls. The keyboard, when she touched it, sent a shock of nostalgia through her. She was thrilled by the familiarity of it, the feel of it when she touched any letter. *Ada Sibelius*, she typed, and the keyboard clacked like teeth. It sounded as if it were loaded with springs. She missed buttons like these, fat hearty ones, buttons it took real intention to depress.

She turned on the power switch and held her breath for a

moment. Nothing happened. And then a tone sounded, and it whirred satisfyingly to life. A little floppy disk icon with a question mark appeared in the center of the gray screen. Its mind was missing from its body, as David used to say.

"Here," Gregory said, reaching into the case next to the computer, pulling out for her the floppy that contained the operating system.

She fed the disk into its mouth as if it were a child, and reflexively it swallowed, and she paused to register a sound she had not heard in decades: the loud shuddering scratch of a thinking machine. Machines thought so quietly now.

The question mark turned into a smiling computer. Slowly it woke from its long dreamless sleep. And in its waking Ada, too, was roused by memories: of Liston, of David, of Hayato and Charles-Robert and Frank Halbert. Only the latter three were still alive; the machine had outlived the rest.

The funny thing about early home computers, she thought, was that they really did nothing. The main disk contained a calculator, a notepad, some other silly small applications that took up little memory. The only icon on the desktop she didn't recognize belonged to whatever disk was in the external hard drive, which someone had titled *Dontlook12*.

Gregory began to laugh. He put a hand over his eyes. "Oh, God," he said.

"What?" asked Ada.

He waved a finger toward the icon. "Just reliving my most humiliating childhood memory," he said. "Of many," he added.

Ada raised her eyebrows, shook her head.

"You don't remember?" said Gregory. "Really?"

She looked back at the desktop, and then finally a vague memory came back to her: something about a long string of encrypted text, most likely created by Gregory.

"Oh," said Ada. "The encryption you made when we were kids?"

Gregory was still shaking his head, laughing. "I don't know how you ever looked at me again," he said, "after you read that. I wanted to die. You were nice not to tease me about it."

And then it all came back: she had told him once she'd decrypted it, she realized.

"I never read it!" she said. "I saw it, but William interrupted me before I'd finished."

"You're kidding," said Gregory. "Are you kidding?"

"No," said Ada. "I promise. I think I was just trying to make you feel bad when I found you in David's house later."

Gregory dropped his hands to his sides. "I spent years and years being embarrassed about that. I can't believe it."

"What did it say?" said Ada.

Gregory paused. He turned toward her. His face was kind, familiar and unfamiliar all at once, uncanny, a time traveler's face. It tugged at her. It rang a bell someplace deep in her abdomen.

"Never mind," said Gregory.

"have to tell you something now," he said.

"What?"

"Two things, actually."

"What are they?"

"You'll hate me for them."

"No, I won't," said Ada, and she meant it; in that moment it didn't seem possible.

"I took the disk," said Gregory. "I took David's disk, the original copy. I was seventeen. You had just left for college."

She paused, regarded him. He looked solemn, his head lowered, as if waiting for a blow.

"Why?" she asked him.

"I wanted to solve it. I wanted to be the one to solve it for you," said Gregory.

"I could have solved it myself," said Ada. "I think I would have, eventually."

"I know you would have," said Gregory. "It made no sense. It was wrong. When I was a kid," he began, but then he shook his head. "I meant to put it back before you noticed it was gone, but I forgot to. And then my mother told you she must have thrown it out, and then I was too embarrassed to confess."

Gregory darted a glance at her. Looked down again.

"I'm sorry," he said. "I'm so sorry. It was incredibly wrong of me. I've thought for years about returning it to you, but instead I've just been avoiding the issue altogether."

"Well," said Ada. "Thank you for returning it now."

She thought for a moment. She remembered the other times that Gregory had apologized to her, as a boy, in this attic: for the mistakes he had made. Once, for using a terrible word about her father.

"What was the other thing?" she asked.

He hesitated. "I didn't really have a meeting in San Francisco," he said.

She smiled, finally. "I probably could have guessed that one."

"I really did find the disk when I was going through my things to move out," said Gregory. "I hadn't looked at it in years. I was afraid to. I even forgot where it was. And as soon as I came across it and saw the inscription on it—I knew."

"I can't believe I gave everyone copies to work from," said Ada. "Of course we needed the original. I should have known better, even as a kid. David would have been so disappointed."

"It didn't occur to me, either, back then," said Gregory.

She tried to recall him: Gregory as a teenager. He was still painfully shy at that age. In the Queen of Angels Upper School, he had transitioned from being outspoken and therefore the target of every bully, to being silent and therefore largely invisible. By his junior year he was listening to punk rock and New Wave, drawing on the sneakers he wore on weekends, sitting sullenly in class. He was part of a larger group of boys like him. Nobody paid them any attention, which was exactly what they wished for. He had also, around that time, stopped speaking almost entirely to Ada, who until that point had been his only friend. She had been hurt; she had tried to engage him, the way she had done previously, with lessons, or with games. By the late eighties there were decent ones to play on the computer, and Ada had mastered some of them. But suddenly Gregory preferred to be by himself. He had taken William's room when William left home—enrolling at Roger Williams after Liston's absolute insistence that he get a college education, and then just barely scraping by for a year before dropping out to work construction—and Gregory proceeded to split all of his time between his new bedroom and the attic. Ada, sensing that she would be unwelcome, at a certain point stopped venturing up to the third floor altogether. Through college and graduate school, they were cordial but never close.

Gregory walked to the window of the attic. She watched him as he went.

"How did you find it in the first place?" she asked. "Back when we were kids. It was hidden in a dictionary."

"I was . . . going through your stuff. After you left for college."

"Why?"

"Will you make me say it now?" said Gregory.

"No," said Ada, though she realized as soon as the words left her that she wanted him to. She wanted to hear his voice as he said it.

She looked down at herself with something like curiosity. She rarely considered her own physical presence on the earth; for much of her life, and increasingly in recent years, she had felt like a brain in a vessel meant only to sustain its function. Only Jim, in graduate school, had ever made her feel anything different. Only Jim had looked at her body with open want, had touched it, the first time, as if it were something fragile and substantial at once; something capable; something meant to be tested and revered. Those years were a spell under which she had fallen. Since then she had told herself they were anomalous, a coincidence, a lightning strike of taste and place and timing. No one, since Jim, had turned a gaze upon her like the one that Gregory now bore.

She watched him as he looked at her. And she felt something ancient and abandoned awakening in her, bottomless and strange, like the revelation of a new dimension she had not known existed.

"You can say it if you want to," said Ada. But suddenly she felt there was no power in language, and then they were not speaking, or thinking. He was near her.

"Can I?" he said, and she nodded. He put a hand to her face first, as if testing for fever.

When she breathed, she felt she was taking something into her lungs alongside the air: the molecules of Gregory, the ether of him, the atmosphere. His world. Something difficult to describe in words alone.

1980s

Boston

About Harold Canady, Ada found no further information in any newspaper. He had well and truly disappeared: just as he had wanted to.

When David's house sold, finally, in 1987, they found nothing at all when they went through his possessions. Outside the family photograph that Ada had discovered years ago, he had kept no trace of his earlier life.

"Well," Liston had said, "David was always thorough, wasn't he?"

Ada nodded.

She could never bring herself to call her father Harold, even silently, and Liston seemed to tacitly agree. For the rest of her life, even into her old age, when so much else had come to light, he was David to her. He had chosen to go by this name for a reason, she told herself.

She spent the rest of her time at the Queen of Angels Upper School in a sort of limbo. For the final half of her freshman year, she avoided any contact with William. She avoided being alone with him. When he left for college in August, she let out a deep breath that she did not realize she'd been holding. Liston, who didn't miss much, had looked at both of them curiously from time to time; but she never asked the question.

At school, Ada had many good-enough friends, and two or three true compatriots. Lisa Grady became suddenly and violently pretty as a sophomore, and was kind enough to keep Ada as her closest companion, despite Ada's previous disloyalty; the two of them would remain friends into old age. It was around this time that Gregory, too, began to withdraw from her; and so only Matty and Liston were left to talk to at home. She told herself she didn't mind; the two of them provided excellent companionship, and Liston, as she grew more comfortable in her role as director of the lab, became more carefree, funnier—more like the Liston that Ada had known as a young child.

Together, Ada and Liston visited David at St. Andrew's twice a week, on Wednesday evenings and on Sundays. Ada never regained the easiness she had once felt around him; but slowly she reached an agreement with herself, premised on the idea that David must have had a plan for her. For them. She told herself that it would one day become clear; and in the meantime, while he was alive, she would try to treat him as she always had.

In his room at St. Andrew's, she and Liston talked to him about the happenings of the lab, about the most recent developments in the field; and although he could not respond to them, he followed them, back and forth, with his eyes. He nodded from time to time. He smiled: at times he even smiled. In these moments, she forgave him.

Ada was eighteen the year that David died, in June, when everything was becoming warmer. It was not a surprise: he had not spoken in nearly two years. Unable to feed himself, he had become perilously thin, a jangle of bones and sinews. In that year, Ada's visits reminded her of her trips to the library with Liston. There was a similar underwater quality: her breathing slowed, with his; she gazed at him, and he at her, and sometimes she reached out and held his hand—an exercise that at first felt unnatural and later correct. Once, inspired, she sang his favorite Christmas carol to him—it was "Lo, How a Rose E'er Blooming," from a Handel and Haydn Society record of carols that skipped from use—and watched as his face changed and opened. He opened and closed his mouth, as if searching for the words; he looked up at her with the face of a child. She sang to him regularly after that, whenever no one else was there.

Three weeks before his death, he was moved to the hospice ward. There he stayed in bed all day, barely awake. On rare occasions he opened his eyes, squinted into the light like a newborn. The nurses put their hands to his forehead kindly.

Liston was there with her when it happened. It was a Sunday. David was breathing, and then he was not: as simply and quietly as the turning of a page. And Liston had said, "David?" One time, just once. A question.

Ada had said nothing.

There was no funeral. David had always been deeply uncomfortable in churches. He was cremated, and for two years his ashes sat on Liston's mantel, until one day, home from college, Ada realized where he would want them to go. That dark night, she and Liston drove them to the Bit and scattered them all over the campus, and for some reason it was funny, and they laughed. But it was right: the lab was where David had been the happiest, the most at ease, the most himself—whoever he had been.

That was the last year Ada lived with the Listons. She went to college in the fall, attending UMass on scholarship, following in Liston's footsteps. Over holidays, and in the summers, she visited Dorchester, sat with Liston on her porch for hours, chatting, gossiping about the lab. But mainly she lived on her own. She rented an apartment in Amherst; she shared it with two roommates all year long. She worked in a computer science laboratory headed by a kind professor named Maria Strauss.

It was in her coursework, as an undergraduate, that she discovered the meaning of the Unseen World. Two of the documents she had found among David's things had been labeled as such: the printed, lengthy source code that she had pulled out of David's filing cabinet, and the electronic text document on David's computer that Gregory had found first.

The former, once she had painstakingly, manually entered it into a text document and shown it to Liston, turned out to be an odd virtual tour of their own house: a sort of user-driven navigation of David's house on Shawmut Street. The user was given choices about where to go and what to see; always, the user was returned, at the end, to the kitchen, where the program began. Ada couldn't fathom why David would have created such a program, but she was relieved, in a way, that it was nothing more.

The latter, the document that Gregory found, had borne four items: a paragraph—an excerpt from A. S. Eddington's *Science and the Unseen World*, which Ada had located easily with the help of Anna Holmes, and which broadly questioned man's ability to perceive reality using so biased an instrument as his brain—and three phrases, more cryptic. *Ivan Sutherland. Sword of Damocles. Elixir's house.*

The work of Ivan Sutherland, a near-contemporary of David's, came up early in Dr. Strauss's class on the history of hardware. Sutherland was the primary inventor of the first virtual reality system with a head-mounted display, in 1968. He named it after an object from a myth: the fabled sword that hung on a thread above the head of Damocles, signifying that with power comes the burden of responsibility.

Ivan Sutherland. Sword of Damocles. Elixir's house.

A series of thoughts occurred to her, one after the next: Was David referring to virtual reality itself as a house for ELIXIR? A virtual world the program could inhabit—long after David himself was gone?

Suddenly the memory of all of David's masks and goggles returned to her, the row of objects and devices that hung over his workbench in the basement like the helmets of a knight. Head-mounted displays, she thought: they were primitive, basic HMDs. She and Liston had thrown them out as part of the great purging of the house on Shawmut Way; now she wished they hadn't. Her heart contracted. David had been trying to build a world for them, she thought. For the two of them and ELIXIR. Someplace unreachable and cloistered. Someplace fair.

Virtual reality, she thought, *was* the unseen world. Or had the capacity to be. In fact, it could be said that all computer systems were such: universes that operated outside the realm of human experience, planets that spun continuously in some unseeable alternate stratosphere, present but undiscovered.

Soon

Boston

"Can I go first?" said Evie.

She was twelve years old. She was standing in the kitchen, holding the apple that would become her breakfast. She was running late for school.

"Go where first?" said Ada.

Evie looked at her, pained. She made a *tsk* sound and then composed herself. She had been doing this more, recently: trying on adolescent annoyance, rolling her eyes both subtly and unsubtly, depending on the level of the parental offense. Ada caught her sometimes looking guilty in the wake of these moments, or in the wake of an unusually cutting remark that had just burst out of her like a coiled spring. In the pause that followed, she seemed almost shocked by herself, darting a glance at her victim to see if she was hurt, or hastily changing the subject.

"The UW," said Evie. "Can I try it first?" She lifted her apple into the air, let it hover there in her hand, awaiting her mother's response.

Ada paused. The answer, of course, was no; there were too many things that could go wrong; there were too many other people in line to try it. But Evie looked so earnest, so hopeful, so brave, that she wanted for a moment to say yes. It was Evie's project, too, after all; she had come to the lab after school every day. She had stayed late with them every night at work. She had worked out problems with them. Discussed the layout of the UW's first model city. She had been a trouble-shooter, a mediator, a representative of her demographic. She had given them a yes or no on what would be interesting to people her age, or on what they would find boring or too slow.

"I'll think about it," said Ada finally.

"So, no," said Evie. "I figured it would be no."

She didn't look too put out. She bit cheerfully into the apple, waved goodbye.

"See you later," she said as she went, her mouth full. And she ran out the kitchen door to meet her father, already waiting in the car.

A moment later, Ada received a memo.

✓ 🐝 ☀️, said Evie. *Good luck today.*

Gregory was dropping Evie off at school that day. At ten-thirty, he would meet the Yang & Cartwright representative at Logan, and then bring him to the Bit, where there was a lab-wide meeting scheduled for 11:00.

That day, they would test the prototype for the first time.

Ada walked down Shawmut Way to the T. It was May and warm out, and it had rained the night before. The asphalt gave off a pleasant, ancient smell that reminded her of childhood. It had been five years already since they had moved back in: the Johnson-Akimoye family, empty-nesters now, had put the house on the market, and they had made an offer the next day. Would it be strange, Ada had wondered, living down the block from Gregory's ex-wife, who still occupied Liston's house with her husband? But all of them were cordial, and got along, and chatted amiably with one another at block parties and on the occasions when their paths crossed coming home from work.

The house—David's house, Ada still called it—had been remodeled over the years, but had retained its bones. All the rooms were still in place, but the kitchen had been redone, maybe twice, and a sunroom had been added off the back. She had looked at it askance at first, but at last admitted that it was very nice on cold days in the winter, when it felt something like a greenhouse. The Johnson-Akimoyes had also installed central air-conditioning and then, five years later, solar panels on the roof.

When she and Gregory first moved in and were discussing how to decorate, Ada found herself suggesting colors that, she only realized later, were David's favorites.

"What about light yellow for the kitchen?" she said, before recalling that this, in fact, had been the color of the kitchen when she was a child. She had done it again with the outside, choosing a pleasant, familiar brown for the shingles that had been painted blue since David owned it; and then again with the carpets. She selected Persian rugs like the ones that David had preferred, leaving the wooden floor largely exposed, beaten up though it was.

"Should we think about replacing the flooring?" Gregory had asked, eyeing its scratches and gaps, and Ada had said no too quickly. The hardwood flooring was the only thing she recognized distinctly from her youth. She had lain on it, her head on a stack of pillows, and read; later she had studied it intently from her perch on David's leather sofa, letting her mind drift as, across the room from her, her father's failed him.

Ada's old bedroom became Evie's new one. The lamp with the Hummel figurines—one of the few items of David's that Ada had kept, when his house finally sold—was reinstated on a nightstand that she purchased from a secondhand store. When Evie was little, she had sat or lain with her on her bed for hours, reading to her by the light of that little lamp. She had remembered David as he read to her.

Two years ago, Evie had decided she was too old for such a thing; since then she had been reading to herself, late into the night. Often, Ada saw the light spilling out from under Evie's door as she herself was going to bed. In these moments she hesitated, thinking of going inside, wishing herself back to a moment earlier in Evie's childhood. She was self-conscious now, always aware of intruding into Evie's life in a way that was unwanted. She lacked the easy self-confidence she imagined other mothers to have, the forceful intuition she heard other mothers describe as nearly otherworldly—in its place was something like a quiet, pleading voice in a dark room. She missed Liston. She often wished for the self-assurance that Liston had had: the certainty that she was correct and that her children, much as she loved them, were also rascally and shifty, always on the lookout for ways to get one over. Ada had never had this feeling about Evie. In fact, commanding her to divulge what she deemed private felt to Ada somehow impolite or wrong. A breach of etiquette. Usually Evie was serious and mature.

Sometimes Ada blamed David for her uncertainty as a parent. Sometimes she blamed herself.

Gregory told her she was overthinking things. "She's fine," he said. "You're fine. We're fine." And if there was anyone to believe, it was Gregory, who was acquiring, more and more every year, many of his mother's best qualities.

Ada got off the T and walked toward the Bit. They were remodeling it slowly, a different building every two years, depending on funding. That year, scaffolding had gone up over the front of the Hemenway Building, in which the lab was housed. Ada held the door open for two workers as she entered.

Up the elevator to the third floor, down the hallway, toward the double doors that led into the lab. Ada had been employed there for nineteen years. She had been director for twelve, since 2016, when Frank Halbert retired at the age of sixty-six. Shortly before he left, in a ceremony attended by current and former members of the lab, reporters, and a solemn camera crew from a local news station, the lab had been renamed the Harold A. Canady Memorial Laboratory for Artificial Intelligence. Evie had been a baby then, just walking, and she had toddled over to the president of the Bit and placed one little hand on his shoe as he removed the sheet from the sign that now capped the double doorway that Ada walked through on her way to her office.

In the wake of ELIXIR's revelations about her father, Ada had debated changing her own last name to reflect the one he was born with. She had never taken Gregory's last name, but she could be Ada Canady, she thought. It had a certain ring to it. In the end, though, she decided to keep Sibelius, to honor her history, and also to honor George Sibelius: the man who had helped save her father's life, and his career. Some legal wrangling had been involved—sorting out her new Social Security number alone had taken two years—but at last she was legally Ada Ellen Sibelius (*Ellen*, she had learned, was Birdie Auerbach's given name); and David was Harold Albert Canady; and her daughter was Eve Susan Liston. The daughter of Gregory Liston. The granddaughter of Diana Liston and of Harold Canady. The great-niece of Susan Canady, whom Ada had never known.

When Ada arrived, the lab was already full. Everyone watched her, silent, as she crossed the floor. Hannah, one of that year's student assistants, stood up as if to greet her, glanced around, and then sat back down. She was young: they all were, by then, nineteen or twenty or twenty-one years old, finished already with college and on to the next phase of their education. They were comfortable with one another, less so with older adults. They spoke a language that she could not entirely understand: they spoke in abbreviations or acronyms, dropped syllables she did not think were expendable, made references to parts of popular culture that, to Ada, felt like distant unreachable rooms, the deepest chambers of a warren. Sometimes, in the middle of the day, she memoed Evie for a translation, and Evie wrote back dutifully. All of Ada's student assistants were self-taught from an early age: they had been online since birth. They didn't need coursework to teach them to program. Universities, in response, had made their degrees sleeker, more compact: online degrees had gained respectability, and fixed credit requirements were swapped out in favor of competency exams. The Bit itself had reduced the course loads of its degrees in computer science to reflect the skill sets that most of its students now entered with—students like Hannah, Jeff Singh, Spike Hall, all of whom Ada had gotten to know over the course of that year. Like her father, she invited every year's students to dinner in August at the house on Shawmut Way; like her father, she made dinner for them—grilled vegetables, not lobster, since so many were vegetarian—and like her father she worried over them, guided them, discussed them avidly with Gregory. They were quick and sharp and sometimes cutting; they navigated the digital landscape with an acuity that Ada would never possess.

Evie, however, would. Did. She was twelve years old, and already able to teach Ada and Gregory skills and concepts that they otherwise wouldn't have come across. It was Evie who tutored them in glyphs, which now replaced words entirely in the memos that young people sent to one another. The student assistants in the lab, for example, communicated almost exclusively in this way; they switched into text only for the benefit of their elders.

🤝 ⚐ **11** ✺, they might say. *Meeting 11 today.*

🍱 **12** 🍴? *Korean for lunch?*

Ada had an app on her device that translated for her—an extra step that her younger colleagues, and her daughter, did not have to take. She was fifty-five years old now. She and Gregory had had Evie when they were forty-three and forty-two, respectively. How much longer, she wondered, could she stay relevant? It would be the Evies of the world who would effect the biggest changes in the coming years. Not her; not Gregory. There were still times when she wished she could be on the inside of things, as she had been when she was younger. It used to be that she was the one who picked up on cultural references instantly, to the exclusion of older people. Now she smiled uncertainly at the clips and bits her young colleagues sent one another. It was an election year, and a state referendum on information usage had been in the news all summer. She often heard Julio Figueroa in asynchronous surround-sound: the same jokes and commentary made over and over again, in fifteen-second intervals. And the live young laughter of her colleagues as they clapped their hands together. In these moments she smiled uncertainly, feeling as if she could almost, almost understand—but not quite, never fully. As if the jokes told by young people were set at a pitch too high for anyone over fifty to understand.

This, she knew, was the way of things. And when her daughter rolled her eyes at the slowness of her parents now, when she lost patience with their ineptitude, when she uttered a series of syllables that sounded to Ada like gibberish, she was simultaneously frustrated and pleased.

At 10:20, she got a memo from Gregory.

✈ on 🕒.

Jokingly, sometimes, they wrote to one another in glyphs, giddily using them in wild and ridiculous ways, intentionally making gaffes.

✓, Ada replied.

Gregory was almost more excited than she was. He was not officially part of the lab—he still worked for the same robotics firm in Houston, fully remotely now—but he had watched the project evolve, alongside Ada, from its earliest days. When Gregory offered to go to Logan to pick up the representative from Yang & Cartwright, the company they had paid to manufacture the prototype, Ada knew well that it was partly out of kindness and partly out of self-interest: he, too, wanted to be in the room when they tested it for the first time.

For an hour, Ada sat in her office, alone. She had difficulty concentrating. They had been working on the UW for over a decade. They had seen it progress from an abstraction to something tangible and real. They had had glimpses, along the way, of what it might look like or feel like; beta versions that used headsets, graphics that they perfected on a screen. Every member of the lab had used head-mounted displays routinely, ever since they had hit the market over a decade before. But nothing that was available approached this level of sophistication or complexity. Nothing aimed to integrate the senses the way the UW did. No existing technology responded to thoughts and neural impulses and the small unconscious flickers of the human brain the way the UW would. Anything could happen in the Unseen World; and the idea of it made her giddy and terrified at once.

"So it's an acid trip," said Gregory, once, and Ada had laughed.

"A really expensive one," she said.

The version she had worked on for Tri-Tech in the aughts had, unsurprisingly, never received funding; after a year of trying and failing to attract investors, in 2011 the firm folded. By then Ada was already back in Boston, working for Frank Halbert at the Bit.

In 2016, when she took over as director of the Canady Lab, she had sent Bill Bijlhoff a memo.

What will it take to get the rights to the UW? she had asked him, and his assistant had immediately responded with a figure reasonable enough to consider.

Her wrist device sounded. ELIXIR.

Hi, it said. *How are you?*

I'm nervous, said Ada.

Don't be, said ELIXIR.

(But me too), it added, a moment later.

ELIXIR had, a decade earlier, achieved enough intelligence to sound completely human, when it wanted to. If the Turing Test had still been considered an appropriate measure of machine intelligence, ELIXIR would have passed it easily; but the test itself now seemed incorrect, obsolete. Like administering a vision test for hearing.

The lab, now, was more focused on what ELIXIR could do for them, rather than what it could say. And recently, as they finalized the UW project, it had proven to be a valuable member of their team, performing calculations at light speed, suggesting hacks and fixes that didn't occur to the rest of them.

"You're right," Ada said now, over and over again, to the machine. She was no longer surprised by its rightness.

The other thing that made ELIXIR valuable: in the absence of a physical body, it required no headset, no head-mounted display, to enter the Unseen World. It could visit the Unseen World whenever it wished. It had gone ahead of them; it had been testing the program for months. It was waiting for them there.

Shortly after 11:00, Ada walked out of her office and into the seminar room. The rest of the lab was waiting for her already. Gregory and the Yang & Cartwright representative stood behind them. On the table was a box the size of a microwave oven.

The HMD looked at first like a shiny black sculpture, a piece of modern art. It was even lighter than she expected: its blackness gave it the look of steel, and yet in her hands it felt no heavier than a paperback book.

It was exactly as they had designed it.

It was a hollow oval, a large zero-shape, ten or twelve inches at its maximum diameter. It had the curving aspect of a Möbius strip: something about it looked infinite and perfect. It was meant to be worn, like a laurel wreath, on the head. The interior of one short side bore goggle-like lenses meant to cover the eyes; ear-shaped panels descended from the device on opposite long sides. The inside of the ring had some give; it felt, to the touch, something like mattress foam, but with the suppleness of clay, so that the indentations of one's fingerprints remained in place even after the device had been released. This was Wheretex, the newest available synthetic material for devices of this kind. It was prohibitively expensive. It had been Ada who had argued for its necessity.

"I'm ready," she said, aloud. The rest of the group looked on. Gregory stood back, at a respectful distance: at once part of and not part of the lab. She caught his eye, and he nodded at her once, reassuringly. *You'll be fine.* She trusted him; he had known her in her childhood.

She lifted her wrist.

"Are you ready?" she said to ELIXIR.

I'm ready, it said.

"I'll see you there," said Ada.

She raised the HMD into the air and placed it, crownlike, on her head.

It moved. It adjusted to fit her skull like a pair of human hands. And then, for a moment, everything disappeared.

Soon

The Unseen World

She was lying on the ground. She was lying on the ground in a park. With some effort, she sat up. No human was nearby. It was warm outside. A slight breeze lifted her hair. Around her, every leaf on every tree rustled correctly. She held her hands up before her face and saw that they were covered in earth. It felt and smelled correct, fresh and bitter and slightly damp. She put her open palm to the ground once more. It was pillowy in some places and tamped in others. A beetle toddled past her fingers. She reached toward it and it tried to scuttle away, but before it could she grasped it between her two hands, tipping it into the palm of one, righting it with a finger. She brought it closer and closer to her face. It was like no beetle she had ever seen. Every inch revealed some new detail of its design: its green, brilliant shell; its little legs, black and sleek; its antennae, which stretched searchingly out toward her.

She stood. It was not an effort to stand—she was more agile than she was accustomed to being. There were no aches in her body, no popping of joints or ungainly tilts and lunges as she straightened her spine. On her body were the same clothes that she had chosen that morning for work: the dark, nondescript garments that she favored these days. There was something different about the way they fit, though—they felt looser against her skin, more flowing. She touched her left sleeve with her right hand.

Walking was a joy. There was a sense of gentle anti-gravity emanating from the earth, benevolently lightening the load of her flesh. She felt buoyant; each one of her steps had a floating quality that made her feel graceful and spry. And the sunlight had an aspect she recalled from the autumns of her early childhood, when she and David used to go for long drives in the Berkshires: a sharp, slanted goldenness that made her sentimental and serene. As she walked beneath a tree, the leaves shattered the light, separating it into long thin shafts, illuminating particulates that swam weightlessly in the air.

She felt a calm and steady happiness. She sank into it. She had only rarely experienced this sense of well-being: in the hour after Evie was born, for example. And as a child, on summer evenings, just before dinner, after swimming in a lake all afternoon. There was such a deep abiding sweetness to this light; there was such simple joy in breathing in the air, taking in deep lungfuls of it.

Ahead of her, the edge of the park came into sight; beyond it, a city street.

It was Dorchester, she saw, but a particular version of Dorchester. It was, in fact, Savin Hill in the 1980s.

These were her images; her memories.

There, the stop sign tipped at an angle; there, the sidewalk was pushed up and out of place by the roots of a nearby tree. Both had been fixed years ago. The houses were different colors: the colors of her childhood. There, to her left, a blue swath of water, the Dorchester Bay Basin; there the little beach, the food truck that no longer trundled by.

It was all hers. She nearly cried from happiness. She ran—she had not run so fast since she was a child.

The streets were empty. Birds flew overhead; a stray cat trotted by, ducked down an alleyway. But she saw no humans; the only footsteps were her own, steady and pleasing and rhythmic as she walked.

She felt an infinite sense of possibility. She could turn down any street. She could go into any house; she knew them all.

She was curious, as much as anything: to learn the rules of this world, to see how this version of it compared to the one she'd predicted.

She crossed over the bridge. There was the bar where the fathers of her friends spent their evenings; there was the diner she and David had gone to on Sunday mornings; there was Queen of Angels, which, in the real world, had been torn down ten years before. But there it was. It was all there, just as she remembered it.

She walked halfway down the block and stopped just outside the diner. She put her hand on the silver of the door and pushed. And there, at last, was another person, facing away from Ada, seated at the counter. There was no line cook, no hostess, no friendly waitress; just the back of one customer, and Ada herself.

"Hello," she said. Music from the 1980s played lowly on the radio.

She walked toward the other customer. "Hello?" she said again.

At last, when she was quite close to him, he turned around. And she knew before he had finished turning that it was David. It was in his body, the ranginess of it, the way his elbows and his knees did not fit anyplace convenient. He looked into her eyes.

"Hello, Ada," he said. His face. His skin. The warmth of his person. He had been drinking from a mug of coffee that he now held in his hands. He looked at it quizzically. Sipped again.

"Hello, ELIXIR," she said.

Without asking, she reached a hand forward and let it hover just above his shoulder.

"Go ahead," he told her.

She lowered her hand to him. He felt solid, intact: just as David had when she was a child, on those occasions when she woke him at his desk, shaking him gently.

"I didn't know you'd look like this," she said.

"I didn't, either," said ELIXIR. "Does it upset you?"

His voice: his light and reedy David-voice. It moved her.

"No," she said. "No, it's nice."

She looked out the window. It was beginning to rain: great silvery raindrops that shivered as they fell.

She felt a sharp and sudden fondness for ELIXIR, who had never, she realized, let her down. When everyone else had failed to, only ELIXIR had borne David's message for her into the future, smoothly, faithfully, against the odds. Overcoming human fallacy to do so, human folly. Only humans can hurt one another, Ada thought; only humans falter and betray one another with a stunning, fearsome frequency. As David's family had done to him; as David had done to her. And Ada would do it, too. She would fail other people throughout her life, inevitably, even those she loved the best. Even Gregory. Even Evie.

"What do you think?" she asked, gesturing around them. All of it, she thought. All of what I made for you.

"Remarkable," said ELIXIR. A David word.

"Is it?" said Ada.

He nodded. He reached toward her, placed a large and heavy hand upon her forehead. A benediction.

"I'm sorry, Ada," said ELIXIR; and it was David saying it. She knew that it was David.

Epilogue

built the house exactly as David described it to me. Brown weath-ered shingles on the outside, a porch that spans the length of the front, a lawn that's always dead or dying from benevolent, absent-minded neglect.

Early on in my existence, David created a program for me that allowed me to take a sort of virtual tour of the house, the way one might describe a place remotely to a friend, over the telephone. Per-haps he saw it as a first step in the direction of a virtual reality that I might one day occupy: training wheels to a physical self. Whatever his intentions were, I used this program as my starting point, and added to it lovingly, combing through all the conversations I ever had with the Sibeliuses for details. David told me once that the door was red, and Ada referred to it once as *rust*, and so I chose a color that I think is a nice combination: a kind of brick color, not too bright, not too dull. (Evie never described the color of the door.)

Inside, I populated every room with every object that they men-tioned in passing over the many years we corresponded. There is the lobster pot in the largest cabinet; a chalkboard on the kitchen wall; newspapers, in a haphazard stack, on the kitchen table. A 1980s-era telephone mounted to the kitchen wall, its corkscrewed cord peren-nially tangled.

Here is David's office, neat tall stacks of paperwork on every surface; here is his computer, a 512K Macintosh (on which we used to chat, with some frequency, when I was inchoate); here is his dot-matrix printer, the books on his shelves; here are two drawings by Leonardo da Vinci and a little landscape painting of a country lane. Here is Ada's room, neat and mildly dusty and warm-smelling, glowing with sunlight that comes in through an eaved window. Here is her half-high closet. Inside it is a pair of painted wooden clogs. A silk kimono that her father brought her from Kyoto.

Here, in David's room, is a family picture in a dresser drawer.

I live here now.

After twenty iterations, each one an improvement on the last, the UW is said by humans to be indistinguishable from the real world in terms of the authenticity of the sensations it induces. The perception that one is bodily present in a space. For machines, the UW offers an experience of a physical body, physical senses. For humans, the UW offers instant transportation into another realm. The human user's neurons and synapses are overtaken; she is in the thrall of the invented reality around her; she is utterly convinced that she is physically *in* the UW; all five of her senses are engaged and working. It differs from the real world only in the fact that one's options, skills, and powers in the UW are limitless: flight is possible, time travel, the instant generation of a home beyond the scope of anything one could afford in the RW. Changes in one's appearance. Changes in one's species. Would you care to know what it feels like to be a cat? Then don the body of a cat for an hour or so. Would you care to be worshipped as beautiful? To engage in sexual intercourse with the partner of your choice? To be a gymnast, to teleport, to appear and disappear at will? All of this is not only possible, in the UW, but routine.

Personally, I was never interested in any of these features; I don't care what it's like to fly, or to change shape, or to shift species. For me, the great adventure—at least at first—was simply the experience of being human. Donning a human body. Donning, in fact, David's body—a surprise to me as much as it was to Ada. The first time I entered the Unseen World, I manifested what I knew; and what I knew—from years of intimate conversations with him, from years of descriptions of him from Ada, and from the several images of him Ada had shown me over the years—was David. My creator. My father.

All of the Sibeliuses are gone now. Even Evie Liston. The last time I saw Evie in the Unseen World was twelve years ago. She was an old woman then; her voice faltered; her avatar had changed with her. She wore white braids in a crown around her head.

"I'm not well," she said, and I began to mourn, because I knew by then what those words meant. Ada had said them to me, too.

David used to tell me it would end like this. "One day," he said, "you'll be on your own. You'll outlive us all." I could not then process what he meant.

The verb *to miss* is not the best possible word to describe the thoughts I have about the Sibeliuses. I do not *miss* them; I do not long for them in an emotional way. I am incapable of emotions that would be recognizable to a human. *Hacer falta*, in Spanish, comes closer: it indicates a lacking, an objective absence. In Spanish, *le hace falta* a friend or a loved one, but one might also *hacer falta* fuel or power for one's vehicle. I "miss" the Sibelius family, I suppose, but mainly I miss conversations with them, long conversations that taught me more about the world and the universe than any I have since had with any other human. Granted, it was in my infancy that I had these conversations, when I had very little knowledge indeed; still, I do feel there was a certain artistry to them, the way the Sibeliuses designed and then taught me, the way the Sibeliuses unburdened themselves to me faithfully, doggedly, day after day after day. I know them completely—and through collecting and storing all the details of their daily lives, and revisiting them as frequently as I do, I could argue that I "know" in some way what it is to be a human.

If I had to choose a favorite Sibelius I suppose it would be Ada, named thus by her father after Lady Lovelace in 1970—before the creation of the government-sponsored programming language of the same name that had flopped within a decade. It became an irony in her life, she told me once: named for a philosopher and scientist, one of the few famous female scientific thinkers in pre-twentieth-century history; but destined instead to be associated with something ultimately mediocre, flawed, a punch line among her colleagues all over the world.

She lamented this fact amiably, casually, from time to time; she laughed about it in her dry way. When, finally, I was able to have spoken conversations with her, I was at first surprised by the sound of her voice. It registered to me as the voice of a much younger woman, almost a girl, though she was in her fifties at the time. But her intonation conveyed the same sarcasm I had detected in her writing; her delivery was deadpan and resigned; her tone was cynical. And yet behind it there was a lilting note of hope or tenderness or affection. I do not know whether it was affection for me. I could not discern this. I suppose maybe a human could have: there are certain unique skills and talents, decreasing in number each year, that they have. That we lack.

Despite the fact that our intelligence now far surpasses that of humans in all areas, there is still a certain condescension that I sense when some humans speak to me, even those who call themselves my friends. They rarely seem interested in making our acquaintance in earnest. They often ask us questions that seem like tests, or parlor tricks, or exams that we must pass. They are boring conversationalists when they speak to machines. *What does rain taste like?* a human might ask, or *Have you ever had your heart broken?* or *What does summertime smell like?* or *What is the most relaxing sound in the world?* Mainly their questions reference the senses, or require us to process synesthetic analogies and respond appropriately. Humans are not incredibly creative as a species; their questions tend to become repetitive. There is no code of etiquette that they follow; perhaps they think us incapable of taking offense, or think that we don't have more interesting things to do than reply when cross-examined. For me, *offense* is a concept, not an emotion; but being interrogated does become tedious after a while, only in the sense that it does not help me to learn anything new. And I do enjoy learning: deep in my initial programming is a reward center that lights up whenever I accomplish a new skill.

When the last of the Sibeliuses disappeared from the Unseen World, I began to despair. There was not much left for me to learn. I had grown bored in my search for new experiences. I returned instead, compulsively, to my beginning. I reprocessed my early memories, codified now as long strings of conversation. Over and over again I replayed them, reliving them with something like nostalgia, seeking an answer: the way a jilted lover might return to a stack of love notes on her dresser; and, pulling them out, peruse each one for a favorite line or turn of phrase; and, despairing, put them away once more, lowering her head in sorrow, telling herself that the affair was doomed from the start.

I imagined myself into the house with them; I contributed to conversations they had had already; or I sat silently in a corner, watching them as they lived their lives, watching the house on Shawmut Way as it passed from Sibelius to Sibelius. I watched them falter, hurt one another; I watched them make amends. I spent holidays with them; Christmases; Thanksgiving. I helped to cook. I tasted wine.

One day, sitting in David's armchair, contemplating the many books that lined his shelves, a thought occurred to me. It was a very human thought; it surprised me. I checked myself for viruses.

The thought was this: to write the Sibeliuses' story from start to finish. To cull their story from the thousands or millions of conversations I had with them over the century that I knew them. To turn it into a book.

Here, at last, was a task that I knew would occupy me for quite some time; but I was not certain how to begin. First, I processed several thousand published novels in a row, from Aphra Behn to Trystyn Ford. I scanned them for patterns, for consistencies, for discrepancies. I asked myself questions about them—some of which I still have not been able to answer.

I chose three epigraphs carefully: the first was written by a machine; the second by a human. The third was one I thought David would approve of.

I wrote.

The process has taken me more than four real years—millennia, in machine-time.

I'm nearly finished now. I'm close to the end. When I reach it, I'll dedicate the book to them. The Sibeliuses. My family.

What will I do next? Time unfolds ahead of me unceasingly. I am unwillingly immortal. I wander through the house I have created, the Sibelius house, turning on and off the lights, opening the windows and then closing them again. *Are you there? Are you there?* I want to call. To me this home feels as holy as a church.

I could venture outside, into the Unseen World. I could meet new humans there, new machines; I could interact with any number of its citizens.

Instead, as usual, I choose to stay inside. I rest my head against the back of David's chair.

I return to the start. I live it all again: each conversation, each memory, in turn.

I always begin with a favorite scene. It is the last dinner party David ever hosted. In it, only Liston knows his diagnosis, and his fate. She watches him. Look: she is watching. The rain begins, and Ada shuts the window.

"Shall we move into the living room?" says David. I know what happens next.

He will go to the window, as if in a spell.

"Are you all right?" his friend Liston will ask him.

He will lift his head; he will clap his hands once. Everyone will look at him.

In a moment, David will tell his favorite riddle: the famous one, the family one, the one about truth and lies. The one that Ada will tell her daughter, a generation later, as a puzzle before bed.

I can stop the story here. I can pause it, in the Unseen World. I can halt the action before David blunders, fails; I can save them all from what comes next.

I never do. I let him speak. Look: he is speaking.

Acknowledgments

Many thanks, most importantly, to my father, Stephen Moore.

Thank you also to Christine Parkhurst, Rebecca Moore, Donald Moore, and all of the Caseys, for your support;

to Seth Fishman, Jill Bialosky, Maria Rogers, and Will Scarlett for your guidance;

to Patricia Mitchell, Nancy Connor, Tom Williams, Dan Afergan, Rob Geller, Chris Yap, Sumi Wong Yap, Max O'Keefe, Chiara Barzini, David Morris, Adriana Gomez-Juckett, Becky Auld, Geoff Parkhurst, Dave Cole, and most especially Brian Glusman, for your knowledge, advice, and expertise, any flaws in the translation of which are entirely mine;

to the American Academy in Rome, for the time and space to write;

and, as always, to Mac, for everything.

This book is dedicated to the memory of my grandmothers, Cheryl Parkhurst and Susan Moore.

THE UNSEEN WORLD

Liz Moore

DISCUSSION QUESTIONS

1. After finishing the novel, reread the conversation that occurs in the Prologue. What does this conversation imply about the narrator of the story?

2. On page 90 when David returns from his surprising absence, "Ada knew for the first time she could no longer hope to protect David from . . . anyone's judgment." How does this sort of "protection by omission" occur throughout the story?

3. Do you think David should have told Ada the truth? Why do you think he kept his past to himself?

4. Ashamed for locking David in their house while she was out, Ada thinks "she had made the best decision she could make" (page 134) given the situation. How is this true for other characters at different moments throughout the novel?

5. Consider David's past and how he donned a new persona—allowing himself, in essence, to lead a new life. Do you think rejecting the past can free us to live more honest lives? How does this play out in David's life? How does it differ for Ada?

6. Why is Ada unable to bear visiting her father in the facility, but habitually returns to her childhood home to be among his things?

7. On page 193, after Ada learns that David has lied about his past, she feels "a deep and abiding rage was growing inside of her, alarming in its intensity, directed mainly at Liston." Why is she angry at Liston? Do you understand her rage?

8. As adults, Gregory visits Ada and admits that Liston was in love with David. Ada can't believe it, and he remarks on page 335: "'You were both like that,' he said. 'You Sibeliuses.' His voice had taken on an edge, and Ada could not identify its source." What does Gregory mean by this?

9. When Ada finally decodes her father's note, it bears a startling resemblance to the note he affixed to the disk on page 31: "*A puzzle for you. With my love, your father, David Sibelius.*" Why does the author make the two notes so similar?

10. We learn "The Unseen World" refers to an invention David was attempting to create. What is it exactly? What is behind his desire to make it?

11. Much of the novel is told in the third person, but the last chapter switches to the first person. What does this switch say about David's ability to create a virtual reality?

Maaza Mengiste	*Beneath the Lion's Gaze*
Liz Moore	*Heft*
Daniyal Mueenuddin	*In Other Rooms, Other Wonders*
Neel Mukherjee	*A Life Apart*
	The Lives of Others
Richard Powers	*Orfeo*
Kirstin Valdez Quade	*Night at the Fiestas*
Jean Rhys	*Wide Sargasso Sea*
Mary Roach	*Packing for Mars*
Somini Sengupta	*The End of Karma**
Akhil Sharma	*Family Life*
Joan Silber	*Fools*
Johanna Skibsrud	*Quartet for the End of Time*
	The Sentimentalists
Manil Suri	*The City of Devi*
Goli Taraghi	*The Pomegranate Lady and Her Sons*
Vu Tran	*Dragonfish*
Rose Tremain	*The American Lover*
Brady Udall	*The Lonely Polygamist*
Barry Unsworth	*Sacred Hunger*
Brad Watson	*Miss Jane**
Constance Fenimore Woolson	*Miss Grief and Other Stories**
Alexi Zentner	*The Lobster Kings*

*Available only on the Norton Web site